Demons In My Bed

Demons of Port Black Book 1

Britt Andrews

DEMONS IN MY BED

DEMONS OF PORT BLACK
BOOK ONE

INTERNATIONAL BESTSELLING AUTHOR
BRITT ANDREWS

Copyright © 2022 Britt Andrews

All rights reserved. No part of this publication may be reproduced, distributed, or transmitted in any form or by any means, including photocopying, recording, or other electronic or mechanical methods, without the prior written permission of the publisher, except in the case of brief quotations in book reviews.

The unauthorized reproduction or distribution of a copyrighted work is illegal. Criminal copyright infringement, including infringement without monetary gain, is investigated by the FBI and is punishable by fines and federal imprisonment.

Please purchase only authorized electronic editions and do not participate in, or encourage, the electronic piracy of copyrighted materials. Your support of the author's rights is appreciated.

This book is a work of fiction. Names, characters, places, brands, and incidents are the products of the author's imagination or used fictitiously. Any resemblance to actual events, locales or persons, living or dead, is entirely coincidental.

Cover Design: Christian Bentulan – Covers by Christian

Formatting: J. McDaniel

Editing: Aubergine Editing

Proofreading: Proofs By Polly

Content Editing: Cassie Hurst

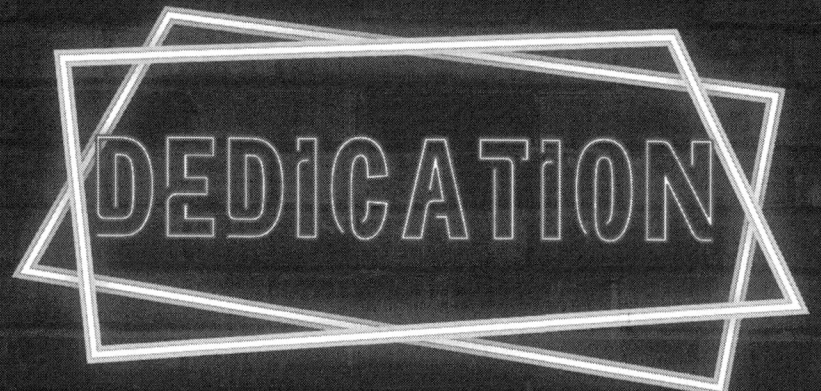

Remember all of those people who doubted you?
The ones who liked to bully and belittle out of spite and jealousy?
Yeah, fuck them. This one goes out to all of US.
The ones who are still here, fuckin' rocking this shit, despite the naysayers.
We're all members of The Exiled now and it's time to let our inner demons run free.

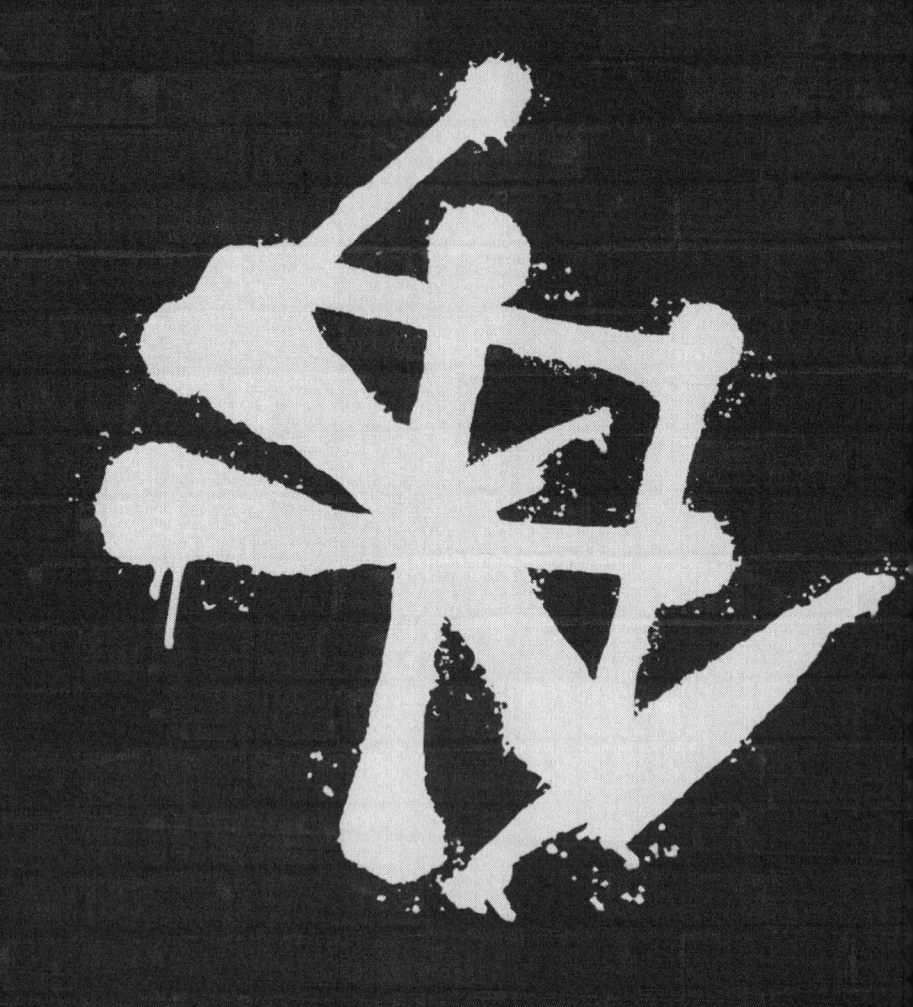

Table of Contents

Trigger Warning
Prologue
1. Palmer
2. Ashland
3. Palmer
4. Rhodes
5. Palmer
6. Talon
7. Palmer
8. Misha
9. Felix
10. Palmer
11. Ashland
12. Palmer
13. Felix
14. Palmer
15. Rhodes
16. Palmer
17. Misha
18. Talon
19. Palmer
20. Rhodes
21. Palmer
Afterword
Acknowledgments

About Britt Andrews
Stalk Britt Andrews
The Magic of Discovery
Also By Britt Andrews

CONTENT WARNING

Demons In My Bed contains epic graphic sexual scenes and the foulest of languages.

Previous SA is referenced but not described in detail.

This book is full of blood, stalking, hunting, knotting, tail play, male on male, group sex, and other fuck hot themes.

It will have you questioning your morals and panting after the anti-heroes.

If you're ready for a damn good time, continue at your own risk. You've been warned.

P.S. If you'd like to listen to some damn good music while you read, check out the Spotify playlist I created while writing. I'm always adding to it when I find songs that match the vibe I'm writing.

Prologue

The time had finally come.

I left the three agents I'd been playing pool with all evening in the billiards room and practically sprinted down the hallway. We'd been having fun, and it had been a while since I'd done anything aside from train, but I let my mind slip back into my working mentality. There was no room for smiles or teasing jokes with smoking hot guys. No, not now. Not when everything I'd been planning for was happening.

My phone vibrated, and I connected the call without even checking the screen. "Vale."

"Ah, Palmer. Good," Asrael—my mentor and the CEO of Montague Industries—murmured, making my spine stiffen from muscle memory and training. "I'll meet you in an hour to get you to your destination. I've arranged for Laurie to do one last session with you. She's waiting for you out on the lawn."

My heart raced. Adrenaline and excitement were taking over. "Yes, sir."

"Listen to whatever she has to say. If anyone can offer you any last minute wisdom for this type of assignment, it's her. See you soon."

The call disconnected, and I shoved it back into the pocket of my gown. Thank fuck for dresses with pockets; even formal ones now came with such joys. Asrael had asked me to meet him here tonight at his seaside castle and being the kind of man he was, he'd required a formal dinner. I'd sure as hell be changing out of this contraption as soon as possible though.

I silently moved down the stairs, freezing in place when I spotted a guy I had absolutely no desire to speak to. Confused, I tilted my head. He should've heard me coming, but was clearly distracted. *By what?* Leaning over the banister, I saw him staring at an image of a woman with long, red hair that would make anyone jealous. He ran a finger over her mouth, and I grimaced. Gross. Whoever she was, I hope she never tangled with that asshole.

The agents who worked at Montague were a family, for the most part. On an assignment, you had to be able to trust your team implicitly. Bryce hadn't been around all that long, and I had a sneaking suspicion he was actually banging Laurie. I had to stifle the urge to gag. Not that I gave a shit about who was fucking who amongst the other agents, but there was just something about him that I didn't trust. That had been one of the first things Montague drilled into our heads when we began our training. Never. Ignore. Your. Gut.

Bryce shook his head and took off in the opposite direction. Thank the stars. Hiking up my skirt, I raced down the remaining steps and slipped through the front door into the night. The castle, which was nestled along the coastline, was completely enveloped by the sound of roaring waves that carried through the air.

That was the thing about the ocean—not only was it big and intimidating, it was also deafening. All-encompassing, the sea could attack all the senses, making sure you were constantly aware of the true master of this world.

I couldn't be near the sea and not think of my parents. The first time I ever saw the ocean, I'd been six years old and on a family vacation. Just the three of us. I'd never forget how when we walked up over a sand dune to see all of that blue water spanning as far as the eye could see, it wasn't the size that scared me. It was the noise.

I clung to my dad's back like a monkey, and he carried me over the hot sand. He must have felt my apprehension, because I felt his chuckles vibrating through his back. He asked if everything was okay, and I just squeaked something about how the ocean was so loud.

My mom stripped off her cover-up and ran past us, laughing as the wind blew through her long, dark hair, her squeals of happiness rising over the beast of the sea. Dad and I watched her jump through the waves, and she waved back at us.

"One day, Palmer, you'll fall in love. I hope you have a kind of love like the ocean—so deep and all-consuming that sometimes, the intensity of it hurts in certain moments. Just like this one." My dad's eyes never left Mom as she laughed and waved at us to get in the water.

"Why does it hurt? Love is happy. That's what my princess books say."

Dad laughed. "It's a good kind of hurt."

My nose wrinkled. "Hmm, that sounds scary. I'll just close my eyes."

Dad swung me around, landing me on his hip so he could look at me. "Let's close our eyes then." I smiled and copied him, bouncing with excitement at this game. "Do you hear it?" he whispered.

"Hear what?" I whispered back, but it was more of a whisper-shout.

Mom's laughter carried through the air on a gust of wind to us, and my eyes popped open. Dad's eyes were crinkled at the corners as he smiled down at me.

"Your mom is my ocean. Big personality, huge heart, endless love... but the thing I love the most is that when everything about her is so big, I can just close my eyes. Even when I can't see her, or feel her, I can hear her. She's the sea and I'm the sand. Always here to catch her when she breaks."

I pondered his words in my six-year-old brain. "Then what am I?"

"Oh. Right." Dad shook his head like he'd forgotten about me. "That's easy. You're the little, stinky, crab baby!" My mouth popped open in disbelief.

"Come on, you two! Don't make me come get you!" Mom yelled out to us as the waves crashed around her knees.

"I am NOT a little, stinky, crab baby! I am not little OR a crab!" Wiggling out of Dad's grip as he howled with deep belly laughs, I peeled off my own little cover-up and handed it to him. He secured my life jacket, and then I was off, kicking sand up under my small feet.

He shouted, *"Does this mean you're just a stinky baby then?"*

"I'm telling Mom!" Glancing back, I saw my dad standing there, just watching us. It took a moment for me to notice that there were other people on the beach, though most of them looked a little strange. Slowly, my dad's focus shifted from me to scanning the beach. He didn't seem alarmed by all the see-through people, so I ran down to Mom, ready to have one of the best days of my childhood.

Being at the beach again felt like fate. Getting the green light for my first mission while staying in a castle right on the shore? Every wave that broke felt as though my parents were right there with me, cheering me on, proud of how far I'd come.

The sound of a twig snapping had me spinning to meet Laurie as she attacked. I immediately went on the defensive—just in time too, because vines exploded from the ground and she laughed, her red hair blowing all around her face like an evil witch. I threw myself backward, narrowly escaping the vines with a back handspring.

One of Laurie's biggest mistakes was that she continually underestimated me. She wasn't the only one. My affinity was a strange one, and without having an element I could call on—the way pyros could with fire, or shifters with their animals, or hell, manipulating the weather and using lightning as a weapon—most assumed that put me at a disadvantage.

The fact of the matter was that every witch or mage had the ability to use magic, and I'd studied harder than my peers at mastering those spells since I didn't have an attacking affinity like most of them. Even Laurie, a green witch, was able to use plants as weapons. Ridiculous.

Her eyes narrowed as she advanced on me, and thorns began to grow on the vines that were reaching for me. Muttering the word "*Indespectus*," I grinned when she shrieked. I was now invisible.

It wasn't a spell that lasted very long, and I didn't like to use it often because it drained me. Fast. But for right now? To best her? Yeah, it would be worth it.

"Well, look at you," Laurie taunted.

I laughed. "Bet you wish you could."

She followed my voice and charged, but I was easily able to evade her. "Didn't take you for the run and hide type," she baited me, letting vines curl around her arms as her eyes scanned the ground, probably looking to see if there were any impressions in the grass.

Unsheathing one of my knives, I stalked closer.

"Show yourself and fight me! If you think you'll be able to beat—"

Her voice cut off abruptly as my blade gently kissed her throat. My spell wore off, and I stepped back, sheathing my weapon. "Good figh—" The world tipped as I was yanked off of my feet by my ankles. The breath was forced from my lungs when my back connected with the ground. Rage was the first thing I felt, the second being a foot stomping my chest down when I attempted to get up.

"Never take your eyes off of your opponent. There are no rules out there. There is no honor. If you're in a fight with an enemy, then you better make sure you're prepared to end them, because as long as they still breathe, they can and *will* come for you."

I blinked up at Laurie as the clouds shifted, shining moonlight onto her face. Her eyes were the most intense I'd ever seen them, and I found myself nodding. The anger I'd felt just moments before dissipated to that familiar feeling between mentor and student. Respect. She was right, and this was something I'd remember in the field.

Don't let them live if they mean to kill you.

She extended a hand down to me, and I grasped it, letting her pull me to my feet. "Any other advice?"

"Yeah. Just one thing. Do whatever it takes. You're a woman and that is your greatest strength." When I lifted a brow at what I thought she was implying, she huffed and smoothed down her clothes. "This is a man's playground we're in. They just haven't figured out yet that while they're running around beating on their chests, we're the ones getting all the information we need from them, *however* we can." She placed a hand on her hip, and I felt eyes on my back.

Glancing over my shoulder, I smiled at Asrael, who was striding toward us like a savior. That's what he'd been for me, ever since he took me in at age sixteen and helped me get to this level.

"Ladies, that was a good fight." He smiled at me and then Laurie. I didn't miss the way she slid beside him, leaving only a breath between their bodies.

"Thank you, sir," I replied, my voice steady.

Laurie smiled up at him, brushing some of her rogue, red hair from her face. The wind picked up though, making her efforts futile. "Here," Asrael offered, tucking her hair behind her ears and then turning to me. I shifted my gaze for a split second to Laurie, just long enough to see her wink at me. "Thanks for your assistance, Laurie."

It was a dismissal. One I expected her to pout over. But she didn't.

"Of course, Asrael. Good luck on your assignment, Palmer." She started to head back to the castle. I was about to thank her, but Asrael spoke first.

"Laurie?" he called over the sound of the waves. She turned and looked back at us. "I'll be back within the hour."

The light of the moon had nothing on her Cheshire grin. She nodded at Asrael and then turned her attention to me. "Remember, Palmer—*whatever* it takes!"

My cheeks heated at the thought of her and Asrael doing gods knew what together. He was like a father to me. Nope, not going there.

"Are you ready to go, Palmer?" Asrael asked, offering his arm for me to loop mine through.

"I've never been more ready for anything in my life, sir."

He gave me a warm smile. "Well then, let's get you to Port Black, Agent Vale."

Chapter One

I adjusted my tits with a shimmy, boosting them up in my skintight, black, leather corset. Fog rose from the street, giving the illusion of what most normal people would imagine phantoms to be like. I'd learned from a young age that the undead weren't that peaceful, or fucking quiet. The mouth breather who'd followed me the past five blocks was a testament to that.

My middle finger flew up over my shoulder where I knew his ripped-off face was waiting. Always with the scare tactics, these ghosts. I wasn't scared of them though, not anymore... Especially not tonight when there was work to be done.

"Bitch," the ghost whispered in his gross, dead voice, earning an eye roll and another quick middle finger appearance.

"Yeah, I'm a bitch, and I have a job to do, so fuck. All. The. Way. Off." Power surged beneath my fingertips, and with a little flick of my wrist, the spirit was blasted away. A shiver worked its way through my spine, and I reached into my matching leather bag, needing some Purell in the worst way. I didn't know if ghosts carried germs, but with the way that one had been breathing on me, I wasn't taking any chances.

Slow clapping had me glancing over to a nearby bench where another damn ghost was sitting. "Ugh," I groaned. "What now?"

"That was pretty impressive. You did me a favor—I've been seeing that guy's hideous face for way too long," the ghost said.

I huffed. "Didn't do it for you, and I'd appreciate it if you'd stay right where you are. Otherwise, I'll do the same to you."

He laughed and stood up. His form shimmered as he moved, like all ghosts. Some were more transparent than others though; I was pretty sure that was down to how long they'd been dead. The soul can't hang on forever. This one though, he was a bit different in the way that I could actually make out his height. Ghosts were usually more fluid, kind of blob-like in their movements, which caused them to distort from super tall to very short in the blink of an eye. This guy's form didn't change shape. He was simply tall. His other features were too shimmery for me to make out though, which was the norm.

"Going to the big party across the street?" he asked, watching me closely.

"Maybe," I replied, looking over to where he pointed.

"Brave girl."

"Nosy ghost," I fired back, and he chuckled. Why was he so damn chipper? He was dead. I decided I'd just ignore him for now. If he wanted to get pushy, I'd give him a good blast of magic and hopefully send his ass to the other side. "Snake, the invitation." I popped the bottle of sanitizer back into my bag and waited for my familiar to scurry up my leg with the invite.

The ghost inhaled sharply. Not an uncommon reaction to my little buddy. "What the hell *is* that thing?"

I ignored the ghost. "Good boy," I praised, rubbing the half of Snake's head that still had fur. Snake was a squirrel who'd met his untimely end after losing a fight with a snake. When I'd stumbled upon him with those twin snake bites in his neck, I couldn't just leave him lying there. My original plan had been to bury him. Imagine how shocking it was when I went to place him in his little grave, and my magic seemed to latch onto him, bringing him back to life.

Up until that moment with Snake, I'd only ever been able to see ghosts, and sometimes interact with them. My mentor and guardian, Asrael, had always suspected I'd be able to reanimate bodies at some point if I continued pushing myself. Testing my magic to the limits of my sanity... and one day, it happened.

So here we are, Palmer Vale: Spirit Witch and her familiar, Snake: The Reanimated Squirrel. An unlikely duo, but holy fuck, have we seen some shit together.

I unrolled the invitation to reread it for the hundredth time.

There were so many questions, so many things wrong with this invitation, but I had to force all of them down because this was potentially my best shot to get close enough to them.

My eyes flicked across the street to where people were lined up to get through the door. Three huge bouncers were manning the door, but it seemed they were letting anyone in who approached, as long as they were dressed... appropriately.

Reaching into my bag, I pulled out the two masks I'd brought with me. One was a lacy, black, masquerade-style one that covered my eyes and nose. The other was a little more extravagant, with black bunny ears covered in little white, shiny gems.

"If you're looking to make a statement, you have to go with those ears," my unwanted, new friend advised me, indicating the more ornate mask with a tilt of his head.

I looked between the two options and tossed the lace mask down on the bench. Maybe some poor fucker could use it for something.

"Good choice."

"I'm going now," I snapped, annoyed. This was a big fucking deal, and I needed to focus—that was difficult to do with the ghosts of this shitstain city's past floating around and harassing me.

Blocking out the ghost's amused laughter, I took in the neon lights that glowed above the door, spelling out one word: Haunt. Bass boomed from within the club so loudly that my heartbeat pounded in rhythm all the way across the street. My fingers tapped against the knife that was strapped to my upper thigh, completely visible. There was no point in hiding weapons going into this lion's den. If rumors were to be believed, we wouldn't make it through the night without at least a few casualties.

"Okay, Snake, listen," I said, holding out my palm for my friend to sit in. He scampered down my arm and obediently stared up at me, listening to every word out of my mouth. "This is what we've been working toward, okay? I'm going in alone, and you're going to find your own way in through the ventilation ducts. Stay hidden unless I call for you. If you find anything that I need to be aware of, just give me a nudge. I don't want anyone to know my affinity. At least, not yet. So we have to keep you hidden."

Snake chittered—his way of saying he understood. He was a great asset to have if I ever needed to steal something small, plus he was incredibly nosy. My magic was what kept him alive, and it gave us a special mental connection, allowing us to let each other know if there was a problem. Or if he missed me, he'd sometimes give me a nudge hug, as I called them. Little tiny hands full of love, hugging me mentally. I wiped the dopey grin off my face and scowled at Snake, who appeared to be smiling knowingly.

"Shut up, Snake," I hissed, and then I felt it. The nudge hug. "Oh, for fuck's sake," I griped before laughing as he jumped onto my chest, burying his little face against my neck. "Okay, yes, little nut prince, I'll miss you too. See you soon."

I put Snake on the ground, and he scampered over to a large tree, disappearing up into its branches. A quick glance at the bench had me relieved to see the ghost had disappeared as well. No distractions, and no turning back now. I double-checked that the invitation was in my bag, along with my burner phone, some cash, and my mask. The bag was a black, leather, designer backpack that I'd pined over for months before I finally broke down and bought it. I wasn't materialistic by any means, but I did appreciate quality and was willing to pay for it.

With a quick roll of my head, I cracked my neck and took my last breath as a free woman. Head held high, I stomped across the street, the heels of my thigh-high, black, leather boots announcing my arrival as I made eye contact with one of the bouncers and held it. Fuck the line—there was no way I was waiting outside. The hunt was on, and I was salivating just imagining all the possible ways tonight could go.

My eyes were laser focused on the bouncers at the front of the line, so much so that I was completely taken off guard when someone bumped into me hard enough to send me staggering to the right. Thanks to the groups of people in line snapping pictures, camera flashes suddenly blinded me, and my vision spun, making white spots dance around.

A big hand grabbed my upper arm, preventing me from slamming into a group of people. I was already tensing, prepared to make a grab for my weapon, when the guy apologized. "I'm so sorry," he muttered, pulling me upright.

I blinked a few times, chasing away the temporary blindness. *Oh.* I recognized him from my research. Frank, one of the gang's higher-up members. He handled shipments and oversaw exports. All illegal, of course. His dark eyes took in my outfit, and I stepped out of his arms, holding my hands out in a 'no, thank you, I'm fine' gesture.

I flashed a fake smile. "No problem. I was distracted."

Frank held up a finger, like a genius thought had just struck one of his two brain cells. "Let me make this right. I insist. Come with me."

Wary of Frank and his motives, I followed two steps behind him until we reached the bouncers. I heard a few "lucky bitch" comments muttered from those still standing in the painfully slow line.

"Evening, gentlemen," Frank crooned, earning a few eye rolls from security. "As you probably saw, I bumped into this sweet thing back there and I wanted to apologize—" A loud ringtone suddenly cut through his words, and Frank fished his phone from his pocket, his face paling at whatever he saw on the screen. "Gotta take this... See you around, sugar."

I watched in annoyance as that slimy ass skittered away, phone held to his ear. One of the bouncers continued checking IDs and stamping hands. I wasn't one to get this far and not get what I came for though. I wanted to be in that damn club. *Now.* I stepped to the side to speak with the other two bouncers and made room for a small chick who was wearing some kick-ass butterfly wings. Oh damn, so shiny. *I want wings.*

"Did you not see the line?" one of the bouncers asked, drawing me out of my momentary pout.

I pressed my palm to my chest and tossed a glance backward at the line. "Oh, I saw it. Did you not see this dress and these boots?" My focus switched to the bigger, black man beside him, who was smirking at me. I could work with that. "I have this too." I pulled the invitation out of my bag and handed it over.

The two of them looked it over, giving me a skeptical look. "Okay..." the bigger of the two said, drawing out the word so it almost started as a statement and ended like a question. He folded the invitation, then tossed it into the trash can.

What the hell? I could tell I was losing them; they were eyeballing me like I was a stage five clinger. Desperate times called for desperate measures.

I was seconds away from being waved off when I squeaked, cutting off whatever words they were about to say. "I think I stepped in gum or something when I crossed the street. Could you take a look for me?"

"Miss, you're going to have to wai—" He abruptly stopped protesting as I lifted my leg straight up, giving him a direct look at the sole of my boot and a straight shot of my cunt. Lace G-strings only covered so much.

"Fuckin' Christ, get her inside. You have a mask? They're required." The other bouncer—who'd been silent so far—reached out to steady me as I lowered my leg.

With a big smile, I pulled out my bunny mask, the white gems reflecting the neon colors of the lights, practically glowing in their settings on the tall black ears. "All set, big guy."

"James, escort this one to Top Tier. I think the bosses might appreciate her choice of mask for the evening," the grumpy, tattooed head guy ordered the smirky, nice one.

Thank fuck. I'm in. I knew the bunny ears would work. Kinky, naughty gangster demons.

My escort held out his arm for me to take, and I stifled a snort. Like this was some kind of upstanding ball for royalty. If dirty, seedy underbelly ever had a face, it would be this city. This fucking club. This gods damn gang. I situated my mask and slipped my arm through James's.

"Welcome to Haunt, where anything you desire is possible. Whatever you're into, or looking for, I guarantee you can find it here."

"Thank you," I murmured distractedly. My eyes were busy sweeping my surroundings. The entrance led to a wide hall with walls completely covered in detailed graffiti. Black lights lit the walls up in flares of neon, every color you could imagine. The music was getting louder, but there was no sign of the actual club yet.

A group of women were just ahead of us, and at the end of the hall, they took a left. We went right. "The main club is that way, but you've been selected to be VIP tonight so you get access to Top Tier."

"What does that mean, exactly?"

"There is an exclusive upper level of the club. VIP guests are the only ones allowed into Top Tier." I lifted a brow, pretending I had no idea why I'd been chosen. He chuckled. "Our bosses have certain... tastes. Let's just say, we think you may be intriguing to them. Isn't that why everyone comes to these parties? To let loose and maybe catch the eye of The Exiled?"

"You mean I'll get to meet them tonight?" I asked, faking my fangirl excitement. I mean, I *was* excited, just not for the reason most of these people would be.

James winked at me. "Definitely. Maybe more than that, if you play it right. Your little boot stunt out there was a nice touch."

We shared a knowing look. I didn't even try to argue, because really, what was the point? He knew I was trying to get in here, and here I was. So I just shrugged.

To my surprise, James bellowed a laugh. "You just might make it out, girl. I like your spirit. Here we are." I released his arm, and he used his thumb to scan us into the exclusive part of the club. "After you."

The door swung open, revealing a flight of stairs. The music swept down the steps, that loud, contagious energy that only nightclubs create reaching for me, luring me into its depths. Vaguely aware of my escort shouting over the booming bass, I did hear him say that everything upstairs was part of the exclusive Top Tier.

When I reached the top of the stairs, I schooled my expression, not wanting to give away my real reaction of *holy fucking shit*. Internally, I thanked the emotionless drones who'd taught me at the academy how to be just like them... because there were writhing bodies. Everywhere. Dancing, humping, fucking. Dancers hung from the ceiling, suspended by ropes, twisting their lithe bodies in time with the music. Strobe lights and flashes of neon lit up the otherwise pitch-black space.

"Enjoy your evening at Haunt!" James yelled in my ear before disappearing back down the stairs. I didn't give him a second thought, moving further into the club, eager to see what an Exiled party was really like. How dark could they really be?

I'd never seen so much leather, latex, lace, and flesh in my life. And the masks. So many fucking masks. Some were your typical, masquerade style, but others were straight out of horror films and nightmares. And then there were the kinks. A quick scan of the room took in bondage restraints, collars, gags, and some things I'd never even laid eyes on before. *Good for them. Damn.*

My brain felt like it was spinning as I neared a balcony. I was in sensory overload, in the best possible way. "Gopnik" by Mareux had everyone grinding, completely entranced by the sultry beat and raspy voice.

I shouldered my way to the front of the balcony, getting my first real look at the expanse of Haunt. It was massive. The lower level was almost like a pit, full of people. The balcony I was on ran in a full circle, about twenty feet above the dance floor. Along the walls, there were alcoves with neon signs shaped into different things. I caught a glimpse of a skeleton, a huge dick spurting cum in flashes, and what looked like a pig snout.

"First time at Haunt?" a woman called out to me over the music, and I swiveled to look at her. Her short, blonde hair was in little pigtails, and she had a pair of wings attached to her back. I realized it was the girl from the line earlier.

"Yeah! Is it easy to tell?" I shouted back, offering a smile and sneakily eyeing those sparkly wings. *Wonder if she made them?*

She laughed. "I think everyone's a little shell-shocked the first time. You saw the sex cells?"

"I'm sorry—the *what*?"

Her head tilted toward the alcove I'd been staring at, which proudly displayed *It isn't going to lick itself* in neon lights. "The sex cells. Each alcove leads to a different room, but the signs give a pretty clear description of what goes on inside. Like that one there?" She pointed at the licking one. "It's for people who love oral sex. Giving and receiving. And it's anonymous. Just head on in there, pull your panties down, climb up on the platform on your hands and knees—or your back—and get serviced. Only your bottom half is visible to the room. Or, you can go take a peek and see if anyone's looking especially tasty to you."

"I think I need a drink or two first," I fired back, flashing a wink at my little, butterfly friend as I ignored the rising heat in my body at the visual she'd painted in my brain.

"Sure thing, doll. But you're gonna want to stay right where you are. They're about to make their entrance!" Her eyes sparkled. I didn't even have to ask who 'they' were. Of course they'd make a grand entrance.

Right on cue, the music stopped and the lights shut off, plunging the club into darkness. The roar of the crowd was deafening, and I'd be lying if I said I wasn't swept up in the feeling, the excitement of what was to come.

"People of Port Black!" a voice boomed through the speakers, eliciting another round of screams. "The Exiled thank you for coming to the party! Are you ready to welcome our city's leaders like they deserve?"

My heart was thundering. I was about to see them. In person. For the first time.

"I said, are you ready to welcome your fucking leaders like the royalty they are?!"

The crowd was turning manic, on the verge of rioting. That's how crazy they were for these psychopaths. *How? Why?*

The sound of a slow heartbeat began thumping through the club, and it seemed every soul in the building was holding their breath. We couldn't see a thing, adding to the anticipation, raising the hair on my arms.

"Here they come," Butterfly Girl shouted, clapping her hands as she bounced up and down.

Five red lights flashed along the balcony, and if I wasn't so used to ghosts popping up in my face without warning, I probably would've screamed as I came face to face with a man in a mask. His face was a skeleton, and his head tilted slightly, his dark eyes boring into mine. Slowly, his painted smile stretched into something that should've been truly terrifying, but I didn't so much as blink.

The longer we stared at each other, the further his smile grew. He was sexy as sin, and I could tell he was shirtless, but I didn't dare break eye contact to look. The club was suddenly plunged into darkness again for a moment before orange lights lit up the same spots.

I blinked, looking around for the skeleton guy, but was quickly distracted by the new dancer before me. A big guy with red hair rolled his hips in time with the beat, making the crowd go wild. The gas mask he wore deterred a closer look at his appearance. He didn't focus on one single person as he danced; this one clearly liked to show off. My eyes trailed down his body to find him wearing a leather tutu, full fishnet stockings, garters, and combat boots. Good gods.

Darkness. Blue lights.

Damn, I'd picked a good spot to stand. Another guy before me, this one with dark hair and a simple masquerade mask. How mysterious. I cocked an eyebrow at him as his eyes narrowed on me, almost as though he could hear my thoughts.

Darkness. Green lights.

"A latex pig mask? Holy fuck!" I squealed, unable to stop my reaction.

The absolutely ripped man before me gripped the railing so hard, his knuckles turned white. I didn't miss the amount of blades he had strapped to his body. As I let my own hand trail down my hip to my knife, I heard a growl over the music, which did things to me that usually required a lot more than just a sound.

Darkness. Yellow lights.

Now a tall man in a black hoodie was inches from my face, in a mask with neon green stitching for facial features. Standing behind the balcony railing, he lifted a hand and pointed directly at me before leaning back and fucking free falling from the ledge. The crowd screamed and cheered as the four other members of The

Exiled followed suit, landing on their feet and promptly taking hold of diamond-studded leashes which were attached to...

Oh gods.

"I'd give anything to be on the other end of one of those leashes!" Butterfly Girl yelled, and I watched as the crowd below parted, making way for the five gang bosses as they each approached the center of the dance floor from different parts of the room.

Each of them held a leash connected to a person—some women, some men, all in either a puppy or kitten mask, all of them crawling on their hands and knees, wagging whip-like tails that were coming out of their asses. How were they staying in pla— *Oh. Oh my shit stars.*

They were butt plugs. *Clench. New kink unlocked.*

I thought I'd seen everything.

I thought I knew what turned me on.

I was wrong.

Of course I knew who these men were. They weren't men at all. They were fucking demons who had been running around unchecked for far too long. Witches and mages were out in the open, coexisting mostly peacefully with humans. Demons were—from what I'd been taught at the academy—a dark secret. Neither the civilians in the magical nor human community knew of their existence, and for the most part, the demons stayed in their own realm: Besmet.

But every so often, demons would slip through the portals, either by choice, or in the case of these five, banishment. They had no right to be here. Killing, maiming, breaking the laws that had been carefully crafted to keep peace between supes and humans... They needed to be neutralized.

I was here for a mission. I'd trained for years and researched for months.

I would do whatever I needed to in order to complete my goal. I'd let these demons into my life and into my bed if that's what it took. I'd expose them for what they were.

And then... Well, then I was prepared to kill them.

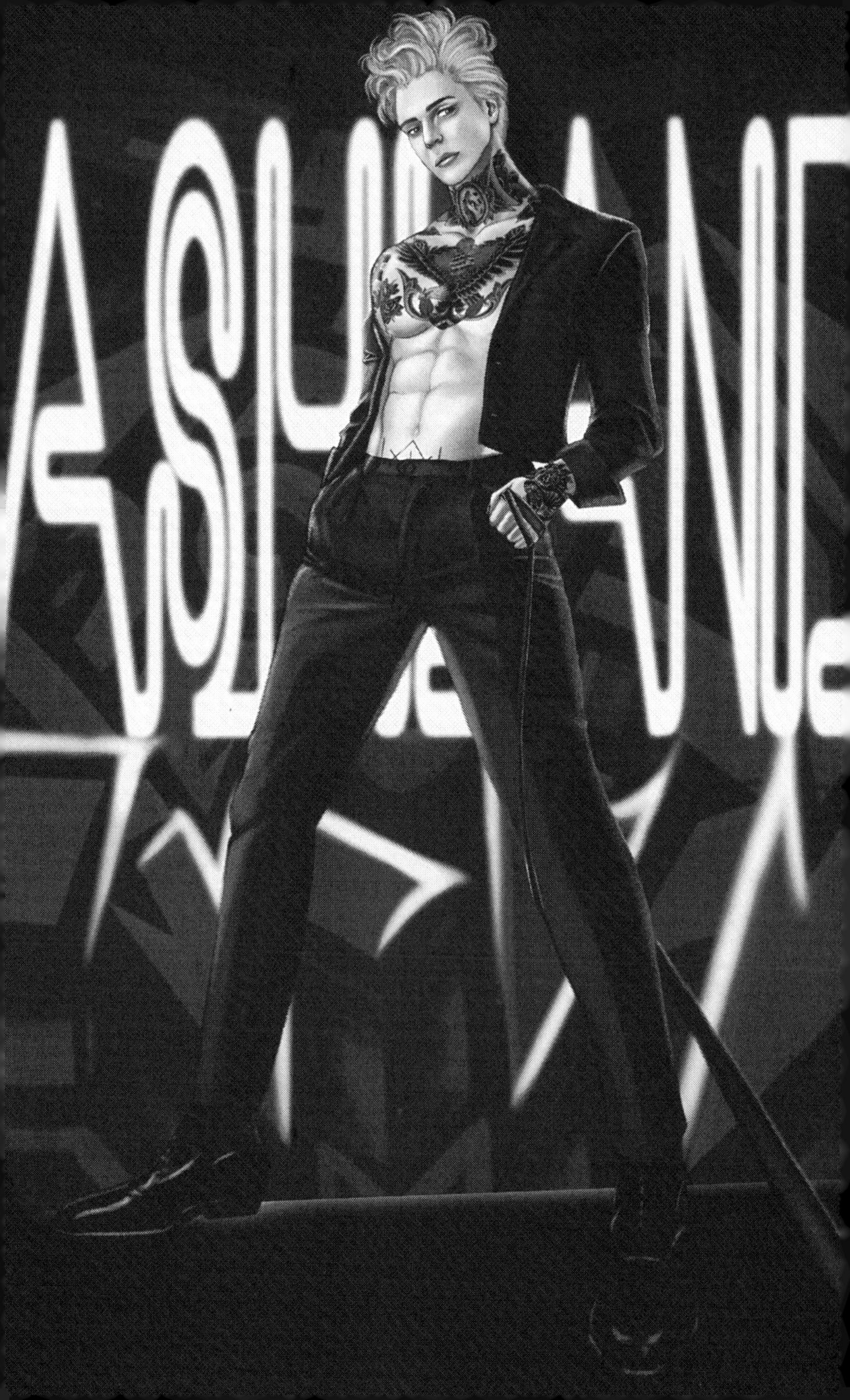

ASHLAND

Chapter Two

The crowd was roaring, stifling the sound of the music, though I could feel the bass thumping beneath the thick soles of my boots. Tension in the leash had me slowing my pace. I'd already forgotten about the big beefy man at the end of it. Looking back at the poor guy, I spotted the fire in his eyes beneath his puppy mask, and suddenly, I was interested again.

This prime piece of Grade A fuckboy human flesh owed me some serious money. Not that I really gave a shit about money; I could always get more of that. What you couldn't get more of was gods damn respect. Any fucker could earn or steal some green, but respect and fear? That was the shit that got my cock hard and my balls aching. Unfortunately for all involved, there was nothing about this particular asshole that got me hard.

I got off on questionable shit, but I wasn't a fucking monster. I'd offered Jack a deal. I'd wipe his debt clean if he agreed to crawl around wearing my collar, on my fucking leash, all night. It was too good for him to pass up, even if the son of a bitch had gritted his teeth hard enough to crack a molar as he agreed. Pride. I fucking loved seeing these supposedly proud men—who were greedy little fucks—degraded to nothing more than my pups.

Jack couldn't see my face, which was effectively hidden behind my black, mesh mask with stitched eyes, but he could certainly see my hands, the way I brought them up my thighs and cupped my junk, eliciting more screams from the crowd. I brought my arms out wide, riling my people even higher. It was all for them, and we were just getting started. I wanted them drunk on the fucking air. Neon lasers flashed through the club, illuminating glimpses of masks and bodies. It was fucking electric.

My gaze lifted to the balcony I'd just free fallen from, and sure enough, a pair of glittering bunny ears were looking right back down at me. Gods, the bouncers knew us too well. *I bet she has a fluffy little tail...*

It had been so long since I'd been in a good hunt. Back in Besmet, the five of us used to tear up the woods, hunting all types of prey. Port Black was a city in the human realm though, and since our race was a secret, it wasn't like we could let our demons out of the bag and terrorize woodland creatures to satisfy our primal urges.

We'd been banished from our home years ago for being a part of the resistance, a group of demons throughout the realm who opposed the tyrannical rule of the monarchy. It wasn't like we were always on that side of things, but some things were just impossible to ignore. Or forgive. Or forget.

"Ash!" one of my boys called out, bringing me back to the pulsing atmosphere of the club. It was probably Talon. Misha never talked. Rhodes wasn't a yeller—at least not in public—and Felix was probably doing inappropriate... or extremely appropriate things to his kittens.

"Let's go, pup," I ordered Jack, tugging on his leash. My eyes widened when the stubborn shit resisted. The people dancing around us froze, immediately recognizing the disobedience. Sighing, I reached up and grabbed the top of my mask, removing it with a harsh tug.

The music died a faster death than a vampire at dawn. My boys were at my back instantly. I didn't need to look; I could sense them there. That's how it had been for so long, and it was second nature.

I stepped forward, still holding the leash. "Jacky, Jacky, Jacky," I said sadly, shaking my head. "I thought we had a deal? Your debt of half a million dollars gone forever, for one night of your submission as a puppy."

My piss-poor excuse of a pup was shaking with rage. Or fear. Who knew?

"Why is he still down there if he's not playing?" Talon questioned, removing his gas mask.

Misha stomped forward, not bothering to take off his pig mask before he bent down and lifted all two hundred and thirty pounds of Jack to his feet by his collar. He slipped his fingers into the harness around Jack's waist, and before anyone could move, the collar, puppy mask, and tail had all been cut.

"I–I'll get the money," Jack stammered, sweat running down his face.

Felix's dark eyes met mine, his deep laugh filling the quiet club. "I don't fuckin' believe this guy, do you, Ash? You think he's gonna pay, Rhodes?"

Rhodes glanced at Jack, looking disgusted. He couldn't stand people who were messy, untrustworthy, or scumbags in general. "I highly doubt it... and he smells like an old Cheeto."

Talon's eyes widened. "But like, flamin' hot or regular?"

"Gentlemen," I interrupted. "Even though this is a valid question—and one I feel we should revisit later—we're in the middle of a party here. So, let's get back to it, shall we?" Misha looked at me, and we moved at the same moment. My blade sank into the left side of Jack's neck, and Misha's sank into the right.

"The Exiled do not abide thieves, cheats, or liars! This man was given a fair opportunity to clear his debt, and he chose to spit in our faces. Let's get back to the party—the night is young and so are we!" Felix shouted as Jack collapsed to the floor. Our minions were already rushing in to drag his body off. Good fucking riddance. I had no place for trash in my city.

Rihanna's "Bitch Better Have My Money" started playing, and I danced my ass the whole way up to the special VIP lounge of Top Tier. I'd just put on a show, and now I was hoping there might be a little bunny up there who'd be interested in putting one on for me... and maybe my boys too.

Felix collapsed next to me, spreading his long legs wide as he removed his skeleton mask. "Fuckin' hell, Ash. Way to start a party. Though I'm a little upset that my kitten time got cut short. I didn't even get to feel their little claws." He turned his dark brown eyes in my direction and pouted. A full-on, pretty baby pout, with his bottom lip jutting out and everything.

The tattoo that wrapped around his neck drew my attention, as it usually did. A feminine hand, squeezing the life out of him. It was an attention-getter, but that was Felix as a whole.

"Quit your bitching, brother. We have all night for you to find some pretty pussies to play with." Talon grinned, jumping up on the low table at our knees. Considering he was built like a Scottish Highlander, the guy moved like a ballerina at times, which explained the tutu tonight. The vision of his leather chest harness, tutu, and gas mask was a whole ass vibe. Though I wasn't sure if it was a high fashion type of vibe or that of a deranged dude who sneaks into your bedroom at night and makes weird breathing noises while he rifles through your underwear drawer.

Either way, a bold choice. One had to respect such flair.

The crowd of onlookers gasped and cheered as he launched himself at the pole rising out of the center of the clear table, neon lights glowing within.

"I haven't seen him yet. No word from the team at the docks yet either," Rhodes piped up, like we were already in the middle of discussing business as he lit up his signature cigar. Thankfully, I knew who he was referring to, and the corner of my mouth lifted with a smirk. The night really was just getting started.

Before I could respond to Rhodes, a server appeared through the mass of people, bringing our drinks of choice. Whiskey for me, an

Old-Fashioned for Rhodes, a pint of beer and a shot of top-shelf vodka for Misha, an Irish Car Bomb for Felix, and an Appletini for Talon.

Of course, our drinks were all spiked heavily with Dragon's Fireball from our realm. Despite being a fucking shithole, it was the only place that could make alcohol potent enough to fuck us up. We were lucky to still have some loyal friends on the inside who could source us a few necessities.

"Listen." I leaned in, not wanting anyone to overhear us, even if it was highly unlikely given the volume of the music. "It's going to work. Tonight, we're going to catch us a rat."

Felix dropped his shot into his glass of beer and whooped before throwing the whole thing back. The crowd who was watching from behind the roped-off area lost their minds as alcohol spilled from his mouth, dripping down his neck and chest. Slamming the glass down on the table, he glanced at me and Rhodes. "I certainly hope it works. Little Bobby didn't deserve to go down like that, man. I gave him the best asshole tatt of my life. *My life!* Now my work is wasted." Felix glanced over my shoulder as he trailed off, eyes glittering with interest. "Be right back."

Misha grunted from the end of the sectional, his gigantic boots kicked up on the table, those watchful eyes taking in everything. He kind of reminded me of that eye that saw everything... What was the name of that fucking movie? *Lord of the Things? The Eye of Salmon?* But in this case, the eye was Misha, and right now, that eye was watching Talon spin around like a ribbon in the wind.

"He's right. Asshole tattoo or not, Bob didn't deserve that. None of our boys do. To know that one of our own is behind the deceit?" Rhodes's upper lip curled, giving him that look of superiority he wore so gods damn well. Daddy. As. Fuck.

Suddenly, Misha stood, pulling a blade from one of the hundred places he had them on his body. Talon was hanging upside down, legs locked, his hands gripping the pole, allowing his back to arch. He froze as Misha reached out toward his abdomen, blade in hand. At the swift slicing motion of Misha's left hand, I heard Talon suck in a sharp breath.

The big male smirked, tucking away his blade and retaking his seat on the sofa. Talon slid down the pole, placing both hands on the table, letting each leg fall gracefully one after the other to the floor before he whirled around on Misha. "What the fuck?!" Talon leaned down, getting in Misha's face.

"Fight or fuck?" Rhodes directed at me as we looked on.

I took a sip of my whiskey. "Could go either way. I got five on fuck."

"You're on," he replied, just as Misha lifted up a thin, black thread, about three inches long.

Talon's gaze bounced from the thread to Misha's face. "You cut a loose thread from my tutu? Oh my gods, please tell me it wasn't hanging there the whole night?" Misha tossed the offensive thread off to the side, shaking his head before taking another drink. "Why'd you do that?" Talon pushed, leaning in further.

I swallowed my laugh when I saw Rhodes opening up his banking app on his phone.

"Pretty," Misha growled, bringing his hand up and letting his fingers trail over the material of Talon's leather skirt. A little tug had Talon tumbling onto the big man's lap.

Then they were making out. My phone vibrated in my hand, and I saluted Rhodes when I saw the notification for the five thousand dollars that had just hit my account. Another notification came through before I could put the phone down, and I couldn't stop the deep growl that left my chest as I scanned the message from Rooster, one of our guys down at the docks.

Rooster: Rats showed. 25. X'd em all.
Me: Get back to Haunt. Good work.

Slowly, I pocketed the phone and raised my glass to my lips. The burn of the alcohol as it slid down my throat stoked my fury to new levels. It wasn't like this was unexpected. Over the last six months, shit had been happening. Money was missing, our rivals—The Scorpions—were thwarting our fucking plans, product was being destroyed, and members were disappearing or being taken out during ambushes when The Scorpions should've had no clue about our plans.

There was only one explanation. A fucking rat. In ten years, we'd never had this issue—yet we were, with a gods damned traitor in our gang. A brotherhood of rejects, the men and women society deemed unworthy, too fucked in the head, not safe for public consumption... We took them and built an empire. Gave them a family, a safe place to let their demons out to play without fear or judgment.

"I'm gonna fuckin' kill him," Felix snarled, rejoining us, phone in hand and lipstick smeared across his mouth and neck.

Talon shifted, crossing his legs and leaning against Misha's chest. "Get in line, brother. I can already smell him. He's close."

I inhaled, taking in a mix of leather, alcohol, sweat, and sex. Just underneath, the scent I was searching for—too strong aftershave and olives. Fucking Frank. I was on my feet in a flash, cracking my neck when I was hit with it. Crisp air, like a fall morning. The decaying of leaves and damp earth mixed with a hint of... cherries?

I spotted her ears before I saw the rest of her as she strutted through the crowd, weaving through the writhing bodies and holding the hand of a small, pixie-like woman. The two darted through an opening, giving the five of us a direct view as they passed right by the ropes separating us.

"Oh my fuck, a bunny. I want it," Talon growled, and I didn't even have to look to know his nails were already sharpening against Misha's thighs.

"Who is she?" Felix asked, coming to stand next to me as we tracked her movements like the monsters we were.

My brow lifted when Frank appeared, clearly en route to us, but the lying fuck got distracted by my bunny. He came to a stop, forcing her and her little butterfly to also stop in their tracks. Frank was a good-looking guy, I'd give him that. Too bad he wouldn't be after tonight.

Focusing my hearing, I was able to pick up their conversation easily. "Looking good, sweetheart. Damn. I'm not surprised you ended up in Top Tier," Frank crooned.

My bunny tilted her head and surveyed Frank, with his shoulder-length, dark hair and strong jawline. Bringing his hand up, he ran his filthy fucking fingers through her long, straight ponytail.

"I'm going to remove each one of those right after I pluck the nails and break each knuckle." We all turned and glanced at Talon, who was now standing on the table, leering at Frank. "*What?*" he demanded, looking scandalized at our expressions. "I'm just letting you fuckers know."

"Don't touch me."

We all heard it. For all of our proclivities, those three words were like throwing a match in the middle of a forest that hadn't seen rain in months. I had to actively work to keep my horns from sprouting and my wings from erupting.

Frank laughed as he ignored her, placing both of his hands on her hips and tugging her hard toward him. Hard enough that her hand left her friend's and her drink sloshed over the rim.

"Frank!" I barked, deliberately letting some of my demon lace my tone. Bunny Baby and Frank both turned to look, and I caught Misha beckoning them over with a crook of one massive finger. His big ass hadn't even left the couch. Frank released the girl as though he'd been burned and moved toward us, but without the bunny. That wouldn't do.

"You too, Bunny!" Talon shouted, doing a twirl.

Rhodes intercepted Frank and guided him roughly, pushing him down on the sofa, right next to Misha. I could hear them talking, but couldn't focus on anything other than the creature stomping toward me in those sexy ass boots that deserved to be licked. Sweet fucking moons, my demon was scaling the cage he was confined within, desperate to get out and devour this sweet treat.

My mouth was watering. My dick was thumping.

And then my eyes met hers.

Murder. They were full of murder.

I tossed my head back and laughed deeply, because holy fucking shit, I think I'd just fallen in love with a gods damn murderess wearing a rabbit mask and fuck-me boots.

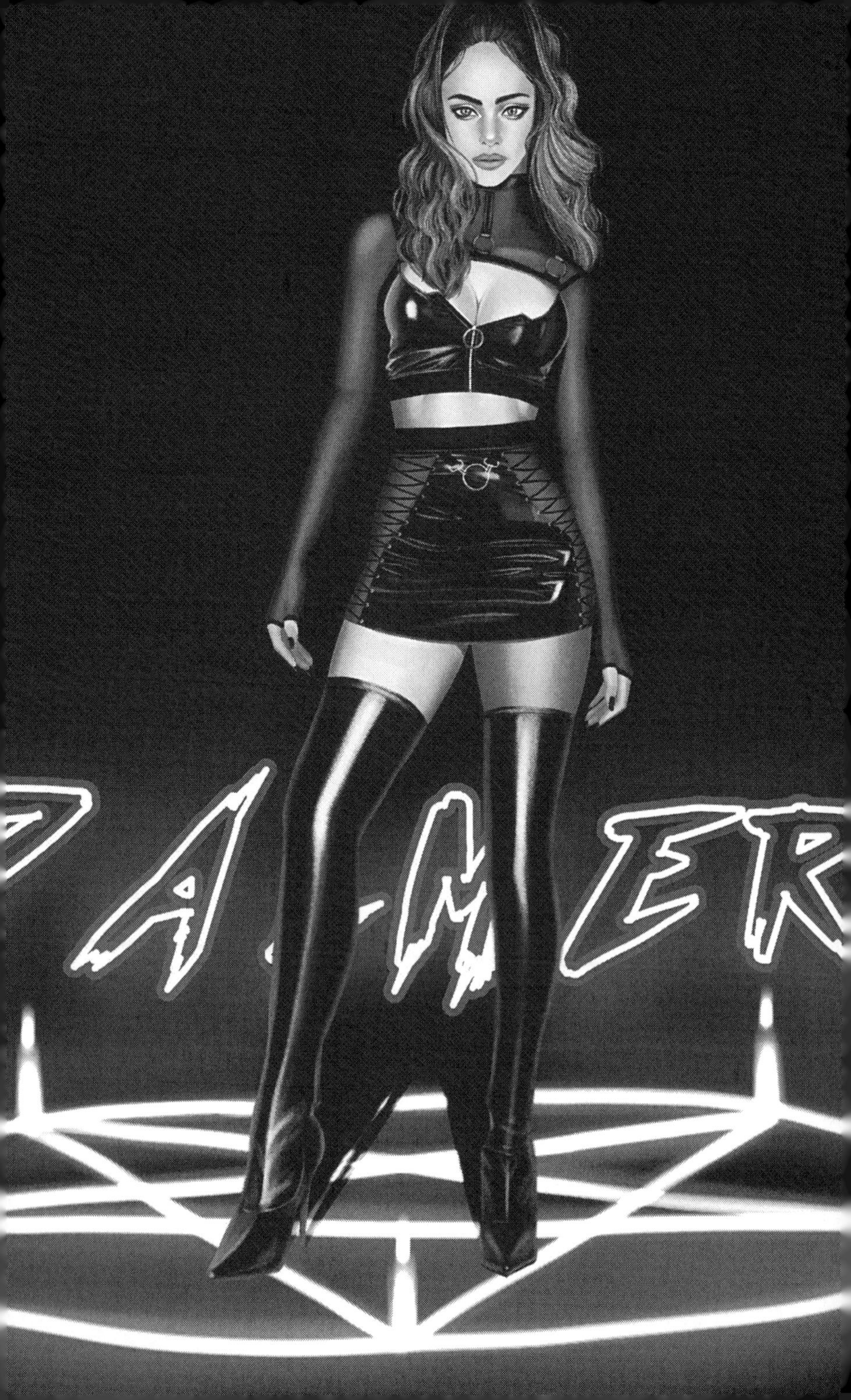

PALMER

Chapter Three

My eyes pierced his as I stormed over, pissed as hell at being summoned like a fucking animal, but at the same time, this was good. *Chill out, Palmer. This is the opening you wanted.* My new friend's hand was sweaty in mine, and I felt the way her fingers trembled with each step we took toward the group of unstable gang leaders. I couldn't blame her. They'd literally stabbed a man in the neck like it was just another day in the office.

I'd heard of them, heard the stories. Anyone who wanted to know could find out; it wasn't like The Exiled hid what they did. Why they did it though, that was what interested me. There was another gang in the neighboring city that was just as toxic, but their city was a bit different. While Port Black was dangerous, it wasn't filthy. The city was kept relatively clean, whereas West Harbor was a mess and just as dangerous as Port Black. It seemed as though The Exiled actually cared about the state of their city, not just their power over it.

Rumor had it that this gang ran the city with an iron fist, and anyone who objected to their rule ended up beaten, missing, or dead. The entire gang fell under the name The Exiled, but when you heard whispers on the street, everyone knew exactly who was at the top of the chain. And I was about to meet them all, live and in color.

Ashland was staring at me so intensely that it was starting to piss me off. I didn't want some murderous, criminal-minded fuckboy staring at me like that. It had nothing to do with the fact that he was even more gorgeous in person than his photos suggested.

At that moment, if I could have spewed fire at him from my eyes, he would've been a pile of ash. In fact, I was wishing like hell that I had a pyro affinity so I could light this bitch up like a charbroiled chicken wing. He seemed to know it too, though instead of recognizing danger, he laughed. Fucking laughed.

"Are you fucking kidding me?" The words were out of my mouth, no stopping them. Ashland's head snapped forward, and another demon—the one usually dressed like a 1920's mobster—appeared at his side, glaring daggers at me. With his mask gone, it made his scowling all the more severe, even though it had only been a masquerade mask. While I'd classify most of The Exiled as hot, I'd call Rhodes handsome or roguish. He was striking in his fancy clothes, but he really was a wolf in designer sheep's clothing.

"Problem here?" he asked, letting his gaze flick down my body before quickly returning to my face.

Ashland shook his head. "Nah, Rhodes. No problem. I was just about to introduce myself to these two. Do you have your handkerchief? That barbarian caused her to spill half of her drink."

Rhodes pulled a silk hankie out of his breast pocket, holding it out for me to take. I tossed the rest of my drink back, then took the small square of fabric, wiping down my fingers and arm.

Satisfied that I got it all, I tossed the hankie back to Rhodes and met Ashland's blue gaze. "Well, what do you want?" I crossed my arms, pushing my cleavage up. They knew I wasn't from here. I could easily get away with pretending I had no idea who the fuck they were and take a shot at their egos in the same strike.

My cute, little friend gasped and gripped my upper arm. "She's not from here. I'm sorry," she stammered, seconds away from dropping to her knees to beg for forgiveness on my behalf.

Ashland waved her off, but Rhodes seemed to take the dig for what it was, narrowing his eyes at me. Good. He'd be the one I could wear down. Fucking dapper, dandy dickwad.

"It's not a problem. We're glad to have you two here tonight. I'm Ashland, one of the owners of the club. Would you like a drink...?" He let the sentence hang, and my friend picked up on the cue, blushing as she gave her name.

"Cherry."

He barely glanced at her. "And you?"

"Palmer."

"Palmer," he repeated, his tongue flicking out to wet his bottom lip. I had to mentally bitch slap myself when my vagina pulsed, hearing how good my name sounded coming from his dirty mouth.

"I'll take a shot of your most expensive tequila. Make it a double. And one for Cherry." I gestured to my new friend.

Ashland's eyes darted over my shoulder, and his chin tilted up. A server appeared two seconds later, eagerly taking his order. My own focus had shifted to the redhead who was currently towering over the group, thanks to the table he was standing on. This was the one who'd been wearing the gas mask earlier. Talon. His fishnets and tutu were on proud display as he leaned back against the pole. He caught me looking and winked. Damn, he was pretty.

"Your drink, Palmer," Ashland purred, drawing me back into his orbit and handing me a shot glass. "Come and sit with us?"

I chanced a look at Cherry, who was eagerly nodding. "Lovely," I muttered, squeezing between Rhodes and Ashland, ignoring the way my hair seemed to stand on end as my skin brushed against them. The second my ass hit the leather sofa, Talon pounced. Literally. Like a tiger in a tutu. His knees landed on either side of my thighs, and I held my glass up, trying to prevent any spillage, again.

Plucking the shot glass from my fingers, he gripped my jaw and tilted my head back. "Don't. Move. Bunny."

My eyes were the only thing I dared to move, and I watched him unsnap a small pouch on his leather harness, pulling out the smallest salt shaker I'd ever seen. "You keep a tiny salt shaker in your harness?"

He chuckled. "I like to be prepared. If I didn't have this right now, you'd be saltless with a double shot of tequila."

"Thanks," I murmured, reaching up to take it from him. The sharp slap came fast, leaving the top of my hand stinging. "What the *fuck?*"

"I said not to move, Bunny. I'll handle this. Now, be still. Next time, it'll be your ass."

I flopped back against the cushions with the top of my hand tingling and my face warm from Talon's surprisingly bossy attitude. The fishnets and tutu clearly had me drawing conclusions about him that simply weren't true. Like, that he was a prissy little bitch who—

All thoughts died as I watched him theatrically lick his lips, the piercings in his tongue glinting in the neon lighting. "Hold my hips, Bunny." I gripped him firmly as he began thrusting his hips, working them in a way that no man I'd ever been with in my life ever had before. I couldn't look away. The creamy skin of his abdomen rolled with each perfectly in sync movement.

Gods damn. I was supposed to be listening in on whatever conversation was going on at the other end of the couch between the bearded knife yeti and that fuckhead, Frank. I needed to hear if they were talking business.

"Uh-uh, little Bunny. Eyes right here. I want to see it when it happens," Talon growled, raising the hair on my arms.

"When what happens?" I rasped, unable to deny how my own hips were beginning to lift. Wetting his lips once more, he lifted the salt shaker and sprinkled it on his mouth. Fuck. Bracing himself with his left hand on the back of the sofa, his right twisted in my ponytail. I was panting, and it really pissed me off.

Talon leaned in, his nose brushing the column of my exposed neck. My eyes rolled when his warm breath hit my skin, and when I refocused, I found myself caught in the gaze of a beast. With his stance wide, Misha looked like he was the size of three of me.

"I want to see the look on your face when you realize how fucked you are. That a little bunny such as yourself should never have walked into a den of monsters," Talon whispered into my ear.

My palm landed on his chest as I pushed him away. "Can I have my drink now, or are you going to talk all night?"

"Salt first. Suck, Bunny." Talon tilted my head by using his grip on my hair and smashed our lips together. Saltiness, apple flavor, and something unique to this demon assaulted my senses. Time froze as we fucked each other's mouths with our tongues, and I cried out when he bit down on my bottom lip, breaking the skin with ease.

Talon pulled back, chest heaving, and took my shot glass. Gods, I needed that drink now. "Open for me, Bunny."

Open for him? What?

He lifted the glass and tossed the tequila back in one fast motion. Outraged, a "Hey!" left my lips before his hand was there, prying my mouth open as his face hovered right above mine. His bright blue eyes pierced me like twin icicles, and the fire of the alcohol lit my taste buds as he spit the entire shot into my mouth. I swallowed it all just as Misha leaned over us and shoved a lime in both of our mouths.

What the hell just happened?

"Mmm," the ginger-haired demon growled, his eyes locked on mine. "There it is. You look so fucked for me right now."

It took everything in me, but I had to recall why I was here in the first fucking place. It definitely wasn't to get unsolicited lap dances or let psychopathic demons spit tequila in my mouth. The mask had worked a hundred times better than I'd anticipated; I'd easily gotten their attention. Now that I had it, I needed to keep it. Everything I'd studied about these creatures alluded to them enjoying not only mask kinks, but more specifically, prey and predator type stuff. I'd been hoping that the bunny ears were just different enough from the usual leather kitten or puppy masks. Seems I was right.

"How do you think you look right now?" I slid my palms up his thighs, heading further north. "You're the one straddling me in a gods damn skirt with a raging boner and nipples hard enough to take out an unsuspecting eye."

A deep, almost lyrical laugh filtered in, breaking our stare down. "Damn, bro. She's got you there. Who's your friend?"

Talon grunted, swinging his leg over me and settling down next to me. "This is Bunny."

"My name isn't Bunny," I snapped, loving the way Felix, Talon's twin, grinned at the harsh tone I used on his brother.

A completely tattoo-covered hand reached for mine, and Felix brought his lips to my skin. "I'm Felix. Pleasure to meet you, Not Bunny."

This one was total goth-boy personified. Dark hair, so dark it must've been dyed. Black fingernails, ear gauges, big, tortured eyes. The pictures I'd seen had not done his beauty justice. He was stunning, otherworldly even. Felix was trouble in a six-foot-three body that was built for fucking and killing. All of the ink was just sexy gift wrap.

"Listen, fellas. You got it wrong. I swear." Frank, the guy from earlier, was stammering, backing away from an advancing Rhodes and Ashland. With a snap of Rhodes's fingers, security was there, taking away a screaming Frank.

"What's going on?" I asked, purposely showing my interest in Frank's situation.

"Not for you to worry about. Now, I have an idea..." Felix trailed off, locking eyes with Misha as the hair from my ponytail was pushed slowly from my shoulder.

My new butterfly friend seemed occupied with a group of men and women on a sofa across the VIP space, so I let myself relax. What the fuck was I doing making a connection with someone while on an assignment? She could prove useful though. Though not a gang member—as far as I knew—she still had valuable information that no amount of hacking or research from behind a screen would've gotten me. Sometimes you needed firsthand information, the good tea from someone on the ground. That was Cherry. I needed to keep her safe.

I raised my chin and stared at Felix. "What's your idea?"

Rhodes and Ashland circled at that moment, invading my personal space as though it didn't exist to begin with. "It's been a while since we've done this..." Felix shared a heavy look with Ashland.

"Do you like games, Palmer?" Ashland murmured, leaning in as if he could suck the answer from my soul.

"Depends on the game."

"We want to hunt you," Felix growled in my ear, startling me. I snapped my face toward his, eyes wide.

"Hunt. Me?" I repeated slowly.

"Beneath the club is a maze of sorts. We designed it for our... tastes." Talon crossed his ankles as he stretched his legs out on the table.

Their tastes. Their fucked-up sexual fantasies.

Rhodes was glaring at me so hard, I couldn't tell if he was getting ready to rip me away from his boys or take an impromptu shit in the middle of the club. Who knew what went down in this maze—none of my research had mentioned anything about it, and that was a red flag right off the bat. It meant this maze was a new development, or that those who knew about it kept their damn mouths shut, or... they never survived the hunt. With the way these guys killed without remorse, it wasn't a stretch to bet on the latter. Most of the people here either worshiped them like dark deities or were terrified of them.

I needed a second to get my head on straight. My face was flushed from Talon's teasing and Felix's flirting. Getting close may have been my plan, but I hated how they'd already worked their claws into me. It had been like, thirty fucking minutes.

My mouth opened to come up with an excuse, some reason to sneak off to the ladies room and think this over in peace, but Rhodes heaved a sigh. "The maze doesn't really seem appropriate for her," he announced, crossing his arms over his broad chest as he scanned my body.

"Excuse me?"

He brought his cigar to his mouth and puffed, letting the smoke waft from his open lips as he leaned in. "My apologies. What I meant was you don't really suit the game. I like a bit of a challenge, not some fangirl groupie who drools over my crew's cocks all night."

I barked a laugh, pushing myself to my feet. Misha was already crowding in, but I didn't stop. Chest to chest with that asshole, Rhodes, I smirked. "I assure you, if I had a cock, it would be them doing the drooling." I plucked the cigar from his hand and inhaled it slowly, letting the red glow of the cherry light up our faces. "You want a challenge? You got it, Mr. Dapper. But let me be clear from the beginning." I spun, making sure to look each and every one of these demons in the eyes. "I'm *nobody's* fucking fangirl or groupie. There's only one person I'm a fan of." I dropped the cigar into Ashland's glass, enjoying the way it sizzled as it went out. Scooping up my bag, I smiled. "And you're fucking looking at her. Now, take me to the maze."

Misha grunted, holding his arm out for me to pass. Spinning, I flipped my hair and I'm pretty sure it whipped Felix and Talon both. One of them definitely moaned.

"Do they have hell-bunnies? Hell-rabbits? Mother of Saturn, I could bludgeon a man to death with this dick right now," Talon groaned, and then threw his head back and howled, setting the entire club into a fucking frenzy.

I didn't look back. I'd learned a long time ago that looking back only kept you stuck in the past.

A forest full of werewolves on a full moon would've been quieter than the roar of the crowd now. The club logos along the walls started to flicker, the lights flashing through every color in the rainbow. Suddenly, they all lit up red, while the rest of the club was plunged into darkness. The signs had one small, sinister change. The letter A was conveniently not lit, effectively changing the name from Haunt to Hunt.

"Scared yet, little girl?" Rhodes whispered, and while it should've been too loud to hear him with the amount of noise, it was as if his words cut right through it all, sending a shiver down my spine. I tried to ignore him, focusing on Misha and keeping an eye out for the stairs or elevator. They had said this maze was downstairs. A deep growl had my heart pounding, though not from fear. I knew Rhodes was right behind me.

"You wish," I muttered. Misha was right in front of us, now keeping an elevator door open for us all to step inside. His massive frame was doing a great job of separating us from the boisterous crowd.

Rhodes chuckled. "You look nervous. I just call it like I see it."

"Yeah? Well, maybe you should pull your monocle out of your asshole and take a closer look." Laughter broke out between the rest of the guys, but a tight grip around my wrist had me coming to an abrupt halt.

"Excuse me?" Rhodes leaned down, putting his face right in mine, his hand completely encircling my wrist. Hell, he could probably hold both of them in one hand.

"I thought we were making assumptions about each other." I lifted my chin as the rest of the guys crowded into the elevator. Ashland's eyes were glittering with excitement, and the twins were still cackling. "You think because I'm a woman riding in an elevator with five men, ready to play some kind of fucked-up game, that I'm scared or nervous. Right? Since I'm smaller than you, I should be terrified?" If steam could visibly blow out of someone's ears, Rhodes would've been smoking more than a tea kettle. "It's not a bad assessment. Pretty fuckin' sexist, though I can see how you arrived there. You simply look like a douche who owns a monocle."

"Kitty has claws... Meow," Felix purred, pulling me back against his body like we were best friends and not two strangers who'd just met each other for the first time. Watching his brother feed me tequila like a momma bird obviously meant he thought of me as family now.

I gave a smug little smile to Rhodes and settled in against Felix. Fuck, he smelled good. *Sweet lemons and fresh paper.* My head swam as I breathed him in, the tension between us all rising as we descended.

The elevator dinged, snapping me out of my haze. "Were you just scenting my brother, Bunny?" Talon purred.

I jumped away from Felix. "I don't know what you're talking about."

"If you want me to scent-mark you, kitty, I will," Felix growled, his eyes flashing with desire as he advanced toward me again. The doors slid open, and I took the opportunity to turn and take a breath. Unfortunately, my path was blocked by a giant.

"Few rules, Bunny. There aren't many in Haunt. Live and let live, and all that. Down here though... it's different. The Hunt is..." Ashland trailed off, his gaze scanning the enormous basement area of the club. "The Hunt is fucking *everything*."

Taking my hand, he led me out into the basement. It was dark and hard to make out much of anything, though the place looked pretty industrial, with exposed pipes and beams running along the ceiling. The walls didn't extend all the way up—the ceilings were much too high for that—but they were still tall enough to make you feel trapped.

"We all like different things and yet, quite a bit of the same things," Ashland continued cryptically, running his fingertips across my shoulder. "At our basest forms, what are we?" I swallowed as the other guys began removing the bits of clothing they had on. "What are we, Palmer?"

"We're animals."

He smiled, his white teeth appearing sharper, deadlier. Standing before me, he slowly slid his leather suspenders over his shoulders, letting them fall to his legs. "We are... And me and my boys? We're carnivores."

"So you want to, what? Eat me?"

Oh, they definitely did. I could already see some evidence of how turned on they were, and I couldn't deny the dampness that was growing between my own thighs. But with each passing second, it was as though the muscles on display in front of me grew. Each roll of a shoulder revealed more rippling bulk. They seemed to be growing, shifting, right here.

"I wanted to eat you up the second I laid eyes on you in the opening act... but I want to fucking hunt your ass down first. I want to feel your adrenaline, and get high on your fear. I'm dying to see you crawl around for me. I want your cheeks red with embarrassment and your ass warm from my hands," Ashland breathed, inches from my face now.

"And I want you to fight me, kitty. Scratch me, maul me, fucking bite me with those little teeth," Felix whispered in my ear, pressing himself against my back. He nudged my head to the side and ran his nose up my neck, breathing in deeply. "Then it's my turn to mark you... so make it count."

Oh my fucking stars.

"I'm going to scare you, Bunny babe. You're going to scream. It's gonna get this cock so hard, fuuuuck," Talon groaned, palming himself over his hot pink jockstrap. "I can hear your squeals echoing already."

My chest was rising and falling rapidly. The scenes they were painting were too good. I hadn't expected my body to react to them like this, and I suddenly felt extremely inexperienced. This was some next-level kinky shit that my brain would never have even come up with.

"Mmm, look at those hard little nipples," Ashland praised. Glancing down, I saw he wasn't wrong.

Misha bent down, his huge fingers looking ridiculous against the tiny zipper on my boots, but he slowly removed them, showing a surprising amount of tenderness as he helped me step out of them. Fuck it, I was here and I was going with it.

He stood, and I walked my fingers up his barrel chest. "And what do you want, big guy?" He just smirked, tugging on one of the bunny ears, effectively removing the mask completely from my face. His hazel eyes darkened rapidly as his pupils dilated. He scanned my face, and my brow furrowed when I thought I saw a flicker of orange in his eyes. *What the hell?*

Misha glanced away from me, looking over at the other guys as he took his time, reaching around his back to unhook his dagger belt and letting it drop to the concrete floor. I raised my leg, sliding my dress up to reveal my thigh knives before going to remove them. Misha stopped me, his massive hand covering my much smaller one, halting my movements.

"He's not a big talker, I'm afraid," Talon piped up. I couldn't see him, but his voice was getting closer. "Blades turn his big ass on, though. Oh, and blood." He paused, and I felt his presence right behind me a second before he stepped around and froze, realizing my mask had been removed. A devastating grin took over his face, and I sucked in a breath as he invaded my space further, his hand brushing a few stray hairs back from my forehead. "Most of all, Big Mishy likes pretty things. And you might just be the prettiest thing we've ever had to play with."

Misha's hand fell away from mine, and with it, the warmth that his touch provided. A shiver ran through my body, but was it from the cool underground air? Or something more... dangerous?

Get your head back in the game. Come on, Palmer.

If I was going to get through this mission and succeed, I needed to focus on my end goal here. Impress Asrael, continue building my skills and proving myself an asset to Montague Industries, and then I'd be able to use the company's resources to track down those responsible for my parents' deaths. Thinking back to the night before I left for Port Black, when I had my final impromptu training session with Laurie, I allowed her words of wisdom to ring through my head.

Whatever it takes.

With my confidence and purpose renewed, I straightened my spine, throwing Rhodes a bored look. Truth be told, I was curious about what he'd be interested in. Moody and broody should've been his tagline. "And Monocle, what about you? What do you want?"

Rhodes leaned up against an exposed support beam, returning the bored as fuck look, but I could feel his dark gaze sweeping over my face, studying me. "I want to watch them find you. I'll watch them scare you and fuck with you." He shrugged. "Fuck you, even. Then, when I blow my load, maybe it'll be on your face."

I raised both hands and flipped that son of a bitch off. "You can try and come on my face, fucker... but I guarantee you I'll be marking your face first."

Ashland released a sound that was bordering on feral as he stepped in front of me, his large body blocking out everything else. I felt his hand tremble as he gripped my chin, turning my face side to side as if inspecting me. "You just keep getting more and more delicious."

Batting his hand away, I placed my hands on my hips and stared him down, despite being much shorter. "You mentioned rules?" I needed to know right away what I was dealing with here. It wouldn't be a hardship to fuck any of them—they were all hot as sin, and if they actually fucked as dirty as they talked? Damn.

I really needed to keep my wits about me though. Their bodies had already bulked up, which would typically raise some red flags for a normal person. As far as I knew, they kept their true race a secret, and I was playing dumb at the moment.

"Mmm, yes. Those pesky little things. Do you have anything you want to say no to before we start?"

I blinked, and a huff of exasperation left my mouth. "I don't even know exactly what I'm getting myself into here."

Rhodes made a noise of disbelief. "I think you know exactly what you're getting yourself into. We fight, we fuck. Don't worry though—we don't fight women."

Oh, that smug, monocle fuckhead. Just grin and smile at him.

"The safe word is the only way to make us stop," Felix explained, adjusting himself with no shame. He was wearing the shortest pair of black boxer briefs, and every inch of him was covered in art. "Feel free to pretend you don't want something that deep down, you really do. When we're down here, everything is consensual. The safe word is the same for all of us."

Wait, what?

Misha caught my surprised reaction and let out a soft chuckle as he pulled his hair up into a bun. And there it was, that little sliver of fear that I'd pushed away.

"Everyone is fair game, Bunny. You're the special prey tonight, but we have a lot of energy to get out, and sometimes an adrenaline rush is just what's needed." Talon's expression was playful, but in all the wrong ways. His dark tone didn't match his facial expression, and it wasn't the first time I'd noticed.

"So, what's the safe word?"

Talon giggled. "Snails."

"Snails," I repeated slowly, making sure I heard that correctly.

Felix pointed at me and winked. "You got it, baby."

"Enough bullshit. Let's hunt." Rhodes stripped down to his dark red boxer briefs and disappeared into the darkness.

Talon and Felix sighed in unison, and one of them mumbled, "He's such a little preppy cunt sometimes." They turned and made to follow the path Rhodes had taken.

"Wait!" I cried out. The twins turned in sync and cocked their heads at the same fucking time. Shit. They needed to chill with the creepy stuff. "How long does the hunt last?"

Talon shrugged. "It lasts as long as it lasts. Usually, until we can't fuck anymore."

Ashland shoved Talon playfully. "Hours, Bunny. We'll count down from fifty. You better get a move on, because you smell like you're in need, and when I catch you..." The big, blond demon made a sudden move and nearly caught me by the wrist as I spun out of his reach.

"Run, little rabbit," Felix taunted. Then they all started howling, and an answering roar—from Rhodes, I assumed—rose from within the depths of the maze.

I ran. Each number that was called out during the countdown lit my blood on fire and had me pushing my bare feet faster. There were stacks of boxes, ladders, and rows of scaffolding—it was like an indoor spy course. My heart leapt at the nostalgic burst of excitement. We had run courses like this daily during training.

I was confident in my climbing skills, so I ran until I heard the number forty being shouted. All of the grips to climb were much taller than me, but that wouldn't be an issue. I'd been running courses like this for years. I was fast, strong, and silent.

Grinning, I ran at full speed toward a crate, jumping on it and launching myself up, my fingertips just grazing the first metal rung on the scaffolding. The count was up to forty-five now, and I could feel my heartbeat in my temples as I pulled myself up using my arms, just enough to get my foot on the bar. From there, it was seconds before I was three levels up and the number fifty was bellowed from the guys below.

Not guys, Palmer. Demons. They're fucking demons. Don't forget it.

"Ready or not, Bunny! Here we come!" Ashland's raspy voice was like an electric shock to my body as I stared out over the maze. Some parts were visible, though just barely. A few blue lights provided a touch of visibility, but it was getting foggy, like someone had set off a smoke bomb or an actual fog machine.

"But don't worry, little Bun-Bun! You'll be coming too!" Talon sang.

Fuck. I sank down on the wooden platform, tucking my legs beneath me. I hadn't expected them all to fluster me so much, but that was part of the job. Training only got you so far. Actual targets were unpredictable and missions like these were risky. All things considered, tonight had gone way better than I could've imagined.

They were interested. Now I needed to figure out how to make them obsessed.

RHODES

RHODES

Chapter Four

My body was ready for anything at this point. Storming away from that little brat and my boys had me seeing red, but it was necessary. I needed to cool the fuck down before I did something rash. Like break her little neck.

The fuck kind of dickhead wears a monocle anyway? I would never, and the thought of myself being caught dead with such an accessory pissed me off. We had a traitor in our gang, and had stabbed a man in the middle of the club earlier, yet here we were, with this bitch in bunny ears.

Where was she from, anyway? I sure as shit had never seen her before. Fucking hell, the others were already simping over her. Even Misha had that stupid Cupid-struck expression.

Nah, something was going on. I was suspicious by nature, and experience had taught me that was the best way to keep air in your fucking lungs. I had many roles within our organization, but mainly, I was a ghost. I moved through the city undetected, spying and using my telekinetic powers to give us the upper hand when it came to business transactions. Especially when people tried to fuck us over.

Though it had been a very long time since anyone had tried—until fucking tonight.

Growling, I slammed my fist into a wooden crate, splintering the damn thing into a million pieces. Liars were one thing that I could never tolerate. I scratched my forehead where my horns were ready to appear at any moment, and they erupted the second the howling hit my ears. Tossing my head back, I let out a roar of frustration.

I couldn't stop thinking about Frank. We'd gotten an anonymous tip about him being the rat, so we'd set a little trap. Arranged this big party to ensure the whole city would be here along with us. Told Frank about a big shipment of guns coming through the port earlier that day, and where we'd be storing it. Ridiculous how easy it was to set the stage. It was way too good of an opportunity for our rivals to pass up.

I was just about to take a left when I heard a soft shuffle. Freezing in place, my head whipped to the right, where the noise had come from. My nostrils flared, and I felt my demon rising at the prospect of prey. All thoughts faded as I caught her scent. Excitement, fear, and arousal with a hint of cherry. Fuck. She was practically blasting the entire maze with pheromones. Pheromones that felt like they were speaking right to my dick, begging me to give chase.

That was different from anyone else we'd brought down here before. Yes, we could tell when someone was turned on, but this... This was something else entirely. My mouth was literally salivating as I padded silently in the row next to her. The counting of my boys was growing louder and more raucous. Reaching a dead end, I eyed the seven-foot-high metal wall, landing effortlessly a second later. Demon perks—excellent jumping skills.

Palmer looked behind her, like she could feel my eyes on her. *Can you, little girl? Can you feel how much I hate you already?* Her blue eyes darted around, and I took in the roundness of her cheeks which should've seemed out of place with how toned she was, but the stars had blessed the woman with curves in all the right places. I had to admit, she was stunning. Her attitude, however? I clenched my fists as my palms itched to light that ass up.

Palmer lingered for a couple more seconds, no doubt listening for any hints that she'd been found, before breaking into a dead sprint right toward a wall. Jumping to my feet, I was ready to intervene.

Was she going to try and knock herself unconscious before we even started? If she didn't want to do this, she could've just fucking said so.

At the last second, it was like she transformed into something else. I suspected she wasn't human, but it was hard to detect what she was, probably due to scent suppressants. A witch of some kind, though witches didn't come with the skills to do what she was doing. I watched with interest as she scaled the scaffolding like some kind of parkour model.

Who are you?

There was definitely something more to her. She dropped down onto her knees, kneeling there silently as the others started calling out to her. Warning her of what was heading her way. She wasn't running though. Hell, her hiding spot wasn't even that great.

Felix, Talon, and Ashland were whooping and hollering, but it didn't last long since the sound system kicked on and "Final Girl" by Graveyardguy and Slayyyter started blasting. Palmer slowly lifted her head, gazing out over the maze, a smile forming as she listened to the words of the song. Dear gods—she was into this. Not only that, she hadn't even startled when the music cut on.

I suddenly smelled metal and instinctively rolled hard to the right, a split second before a dagger would've nailed me in the thigh. "Fuck!" I continued rolling right off of my perch, because I knew as soon as I stopped, Misha's big ass would be on me. I'd been so distracted that I hadn't even noticed him sneaking up on me. If Palmer had any sense, she would've run the moment I gave up my position. Unfortunately, I couldn't see her hiding spot anymore.

Landing on my feet, I threw my arm up to block the punch that I knew was coming. My entire body vibrated from the force of Misha's strength, but I was faster. Dropping down, I spun and swung my leg wide, hoping to knock him off his feet. He laughed as he jumped, easily avoiding contact.

A massive foot came at my head, but my hands found purchase on his boot, and I twisted hard. Misha threw his body into the movement, leaving the ground as his body rotated into a sideways flip. Taking advantage of the space, I hopped up, scanning the area for any sign of the others. The sound of blades being unsheathed made me groan.

"You know I hate when you use those fucking things. It's cheating," I growled, circling one of the deadliest demons I'd ever known.

"Pussy," Mish grunted, as he flicked his wrist and sent a dagger sailing past my head. A squeal, one that was certainly not from any of us, had Misha and I frozen in our stances.

"Did you..." I spun to look and was surprised that I didn't see Palmer lying injured on the ground. Misha stormed over to the pathway and knelt down, picking something up from the floor. "What is it?" I got closer, just in time for him to hold up a little clump of hair, maybe half an inch long. "You fucking sliced the end of her ponytail off? On a run by?"

Misha grinned and lifted the hair to his nose, taking deep inhales of her scent. His damn eyes rolled back in his head, eyelids fluttering before snapping back open, and his irises flashed orange. Oh fuck. A calm Misha was dangerous enough, but a feral Misha, the one with orange eyes, who could bulk up to three hundred pounds of muscle in a flash? Fucking lethal.

His entire body shivered as he shoved her hair into his pocket, staring off in the direction she'd run. I was about to open my mouth to tell him we could hunt her together, but we both heard a soft thump, like someone falling or getting knocked over.

Hunt, hunt, hunt.

Oh gods, I wanted to catch her little ass and order the others to punish her. A mouth as sassy as hers deserved to be stuffed.

Mish took off in a flash, heading to inspect the noise, and I followed at a slower pace. I wanted to catch her, but I was also interested to see what she would do before that. The music had changed to "Succubus" by NIGHTMÆR, further setting the stage for whatever was to come.

Maniacal laughter suddenly echoed as Talon and Felix tore into my line of sight, both of them laughing their asses off. "Would you two shut the fuck up?" I hissed, and Felix flipped me off while Talon made a great display of pretending to jack himself off.

"Did you see her yet?" Felix called as they made their way over to me.

I nodded. "Yeah. Spotted her when she ran through during the countdown. Misha got a hit on her."

Their eyes lit up with fire. "What kind of hit?" Talon demanded excitedly.

"Launched a dagger that missed my ear by an inch and hacked off the end of her ponytail as she sprinted past."

"Gods, that beefy brute. We need that hair to pull so we can hold her mouth where we need it. He can't be chopping it off like that," Felix grumbled, looking put out.

Talon popped his hands on his hips, his dick hard as a rock and barely contained within his jockstrap. "Which way did they go? How is big Mishy now? Is he"—he leaned in closer, his body trembling with excitement—"unhinged?"

I laughed and started back down the path I'd been on before the twisted twins showed up. "Unhinged? He's fucking feral, Talon. Bulged up like a fucking pufferfish with the eyes of a monster."

Talon, unsurprisingly, moaned. "Gods above, I love when he gets like this. Come on, I want to see him manhandle her little ass."

I couldn't argue with him. It was exactly what I'd been hoping to see when I followed him. "Where's Ash?"

Felix shrugged. "Took off not long after we entered."

A long howl pierced the air, answering my question. "There he is. Sounds like he found something interesting."

Talon clapped. "Then let's shut the fuck up and go find out what it looks like when five demons fuck a little bunny rabbit!"

A scream. Fuuuuck. That little wail of terror was like a shot of epinephrine straight to my cock. All three of us growled and took off, scaling the scaffolding and other obstacles like spiders. Didn't matter that I didn't trust her and that I really didn't appreciate her smart mouth—I was the hunter and she was my prey. That scream was like the holy grail of aphrodisiacs.

Reaching the top of the scaffolding, I was able to scan easily, and the sight that greeted my eyes nearly had me exploding. Palmer, on her ass, scooting away as quickly as possible from a slowly advancing Ashland.

"Come back here, little rabbit!" Ash chuckled, twisting something in his hands. I jumped the ten feet to the next row of scaffolding for a better look, seeing right away that it was rope. Silk rope, by the looks of it. "I just want to tie you up before I eat you. It'll be easier for my boys to hold you still for me."

I saw him before she realized he was there. Orange eyes glowing in the shadows were his only giveaway. She was going to make her move any... second... now...

Palmer spun and braced herself on her palms, pushing herself forward to her feet. Misha stepped out just in time to snatch her by the ponytail he seemed low-key obsessed with. Her shriek and growl of anger had my head swimming. "Let me go!"

He didn't. In fact, he tossed her over his shoulder like a fucking caveman and slapped her ass. Hard.

"Fuuuck me, little rabbit. You smell like you're drenched. Are you?" Ashland asked as he sauntered over to Misha.

"Fuck you is right, asshole."

"Did someone say fuck my asshole, right?" Talon jumped down from his hiding spot, landing right behind Misha. Palmer lifted her head and flipped him off. "I'll gladly fuck that little ass, Bun-Bun."

"That isn't what I said," she barked, thrashing against Misha's ironclad grip. She wasn't going anywhere, and she knew it.

Felix landed next. "I think that's exactly what she said. You want us to do bad things to this pretty butt?" He ran his fingertips over the backs of her thighs, and I heard the sharp inhale of air, along with the blast of arousal scenting the air. It seemed to pulse from her very being, and gods, she smelled divine. My hands had a mind of their own as they slipped inside my boxers; I couldn't stop myself.

Squeezing hard, I practically purred as I pumped my cock through my fist. Such a helpless little lamb, at the mercy of beasts who wanted to pry her legs apart and split her in two on their fat dicks. *Could she take more than one of them?* My balls tingled, and I twisted my palm over the tip of my cock, gathering up the wetness there before smearing it down over my veiny length. *Fuck yeah.*

Somewhere in the back of my head, a voice was whispering that my reaction to her wasn't normal. That none of our reactions were normal. We'd hunted plenty of people before, but this heady fucking high was next-level.

Dropping down on my ass, I let my legs dangle from my vantage point and worked my dick, anxious to see how this would play out. I'd feel better after I got off and we all got her out of our systems.

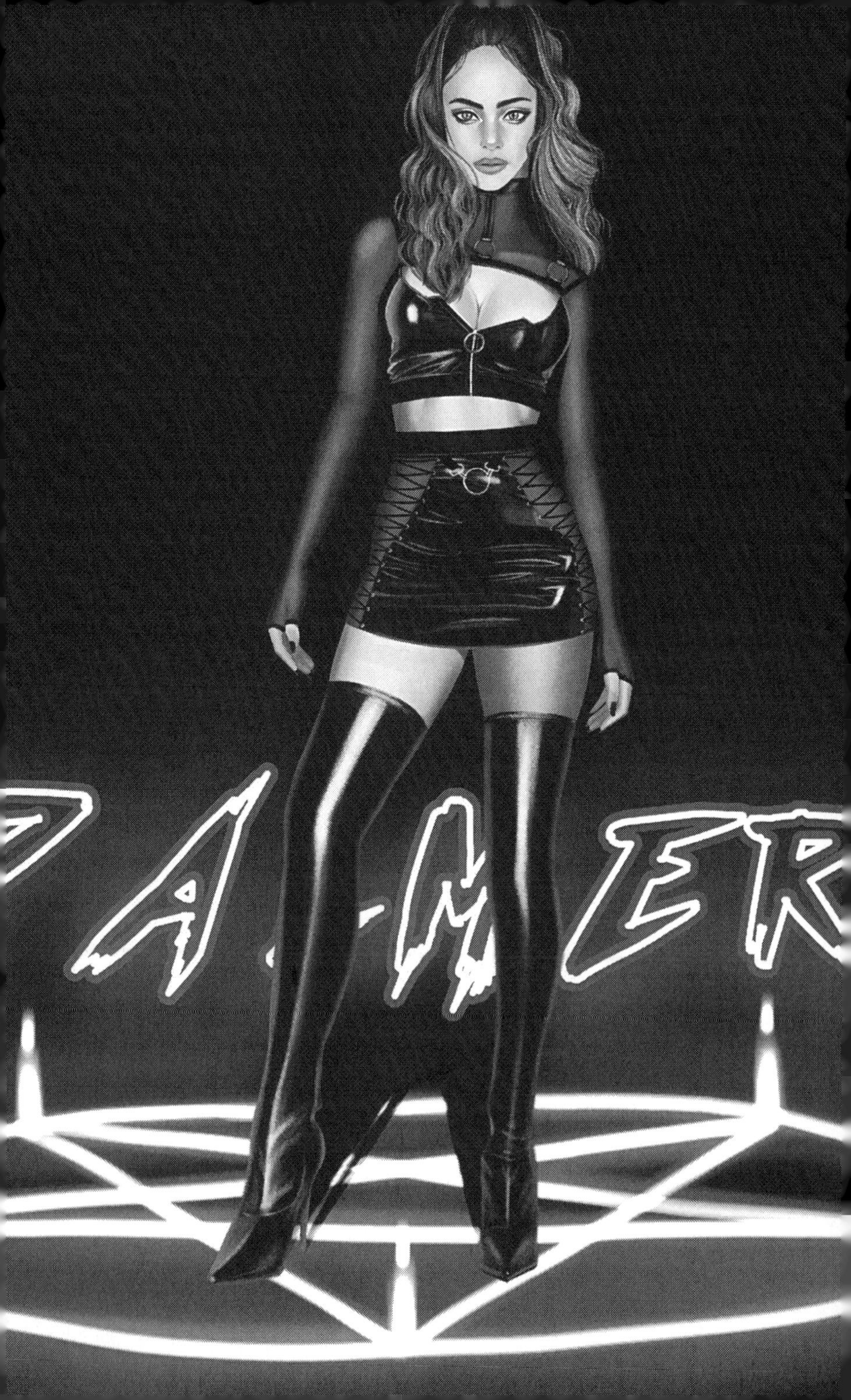

PALMER

Chapter Five

Don't fight them, Palmer.

Fuck. I wanted to fight them. I wanted to kick their asses and get myself off later, thinking about how shocked they'd be. But I couldn't show my cards yet. I didn't want them to know I could fight, because that would lead to questions that I didn't need asked. Asrael, my mentor, had sent me here for a purpose. He believed in me, and I wouldn't let him down.

Misha's palm landed on my ass for the second time, and I couldn't stop the squeal that rose from my throat. His muscles rippled beneath me as I braced my hands against his bare back. Without giving it a second thought, I pulled my hand back and smacked his ass as hard as I could. Everyone went dead silent.

"What?! He's allowed to slap my ass, but I'm not allowed to spank him back? Fuck you guys!"

Slowly, Misha pulled me down the front of his body, letting my feet just brush the floor. On my way down, I felt every oversized bulge of his massive form. His eyes were orange, and I jerked back from him in surprise—at least, I tried to, but it was no use. His hands were gripping my shoulders, and he leaned down so close to my face that his beard brushed my skin.

"No."

"Oh, you're talking now? Well, anything you do to me is fair game for me to do to you. How about that, you overgrown tree frog?"

He narrowed his eyes as Talon and Felix's laughter broke through the tension. Those orange eyes darted all over my face before he sighed.

"What are you doing? Don't pat my head like that." I flailed my arms, batting him away. How dare he pat me on the head like a naughty kid.

Smiling, he grabbed my wrists and held them together over my head before nodding to Ashland. Realization hit, and I tried to squirm, but my wrists were bound in a flash. I was being carried over to an exposed beam that conveniently had— *Oh shit.*

"No, no, no," I chanted as my arms were lifted, and the rope slipped through a large metal hook. "You barbaric, cocky..."

"My cock is indeed quite barbaric, kitty. Did you know I'm an artist?" Felix questioned, stepping behind me. It was a struggle not to close my eyes when his warm breath hit my neck. "I want to see my new canvas."

My skirt was literally ripped off, leaving me there in my black thong and corset. I knew I looked good—I worked out every day—but hearing the groans of these four huge demons as they laid eyes on my nearly naked body did amazing things to my confidence. My body was shaking with a mixture of fear and desire so potent, I felt like I was having an out-of-body experience.

"Such pretty skin," Felix praised as his hands slid from my arms down to my waist. Every nerve ending in my body felt electrified, the anticipation of what was to come driving me insane.

"Felix," I whispered, unable to stop myself from sounding desperate. Ashland prowled closer, coming to stand directly in front of me. I watched, mesmerized, as he reached out and wrapped his hands over Felix's. His ice-blue eyes flicked from my face to over my shoulder.

"I think she needs something from us, Lixy." His eyes came back to mine. "Don't you? Tell us what you need."

I squeezed my thighs together, trying to generate some friction to soothe the inferno of need that was growing with each tension-filled second, but it was useless. Ashland reached out and grabbed my cunt, gripping me like he owned me. Like this pussy already belonged to him.

"Ash," I moaned as he flexed his hand, causing me to lose my precarious footing and sway harder against him.

"Your pussy is so fucking hot for us, little rabbit. Does that embarrass you? That we know how turned on you are? There's no hiding the truth." Yeah, I wasn't interested in hiding anything anymore, not when the pressure of his hand on my clit felt that amazing.

Felix's lips landed on my neck. Something sharp trailed up my thigh, and a blink later, my corset and thong were laying on the ground. Cool air hit my nipples, pebbling them even further.

"Please," I mumbled, past the point of caring that I was now begging.

Talon darted in and snatched something by my feet, earning a snarl from Felix and Ashland both. Smirking, the ginger demon brought my destroyed thong up to his face. My eyes widened as he shoved the lace against his nose and inhaled deeply before running his tongue over the material. *Oh Jesus.* He was licking my underwear.

What happened next, I wasn't quite sure, but it felt like all hell broke loose. Ashland and Felix jumped on Talon, the three of them fighting like dogs over my thong. The sounds they were making were blood-chilling, snarls and growls that only the most dangerous of creatures could create.

Looking around wildly, my eyes landed on Misha, who was watching the fight with interest but was still making his way over to me. "Why are they fighting like that?" I gasped when Felix landed a particularly brutal kick to Ashland's chest.

Misha stared down at me. I wasn't really expecting an answer. They weren't joking when they said that he didn't speak much. Like, at all.

"They fight for you."

My eyebrows lifted at that. He'd given me more than one word. "Why though? I thought you guys were into the whole 'sharing is caring' thing?"

Misha grunted, reaching out and taking hold of my hips. "First taste."

"First... Oh. *Oh.* They're fighting over who gets me first?" I glanced over to see they were now nothing but blurs of fists, feet, and violence. My own feet suddenly left the ground, drawing my attention back to the big guy before me. "What are you doing?"

"First taste," he growled, sliding his hands under my ass and encouraging me to wrap my thighs around his shoulders. The others were going to be pissed when they realized their fighting had caused them to—

"Oh my *fuuuck*," I cursed as Misha's tongue swiped through my pussy, top to bottom. The sound he made sent rough vibrations through my clit, and I was a little concerned he might actually take a bite out of me.

"You son of a bitch!" Ashland yelled. The sounds of the fight came to an abrupt halt as the three of them turned and got an eyeful of me grinding my cunt against Misha's mouth, wrists still suspended from the ceiling.

Talon was behind me in a flash, his hands on my nipples, twisting them between his fingertips and sending jolts of pain through my body. "Fucking hell, Bun-Bun. What a sight this is. Do you like how he eats that cunt?"

"Yes!" I cried out as Misha's lips sucked hard on my clit, causing me to bow back against Talon.

"That's it, give us those sounds," Felix purred, taking a spot at my side. My head fell back onto Talon's shoulder as he continued tugging at my sensitive nipples. "Fuck, you're such a pretty little thing. All trussed up and nowhere to go."

The dirty talk was doing it for me. Oh gods, I was shamelessly humping Misha's face now but all it seemed to be doing was spurring him on. The growls coming out of his mouth were just as powerful as the filthy words the others liked to use.

"How's she taste, brother?" Ashland asked, staring at where Misha's tongue was buried between my legs. Suddenly, something was stretching me, making me moan low and deep. The sensation was gone just as fast. My eyes flew open, and I stared, fascinated, as Misha lifted his hand to Ashland's lips. I could see my wetness glistening on his fingers, and *oh my fucking gods.* Ashland opened his mouth, sucking Mish's wet fingers between his lips.

"Oh fuck, Misha. That looks so sexy," Felix whined. Actually fucking whined. He was right though. My body was winding higher and higher watching Ashland suck and lick Misha's fingers while he ate me out.

"Eat her off his fingers, Ashy boy. Fuuuuck me. My cock is aching, Bun-Bun. I need to fuck you soon." Talon whispered the last part in my ear, and I couldn't hold back my eruption another second. I fucking detonated. My thighs tightened around Misha's head so hard that had he been human, I could've done some real nerve damage.

Misha pulled back, leaving me a dripping, panting mess. His eyes glowed orange, and that's when I noticed them for the first time—a pair of horns that were barely visible along his hairline. His beard was slick from my orgasm, and he made absolutely no move to wipe it clean. As good as it was, I was desperate for more.

"Someone fuck me. Now."

Felix barked a laugh, letting his hand slip up to my jaw. Angling my face toward him, he didn't hesitate before crushing his lips to mine. He was a total bad boy in every sense of the word. The tattoos, the fucking swagger, the way he was fucking my mouth with his tongue...

"Was she giving us orders? Did I hear that correctly?" Ashland sounded amused, but his tone held an undercurrent that had my inner witch trembling, because *oh shit, I'm probably in danger.* I sank my teeth into Felix's bottom lip, earning a growl and a deep groan from the sexy demon. He turned his attention to my throat, licking and sucking his way down to my breasts.

"She definitely was. Didn't even say please," Talon tsked.

"Please. Please, Talon."

"*Please. Please, Talon.*" That was my voice. Repeating my begging.

What the hell? "Who said that?"

Talon trailed a finger down my cheek. "One of my many talents, Bun-Bun... but I want to know about you. Tell me, have you ever been the filling in a twin sandwich?"

I shook my head. "I've never done anything like this before."

"Good. You're gonna be a vision with my brother's cock in your mouth and mine in that sloppy cunt." Talon lifted me, removing me from the hook finally. Even though they'd been holding me up the majority of the time, my arms still felt like jello. He carried me over to a wooden crate that conveniently was just the perfect height to bend me over. I didn't wait for instructions; I was delirious with the need to come again, so I bent over and stuck my ass out.

"Mother of fucks, look at that ass," Talon gasped, and I smirked, loving the praise he seemed to like giving me.

"Get that dick inside her, man. Fuck her good," Ashland gritted out, taking his cock out of his briefs. I couldn't look away from him as he stroked himself. Not even when I felt Talon's dick pressing against me, seeking entrance. Not even when my head was jerked to the right position by my ponytail, and Felix slapped my mouth hard with his fat cock.

My lips fell open, and my mouth was instantly stretched wide around Felix, who didn't waste any time working his way in as deep as possible. Oh, these demon boys were going to fucking wreck me. Any hope I had of this not being the best sexual experience of my life vanished, and all sense of time and space evaporated as Talon sank into my pussy. Hard. No one inch at a time bullshit.

He claimed me in one fucking thrust and one slap of his balls against my clit. My eyes widened, and I tried to pull back slightly from Felix but he was relentless. They both were. Their thrusts at first alternated, but soon they found a steady, punishing pace, pumping their hips and fucking me so good, I wondered if I'd actually been possessed by them.

Spit ran down my chin, while the sounds of my mouth and pussy echoed throughout the cavernous basement.

"Such a good little whore for us," Ashland purred, running his hand down my spine, causing my back to arch like a fucking cat. "Spit." I didn't have to ask who or what he meant by that, because warm saliva landed right on my tight asshole, thanks to Talon. "Relax, little rabbit. I wanna feel you from the inside."

I was going to die. My whole body shook as Ashland swirled his finger against the rim of my ass, and as he breached me, I whined around Felix's dick.

"Shhh, Bun-Bun. Take it like a good slut. My good little baby bunny. Open that hole, that's right."

For the second time, I exploded like a volcano.

TALON

TALON

Chapter Six

Sensual, sinful, seductive, silky fucking stars of bliss.

That was how the inside of my little Bun-Bun's pussy felt. My demon cock had died and gone to the highest of slippery heavens. She was just so fucking responsive to every touch, every word, especially when one of us praised her. I thought I'd died and gone to Hell when I saw her face for the first time, but I could now say with absolute certainty that she'd never look more beautiful than she did while being worked over by us. I could already tell the others were just as fucked as I was.

I wonder if she'd allow photos? I could flip her over and bury myself in her pussy, then let my tail slip inside of her tight ass. What would her pretty little face look like then, being forced to take all of me? My cock jerked, spraying out pre-cum like it was confetti.

"That's it, open up. Let Ash feel that ass, babe," Felix crooned, stroking his fingertips over her face. I met my brother's eyes as he drove into Palmer's mouth, and he lifted a dark brow.

'She's fucking exquisite, Tal.'

'Gods, you don't have to tell me. Wait til you feel her cunt. If I had a soul, it would've been squeezed out of my cock by now.'

'Well, I propose a swap then.'

'Get fucked, Lixy.'

"Secrets are lies, boys," Ashland scolded, leisurely circling his finger and earning us a high-pitched mewl.

Misha stalked over and stood right next to Felix, slipping his boxers off and letting the heavy weight of his dick out. Finally. Mishy wasn't built like most boys. He was like a mountain of a man, one you could climb and then brag about later that you'd survived to tell the tale. His abdomen wasn't ripped or even defined—he was just a solid fucking block of muscle. Including his cock.

"Damn, Mishy. Look at that fucker. Let her lick it." I wanted so badly to flip her over so I could see what that would look like, her sucking two dicks... but then I'd lose my firsthand view of her little booty hole, so nope. Call me a selfish prick, whatever.

Felix shifted, letting the poor bunny have a breather as his dick slipped out of her mouth.

"Gods," Palmer panted, her breaths coming out of her in time with my thrusts.

"I'm so close right now, Bun-Bun. You're so sexy. I love seeing you used like this. Do you have any idea how beautiful you look right now?" My hips faltered, and Ashland winked at me, wiggling his free hand at us before slipping it underneath Palmer in search of her clit.

"Please, oh please!" she shouted, dropping her forehead down and pushing her ass up even higher. "Like that, I'm gonna— Oh, yes!"

"Milk him, Palmer. Earn that cum, babe." Ashland continued rubbing her, whispering his filthy words.

My entire body jerked, riding out the waves of Palmer's orgasm. The rhythmic clenching of her body, urging mine to flood her, fill her, mark her. My head rolled back, and a rumble built in my chest. A roar left my mouth at the same time I began shooting my hot load deep within my sexy bunny. Zings of pleasure zipped up and down my body as I continued rocking against her, desperate to keep our connection just a little bit longer.

I'd had a lot of sex in my life, but nothing had ever come close to feeling like this. My cock was throbbing, despite my balls feeling considerably lighter. "Fuck, Bun-Bun. Fuck back on me." I gripped her hips and pulled her back roughly.

"Talon!"

Oh shit. *Oh shiiiit.* I looked down, wide-eyed. I had certainly never had this happen before.

"Oh my gods, it hurts," Palmer squealed, trying to crawl forward. To get away from me.

The others wore matching expressions of confusion, and Ash looked down, getting a good glimpse at my predicament. "What. The. Fuck. Talon?" he growled.

"Don't you fucking growl at me, dickface."

Palmer was squirming like a worm on a hook. Ha. She kind of was.

"Shhh, Bun-Bun. It'll be okay. I've got you."

Felix came around now. "Don't you dare, Talon. Back away, man. You'll tear her up, bro."

I narrowed my eyes at my brother. Who was he to tell me what to do? She had a safe word and if she didn't like it, she could say so. All I could do was think about how amazing it would feel to push in just a tiny bit more, and then we'd be...

"Back the fuck up," Misha warned, spinning a wicked-looking blade as he approached.

Palmer turned her head back, eyes wide. "What's happening right now? Are you trying to fist me without lube? What kind of animal—"

Rhodes chose that moment to make himself known. He landed right at Palmer's head. "Listen, little girl. You need to be very quiet and very, very still. This is important. Don't speak." He pressed a finger over her lips, and my body was officially rioting against the amount of self-control I was having to use right now.

"Let her go, Tal."

"Don't do it."

"Back up."

"Son of a bitch!" I roared, easing my swollen cock out of my treasure and stumbling back. Palmer spun around, sitting on her ass, knees pulled to her chest. She looked unsure, confused... "Gods dammit!"

I couldn't have stopped it. Nothing could have.

Wings exploded from my back, my horns erupted, and my tail snapped out like a fucking bullwhip.

"Holy shit," she gasped, taking in my demon form, but that wasn't what made her shriek. No, it was when the other four also simultaneously demoned out, leaving her naked and surrounded by huge ass monsters with huge ass dicks.

"Palmer," Rhodes warned, sticking out a hand to what? Comfort her? Subliminally tell her to calm her tits?

Mishy was stalking over to me, and I couldn't focus on the repercussions of our situation because his normally incredibly, impressive erection now resembled a baseball bat. *Oh hello.* That could stun an unsuspecting... My face jerked to the side from his fist. Spitting out a wad of blood, I reared back and slapped him right across the face.

"That was fucked up, Mishy. I was dick-stracted and you knew it!"

"What have you done, Tal?" he asked, his voice low and his accent strong.

"What the fuck are you?" Palmer's high-pitched question broke our stare down.

Ashland ran a tatted hand over his face. "Wait right here, little bunny. Nobody is going to hurt you, okay?" She didn't look convinced, and he turned to the rest of us. "A fucking word. All of you. Now."

"Oh, Daddy's mad." I pouted, shuffling over to the corner where Ash was headed.

"Can you be serious for two gods damn seconds?" Rhodes asked, staring at me like he wanted to fight. I licked my index finger and pressed it to my pierced nipple, making a sizzle sound.

We stood in a circle, our wings creating a nice barrier so my Bun-Bun wouldn't be able to peep in on our demon dicks. Ash huffed with impatience. "Talon, what happened?"

I threw my hands up. "I don't know. One second, I'm balls deep in the sauciest pussy I've ever felt, admiring her little booty hole—"

"Talon," Ashland growled.

"I popped a fucking knot, bro."

Felix's eyes widened comically. "Popped. A. KNOT?"

"I've never had it happen before. It felt so good. Too good. It was halfway inside of her before I realized and stopped."

"And now she's seen us in our real forms," Rhodes added. Being Captain Obvious was one of his favorite pastimes. "You know what that means."

Ash growled. "I want to know why he popped a knot over her. That's... bizarre. Have you ever had that happen?"

Rhodes was silent for a moment, but we all knew the answer. No. No, he hadn't, because we'd talked about this before. Knotting was what happened when our cocks felt like the person they were fucking was breedable. Or, once you were mated to that person, your dick would always inflate like a balloon during sex. Since demons didn't have fated mates outside of our own race, that clearly wasn't the case with Palmer. Seemed like my cock had gotten carried away and wanted to try and breed that little bunny. I sighed dreamily, just thinking of her wriggling around on my knot, unable to get away.

Rhodes finally spoke, answering Ash's question. "That's irrelevant. She's seen our demon forms. She knows what we are."

"No." Misha crossed his arms over his chest, sending a challenging look at Rhodes.

"Regardless of her seeing us or not, there's something different about her. You can't deny that. None of you can," Felix said, glancing over to check on Palmer.

"What do you propose we do?" Ash asked nobody in particular, running his thumb over his jaw as he thought about the question himself.

Rhodes snorted. "Kill her."

Misha exhaled hard, reaching for his blades. "No."

"You keep saying no. No what?"

"Harm her, I'll cut you."

I barked a laugh. "Fuck, Mishy is smitten. It's okay." I held my hands up when he shot me a dirty look. "I am too! My cock nearly *knotted* her." And gods damn, it would've been glorious...

Rhodes broke away from the circle and started pacing. "Well, we can't let her go. She could ruin everything!"

"So we don't let her go..." We all looked to Ashland, who was nodding slowly. "We won't let her go. We'll keep her. She'll be ours."

"What do you mean, *keep her?* You can't be serious, Ashland. You can't just fucking keep people because you feel like it. We don't know this woman. We don't even know what kind of witch she is, because trust me, she isn't human."

"Rhodes, you're being a real cunt bag right now, and it's totally bringing down my knot. Can you just dial it back a tad?" I looked down at my little baby knot. It was cute, but it wasn't the wrecking ball of pussy destruction it had been a minute ago, and that made me sad.

"I'm going to fuck you up if you don't get your shit together," he snapped at me. Grumpy jerk.

"How would it work?" Felix asked Ash. Good. I knew he'd be on board.

Ash smirked. I smirked. We were just a couple of smirky boys coming up with grand plans. *Fucking love his crazy ass.* "I'm going to do what I do best. I'm going to make her a deal."

Deal making was one of Ashland's powers. He was scary good at them, always coming out on top. Look at that poor wannabe pupper earlier—started the night with the world at his fingertips, and now he had no neck. Because it was stabbed. Twice.

"I think this is a mistake," Rhodes announced.

"We'll vote on it. All in favor of keeping the bunny, say aye."

Misha, myself, and Ashland all voted immediately, a resounding aye. Felix wiped his hand over his head. "It's not that I'm against this, because I'm not, per se. I'm just wary because something feels different. Right? How many people have we shared in the past? Yet this has *never* happened. I think we need to be careful."

"We can still be careful without killing her, and if shit goes south, we can reevaluate later. I'm not against killing someone who's a threat to us." I rolled my eyes. "Obviously."

My brother studied my face, looking for... what? I had no idea. But he must've found it, because he nodded. "I'm in."

"Idiots," Rhodes spat. "I'll be in the gods damn penthouse; I need to decompress. But I'm telling you right now—if I see her doing anything shady, I'll end her, and you four can suck my cock in thanks."

In a blink, he was gone. I guess he wasn't concerned about her seeing him jump now that the secret was out. As demons, we all had an ability called jumping, which allowed us to teleport. Since our true nature was a secret, we didn't get to use it all that often in Port Black.

"He'll come around," Ash said, waving off Rhode's grumpy dick energy.

Misha was done waiting around. He closed his eyes, and his demon form disappeared. Leaving us standing there, he made his way over to Palmer. She was sitting on the edge of the crate, her legs dangling now. I studied her, surprised that she hadn't tried to run yet, though I decided she was probably just in shock. Her impossibly wide eyes watched Misha suspiciously as he approached.

Ashland sighed and forced his demon away too. "So, let's go make ourselves a deal."

Felix and I trailed behind, not quite ready to return to our other forms. I loved letting the beast out of the chains. *'How did it feel?'* he whispered inside my head, one of the little perks that the two of us shared since we'd shared a womb.

I side-eyed my brother. *'How do you think it felt?'*

He grinned. *'Fucking fantastic?'*

'Better than fantastic. Whatever that is.'

'I hope we aren't making a mistake,' Felix mused apprehensively just as we reached the others.

I shrugged. *'We always make mistakes, brother. Or have you forgotten how we earned our fucking name?'*

He froze and turned to me. *'How could I forget?'*

'Exactly!' I punched him in the shoulder. *'But we always come out on top, don't we?'*

"One of you better start fucking talking, because if you're going to kill me, you're going to have a fight on your hands," Palmer informed us, sliding off the crate and standing naked at her full height, which looked to be an impressive five-foot-two without heels.

She was so damn feisty. Not my usual cup of tea, but maybe that was because I'd just never had a good enough sampling before? Either way, my knot pulsed at her attitude.

Eep. Sassiness is the key to knot growth? Interesting.

"Talon? Did you hear what I said?"

"Huh?" I blinked, allowing my brain to come back online after the epiphany I'd just had. Palmer huffed like a baby goat and raised her hands, like we were gonna fight or something. "What are you doing? Put those hands down."

Ashland chuckled. "She said she's going to fight us if we try to kill her."

"Okay, first of all"—I held up a finger—"that sounds really fun, especially if we can do it without clothing. Second of all, nobody's going to hurt you. Tell her, Lixy."

My brother reached out for our girl, and she *snarled*. Oh my stars, pretty sure I felt hearts explode in my eyes. I no longer had circular pupils; they were now heart-shaped. Or bunny-shaped.

Felix sighed, running his rejected hand through his dark hair. "Palmer. Listen, things got a little out of hand earlier. That wasn't expected. In a perfect world, you never would've seen us… like this." He fluttered his wings and whipped his tail in demonstration. "But here we are. Lucky for you, we want to make a deal."

She eyed him warily, like he didn't just tell her *hey, good news! We aren't going to kill your ass!* No, she was stink eyeing him, like she'd witnessed him put the toilet paper under instead of over.

"I'll be the one arranging the agreement," Ashland piped up, drawing her evil eye to him. I wonder if that'd cause eye strain or premature wrinkles. Lowering my eyelids, I attempted to match her expression while Ash continued. "No funny business, I promise. You just can't tell anyone about what you saw here tonight. We don't know you well enough yet to take your word that you'll stay silent. I propose you stay here with us for six months while we evaluate our relationship. If you break our agreement, there will be... consequences. We enjoyed tonight and wouldn't mind a repeat sometime. Can't do that if you're unavailable."

Palmer snorted. "*Unavailable.* Right." She crossed her arms over her chest. "You mean dead."

"I was trying to be delicate about it, but yes."

Yeah, this was not a good position for someone to hold for long. My eyelids were beginning to twitch! How the hell was she doing this?!

"Let me get this right—you don't want me to tell anyone who you are, but you also don't want to kill me."

We all nodded.

"You want me to stay with you for six months and fuck around some more."

We nodded harder.

"Okaaaaay..." The word dragged out, and I didn't miss the wolfish grin on Ash's face—probs thinking about what it'd be like to fuck her with a knotty knot. "Then why the fuck is Talon looking at me like he's going to go murder city on my ass?!" she shrieked, pointing an accusing finger at me before turning on her heel and sprinting away from us.

"Ah fuck," Felix muttered, as Palmer snatched her shredded clothing from the floor before disappearing back into the maze.

"Dammit, Tal. What the hell, man?" Ash looked over at me, then immediately reared back. "The fuck kind of face is *that?*"

I relaxed my facial muscles and let out a groan of relief. "I was trying out a new look and it didn't take, okay? Fuck off my dick."

Felix laughed, then pinched the bridge of his nose with a sigh. "Well, we have a bunny to catch... again."

Ash's phone started ringing, and I saw Rhodes's face on the screen just before Ash accepted the call. "Yeah?"

"We have a problem." Rhode's voice filtered through the speaker.

"What kind of problem?"

"You guys are gonna want to get down to the dungeon. Our little rat is running his mouth."

"We'll be there soon." Ash ended the call. "Felix and Talon, you're with me. Misha, fetch our bunny," he ordered, already heading for the exit.

I held up my palm, stopping him. "But the deal? Shouldn't we finalize that shit first?"

Felix chuckled and shook his head. "Ash got her, bro. While you were busy making your 'I'm shitting so hard right now' face."

I thought back quickly. "Oh, you smooth bastard." An evil little grin sprouted on my mouth. "Good work." She'd repeated the deal back to us, to which we'd all nodded—sealing our agreement when she said okay. Fucking beautiful.

Misha stalked away, heading for the same path Palmer had disappeared down. I had no doubt he'd catch her. As much as I wanted to catch her myself, I really wanted to go fuck up that little rat bitch in the dungeon. And with the way my dick had acted around my little Bun-Bun earlier, it was probably for the best that I gave it a little breathing room to chill the fuck out.

Felix and I pulled our demons back inside, and I rolled my shoulders, adjusting to the loss of my wings and tail. Ash slung his arms over our shoulders, and the three of us headed the opposite direction.

"This is the best night of my life," I whispered, before tilting my head back and howling, hoping my little Bun-Bun would recognize me. If not, no big deal. I had six months to brand myself on her fucking soul, and I was going to own her.

Every. Fucking. Piece.

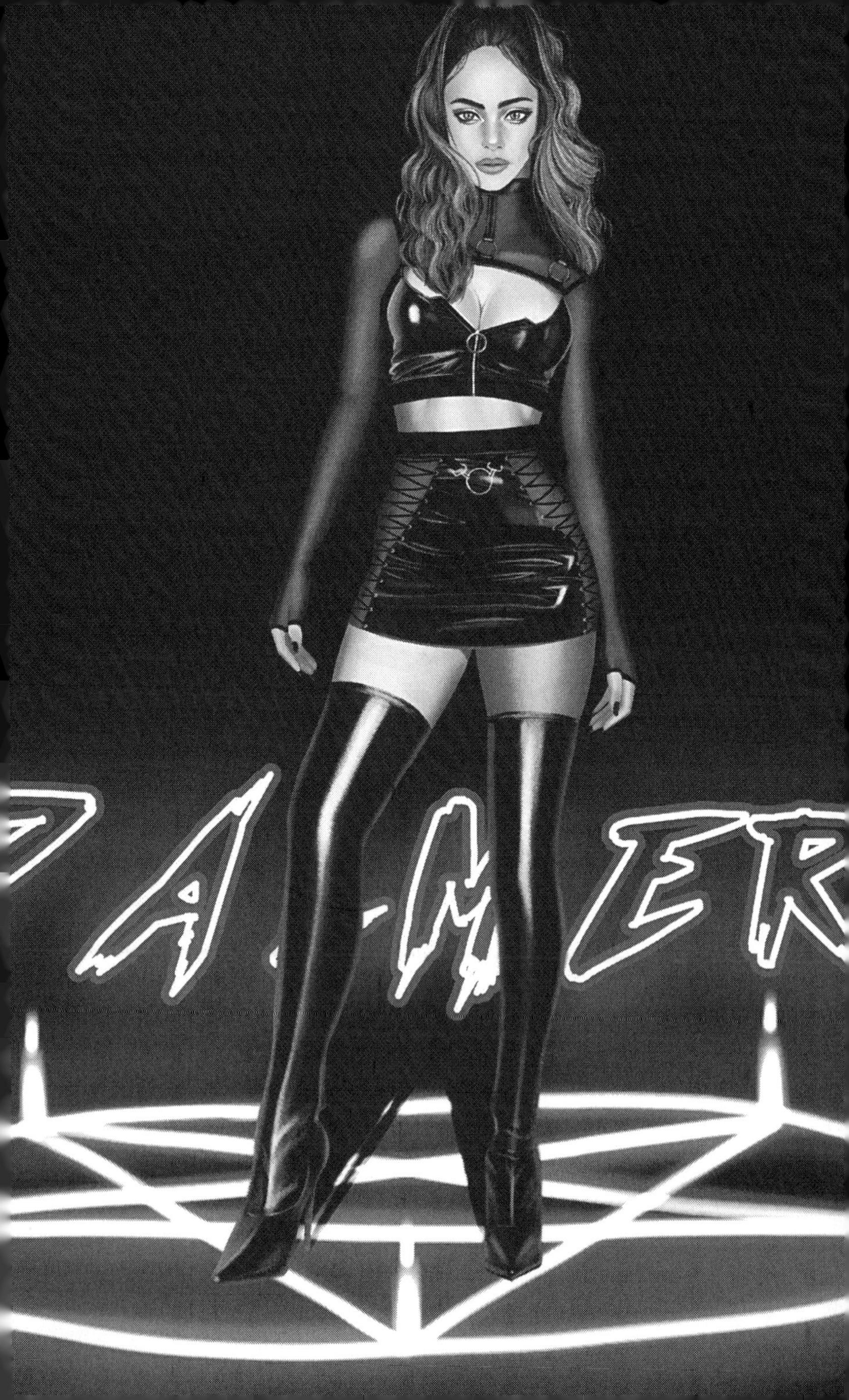

PALMER

Chapter Seven

This was not going to plan. I mean, it kind of was—my aim was to get close to them, after all—but not quite the way I'd envisioned during all the time I'd spent planning this mission. We weren't trained to fuck our targets as a way to succeed, though it was definitely part of the training we'd gone over. Sex got things done. One of my mentors, Laurie, was one of the best I'd ever seen with her ability to use her sex appeal to get what she wanted. Asrael was a victim of hers, and I wasn't even positive he realized it.

So, I'd known I was likely going to have to use my body to win them over, but I hadn't anticipated their level of depravity. Or the fact that they'd made me wetter and hornier than I'd ever felt before. Not only had I fucked them, I'd enjoyed it. The evidence of that was still between my legs, and I could feel the slickness with each step I took as I ran away from them.

Sex to me wasn't a huge deal. I wanted to get fucked, I got fucked. It was when things took on a more emotional angle that I tended to get weirded out. Emotions could be used against me, and I had no interest in the dangers that brought.

Six months. That was a good time frame. I would need to discuss that with Asrael, of course, but I could accomplish a lot in six months from the inside of their organization, though I'd be damned if I agreed to some kind of demonic deal before thinking over every angle. I didn't see Asrael having an issue with the time frame, especially since the estimated end date for this assignment was still to be decided.

Plus, seeing all five of them shifted in their true forms had scattered my brain worse than tossing birdseed in the air during a hurricane, and I needed some time to flush out what the hell they were up to.

They were dangerous, no matter what—I'd known that going in. I'd seen some pictures of demons before from Montague's CCTV. My employer was a multibillion dollar company that had the highest tech out there and held nothing back when it came to the pursuit of dangerous supernaturals.

Seeing the men who had just been fucking, licking, and fingering me shift into these... creatures? It was like throwing a glass of ice water all over my sexed-up body. A slap from that cruel bitch, reality. Knowing and seeing really were two different animals, and I was livid with myself for letting myself get so off track.

I hadn't wanted to show them my fighting skills yet, so I did the only thing I could do—I fucking bolted. Talon had been looking like he was about to do something horrible to me, and I wasn't about to stick around and find out what.

A howl pierced the air. "Fuck. Fuck. Fuck," I cursed softly, darting around a corner. If I could reach the actual wall, then I could find a door or something to get out of here. Reaching the end of the path I was on, I turned left and had to stifle a whoop of excitement. An elevator was straight ahead. Sprinting with everything I had, I reached the doors in seconds. There was only one button so I pushed it repeatedly, bouncing on the balls of my feet. "Come on, hurry up."

I reached for my bag on autopilot, frowning when I remembered I didn't have it. I'd left it back at the start of the maze. The sad excuse of my corset barely wrapped around my naked upper body and my ass was bare as the day I was born. Awesome.

Suddenly, the hair on the back of my neck lifted. Someone was watching me, and the fucking elevator was taking a century to get here. Should I run? Fight? The decision was made for me when a big arm wrapped around my waist, lifting me off the ground. Misha reached out with his free hand, pressing it to a scanner that was completely hidden from view until touched, right above the damn button.

"Put me down!" I squirmed and snapped my head back, trying to get his face. Fucker didn't even react. I was nothing more than a pesky gnat to this grizzly bear.

The doors opened, and he walked in, holding me snugly against his body. He put his palm on another hidden scanner and the doors closed, sealing us in. He released me, and I spun around, shoving him with both arms as hard as I could. All that did was piss me off more because he moved exactly zero inches.

He lifted a dark brow and stared down at me. I'd never seen a man his height before—he had to be pushing seven feet. *Where does he even buy clothes to fit?* I opened my mouth to tell him off, but just then, a ding sounded and the doors slid open. Glancing at him, I waited half a beat before tearing out of the elevator, only to skid to a stop almost immediately.

We were in an apartment. A huge, gorgeous apartment. Sleek, black leather furniture filled the sitting room where I was standing. A massive TV took over one wall, the others covered in more artwork than I'd ever seen in the span of my entire life. In one room. Canvases of all different sizes decorated the walls in varying styles, though now was not the time to take a closer look.

A kitchen was to my right, matching the modern style. It looked as though it was never used. How people lived in such clean and uncluttered homes was always mystifying to me, because no matter how hard I tried to keep my living space organized, it never seemed to work. I fought the urge to dash into the kitchen and upend some flour and sugar all over the place, just to be petty.

Misha walked past me, unaware of my devilish thoughts, and made his way to a spiral staircase. It had obviously been made extra wide to accommodate the extra wide male now going upstairs. Clearly, he wasn't even worried about me trying to escape. The elevator would be the obvious way out, if it weren't for the damn hand scanner, but there had to be an emergency stairwell somewhere. I'd have to play it cool and see if I could find it. I didn't like not knowing my exits—that's how you ended up dead.

The footsteps had stopped, so I dared a look and found the big demon standing halfway up the stairs, staring down at me. "What? You think I'm going to follow you around like a puppy? Get fucked, big man."

He didn't respond. Instead, he simply began descending the stairs at a slow pace. Slow enough that I was second-guessing getting mouthy with him, but I held my ground. Misha stopped right in front of me, and in a flash, I was dangling over his shoulder for the second time tonight.

"You can't just carry me around whenever you want!" I screeched, pounding my fists against his back as he climbed the stairs. We walked down a long hallway until we reached a set of double doors. I was well and truly livid by the time he tossed me down on a big bed. "If you think we're fucking, you have another thing coming, asshole!"

He snorted and turned, heading to an open door on the other side of the huge room and disappearing through it. I scanned the room quickly, taking in the setup. The walls were painted matte black and there were knives everywhere, the dark background making the metal look even sharper. So this was his bedroom then.

The furniture was beautiful, dark-stained wood that I wouldn't have been surprised if it was handmade. This bed certainly had been custom-made. It had to be ten feet long and ten feet wide.

The sound of water running came from where he'd vanished. The fuck? He'd just left me here unsupervised to go take a shower? Slipping off the bed, I stormed over to give him a piece of my mind. "You have a lot of nerve, you know that? Disappearing to take a—Oh."

A very naked Misha was kneeling over a massive tub, adding bath salts to the water. As I got closer, I could see there were already bubbles swirling around. It smelled heavenly, like lilac and fresh cotton.

"I didn't take you for a bubble bath kind of man," I murmured.

"You have no idea what kind of man I am," he replied, and I felt my mouth open in shock.

"I guess not. I didn't think you talked."

He shrugged. "I talk when I have something to say."

I loved his accent. It was Russian, which raised more questions in my mind, but I'd have to wait for another time to start digging into personal history.

When the water was to his liking, Misha rose from his knee and walked over to a large closet, retrieving two towels and a couple of washcloths. Did he think I was going to get in there with him? I watched warily as he set a towel and washcloth on a small table beside the tub, keeping hold of the others as he turned to face me. He opened his mouth, then paused, before closing it again. With a curt nod, he walked past me, hanging his towel on a hook next to the huge shower.

"What are you doing?"

He looked over. "Showering."

"But... your bath?"

"Enjoy." He disappeared into the shower.

He ran this bath... for me?

"Hey, wait!" I sped over and nearly choked at the sight of a dripping wet Misha. His ass was maybe the juiciest ass I'd ever seen on a man... and it was all wet and shiny. I trailed my eyes up to meet his as he looked back over his shoulder. "You ran that bath for me? Why?"

He turned, giving me a full frontal view as he tilted his head back, wetting his long, dark hair. "I wanted to."

I wrung my hands together, unsure of what to say next. This was weird. I didn't like it. What if he felt like I owed him something if I accepted the bath? Deciding to make sure it was clear that this was a gift with no strings, I opened my mouth at the exact moment his dick twitched.

And I'm out.

I dashed back to the tub, and I could've sworn I heard him laughing. Well, fuck him. I couldn't think with that horse cock staring at me. The bath would be a small sacrifice if it meant I'd get a second to myself without having to see that thing.

I quickly removed the pathetic remains of my corset, dropping it on the floor beside the large tub. Stepping into the hot water released a moan of satisfaction from my throat. My body was aching from all of the physical shit I'd done earlier, the running and the sex. *Oh gods, that sex.*

I leaned back and pressed the button to turn on the jets, letting the water pressure massage the hell out of my muscles. I closed my eyes, but kept my hearing sharp because I didn't want to give Misha an opportunity to sneak up on me. Or any of them, for that matter.

So what did I know? That The Exiled were truly demons, were into kinky sex, and had no fucking problem stabbing a man in the neck in the middle of a crowded nightclub. They were loyal to one another, despite clearly enjoying fighting each other. Supposedly, they didn't want to kill me, but that could change in the amount of time it took me to sneeze.

I needed to calm myself and focus on my objective. That had me thinking back to when Asrael had started training me for this very moment. I was ready. I'd do whatever it took to prove myself to him.

"Palmer," Asrael greeted me, as I stepped into his office at Montague's headquarters.

"Sir," I replied with a nod, sinking down into a chair when he motioned for me to sit. I was shitting bricks. Earlier today, I'd participated in a mock mission, and not long after, was told to come up to see the big boss. I was concerned that I might get accused of cheating to gain intel, having used my ability to converse with the dead to ask the lingering spirits if they'd overheard or seen anything. Some of the others on my team had given me disgusted looks, but the way I saw it? In the field, nobody was going to give a fuck. It was up to me to get intel however I wanted, just like they could use their powers as they needed to.

He stood in front of his desk, his dark eyes staring through me. "Great work today. I was watching. Did you know that?" Asrael had always been kind of a father figure to me since I'd arrived here as an orphan many years ago, after my parents were killed.

"No, sir. Thank you." My heart was pounding. If I impressed him, he might let me start taking real assignments. I was fucking ready.

"Your powers seem to be getting stronger. Very smart to use your affinity in any way possible. Your hard work is paying off."

He was right. They were getting stronger. After the amount of training hours I'd been putting in, they'd better be.

"I have an idea. There's an assignment that I think you'd be great for, but it's still a ways off from being pursued. It's in the early stages right now. Surveillance and planning. You know I have eyes and ears everywhere."

I nodded. Montague had their hand in everything, it seemed. Known for their endless pursuit in the studies of magic and how to not only boost affinities, but potentially alter them? It was groundbreaking in every way, and Asrael was relentless. Montague also had one of the best training programs for magically gifted people who wanted to protect the world from supernatural threats. That included other witches, mages, and as I was about to learn, demons.

"Have you been able to communicate with them?" he asked, his eyes sharp as he studied my face. I didn't have to ask who 'them' was; he meant the spirits who plagued me.

"A little, yeah. At first, it was just images, glimpses of their lives, things they'd push at me and want me to know. Or visions of other things, like how they'd kill me if they were still alive. It's getting easier and easier to hear words now, though. I'm confident that continuing to work hard will unlock that power."

Asrael smiled. "I'm proud of you. You've come such a long way." He reached out and pushed some of my hair behind my ear. "You're growing up so fast, Palmer. Makes me feel old." Chuckling, he turned and headed for the minibar. Old? He looked to be maybe forty, not old at all, and he was handsome from an objective point of view. "Have you tried to talk to your parents?"

The question caught me off guard, and I whipped my head over to look at him. We never talked about my parents. It wasn't like it was forbidden; it just wasn't a topic I enjoyed lamenting over. The past was just that—past. I was over what had happened. I'd tried for years to get the spirits of my parents to contact me, to tell me who'd done this to them, but it was total radio silence. What good was my gift if I couldn't even use it to get answers about the murder of my own family?

"Not in over a year. I failed to see the point in expending the energy to try anymore."

Asrael turned to face me, now holding a tumbler of whiskey. "I know it's frustrating for you, but I really am impressed. A good agent knows how to make the best use of their time, and you've clearly been using yours wisely. In the meantime, I'd like you to go on your first assignment. It's low risk, but I want you to get your feet wet. You'll go with Hunter."

I had to suppress the urge to squeal. Hunter was my best friend and had already been active in the field for a year now. "Yes, sir. Thank you."

Asrael smiled at me, and the pride in his eyes had a blush rising to my cheeks. I wasn't always the easiest person to get along with, but he had always gone out of his way for me and made me feel like I truly belonged here—like I had a purpose. I would pay him back the only way I could: by being the best gods damn spy Montague had ever seen.

I'd left that night with Hunter, and the two of us absolutely crushed the assignment. I smiled at the thought of my big, best friend, with his curly hair and emerald green eyes. At six-five, I'd always thought he was the biggest man I'd ever seen, but Misha blew that out of the water.

Hunter had also been taken in by Montague Industries when his mothers and brother were killed in a fiery explosion during a family vacation. A leaky gas valve or something had sparked, causing their entire wooden cabin to go up in flames, killing his family. He'd been just ten years old when he was taken in, but he was one of the strongest mages I knew.

Opening my eyes, I jolted upright, sending the bathwater sloshing over the edge. Misha was standing right in front of me with a towel around his hips and an inquisitive look on his face.

"How does a person your size move so silently? It makes no sense," I muttered, leaning back and attempting to calm my heart.

"You're smiling. Why?"

I grabbed the washcloth and squirted some bodywash on it, rubbing it together as I pondered how I wanted to answer his question. "I was thinking about my best friend."

Without responding, he turned and walked to the large double sink and grabbed his toothbrush. I started soaping up my shoulders while observing him.

"We grew up together," I told him, wanting to keep the conversation flowing for some reason. He'd already spoken more than I thought I'd ever get, so I wanted to try and keep that going. His eyes flicked to mine in the mirror as he started brushing his teeth. "I miss him."

Misha coughed and spit out a mouthful of toothpaste in the sink, then whirled around. "Him?"

Oh, he doesn't like that.

"Yes, him. He's a man."

"No."

I lifted my brows. "No? What do you mean, no?"

He rinsed his mouth quickly, then stomped over to the tub. "Five minutes."

My mouth gaped. "*Excuse* me?"

Misha turned and left me staring as he walked out of the bathroom. The sounds of dresser drawers slamming reached me, and I rolled my eyes. What a weirdo.

Still, I needed to wash my hair, so I set about doing that before Mr. Moody could return and make me get out of the tub with a head full of suds. Rinsing my hair, I sent out some love to Snake via magic, just to let him know I missed him too. I'd reveal him when the time was right. Since they didn't know what my affinity was yet, I might as well keep it a secret for as long as possible.

Feelings of adoration and relief were returned to me from my little buddy, and I relaxed a bit, knowing that he was okay. Snake could take care of himself, but I'd be lying if I said he wasn't also kind of fucked up. He tended to scare the hell out of those who saw him and really prided himself on making people piss their pants.

"Out."

Sighing, I hit the drain on the tub and stood, letting the bubbles run down my skin. Misha grabbed the towel he'd already gotten out and tossed it at me before disappearing again. Gritting my teeth, I stepped out onto the plush bath mat and dried myself. My hair was a long, wet, tangled mess so I set out to find a brush, and maybe a robe. I hit the jackpot in the cupboard where Misha had gotten the towels from earlier.

A big, fluffy, black robe was folded and sitting on a shelf, prime for the taking. Helping myself, I slipped into it and huffed a laugh at how fucking long it was. It was like the bridal dress version of a robe, complete with a train. I wasn't surprised to find a little box full of hair care items—Misha's hair was pretty long for a dude. I sprayed some leave-in conditioning spray on my head and got to work brushing out the mess. The smell was intoxicating, like hints of tobacco flower with a sharp undertone of steel.

Once that was done, I figured it was time to bite the weenie. I silently padded across the floor, my robe trailing behind me. All was quiet in the bedroom, so I peeked around the corner and nearly ran for the tray of food that was sitting on the coffee table next to a sleek, gray couch. Steak, potatoes, steamed broccoli... Oh gods. My stomach growled like a lion chasing a gazelle.

The bedroom door opened, and Misha appeared, carrying a second tray. He froze, taking in my outfit, and his nostrils flared. Was he sniffing the food? Or me? I studied him right back—the loose, black tank top and dark gray joggers were a dangerous combination.

"I didn't have any clothes so..." I held my arms out, letting the sleeves fall over my hands. He didn't look impressed.

"Eat." Misha sat the second tray down and plopped himself on the couch, not wasting any time in digging right into his steak. I was fucking starving; I didn't need to be told twice. I sat down beside him, and the two of us stuffed our faces in silence.

The plates were so loaded with food that I only got about halfway, but holy hell, I was stuffed. Groaning, I flopped back on the couch, holding my belly. "Gods, that was good."

Misha was still going strong, and I nearly choked when I looked over and realized that he was on the last bite. His plate was wiped clean. Turning to me, he gave me a glance and then stole a look down at my plate. Pointing at my steak with his fork, he lifted a brow in a silent question.

"Go ahead." I was both impressed and horrified as I watched him methodically slice through the meat with a knife clearly better suited for hunting the actual dinner itself. This guy was fascinating to me, and I wanted to see if I could break through that hard outer shell. "I think I'm pregnant with a steak baby."

Misha paused, a big hunk of meat an inch from his mouth, and he slowly turned to stare at me like I had five heads. His eyes dropped to my stomach, then back up to meet mine. "Impossible," he grunted, dismissing me once more in favor of food.

I barked a laugh. "I was joking. Of course it's impossible." He didn't respond. Shocking. He was so stoic and serious, which just made questions pop up in my head like confetti. For starters, why didn't he like to talk? What was with the knife obsession? Exactly how tall was he? I knew he'd gotten even bigger in his demon form, which honestly should've been illegal.

And don't even get me started on all the questions I had about their demon forms. *So, so many questions.*

I wondered when the others would be back. The apartment was huge and spanned a few floors, judging by the peek I'd had up the staircase, so did they all live here together?

My eyes were growing heavy, thanks to the big dinner and the inevitable adrenaline crash that was hitting me like a freight train. Though sleeping right now would be dangerous and foolish.

Misha shifted on the couch, and I opened my eyes, not having realized I'd closed them to begin with. As I peered up at him, he came closer, scooping me up like a princess, and walked us across the room to his bed. I was just so tired. The robe I was wearing completely engulfed me as he laid me down, studying me for a moment before I felt my eyes drift shut again.

"I shouldn't sleep in your bed. I can just have a little nap on the couch, and then I'll get out of your hair!" I called out, not knowing where he'd gone.

"Shhh," he whispered, making me jump because he was *right there*. His large hands wrapped around my shoulders, and he pulled me into a sitting position. I allowed it since my body felt like it weighed a metric fuck-ton. The tie around my waist was tugged open, and I blinked sluggishly as the plush fabric slid off my shoulders and something was slipped over my head.

Misha guided my arms into a massive T-shirt that had the Haunt logo across the chest. I breathed in a deep breath, feeling very cozy in the soft, worn, cotton shirt. He held up a pair of boxer briefs, but I waved him off. "Sleep," I rasped out as I let myself fall back and sink into the pillows.

The blankets shifted, and suddenly I was covered up. Something in the back of my head was niggling at me but it was just out of reach. There was only one other time I'd ever felt like this, and that had been when...

My eyes flew open. "Misha!"

His handsome, rugged face came into view, and he looked... concerned.

"D–did you d–drug me?" Fuck, I could barely speak. My heart was racing, and a cold sweat covered my skin. *No, no, no.* I didn't get a chance to hear his answer as darkness crept in and doused everything.

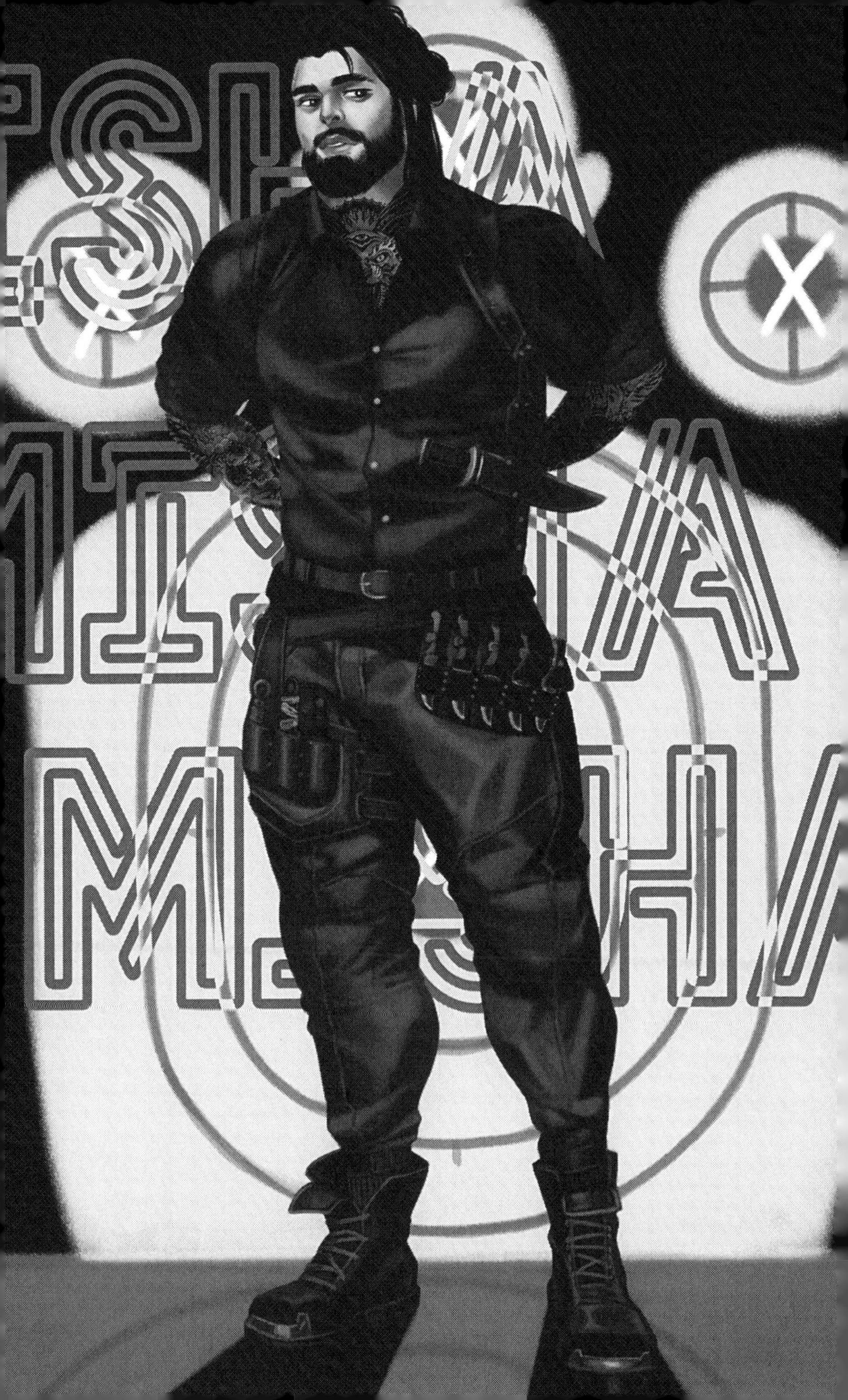

MISHA

Chapter Eight

She was asleep. Though she'd looked terrified just moments before she gave in. Why?

Looking down at her, I took in the way her dark hair fanned across my pillow. The rosy blush on her cheeks, her dark eyelashes that rested against her cheek as she slept. So. Fucking. Pretty. And tasty as hell. I sucked my bottom lip into my mouth, hoping to still catch a taste of her.

Talon had almost claimed her. Fucking hell. I'd never been around another demon during something like that, and I was thankful it hadn't actually happened. Because I was interested. *Very*. I'd already spoken more words to her than I'd used in the last two months combined. If the others had been here, I wouldn't have had to. They ran their mouths enough that I didn't actually need to use my voice.

I pulled my phone out of my pocket and checked for any messages. There were none, which could mean a few things. They were busy killing Frank, which was possible, or they were in the middle of torturing Frank, which was probable. Or, they'd already done both of those things and were working on figuring out the rest of the mystery involving his betrayal.

Grunting, I sat on the side of the bed. Probably for the best I was up here and not down there. I hadn't received my nickname for nothing, though I was a little annoyed that I was missing out. I enjoyed cutting people up. I'd accepted it a long fucking time ago, and when I'd ended up with the name "The Carver," I embraced it. The gang members just called me Carver. Suited me just fine. If everyone was scared of you, they didn't try to make conversation.

Soft snores drifted to my ears, and I looked back down at Palmer, recalling the panic in her eyes right before she gave into my influence. I'd wanted her to relax, not freak the fuck out. "Ugh," I groaned quietly. *I'll just get in quick and make sure she's okay.* If not, I could help. I let my eyes fall shut, and my power pulsed out, searching.

I stepped into the void and waited for the connection to flare. The walls of her dreamscape began to materialize. She was in a dorm room, lying on a twin bed. Her clothes were definitely club clothes, and with the way her leg hung off the mattress at an awkward angle, I knew something was wrong.

Her eyes were wide open, her breathing rapid. The door of the room swung open, and she started muttering the word "No" repeatedly.

Who the fuck was it? I couldn't see the man, but I knew it was a man because of the room. It smelled like a dude's room, plus the shoes by the door were clearly men's shoes. I started to see red, because the only time I got scents in a dreamscape was when something was based on a fucking memory. Whatever this dream was, it was a real event she'd gone through. Some fuckwit had drugged our bunny and scared the hell out of her?

And I'd basically just done the same thing. Fucking fuck.

"Palmer," I commanded. Her big blue eyes locked on me, and the entire dream evaporated. "You're safe. Think of something that makes you happy. Something good."

"Misha? Am I dreaming?" She pushed herself up and stood, the bed she'd been on disappearing. We were now standing in the middle of a thick pine forest, with a fresh layer of snow on the ground and more falling.

"Yes, it's just a dream."

"B–but you drugged me..."

"I would never do that, kukola. I only wanted to help you get some rest. It's part of my magic," I explained. "Had I known..."

"Hey, you're talking a lot," she said, eyeing me suspiciously. "Are you sure you're the same Mishy Bear?"

I balked at the name. "Mishy Bear?"

She shrugged. "Yeah. You're big like a bear. It works."

I really didn't think it did, but she was smiling now, so I let it go. "Where are we?"

"The woods behind the house I grew up in. It's my favorite place in the whole world. Winter was the best, because the snow would come and cover up all of the dead debris on the forest floor. Leaves, twigs, animals... Everything was wiped clean with sparkling snow."

I looked around and shuddered. It had been a long fucking time since I'd been around snow like this... and it wasn't something that brought up good memories for me.

"I'd sit out here for hours and watch for animals. I love squirrels—they're my favorite." She was staring out across the landscape. She seemed to have calmed down enough that I felt okay about bailing. I didn't say a word, just simply slipped away, like an illusion of the dreams people created.

If she remembered anything, it would just be that she'd dreamed and I was there. I could make it so that she'd remember the full extent of the dream—it was one of my favorite fucking torture devices to use against our enemies—but I didn't want her to know that much about me yet.

Knowing she'd be asleep through the night, I rose from the bed and snatched my holsters, then headed over to my bookshelf. I had things to take care of before I grabbed a few hours of sleep for myself. A decorative mirror sat at the same height as my face, and I positioned myself so my entire face was in the frame. A few seconds later, after a click and a whoosh of air, the bookcase swung open.

My body instantly relaxed as I stepped inside, letting the door close softly behind me. This was my favorite place in the world. I wasn't just good with knives, I was the *best*. Hitting the lights, I surveyed my workshop. It was perfectly clean, with the metal gleaming beautifully as I passed by shelves and tabletops full of weaponry and tools.

The snow scene from earlier was still eating at me, and I cursed, dropping my daggers into the stainless steel sink to be cleaned. I hated that it had been so fucking long, yet still those memories could get to me. I got to work, cleaning my weapons and returning them to their rightful places on the walls. The stuff I had on display here in this room were all collectible or antique items that I'd acquired from both this realm and Besmet.

It had been a damned long time since I'd set foot in my home realm, and I really had no desire to return to the fucking shithole so long as King Thane was still ruling it. I'd been one of the lucky ones who grew up far away from Naryian and all that monarchy bullshit.

Besmet, the demon realm, was separated into six sections. I was from the northeast, Kyalta, where it was colder than a witch's tit eighty percent of the time, with snow that piled up high enough to freeze my nutsack.

Growling, I slammed my fists down on the counter. I didn't want to think about Kyalta. I'd escaped there, but sometimes it seemed like my mind would never be free of the horrors I'd endured.

"Boy!"

My stomach sank at the sound of my father's voice. He sounded angry, which he always was. I'd learned a long time ago to predict his mood based on his level of irritation. Mad, furious, livid, or raging. There was nothing else, only shades of anger.

"Yes, sir?" I asked, crawling out from under the table, where I'd been playing with a toy dragon the neighbor had whittled for me.

"We have work to do. Let's go. Leave that stupid toy."

I didn't want it out of my sight. Every toy I got always ended up going missing, or my father would break it as a punishment. I never disobeyed him or talked back like the other boys in the neighborhood, but somehow, I was always in trouble. Nothing I did was right, and even at ten years old, I knew my father saw me as a burden.

It took a lot, but I put my dragon on the table and followed my father outside. The icy wind hit my face, making me gasp. My eyes always watered when it was like this, and I hated it. We had a workshop behind our small, stick cabin that was barely big enough for the both of us to squeeze into. My father was the best blacksmith in our village, and I had become his apprentice the moment I could lift a hammer.

The only time he acted like I was halfway decent at something was when we were in this shed. He taught me everything he knew, the techniques required to produce the best blades in Besmet.

"There's talk of the monarchy wanting to bring in a new royal blacksmith to create a new variety of weapons for their army," my father told me as he examined a broadsword he was in the process of making.

"But you hate the monarchy," I replied, grabbing the dagger I'd been working on.

He grunted. "Not as much as I hate living in this fucking shack. It could be my ticket out of here. My name is known throughout the realm already."

I didn't miss that he'd said it would be his ticket out—not ours. Though I didn't dare question his choice of words. His temper was unpredictable, and I preferred not to give him any reason to blow his lid.

"Do you think they'll send people here to meet you?"

"If the intel I received earlier was right, they're already on their way. When they get here, I need you to be on your best behavior. Do you understand me? I will not have you fucking this up." He brought the hammer down on the glowing, red steel.

"I understand."

"Good, because, Misha? If you ruin this for me, I will make your life a living hell."

Like it wasn't hell already... but I believed him. So I nodded, getting to work.

Two days passed without incident, and I was in the forest playing with my dragon, thrilled that I still had it. I'd been gone for a while, and the sun was now beginning to set, so I wove through the pine trees, trekking my way through the snow.

As I stumbled out from the woods, I saw my father standing at the door of our workshop, holding up the dagger I'd just finished earlier. It had turned out even better than I'd hoped, and was by far my favorite piece. The blade curved like the waves I'd once seen at the coast with my mother, back when she was still alive. I'd fashioned a handle with pointed tips that you could slip your fingers through. I was hoping to create another, to have a matching set. If a demon were to have one in each hand, his fists could be as deadly as the blade.

My father held the dagger up, examining the craftsmanship, and I swallowed hard, hoping like hell he found no issues with it or this would be the end of my wooden dragon. I couldn't take it anymore! Did he hate it?

"Father!" I shouted as I rushed across the snow. He glanced up, and a strange look crossed his face just before he started shaking his head. Oh no. "I finished the dagger this morning, and I only meant to take a little break. I'm going to make the second one now. I'm sorry."

The words had flown from me so fast, it was a wonder he even understood what I said. But he heard. So did the royal army soldiers who were perusing our workshop. I hadn't seen them.

A soldier stepped out of the shed and pointed at the dagger I made. "Boy." He turned to me. "You made this?"

I took a deep breath, swallowing roughly. I could feel my father staring at me, but I didn't dare look. "Yes, sir," I answered honestly, fear making my voice shake.

Another soldier stepped forward, arms crossed. "Nikolai," he said, addressing my father. "The crown does not tolerate liars."

My mouth opened, but my father cut me off. "He's an imaginative boy, and rest assured, he will be disciplined appropriately."

Fear took over. I didn't want to lose my toy!

I looked at the soldiers and threw my hands up. "Why would I lie about making this dagger? I spent hours on the design and burnt eight of my fingers and part of my hand! Look, I even put my initials on it!"

My father's face was so red, I was worried he was actually going to explode. The soldier held out his hand for the weapon, and my father reluctantly handed it over. The group began examining the blade, and I glanced over to my father. His horns were slowly growing, and he held a finger up to his mouth, telling me to be quiet. I could already see the anger in his eyes.

But I wasn't a liar. Why was he so pissed?!

"So tell me, Nikolai, why is your son convinced that he's the one who made this, when you told us it was your design?"

Shit. My mouth fell open. He'd told them he made it?

"This dagger is a work of art. If you are indeed lying, then you're not the best blacksmith in Kyalta. Your son is, and he's, what? Eleven years old? On the other hand, if he's the one who's lying, then you have an eleven-year-old you can't handle. Both situations are problematic. King Thane doesn't tolerate any complications in the capital."

I didn't know what to say, what to do.

"Obviously, the boy is lying. He's been a bit of a troublemaker since his mother passed away," my father explained, and I tried to step into the shadows in a corner. Anything to disappear.

"Hmm. Well, I think what we'll do is take this weapon and let His Majesty look over it. If he's impressed, we'll return. In the meantime, get control of your son."

My father nodded. "It won't happen again. Please, give the king our regards."

The soldiers left without another word, taking the dagger with them.

My feet wouldn't move, and oh my gods, I'd never wanted to run so much in my life. I stayed rooted to my spot, my father beside me. We watched the soldiers extend their wings and shoot up into the sky.

"What did I say, Misha?"

"I didn't know they were here! I swear—"

My face whipped to the side, the rest of my body following, as the back of his hand connected with my cheek. Tears instantly welled, but I forced them away. It would only make this worse.

"You have a problem, Misha. You talk. Too. Fucking. Much."

A foot caught me in the stomach, and I yelped, curling in on myself.

"We're going to solve that problem, so that the next time opportunity comes knocking, you can't FUCK IT UP FOR ME!" he roared, his eyes glowing orange.

"Father, please," I croaked, trying to catch my breath. His hand closed around my ankle, and I felt myself being dragged across the snow toward the doors built into the ground. They led to a bunker. I did not want to go down there. "No, please! I'm sorry! I'll do better!"

He didn't listen, just leaned down with one hand and ripped the doors open, and then I was rolling down the wooden stairs, landing hard on the cold, dirt floor. Glancing up, I saw his silhouette with the sunset sky behind him. Without a word, he slammed the doors shut, leaving me in pitch-black darkness.

"FATHER!"

Growling, I pushed the memory away and started grabbing supplies to create. I needed to take out some aggression. Anything to get the echoes of my childhood out of my fucking brain.

HELIX

FELIX

Chapter Nine

Group sex and murder.

Wouldn't be too unlike any other weekend, except for the fact that I was staring into the face of a fucker who wasn't long for this world, and that was because he was a fucking asshole rat.

"I swear to FUCK I didn't do shit!" Frank screamed, his face a sweaty mess.

Ash picked up a pair of bolt cutters. "Yeah, see, we know you did, Frank."

"And not only do we know for sure it was you... but you touched my Bun-Bun tonight. For that alone, I'm gonna have to take those hands, Frank," Talon explained with a sigh.

"What's a Bun-Bun?! I didn't mean to touch something that was yours, Tal!"

I scooped up the blowtorch and pressed the button. "But you did, Frank. That girl earlier? With the bunny ears? The one who clearly said 'don't touch me?'" My eyes rolled when his face paled. He remembered. "Now, since we know you're a fucking snitch, there's a little issue that needs to be taken care of first. You took an oath when you joined this gang, this family. What was the oath, Frank?"

"P–please," he begged, shaking his head back and forth as I approached.

"That's not how the oath starts," Rhodes barked, making Frank jerk against his restraints. We'd tied his ass to a chair that was bolted to the floor. Usually, it was the hot seat reserved for our enemies, though I suppose Frank was that now.

With the fallen, I rise
With the broken, I cry
With the lost, I find my own
With the outcasts, I am home
With the forgotten, I remember
With the chaos, I am centered
With the wrong, I find the right
With The Exiled, I will fight

"Damn, that's like music to my ears every time I hear the words." Ash grinned and tilted his head back, taking a moment for himself. It was still hard some days to comprehend everything we'd accomplished.

"When you joined, you made a promise. A vow. One to protect the gang with everything you had. Do you think you kept your word?" Talon asked, and Frank sputtered. He knew he was fucked.

"It's on the base of his neck. Get rid of the shirt," I ordered, and my heart began to pound in anticipation of what I was about to do. Ash and Talon cut away his shirt, my brother throwing in a nice slap across Frank's face for the hell of it.

"No! You don't understand—I didn't have a choice!"

"Everyone has a choice, Frank. When you joined up, when we fucking welcomed you, I put art on your skin. A symbol of your dedication and loyalty to this family. Even though you won't be walking out of here tonight, you don't deserve to go into whatever pitiful afterlife awaits you with our mark on your gods damned flesh!"

The blowtorch lit up, the flames so hot they turned blue. Nothing pissed me off quite like my artwork being destroyed. Even though it wasn't a particularly large or intricate tattoo, I still treasured it. But it was my hand that had given it to him, so it would be my hand that erased it.

Frank screamed like the little bitch he was as his skin bubbled and the tattoo was effectively burned away. The screaming suddenly cut off, and I knew he'd passed out. Letting the flame die, I stepped back.

About six months ago, we'd had a deal go south in a bad fucking way. Lil' Petey, one of our best street runners, ended up dead. Rhodes had already been suspicious before that since he'd been noticing some discrepancies in the amount of product we were importing. Then after we lost Pete, more and more of our plans began to get fucked up.

There was just one thing that I didn't understand. All of the shipments that had been short were related to a secret project we were working on. Only the five of us knew what we were creating. Well, and a scientist. But it seemed that the people Frank had been working with were interested in far more than just drugs, cars, or money. They'd had months to make a move on those supplies, and yet the only things taken were rare powders, minerals, and other ingredients.

Shit didn't add up—especially because a lot of the items in question were from Besmet, and most people here wouldn't know what the hell to do with them.

My focus came back to the here and now when Rhodes threw a bucket of ice-cold water over Frank.

"*FUCK YOU!*" Frank shouted, and I glanced over at Tal. Now that he'd realized there was no way out of this, Franky boy's true colors were about to bleed out faster than blood from a severed artery.

"Now, now, there's no sense in that. You can start talking, and this might be a little less painful for you..." Ash trailed off, spinning the bolt cutters. "Or you can continue like this, and I'll use these to cut off every toe, every finger, and your nipples. Your call."

Frank chose that moment to spit on Ashland. That was a horrible fucking decision. Maybe it was the adrenaline, the betrayal, the smell of sweet bunny pussy still lingering, driving us all insane... Either way, the second that wad of saliva hit Ash's shirt, all hell broke loose.

Ash's clothes were shredded as he shifted into his demon form, right there in front of Frank. The scent of piss and shit hit next, and I wrinkled my nose. Piss I could understand, but shit? Jesus, Ash wasn't that damn scary.

In a blink, Ashland got to work removing Frank's fingers. I leaned back against the wall and let him do his thing. You don't spit on a man and not expect repercussions. This was the twenty-first century, not the Wild fucking West.

"Scorpio! It was Scorpio!" Frank screamed, just in time to save his thumb. For now.

"*What* was Scorpio?" Ash snarled, his voice deeper and louder than normal.

Frank started sobbing, and I heaved a bored sigh. "Answer the gods damned question!" I bellowed, sick of all this dicking around. He was a dead man, and we all knew it.

"He offered me a lot of money for some intel. I didn't mean for Pete to get hurt! They didn't even want the high market shit, just some random shit!"

At that, Rhodes looked up, his eyes glowing.

"What the fuck are you?!" Frank shrieked, his terrified gaze flicking between Ash and Rhodes.

"We," Rhodes corrected, walking over to stand beside the big, blond demon. "We are demons. And you are fucked." He shifted, earning another scream from Frank. It didn't hit the same as Palmer's screams though, and I was temporarily distracted by thoughts of her as I wondered what she and Misha were up to.

My brother—not one to be left out—joined Ash and Rhodes, and within seconds, all that was left of Frank was a big bloodstain and random chunks of bone and skin. Fucking gross. Ashland had probably let a little of his biokinetic power out, essentially turning Frank into mush as they ripped into him with their claws.

"Damn, you guys went hard on that," I mused happily, nodding to the stain of Frank. The three of them were breathing heavily, their tails swishing back and forth in agitation. "Feel better now?"

Rhodes flipped me off with one massive claw, making me smirk. "I didn't see any point in waiting. We knew he was guilty."

Back when we first started suspecting Frank, we'd come up with a plan. We set up tonight's big party at Haunt, which meant nearly the entire city and our gang would be here. We then tasked Frank with doing a check-in at the docks for an incoming shipment, just to make sure we had enough space to store it all. Frank drove out yesterday to assess the area, and Ash had let slip to him that the shipment was arriving tonight. Conveniently, we'd all be at the party at that time.

When the text came through earlier, that sealed his fate. He was the only one who'd known about the shipment—which was fake. We'd told our best soldiers to patrol, but to stay hidden. Sure enough, twenty-five thieves had shown up... and now they were dead. If Scorpio's boys were behind it, we'd be able to get confirmation easily enough by checking their tattoos.

"Fucking Scorpio," Rhodes spat, flinging blood from his hands.

"Why the hell would he be making a move like this now? Not only that, but why is he interested in what we're up to? I mean, the weed and cars I could understand..." Talon bent down, scooping up a part of his shredded shirt and using it to wipe off his face.

Ash was still staring at the remains of Frank, like he wished he could bring him back to life just to rip him to shreds all over again. "Yo, Ash, you okay?" His eyes snapped to mine, and I saw a flash of sharp teeth. "Okay, someone needs a cold shower. Come on, bro."

He stared at me for another minute before shaking his head. "Fuck, that was intense. I was so gods damn pissed!"

"Well, he's dead now. Deader than dead. We got what we needed, now let's go clean up. How do you think Mishy is faring with our bunny?" Talon asked, throwing his arm around Ash's waist and leading the way to the communal showers we had down in this area. I'd insisted on those. I didn't want blood and mud and who knows what else dragged through the club or the rest of the building.

"I'm sure he talked her ear off," Rhodes grumbled, and Tal tossed up a middle finger at him.

My skin was fucking crawling from being near them right now in their filthy state, and I zoned out as we entered the showers. I needed a gallon of soap and an endless flow of scalding hot water, and then I needed my studio. I was wired; there was no point in pretending that I'd get any sleep once we headed upstairs.

Rhodes appeared in my stall just as I was about to walk in. "You good, brother?" I nodded, pissed that he'd even noticed my internal distress. "Here, they're new." I looked down as he handed over a bag which held a green loofah, a black washcloth, a bottle of exfoliator, and a variety of soaps and shampoos.

"Thanks, man." I took the bag and went to turn my back, but he grabbed my arm.

"You can always talk to me, ya know?" His eyes shone with sincerity.

I appreciated it, I really did... but no. I couldn't.

I nodded silently, and he left. I showered, listening to Talon singing about hunting rabbits in Elmer Fudd's voice, and Ashland laughing like a lunatic. I wasn't quite sure what to make of Palmer yet, but luckily, I had six months to figure that out. Not that it'd be a hardship to have her around—she'd sucked my cock better than anyone ever had before.

"Cheers to that," I whispered, and got to work scrubbing my skin raw.

****

Freshly showered and down one layer of skin, I sank into my leather chair and picked up my sketchbook. I'd never liked getting dirty, even as a kid. No fucking thanks. Other kids had lived to play in the dirt and the sandy beaches just outside of our village. I happily sat my ass on a chair well above the gritty sand and spent my time drawing instead.

My pencil skated over the paper as I thought back to those days. It had been so long ago that some of the details were lost to me now, while others were stamped in my mind like it was just yesterday—like the fact that our parents had been so embarrassed by my aversion to doing things that "normal young males" enjoyed. We'd grown up wealthy. Incredibly so, and with that came certain expectations. Our parents had been big into appearances.

When our powers manifested at age seventeen, and it turned out we were both capable of shapeshifting and voice mimicry, I thought for sure that would get them off my ass, but it only made it worse. Shapeshifting was a highly sought-after skill in the realm, and the monarchy often tried to recruit as many shifters as possible. Shifters made excellent spies, for obvious reasons.

"Thank you for the invitation, Your Majesty," my father said, bowing to King Thane. We all followed suit.

The king waved him off, standing from the throne. "Thank you for bringing your boys here to meet me on such short notice. The stars have truly blessed your family by bestowing such gifts upon your sons."

My mother smiled. "Yes, they certainly did. When we learned of their capabilities, we knew right away they'd be great assets to the crown."

A door opened somewhere in the throne room, and we all turned our attention to the man who was striding toward us down the long, red carpet. He had a full head of dark hair and equally dark eyes that seemed to hold the kinds of secrets you hoped to never learn.

King Thane raised a brow at the newcomer. "So good of you to join me! Come, meet this lovely family who brought their sons to answer our search for shifters and mimics."

The king's brother finally reached us, and he lifted Mother's hand, kissing her knuckles. "Welcome to Naryian, ma'am." He turned and took Father's hand in a strong shake. "Thank you for coming—I trust your journey was safe? We can never be too careful these days."

"Aye," Father responded. "Safe and sound. Though it did take a bit of time and the winds were not on our side."

The king's brother chuckled, clapping Father on the back. "Of course. These storms lately have been unprecedented. Let's get you situated in your quarters. We have several masseuses and some hot springs that will work wonders on those muscles."

Our parents were nodding eagerly. We were already well-off, but this was a huge move up in society for them. Being here in the castle, with the king of all people... Well, Mother would probably mark this as the best day of her life, topping even the birth of her sons.

"Shifters and voice mimics? Quite the combination," the king's brother said, stepping in front of me now. His dark eyes slid down my face to my feet and back. He paused, and Tal cleared his throat.

Oh right. Respond.

"Felix," I blurted out, and I could swear I heard Mother groan. "Forgive me, sir. I meant to say 'My name is Felix and it's nice to meet you.'"

"I knew what you meant, don't worry." He smiled, and his features softened, making his dark eyes lighten a bit. "Well, Felix, it's nice to meet you too." He stuck out his hand, and I slipped mine into his. Before I could blink, he had moved on to Talon.

"I'm sorry," I piped up, earning myself a discreet jab in the kidney from my father. "I didn't catch your name?"

King Thane bellowed a laugh, and the dark-haired male smiled at me once more. Only this time, it wasn't soft. It didn't lighten those eyes. No, this one chilled me to the fucking bone. It's why animals should never smile, especially not the scary ones. Wolves, bears, dragons...

"I'm Asrael."

"Fuck," I growled, dropping my sketch pad on the end table. This wasn't going to work. I ran my hands through my hair and made up my mind. *Fuck it.*

I threw on some black joggers and a long-sleeved, black T-shirt, before slipping my feet into my neon green Converse, which had some splashes of paint across the tops. They were worn and comfortable, and best of all, my body recognized that feeling of relief. Like hugging an old friend or happily settling into a routine, because no matter how disorganized you were, sometimes you needed that little taste of *predictability* to keep yourself grounded.

Anytime I put these shoes on, it meant I was going to paint. I flung open the coat closet and grabbed my equally broken-in, dark gray backpack, which was covered in patches and pins that I liked to collect from all over.

The best thing about painting—aside from the rush I got from scaling buildings and bridges—was the fact that I was able to completely blackout. Nothing could reach me when I was working on a piece, and that sounded like the perfect fucking distraction right now.

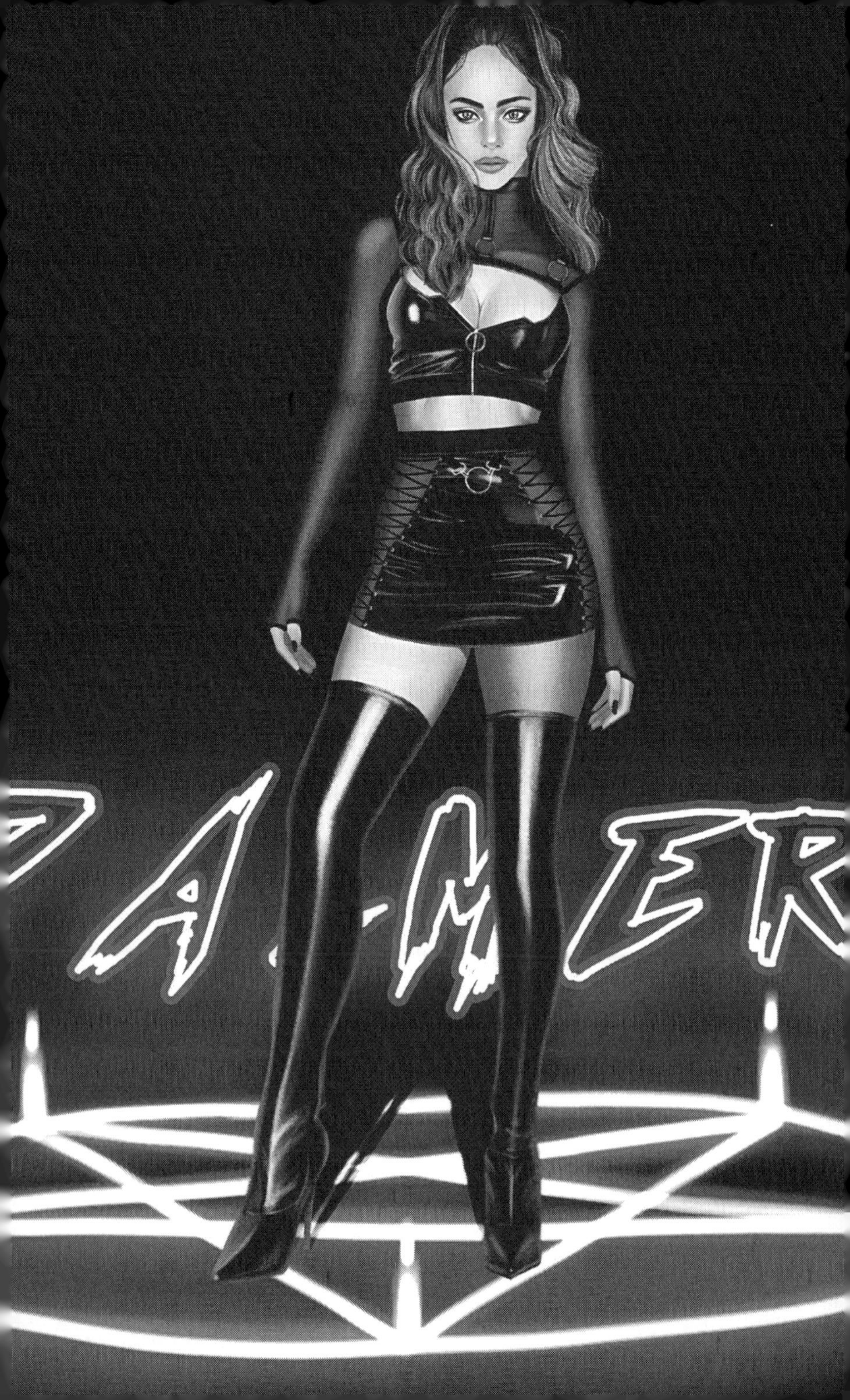

PALMER

Chapter Ten

I was suspended in that glorious moment between sleep and wakefulness, where your dreams feel like reality but you're left without the pressures of real life to sully your hopes.

The chill of the snow was giving way to the warmth of being wrapped up in a nest of blankets. The gentle swaying of the branch I was perched on melted away, and my eyes fluttered open, revealing a room that I didn't recognize. Blinking, I tried to clear my mind and focus my vision. That swaying I'd felt moments before was starting again, and my eyes popped open wide when my brain fully came back online. Gasping, I flipped over and came face to face with a grinning red-haired demon.

"Top o' the mornin' to ya, Bun-Bun," Talon greeted, flexing his hips again, causing my body to sway once more. Was he... micro-dry humping me?

"Talon!" I shoved his bare chest. "What are you doing?"

"No need for violence this early in the day." He propped both hands under his head and stared at me innocently. "I came up here last night and was pleasantly surprised to find you passed out in big Mishy's bed, all sweet and snoring."

"I don't snore."

"Anywho, Mish is still in his man cave, and what kind of gentle-demon would I be if I left you alone in such a big bed?"

"Uh, the best kind? Typically, you don't just get into bed with women who can't consent to—"

He smiled. "Yes, I am the best. Thank you, Bun-Bun. Sometimes a male just needs to hear that from a woman."

I inhaled deeply, feeling frustrated as hell. He had the worst case of selective hearing I'd ever encountered. Glancing down, I was relieved to see that I was still dressed. I knew from my research over the last several months that they didn't condone rape—in fact, they were heavily against it and had made examples of rapists. Publicly. Which was something I would almost say I appreciated, but really, that was the way everyone should be when it came to sexual assault. I wasn't quite ready to bow down and kiss anyone's toes for doing the right fuckin' thing.

All of that flew out the window when Talon flung his covers back and revealed his completely naked body. I choked on whatever words I'd been about to speak.

"Don't worry, I always sleep in the nude. We all do," he informed me with a wink, swinging his legs off the bed and hopping up. His ass flexed as he stretched his arms above his head.

"Why shouldn't I worry about that?"

"Ah, well, I just meant it's not like a 'you' specific thing. I would've been naked regardless of whether you were here. See?"

"Uh-huh," I mumbled. I did see. Saw his creamy skin dotted with reddish-brown freckles, and the muscles beneath that rippling with every movement he made.

Enough! I slammed my eyelids shut to block out the view. It didn't help. All it did was bring back to life the very real events that had happened last night in that sex maze.

A phone started ringing, and I cracked my eye to steal a peek. Talon swiped a phone from the table and answered it.

Okay, I needed to think while he was distracted. *Think, think, think.* Last night, I'd been convinced I needed to get out of here, but in the light of day, that wasn't really looking like my smartest option... Though I also didn't want to seem like I was trying too hard to stick around.

As of right now, *they* were the clingy ones, not me.

"No, I haven't seen him since last night."

I perked up. Who hadn't he seen?

"Shit, man. You know how he gets sometimes. I'd go, but I have a meeting downtown."

A meeting, hmm?

"Yeah, I'll tell Mish. Okay, yeah. See ya in a bit."

"Is everything okay?" I called out as I rolled to the edge of the bed.

Talon grumbled. "Yeah. Felix is missing."

"Missing?" I questioned, surprised.

Tal turned to face me, his dick hard as a post and pointing right at me. "It's nothing to get concerned about. Trust me, Bun-Bun. I know my brother."

The sound of a door opening had me spinning on my heel, just in time to see Ashland blow into the room like a bat out of hell. He came to an abrupt halt when he saw Talon's state of undress and me standing there in Misha's T-shirt.

"Nobody thought to invite me to the party?" He crossed his arms over his white button-down shirt that was half tucked into a pair of burnt orange dress slacks. I squinted, looking closer. Velvet. They were fucking velvet, burnt orange dress slacks.

"There was no party, Ash. Just some snoozing, and maybe I did a little scenting..."

I whipped around to Talon. "A little what?"

"Come with me, love. I'll get you something to wear and we can head out," Ash told me, holding his hand out for me to take.

"Um, I was planning to go ahead and get out of your hair. Just need to find my shoes and bag—"

Ashland stepped closer and took my hand. "Don't be silly. You're with me today. We're going to find Felix."

Excellent. I'd be able to stay close to Ashland and hopefully dig around some more. I made sure to keep my emotions off my face—obviously, I didn't want them knowing that was how I felt. "But why?"

Talon and Ashland exchanged a look, and then started laughing. Ashland took a breath, shaking his head. "Come on now. You saw *us* last night. You didn't really think we were going to just let that go, did you?"

"Oh, right. Well, I don't give a fuck about your little"—I held up two fingers to make horns—"*problem*. I don't care what you are. We had fun, and now I'm ready to leave. So, thanks for the dick." I walked past Talon in the direction of the bathroom, only to be caught off guard a second later when the fucking bookshelf to my right moved, nearly clipping my arm.

Misha was standing there, looking sexy as sin with his hair pulled up in a bun and a set of blades clenched in his massive fist.

"I'll be back. I'm going next door to grab some clothes for her," Ash called, but I was stuck in the dark gaze of a hell beast. Misha took a step out of whatever cavern he'd been hiding out in, and I stepped back slowly. Something about the look in his eye was screaming at me to be cautious.

"Hi, Misha," I mumbled, taking another step back.

He grunted and kept coming for me. I glanced over at Talon, who was now leaning against the wall, observing the situation with amusement, if the way his mouth was hitched up was any indication.

"D–did you sleep?"

Another grunt. I was about to run into the wall.

Was he pissed at me? His eyes were narrowed, and judging by the way his chest was heaving, it damn well seemed like it. "Thank you for letting me use your bed," I stammered, and a growl left his mouth the second I said the word "bed."

His hands were on me in a flash, and I was hoisted up. My legs wrapped around his thick body instinctively, causing his T-shirt to ride up, leaving my lower body completely exposed. I didn't mind one bit when his hands gripped my ass as he walked us to the couch where we'd eaten last night. That was when I noticed a tray of breakfast foods sitting there, and my stomach immediately rumbled.

Misha threw a dirty look at Talon that I didn't understand, and from the confusion on Talon's face, neither did he. "The fuck was that look for?"

Misha didn't respond. He simply arranged me in his lap and leaned over, pulling the table closer. He stabbed a strawberry with a fork, then brought it to my mouth. My eyes flicked to his. He wasn't fucking around. I opened my mouth and accepted the bite, surprised by how sweet the fruit was. I reached for the fork, able to feed myself, but earned a warning growl for my effort.

"Just let the man feed you, Bun-Bun. It's making him happy. He already looks at least seven percent less pissed than he did when he came out here."

I settled back against Misha's chest and did what Talon suggested. It was awkward as hell, but I was willing to allow it if it led to them trusting me faster. Plus, I got a lot of food. I ate fruit, eggs, bacon, and toast. Everything that was offered, I ate. I didn't want to see Misha pissed off, and there were several times I could've sworn that he was smelling my hair and throat.

"Oh, for the love of *fuck*..."

"Good morning, Monocle. You're looking dapper today," I greeted Rhodes, who looked like I'd just pissed on his loafers. Ashland chose that moment to come back, a stack of clothes in hand.

"You're hand-feeding her? Have you lost your gods damned mind, Misha?" Rhodes boomed, his face turning as red as a tomato.

Tension in the room rose fast, and the calmness that had descended while I was eating now evaporated to nothing. *Thanks, Monocle.*

"I'll just... get dressed then," I said softly, sliding off Misha's lap and tugging my shirt down. "Thank you for breakfast." I held my arms out to Ashland, and he handed over the clothes. Bundle in hand, I made a beeline for the bathroom and closed the door just as everything boiled over.

"You're all fucking fools!" Rhodes shouted. "We know nothing about this woman, yet here you are, acting like she's the stars' gift to our fucking crew!"

I wasn't sure who was growling now, but it was more than one of them. My heart was pounding. Rhodes might prove to be a problem if this was how he was going to act.

"You want to keep the woman, and yet when I come out of my shop, she is clearly starving! I will not tolerate it!" Misha bellowed, and my mouth fell open. I mean, I was not starving. Not by a long shot... but also, he was yelling. A lot.

Rhodes laughed without humor. "Ah, Misha. Don't think I didn't notice she was also wearing your shirt and smells of your bed. Are you claiming this pet as yours then?"

"I think the fuck not," Ashland snarled at the same time as Talon shouted, "No!"

"He's scent marking her more than a dog pissing on a fucking fire hydrant!"

I really needed to find out what it meant to be scent marked by a demon.

"You're jealous." Talon's voice was steady.

"And you're all delusional. Talon, I'll be waiting in the garage—we have a meeting. Put some fucking clothes on." A door slammed a moment later, and there was nothing but silence.

Shit.

The hair on my shoulder moved, like a soft breeze had decided to move through the inside of the bathroom. My eyes flicked to the windows, which were closed. Twisting around, I came face to face with the ghost I'd met last night before entering the club. *How did I not feel him there?* Typically, I would sense a ghost from across the room. My scalp would tingle and goosebumps would erupt once they got within twenty feet of me.

I was off my game, and I was *never* off my game.

"He's right. The other one is jealous," the ghost said, a smile forming on his translucent face.

I snorted and walked to the sink. "How would you know?"

The ghost glided up beside me, and we stared at each other in the mirror. "Because I am too."

"A jealous ghost?"

He chuckled. "What? I can't have feelings?"

"Please, be my guest. Have all the feelings you want; I'm just not used to the dead telling me about their emotions. Mostly they just yell at me, call me names, try to scare me—shit like that," I explained, pulling Misha's shirt up over my head.

Ghost boy turned around, and my brows pinched together. "I didn't see anything, I promise," he mumbled, and I could've sworn his ghosty ears were turning red.

Wow. A virgin ghost? I dressed quickly, and the ghost remained, strangely enough. It took a lot of energy for spirits to manifest themselves like this, let alone actually communicate.

"You must be pretty strong," I stated as I scrubbed my face. "Most ghosts would've been wiped out after a minute or two of this, and yet, here you are."

He crossed his arms and studied me. "I'm pretty motivated."

"Motivated? To do what?"

"To talk to you. I've been alone for a long time."

"Palmer? We need to leave in ten!" Ashland called through the door.

"I'm taking a shit, fuck off!"

I turned back to my ghost buddy, but he was gone. Sighing, I got to work braiding my hair. They'd given me more Haunt apparel to wear. I was relieved to see tags attached, so it wasn't like I was wearing someone else's clothes. Even the sports bra and underwear still had tags affixed; I assumed they probably kept spares in the club for the dancers.

With a last glance in the mirror, I straightened and headed for the door. Day one of the infiltration was underway. It was time to get my head in the gods damned game.

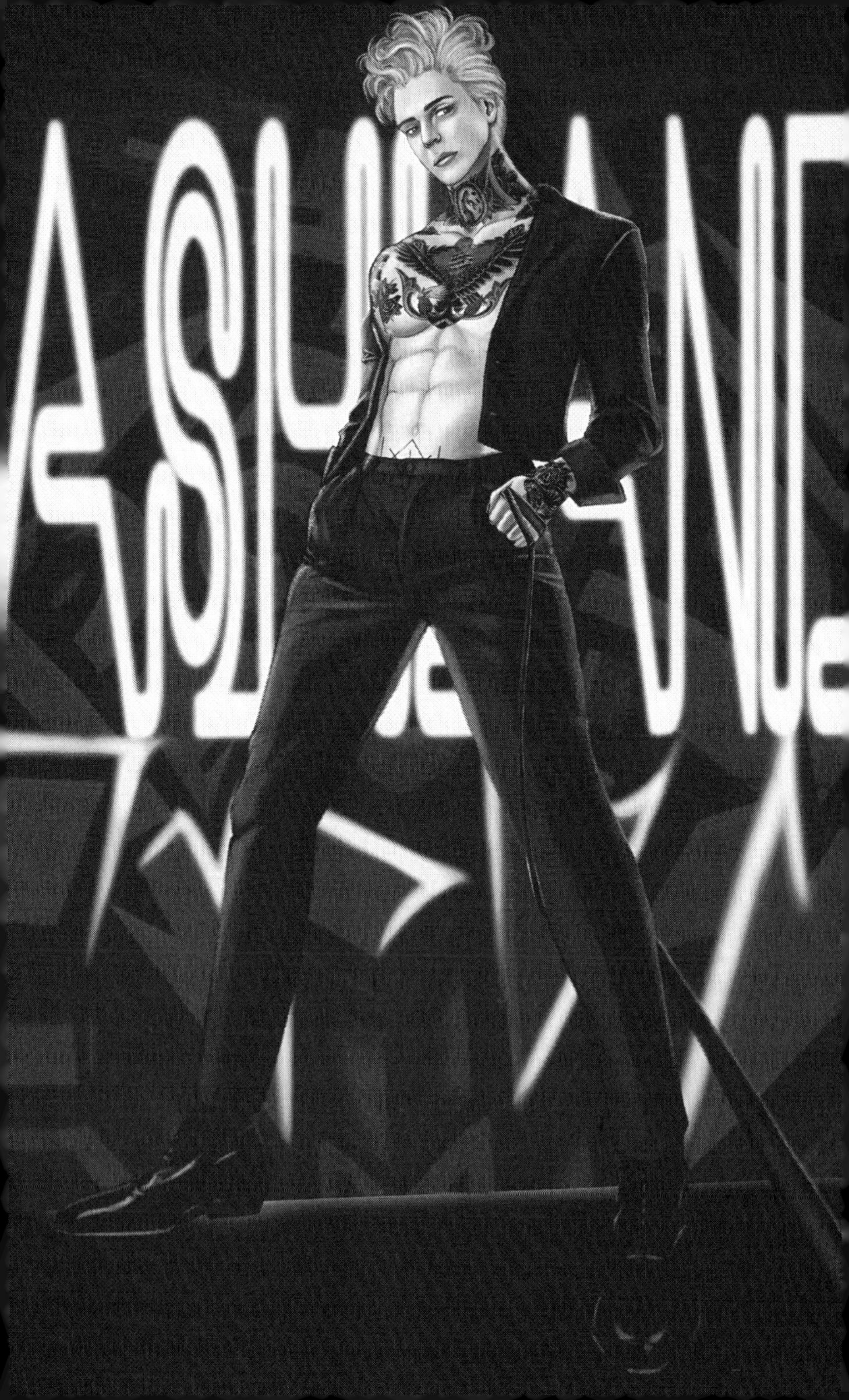

ASHLAND

Chapter Eleven

Palmer exited the bathroom looking refreshed and sexy as hell in the clothes I'd gotten for her. A neon orange, racerback tank and a pair of black leggings shouldn't have looked that damn good. I made a mental note to stop today, if we had time, to get her a new wardrobe. If she was going to be attached to us for the foreseeable future, she'd need to look the part—though apparently, she looked good in anything.

"Everything okay?" she asked, glancing from me to Misha. Rhodes and Talon had taken off while she was getting ready, and I was relieved there wouldn't be another argument so soon.

"Just peachy," I replied, holding my arms out wide. "Nothing like a little verbal sparring to get your day started."

Misha stood and took a deep breath. "Here." He held out his hand to Palmer, and her eyes widened. "For you."

She stepped closer, holding out her hand. Misha placed two blades on her palm and then hightailed it across the room, heading for his cave.

"Misha," she gasped, lifting one of the twin blades. The small handle was a bunny ear, completely encrusted with diamonds and other sparkling gems. "Where did you get these?" Tearing her eyes from her gifts, she looked up and realized Mish was long gone. "Where did he go?"

"He's got shit to do. So do we. I grabbed your thigh holster last night; it's on the bed. Those should fit in it nicely." I nodded toward the daggers.

"They're so fucking pretty," she breathed, spinning them between her fingers. The metal was nearly black—he'd really gone all out. "Wait a second. You're letting me have weapons?"

I couldn't help the laugh that escaped. "Oh, love. You don't scare me. Let's get the fuck out of here."

Once she had properly affixed her new babies to her leg, we were striding side by side through the penthouse. Each of us had our own section of the penthouse, with a few shared spaces. Everything out here in the shared space was sleek and modern, just how I liked it. Black leather with stainless steel accents.

"So, you all live here?" my little rabbit asked, her big, blue eyes darting around, taking it all in. I couldn't stop myself from looking at her uncovered face. When I'd first noticed her in that mask last night, I knew she was attention-grabbing. I'd been curious about what she'd look like with the rest of her face revealed, but I hadn't been prepared to be so stunned by her.

Shaking away my thoughts, I cleared my throat and tried to recall her question. Right. She wanted to know if we all lived here. "We do," I answered, pressing my palm to the scanner. "We have places outside of the city too."

She huffed. "Of course you do."

I lifted a brow at the hint of what sounded like disgust in her tone—something to explore later. We stepped into the elevator, and I hit the button for the underground garage.

She shifted from one foot to the other. "Are we going to talk about last night?"

I grinned. "I'm happy to talk about last night, love. Fucking brilliant night."

The doors slid open, and I could feel her glaring at my back as I stepped out into the cool garage. "That's not what I meant and you know it."

"We can talk about whatever you want to talk about." I spun around and held a finger to her lips, cutting off her words. "*After* we get in the car and on our way."

Her eyes narrowed as she stared up at me, and I felt my dick waking up. My eyes dipped to her slender throat, making me wonder how sexy she'd look with a collar... My hand trailed from her mouth, alongside her jaw, and down to her neck. So dainty.

"Ash," she breathed, and my gaze snapped to hers. I reluctantly released her throat from my grasp.

I swallowed roughly and silently counted to five. I needed to calm down or I was going to demon out right here and fuck her in my natural form on top of the nearest vehicle. "Come on." I turned away from her, walking hastily to my vintage Aston Martin DB4. I hit the unlock button and the car beeped, the lights flashing. Thank the stars for technological upgrades.

Opening the passenger door, I waited for her to slide in. Once she was inside, I closed her door and slowly made my way to the driver's side. There was something about her scent this morning... It was driving me insane. *It was driving you insane last night, too.* I got in and fired up the engine.

"Where are we going?"

I chanced a look and found her scanning the garage. Thank fuck she couldn't tell how on edge I was. "To the docks," I answered, pulling the car out of the underground garage and onto a fairly vacant street.

It wasn't quite noon yet, but the sun was shining. For now. That was the thing about living in Port Black—the weather changed frequently. It was often raining and gray, which explained the vacant streets. People would probably be down at the beach, enjoying the sunshine while it lasted.

"What are you?" Palmer blurted out ten seconds into our drive.

I shifted and tossed her a look. "What do you think I am?"

"A monster."

I chuckled. "I'm not going to argue that one, but no, little rabbit. I'm a demon. So are my boys, as you saw."

"I didn't know demons existed," she replied, studying my profile closely, like I was going to shift and corrupt her any second now.

"And what? Only your kind is able to exist?"

She slowly turned in her seat to face me. "My kind?"

"Oh please, I know you're not human. You're a witch. I'm just not clear on what your affinity is."

There were witches and mages, and each of them was gifted with an affinity. A specific type of magic exclusive to their person. There were so many different types, but sometimes I was able to smell what kind of magic a witch was capable of. Fire, for example. Or water.

Whatever magic Palmer had, it was one I hadn't run into before—and that was saying a lot. It reminded me of the way the earth smelled during autumn: decaying leaves, damp earth, and crisp air. While I wasn't a fan of smelling anything that I'd typically describe as decaying, her magical scent almost felt... cozy. Calming.

"Alright, I'm a witch, yes. Am I in danger when you're... a demon?"

"Yes." We reached the docks, and I pulled up to the security building, killing the engine. Reaching over, I took her hand. "But love, I'm always a demon." With a grin, I kissed her knuckles.

"So I'm not safe with you?"

"I highly doubt you'd find somewhere safer to be than surrounded by five ruthless demons. Now, let's head inside. I have a few things to take care of before we go find Felix."

She groaned. "You're confusing."

I shrugged. I could accept that. We got out of the car, and I led the way to a large open garage door.

"Wait!" Palmer suddenly shouted, and I cringed, turning slowly to face her with my ear ringing. "Sorry, I got excited. Forgot how close you were to me. But I have some more questions before we go in there." She blinked up at me, and damn it all to hell, I'd give her whatever she fucking wanted if as long as she kept those deep blue eyes on me at all times.

"Go on then," I said slowly, wondering if I was going to regret this.

She bounced on the balls of her feet, chewing on her lip as she thought. My eyes zeroed in on that little display, and suddenly I wanted to feel her juicy lip between my own teeth. I wanted to feel everything she had to give me. Especially that pretty little—

"Where are demons from? How long have you been here?" Her eyes widened. "How long have other demons been here? There are other demons, right? Why are you here of all places?" My mouth opened slightly as she rambled, like she barely took a breath before launching into the next question. "How old are you guys anyway? Okay, that was rude. Blink once if you're under five hundred and twice for over."

I didn't move a muscle.

She released a huff of annoyance. "Fine. But why do you call yourselves The Exiled? There's gotta be some kind of story there, right? And those tails, do you use them as weapons during fights? If it gets chopped off, does it regrow, like a crab leg?"

"And you're done." I stepped into her space, tucking her beneath my arm. "Do you suffer from low blood sugar? I believe you may be in need of some sugar."

Palmer released a husky laugh that was like a slap right to the shaft. Not a bitch slap, but like, a sexual slap that stung just right. I filed that idea away for another day.

"No, I don't have low blood sugar. I just haven't had a chance to really process everything or ask questions, and I didn't want to miss my chance."

Most of that shit I wasn't telling her—or anyone for that matter—but I could answer a few of her burning questions. "Of course there are other demons here. You probably interact with at least one demon per day without even knowing it. That's the average estimate, anyway. We're from the demon realm, which is called Besmet. We go back and forth through a portal."

Her eyes bounced around, as if the portal was going to jump out and snare us without warning.

"Don't worry, little rabbit. Even if the portal was here, we wouldn't be able to go through. Well, actually, you could if you had a demon escort who wasn't banished."

"Banished?"

"And that's the last question I'm answering right now—why we chose The Exiled for our name. Getting ostracized from your homeland tends to leave a lasting mark, wouldn't you think?" This wasn't a topic of discussion I particularly enjoyed. Brought up too many memories... especially of people who I'd thought loved me. That just wasn't a road I could travel down right now. Or preferably ever.

Her little mouth opened, clearly to ask more questions, but I cut her off, ignoring her scowl. "Before we go in, I need you to understand that whatever you see or hear is confidential. Under no circumstances are you permitted to share anything with anyone. Got it?"

"Yes." She snapped her fingers, then popped her hand under her chin as though some genius thought had just struck her dumb. "In fact, I have a better idea. Why don't I just stay out here, and then I won't see or hear anything I'm not supposed to?"

I laughed. "Nice try, love. Get inside."

"Aye! Boss is here!" I heard the shout as we approached the door.

"That's right. Look alive, ladies and gents!" I hollered, waltzing into the warehouse like a fucking god. "Heard there was some trouble last night. Anyone wanna show me where?"

One of our more promising mage members with an interesting affinity jogged up, eager to prove himself. "I was here last night when it went down. Happened exactly like Rhodes speculated. We had all the lights off, and it didn't take long before I sensed people snooping around."

I placed my hand on the small of Palmer's back, guiding her with us as we walked through the building. Pallets were stacked up all around us, containing anything and everything from car parts to guns and ammunition. Those weren't the most important items though.

"Tell me again how many there were, Roost?"

The kid grinned. "Twenty-five. Can you believe that shit? Anyway, I shifted and started taking out who I could." Palmer's brows lifted at that, and he laughed. "Name's Rooster. Rattlesnake shifter, at your service."

"That's... not what I was expecting with your name."

"Ah, yeah. Well, Carver gave me the name. I thought it was because I was always up at the crack of dawn, but turns out he just thinks I'm a cock," he explained, making Palmer laugh. I hid my own smirk. I had a reputation to maintain, and this wasn't the time for grins. Rooster led us to a slip at the back of the building that had a boat tied up and ready. "They're all on board, sir."

I nodded and turned to Palmer. "Stay with Roost. I need to go on board and check out something real quick." I glanced at him. "Make sure she's safe, and for the love of fuck, don't let her disappear. If a single hair on her head is out of place when I get off that boat, someone will be answering for the disrespect with blood."

"Understood," Rooster said at the same time Palmer muttered, "Jesus." But that was fine with me. She needed to learn right away that when I meant business, that was the end of it.

One didn't just build a fucking empire being a limp dick, spineless jellyfish. No, I had expectations and I set them clearly. No chance at anything getting misunderstood that way. Maybe it was the discussion earlier about Besmet, but all of that just ran through my head in my father's voice—or I should say, adoptive father. He'd taught me everything I knew and was the smoothest liar I'd ever known.

Nodding to them, I stepped on board and tugged out my handkerchief. I could already smell the stench of death; I needed to do this quickly. The door to the small room in the belly of the boat squeaked as I tugged it open, and I stepped through, letting it slam behind me.

"Fucking hell," I cursed, trying to breathe through my mouth. Squatting down, I ripped the shirt of the first man I came to, looking for a clue about who he belonged to. Right there on his chest was all the confirmation I needed. A tattoo of a black scorpion with bright red blood splatter along its body told me that these men did indeed belong to Scorpio.

My lip curled up in disgust, and I fought against the desire to roar my challenge back to that fuckhead. He wanted a war? He was going to get one.

I got the fuck out of there, my boots landing solidly on the wooden dock as I tucked my silk hankie away and inhaled a deep breath of fresh air.

"Ya know, I expected you to have a fancier boat," Palmer called out, and I was pleased to see that she was standing exactly where I'd left her.

Roost and I both laughed. "Don't worry about that, love. This?" I pointed to the little boat that was quite literally on its last legs. "This is what we like to call a corpse cruise."

"A corpse cruise?" she repeated, her eyes looking at the boat with new interest.

I glanced over to the kid, giving him a nod, and he walked back inside without another word. I stopped in front of Palmer and pushed some of the loose strands of dark hair from her forehead. "We run this city. There isn't anything off-limits to The Exiled. It's taken years of work and dedication, but this is what we've built. My boys, and me. We created a new family, a new home. When someone threatens that…" I had to suppress my demon. "I can get a little *territorial*. Possessive."

"And what? You just kill people who so much as look at you wrong?"

"Fuck no," I all but growled. "We're not heartless beasts, Palmer. However, stealing and lying? We have no use for liars and thieves."

Her blue eyes shifted as she stared at something behind me. Was she looking away deliberately? That captivating gaze returned a split second later, and the paranoia dissipated as quickly as it had come on. Fucking Rhodes was getting in my head.

"Then we're agreed on that at least. So what is a corpse cruise?"

I couldn't stop the grin that took over. "Come with me, little rabbit."

****

"But there's nobody on that boat! It's going to—"

"Shhh," I whispered, pulling her body against mine. Her little ass rubbed against my cock, and I swallowed a groan.

We watched as the boat sped further and further away from the docks, into deeper water. Closer to Scorpio's city, just across the bay. I bent down and grazed my nose along Palmer's neck, enjoying the shiver that worked its way through her body. My lips met her warm skin and all I wanted was to devour her. The sweetest little huff of desire, mixed with her irritation at wanting me, was all the encouragement I needed.

"Touch yourself," I murmured into her ear. She twisted to look up at me, her cheeks flushed with need and perhaps a smidgen of embarrassment.

"Ashland," she chastised, ready to pull away from me, but not yet.

"I want you to come on your fingers right here, with me and my fucking city at your back. I can't think of anything hotter," I whispered, pressing my hips against her ass so she could feel the truth of my words.

She blinked and looked away. "Someone might see us."

"Good," I growled. "I hope they fucking do. I hope they see what they'll never fucking get. Now, *touch yourself.*"

Her breath came out shaky, but she obeyed. As she turned back to the water, I felt her slip her hand into her panties and heard the gasp from her lips as she played with her pussy.

"That's it, love. Rub that wet pussy for me," I rasped against her neck, my eyes on the boat that was getting smaller and smaller in the distance.

"Oh gods," she moaned as I cupped one of her breasts and squeezed.

"Do you have any idea how badly I want to fuck you? From the moment I saw you last night..." I rolled her nipple between my fingers, and she arched her back. Almost there. "Seeing Talon's cock disappearing into your tight little body? Fuck, I could come right now. Maybe I should paint your face, little rabbit? Mark my little whore so my crew knows who you belong to."

"Ash," she panted, her movements becoming jerky.

I reached into my pocket and flipped the little remote control over, letting my thumb rest against the button. "I can't wait to see my cock fill up your ass."

That did it. Her entire body stiffened as she cried out. At that exact moment, my thumb pressed down, and the boat in the distance blew up into a million pieces. Palmer jumped at the sound, her body still shuddering as she spun in my arms, staring up at me with her mouth open.

Smoke billowed up to the sky. I hoped that fuck, Scorpio, was staring at the wreckage, knowing that he'd just lost twenty-five soldiers. I hoped he realized that we knew what he was up to and that he'd started a fucking war.

Reaching down blindly, I took Palmer's wrist and brought her fingers up to my mouth. *Her fucking scent...* My mouth watered as I took in two of them and sucked hard. My tongue lapped and teased, making sure I claimed all of that deliciousness for myself. With a groan of sexual frustration, I popped her fingers out of my mouth. There was no time to fuck her the way I wanted to right now, so this would have to wait.

"Let's go find Felix."

"But... what about the—" She turned to look out at the sea, but there was nothing left of that boat. Even the smoke was nearly gone.

"Oh, and love? They were definitely watching." I winked and headed back inside, thoroughly enjoying the names she was calling me.

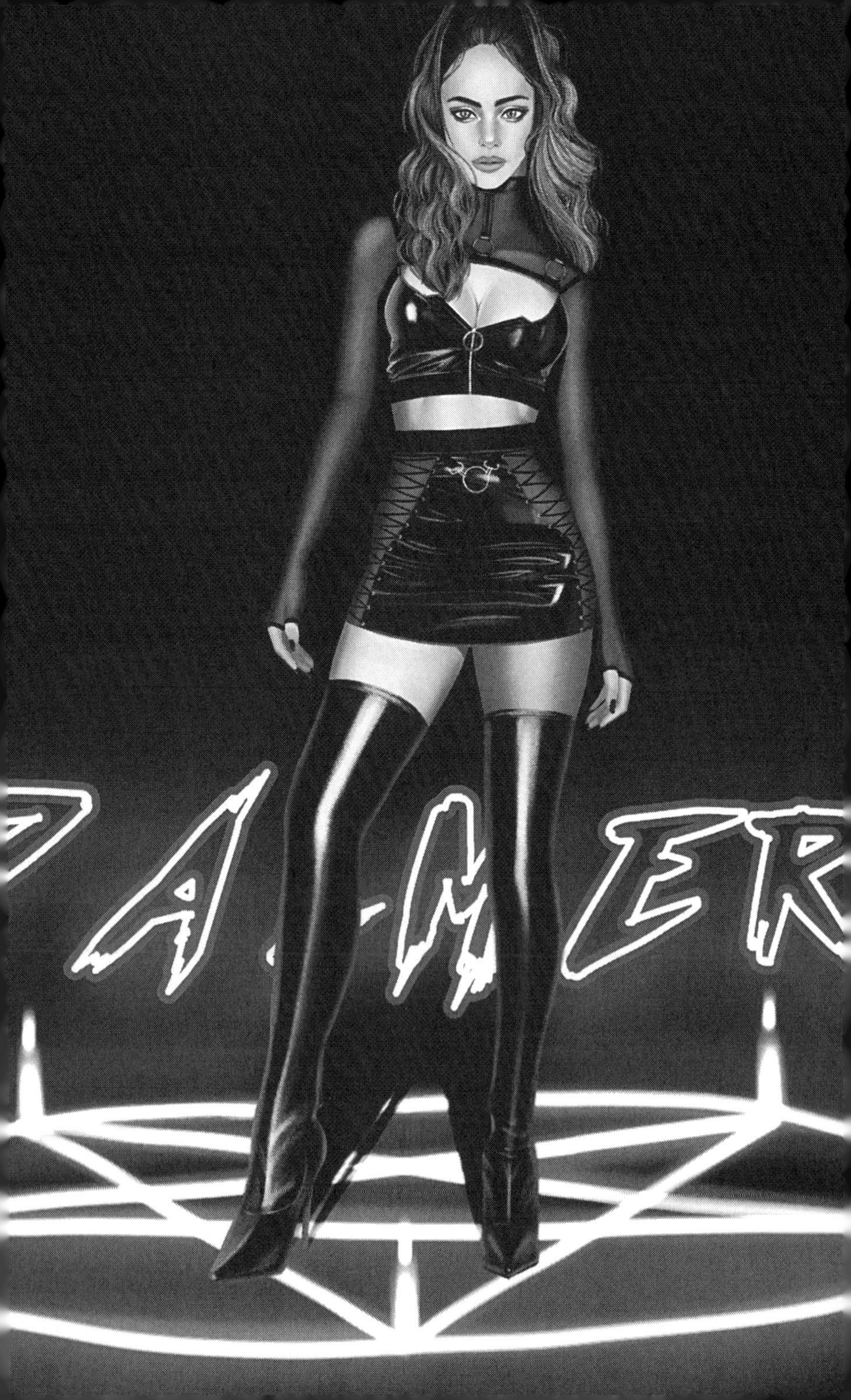

Chapter Twelve

Ash walked away, chuckling like he was the world's funniest fucker. He wasn't.

My spine began to tingle and I looked over my shoulder, unsurprised to see a ghost standing at the end of the dock. I'd already seen several since stepping foot out of Ash's car. None of them had been strong enough to hold their forms for long or able to speak. This one though, he looked pissed. His form flickered like a lightbulb about to meet its doom, and he was right in front of me in a matter of seconds.

He seemed to be in his forties and he looked rough, like life really hadn't been kind to him. His shaved head was covered in tattoos, and his shirt was ripped open, revealing a familiar tattoo: a black scorpion with bright red blood splatter along its body. Interesting. The rival gang across the bay, The Scorpions, were run by a criminal mastermind who went by the alias Scorpio. They were like the diet version of The Exiled, and as far as I knew, not demonic. Just shitheads.

Nobody knew Scorpio's true identity, since he never went anywhere without a mask. Usually, he went with a black, leather mask that was studded all over with spikes. It covered his entire face, except for his eyes.

For the most part, it seemed The Exiled and Scorpions steered clear of each other, keeping to their own sides of the bay. So then why was I staring at a big, dead gang member from Scorpio's crew on one of The Exiled's docks?

"What happened to you?" I whispered, even though a quick look showed me Ash was busy chatting with some people near the building.

"Fuckin' set up. Was supposed to be in and out. Grab the product and go, but they knew we were coming," the ghost grumbled, looking at his hands in wonder. He was a fresh one. I could always tell by the level of confusion at their new form.

"What product?" I pushed, knowing this could be valuable information. He narrowed his eyes at me, and I rolled mine in response. "Oh come on. You're fucking dead, dude. There's no loyalty in death."

"Guess you have a point. Wouldn't be dead if the intel had been good. Scorp is getting greedy. Exiled are up to something—researching and experimenting. That's all I know." His form started fading, and he looked at me with wide eyes.

I inhaled and decided I'd help the poor soul. "Don't fight it. Your time here is over. Just let go." I whispered a few incantations under my breath that usually aided souls in crossing over to the next plane of existence. Even though my affinity was rare, there were a few texts out there that had some helpful information, and I was like a sponge, eager to soak up and learn everything I could to harness my magic and use it to its fullest potential.

"Everything okay, love?" Ash called just as the ghost vanished.

"I'm not your love, asshole!" I shouted back, and was met with a chorus of both laughter and gasps of surprise from his crew at my blatant name-calling.

So The Exiled were researching something. Could this be what Asrael was wanting to know more about? The whole mission was somewhat vague, which told me that while Asrael might've known they were up to something, it was clear he had no idea what.

"Fuck off, Hunt. I'll see you later for dinner." I laughed, *punching my oldest friend in the arm.*

"You're getting stronger, Vale. That felt more like a punch and less like a mosquito bite," he teased, and I flipped him off, opening the room to my dorm and slamming it in his smug face.

Damn right I was getting stronger. I'd been busting my ass at the gym every day and going on as many challenges—mock and real—as possible. I was eager to prove myself, and I loved the validation.

"You're awful close to that boy."

I shrieked and spun around, reaching for the dagger that was hidden in the waistband of my shorts. Asrael was sitting in my desk chair, spinning his own knife around his fingers.

"You surprised me," I breathed, abandoning my weapon in favor of a bottle of water.

"Then that's your first mistake. You should never let anyone surprise you, Palmer. If they can do that, they can beat you."

I lifted the bottle to my mouth and chugged half of the cold liquid. "You're right. Won't happen again."

"I have something for you." He stood and picked up a manila folder that was on the corner of my desk. "These are the targets in your upcoming mission. This is the one you've been training for. It won't be easy—they're sneaky, smart, and powerful. You'll need to learn as much about them as possible before going in. This is enough to get you started."

My eyes fell to the folder, and it took everything in me not to snatch it from him. He must've sensed my eagerness because he held it out to me with a smile. "I knew when I met you that you were special. The only reason I've waited so long for this mission is because I knew you'd be the perfect person for the job. I just had to be patient and wait for you to be ready. I think you're ready. Do you?"

"I've never been more ready for anything in my life, sir."

"That's my girl," Asrael replied, pride shining through his words. He brushed past me and went to open the door.

"Oh, sir? There was something I wanted to bring to your attention..." He leaned against the door and nodded. "Well, um,

I got another package yesterday. I'd hoped, since it had been a few months of silence, that it was finally over."

Asrael's face darkened. "Where is it?"

I walked over to the chest at the end of my bed and opened it, removing the small cardboard box. "Here," I said, handing it over.

"What was it this time?"

My face flamed. "More love letters. Lingerie. Some toys..."

"I'll handle it. I'm sorry this is happening. I really thought that removing him from the academy would've put an end to this... obsession."

"Me too. I'm still glad he's gone."

His face tight, Asrael took away the offensive package, leaving me with the folder that started an obsession of my own. The Exiled.

And now here I was, sleeping with the enemy. These murderous and fully-fledged psychos who had no remorse or sense of right and wrong.

"Here, take these and start distributing them," Ash said, handing Rooster a stack of what looked like tickets. "Fight night. Tomorrow night at the flats. I want the other gangs to join us."

Whoops and cheers went up at the idea of a fight night, but what had me interested was the mention of other gangs. What was his angle here?

"Other gangs?" I asked, picking my nails like I was bored to death.

Ash grinned at me. "Yes, love. There are what's known as the big four in this area: us, Scorpions, Buzzards, and Rampage MC. Every so often, we'll have a gathering of everyone, just some friendly competition. No killing. You'll love it."

Smart. He was using this as an opportunity to draw out Scorpio and possibly dig up information in a supposedly safe setting.

"I'm afraid I have plans. Won't be able to make it," I lied.

"Plans? With who?" Ash demanded, his voice on the edge of a snarl.

I shrugged. "Anyone but you."

Ash slowly smirked and took a step closer, crowding my space. His finger brushed my chin, tipping my face up so I had no choice but to look into his eyes. After a beat, his thumb brushed over my bottom lip. "You're such a little liar. You can act as if you don't like me all you want, but the taste of your orgasm on my tongue right now says otherwise."

His hand fell away, and I gaped up at him like a pissed off fish. Reaching down to adjust himself, he went back to talking to his crew. I wanted to claw his bastard eyes out.

The emotional whiplash I was experiencing with these guys was ridiculous. I was beginning to think *that* was actually what made them so dangerous. I was a fucking trained professional, yet it felt like my brain had been scrambled from the second I walked into Haunt last night.

"Right then," the asshole said, clapping his hands together before tossing me a bored look. "Let's get the hell out of here."

I just glared back. I didn't feel like talking to him at the moment.

Ash ignored me, turning back to his gang. "Great to see everyone still standing today. Excellent job last night. See you all tomorrow night!"

You'd have thought he was a celebrity with the way these people fawned over him. Charisma clearly went a long way in manipulating people.

He reached for me as he got closer, but I dodged his hand like it was covered in dog shit. *Don't touch me, sexy demon hand.* I knew where that would probably lead to—yet again—and it was ridiculous.

He raised a blond brow at my sudden movement. "Mosquito or something?"

"Yeah, a big, blond one with tattoos and velvet freaking pants."

"Palmer, you are hilarious. A mosquito? Honestly? I've clearly got a mothman aesthetic going on here. Get yourself together."

Once again, I was left staring at this creature like I was the dumbass and his insanity was the truth. I stomped out to the car, letting myself in while the prince of criminals waved to his underlings. I really needed to locate my phone when we got back to Haunt. It had been in my bag, but seeing as how I hadn't gotten that back yet, I bet my phone was still down in that maze. There wasn't anything incriminating on it, so that really wasn't the issue. It just wasn't normal for a twenty-five-year-old woman to not be demanding her phone.

Ashland folded his big body into the car and pressed the ignition. "Ready to find Felix?"

"I guess. Hey, do you know where my phone ended up?" I asked, not looking at him as I fiddled with the hem of my shirt.

"I was wondering when you were going to ask." He reached into his pocket and pulled out my phone, handing it over. "Most people would've been clamoring for it the second their eyes popped open. Or hell, last night even." He merged onto the highway and shifted gears, letting us fly past the cars that were already cruising at high speeds.

I immediately unlocked it and pretended to be checking messages and social media. "Yeah, well, I was a little distracted. Last night... and this morning." It was the truth.

His icy-blue eyes flicked over to me, and I desperately tried to douse the heat that was climbing up my neck. "I like when you blush like that. I like it even more when you do it in public," Ashland confessed as his tatted fingers stroked the gear shift.

I huffed. "What? Why?"

"Because, love, it's the sweetest kind of physical validation that I affect you. I loved how red you got at the warehouse—my whole crew saw you blushing and knew it was because of me. You were already flushed when you walked up. Post-orgasmic glow is a real thing. You just looked fucking delicious standing there like that."

"Jesus, Ashland. You have real issues, you know that?"

He barked a laugh and switched lanes. "That may be true, but so do you. I wanted you to touch yourself back there and guess what? You fucking did. So don't be a hypocrite. I'm honest about what I like, are you?"

I paused just before I ripped his head off. Was I? "Maybe I'm still learning what I like."

"Yeah? Aren't we all? Nothing wrong with that. Live a little." He reached over and patted my thigh. "Something tells me you haven't ever really let loose before."

I didn't respond, mainly because he was right. It was hard to "let loose," as he liked to call it, when you were raised in an environment like Montague. I'd been training to be a spy for so long that it had been my primary focus since I was sixteen. Before that, I'd focused on my schooling, mastering magic and academics, with the goal of being accepted into the training program when I was old enough. Here I was on this mission, and it was like someone pushing a five-year-old into a candy shop and telling them they can only look. No touching, tasting, or anything else.

My attention was drawn to the city as we neared the next exit. Gray skies were moving in, which wasn't surprising. Pretty weather wasn't something that belonged here. It wasn't until we had left the highway behind and were flying down a road that had seen better days, that I saw something odd. I leaned forward in my seat, squinting at the lighthouse that seemed to pop up out of nowhere at the end of the road.

It was hard to imagine what it would've looked like in its original glory, because now? Now it was covered in graffiti. Really, really awesome graffiti. Murals, portraits, words—there was too much to take in at once, and we were still too far away for me to appreciate it the way art like that deserved. It wasn't until my gaze started rising that I saw it... and then him.

"Oh my gods," I gasped. "Ash, is that—?"

"Yep. Crazy motherfucker's at it again."

"Again?" I balked, frantically looking back up to see Felix near the top of the lighthouse, scaling the side of it like a spider. "What the fuck is he doing? He's going to fall and break his damn neck!"

Would make my life a lot fucking easier if he did... but I chose to blame the fear I felt on the fact that I didn't really want to see anyone, demon or not, fall from a height like that and be turned into blood splatter.

"Yeah." Ash sighed. "Felix gets like this sometimes and he just needs to let out a little steam. This is his safe place. He's got the inside set up pretty sweet with a kitchen, bedroom, and bathroom. Sometimes a man needs his own cave when he's feeling fucked over something, ya know? Now listen," he said, putting the car in park at the base of the lighthouse. "There's a chance he's not going to be thrilled to see us. Especially if he's in the middle of creating. Gets real bent out of shape at times if his routines are interrupted before he's done. So if he snaps at you, don't take it personally."

"Okay," I replied, reaching for the handle of my door.

We got out and met at the front of the car. Looking up at the expanse of the building, I nearly fell backward trying to see the full height. Felix was all the way at the top now, paint cans in hand as he finished what he was working on. It was too difficult to see from this angle.

"Let yourself in. We'll be right there." Guiding me to the door, Ash ushered me through it. "Remember, if he's being a little bitch, it's not because of you. It's because sometimes he's actually a little bitch." With a wicked grin, he slammed the door, and I heard muted shuffling along the walls. He was probably out there pulling a Spiderman stunt, too.

I figured I may as well look for the bathroom while those two idiots were occupied. Taking in Felix's lighthouse apartment for the first time was an experience. They kept this place well hidden and to themselves, because I'd never read a thing about it in any of the recon reports I'd gotten about these guys.

Taking in the space, I let out a low whistle. Ashland was right; it was a pretty sweet setup. The walls were covered in paintings, hung directly on the bricks. Made sense—with the curved walls, it would've been difficult to hang traditional canvases. One particular painting was a large landscape with a beautiful castle and dragons soaring through the air. The most interesting thing about that painting was the huge red X that had been crudely spray-painted over the entire thing and the words *RISE UP* done in a traditional grunge graffiti style.

There were couches in the middle of the space and a television mounted to the wall. Covering the ground was a huge rug, which would've appeared to have been made from polar bear fur, if polar bears had long hair. Clearly, it was synthetic but I'd be damned if it didn't bring the room together. The couches were neon green leather, and there were other pops of neon scattered throughout the ground level. As much as I wanted to snoop, I really needed to pee, so when I spotted a door I didn't hesitate.

"Oh thank the gods," I sighed as I opened the door to reveal a small, but nice, bathroom. A vintage clawfoot tub sat against the wall, and I actually wasn't surprised to see neon paint splatter all around the outside of the tub. It appeared Felix was some kind of unstoppable art force when he was taken by his muse.

A loud boom and subsequent growls had me nearly peeing my pants, so I hurried and finished up. What had set Felix off after I saw him last night? A flash of the memory of me on my hands and knees, with him thrusting his big dick in and out of my mouth made me curse, and I pressed a little too hard on the soap dispenser, knocking it off balance. The ceramic broke as soon as it hit the sink basin. Fantastic.

I scooped up the small trash can and set it on the counter. Luckily, most of the ceramic pieces were large chunks and easy to dispose of, but as I reached for the last piece, another boom from above my head startled me, causing me to cut my hand. "Fuck!"

I flipped the water on and stuck my hand underneath, already seeing blood. With my other hand, I opened the medicine cabinet in search of a bandaid. I didn't see any, but did see several pill bottles and even more bottles of lubricant. What in the hell?

Leaning in, I read the names of the medications, a little confused to see the drug names lorazepam, oxycodone, ritalin, and clonazepam. Demons took human medications for anxiety, ADHD, and pain? That didn't seem right to me, but I didn't get a chance to look any closer because the bathroom door suddenly slammed open.

"What in the actual fuck?!" I shouted. "I could've been wiping my ass or something!"

"I smell blood. What happened?" Ash's chest was heaving, and his eyes appeared to be glowing.

"I cut my hand when you two decided to wrestle around upstairs," I snapped, holding up my hand. The cut along my palm was jagged and bleeding pretty heavily now.

Ash snagged a hand towel from the hook next to the sink, wrapping it tightly around my palm. "Come on, this needs cleaning up. There are supplies in the kitchen."

"Where's Felix?" I wondered out loud as I followed him out of the bathroom and up a set of stairs.

"Finishing his project. He's almost done, and I decided it was better to just let the fucking madman do his thing instead of damaging the lighthouse further."

Once we reached the landing, the wooden floor expanded outward, creating a sort of loft. A kitchen and dining table were all that were on this level, but it was all high quality.

"Come over here, love. Let me see that hand." I shuffled to where Ash was standing, next to a large kitchen island with a butcher block top. He grabbed my hips and lifted me without any effort, sitting my ass right on the island.

"The chairs over there would have sufficed, I think." I pointed toward the dining table.

"Oh, I'm sorry. Are you the doctor here or am I?"

The laugh that slipped out couldn't have been stopped, and our eyes collided. The surprise in his eyes at my laughter had me freezing up. He was so damn intense.

I swallowed the lump in my throat and shook my head. I was going to just roll with it. They were weird as fuck, sexy as hell, and evil as sin... I could fight it and potentially screw this entire mission, or I could embrace the crazy and roll with it. Let loose, as Ash had said in the car.

"Fine. What's the prognosis, doc?"

A slow grin spread across his face, making him look angelic, in a monstrous way. "Well, I'll need to take a closer look." He flipped my hand over and slowly unwrapped the towel, causing me to wince as he pulled the fabric away from the cut. "Hmm."

"Hmm what? What does hmm mean?"

"It's pretty deep. Sliced yourself good. I better clean it." He turned and opened a cupboard, removing a few bottles that I couldn't quite see. "Here we go."

"Tequila and vodka? We getting drunk?"

"One is for you to drink, the other is to clean that hand. It appears Lixy doesn't have much in his first aid kit, so this will have to do. Can you handle it?"

I tilted my head and smirked at his cocky ass. "I can handle anything."

"Oh, love. I knew that the moment I laid eyes on you last night. Now, put your hand over here—hold it over the sink." He opened the bottle of tequila and handed it to me. "Drink some of that."

I brought the bottle to my mouth, downing several gulps and feeling the instant warmth spread throughout my body. My palm was throbbing now, and I knew it was only going to get worse in a few seconds. I took another healthy swig. "Aren't you having any?"

Ash removed the top of the vodka bottle. "What kind of doctor would I be if I drank on the job?"

I giggled.

Full stop. Oh fuck. I could hear the theoretical brakes screeching in my head. I was not a giggler.

"That was cute," he said, booping me on the nose. I swear to gods my eye twitched, and I found myself eyeing the knife block. "You're all over the place, aren't you, little rabbit?"

"Thinking about slicing you up and putting *you* all over the place, to be honest." Ash gave a full-bellied laugh and tipped the vodka bottle, splashing my hand. I hissed like a feral cat and swung at him with my other hand. He stepped back at the last minute, effectively dodging me. "Motherfucker!"

"I prefer bunny-fucker, if I get a choice."

I cradled my stinging hand to my chest and took a few deep breaths. "That was worse than I thought it would be. Not gonna lie."

"Have another drink. I'm going to try to heal it next and if I can't, well, you won't like what comes after that."

I was downing more tequila before he finished his sentence. "Okay, let's do this."

He took my hand once more and brought my palm to his face. *What the heck is he—*

His tongue snaked out. His very long, *abnormally* long, tongue. A feather-soft pressure made goose bumps erupt all over my skin as he traced the cut ever so gently with his tongue.

"The fuck are you two doing?" a voice boomed from my left. My head snapped around, and I saw Felix climbing into the space from the window. He was shirtless and covered in paint. His eyes tracked Ash's tongue, zeroing in on my hand.

A deep rumble came from Ash as he stared at Felix, never stopping the movements of his tongue. "Hey!" I snapped at Ash, tugging my hand away from him. "We don't growl at people like that."

"I'll growl at whoever I want, whenever I want."

"Why are you bleeding?" Felix asked me, ignoring his idiot friend.

"It's not that big of a deal, just a small cut. Ash said he was going to try to heal it, but he was just making out with my hand like a fucking creeper." I shot said creeper a *what the fuck* look.

Felix sauntered up to me, still ignoring Ashland. "Let me see it."

I huffed, getting annoyed now about all this attention over a stupid little cut. "Here ya go." I shoved my hand in his face, but froze when I saw the tattoo on his neck. "Oh my gods..." I lowered my hand and placed it on his neck, right where a tattoo of a woman's hand wrapped around his throat.

"How did I not notice this the other night?" I laughed, now starting to feel the liquor.

"You got her drunk?" Felix shot Ash a side-eye, and I felt the muscles in his neck twitch.

Crossing his arms, Ash stared at us. "She has a deep cut and I had to sterilize it. Liberties may have been taken with the tequila bottle."

"Liberties. Ha. What are you, a hundred? Grandpa..." I muttered under my breath, teasing him.

"She thinks you're only a hundred? *Nice.*" Felix winked at Ash, who was standing taller now all of a sudden. "But she also called you grandpa. That's a first."

Ashland rolled his eyes. "I don't fuck like a grandpa."

"No, no you don't," Felix agreed, and I tightened my hold on his throat. His dark eyes came back to mine. "You wanna strangle me, baby?"

Did I? My hand did look good wrapped around his neck. I decided to play it by ear. Roll with it, let the hands fall where they may.

"Why are you out here all alone? People were worried," I said, changing the subject and removing my hand. I spied a smear of blood on his throat. "Can I have a damp paper towel? I got a little blood there." I looked down and blinked a few times, making sure I wasn't seeing things. My cut was closing right before my eyes. "Hey, look! No more bleeding!"

I held my palm up, but the smile on my face quickly fell when I saw Felix's face. He'd gone white as a sheet of paper, and Ashland muttered a quiet "Fuck."

"It'll come off; it's just a little bit. Come here." I reached for Felix and pulled him toward me. When no paper towel magically appeared, I decided to just take things into my own hands. I darted forward and licked the blood off his neck. "There. All gone. Nice and clean."

"How did you know that's what was bothering him?" Ashland asked, a slightly suspicious tone to his voice.

"My best friend doesn't like blood either. He acts the same way," I explained smoothly. I did remember reading from multiple reports that Felix did have a bit of a clean freak gene, but I hadn't realized it extended to blood. It definitely didn't apply to paint though, by the looks of him.

"It's not that he doesn't like blood. He just doesn't like it being on him," Ash clarified, while Felix continued to stare intently at me.

Looking into Felix's big, brown eyes, I whispered, "Do you forgive me?"

His body seemed to vibrate for a second before his wings and horns popped out with a snap. He had me scooped up and pressed against his body in the blink of an eye. I squeaked as he carried me to the stairs and began climbing them at what seemed like two at a time.

"Felix! What are you doing?"

"I need to fuck you."

Oh. What? Then his dick flexed. *Son of a bitch.*

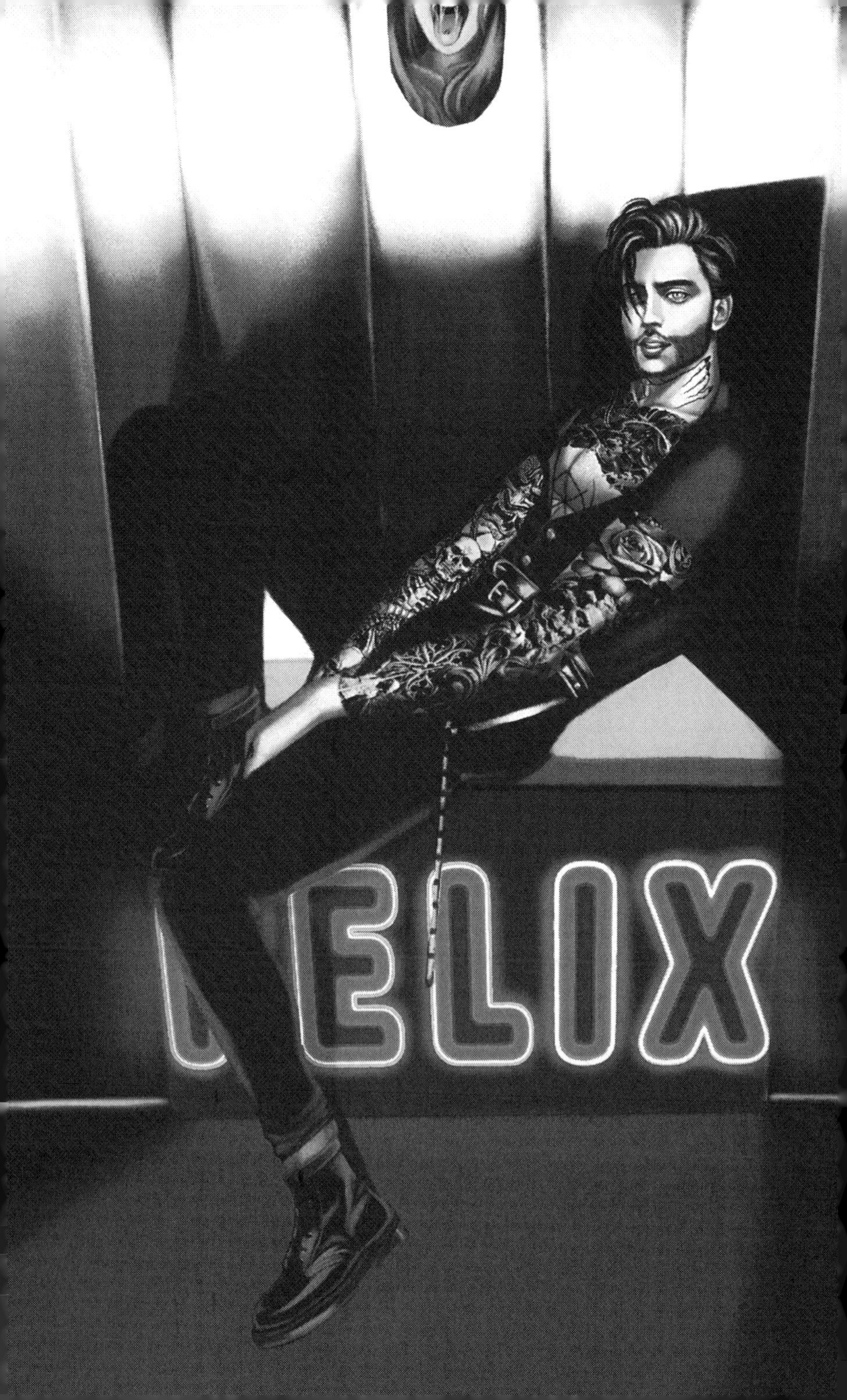
ELIX

FELIX

Chapter Thirteen

I thought I'd gotten it all out during the hours of painting and keeping myself from plunging to my death, but no. All it took was a little smear of blood, and here I was. Actually, that wasn't accurate. Yes, the smear set me off, but it was her leaning in and fucking licking my neck like that. Cleaning me up, like she knew my discomfort and wanted to fix me as soon as possible—that was what had me racing up the stairs right now, with one goal in mind.

Ashland was right behind us; I could hear his growls. He could fuck off.

Palmer tightened her thighs around my hips, which caused her to rock her pussy against my body. "Fuck, baby. That's sexy as fuck," I groaned. My hand gripped her ass, pulling her tighter against me. "I can feel how hot that pussy is."

"You have a filthy mouth," she rasped as I laid her down on my bed. Smirking, I grabbed ahold of her leggings around her ankles and tugged, enjoying each inch of exposed flesh that peeked out at me. I was about to press a kiss to her ankle when I was jolted sharply to the side.

I snarled. "What the fuck?!" My lip curled up, and my wings shuddered, ready to fight.

Ashland responded, his own wings snapping out. "She's *mine*."

My nostrils flared as I stared down my best friend. "Doesn't look that way right now, brother."

"Felix, I swear to fuck..."

"Excuse me? I am not yours, dickhead!" Palmer shouted, and I smiled smugly at Ashland. "And I'm not yours either!" We both turned away from each other to focus on what we both wanted. Her.

"He doesn't get to just climb in through a window like King fucking Kong and steal away my woman like this!"

"Okay, fucker—"

Palmer held up her hand. "Why was sharing last night fine, but right now it's a problem?"

We both paused. Why *was* it a problem? It had never been a fucking problem before. What was different?

All thoughts died a fast death when she let her legs fall open. "What do you think, boys? Can you play nice?"

"So nice," Ashland whispered, stalking his way to the bed. He pulled up his shirt, revealing his washboard abs.

"Uh-uh... I don't believe you."

Ash froze, looking from her to me. I hooked my thumbs in my sweats and pushed, letting them slide down my hips. My cock bobbed now that it was free. I had no problem sharing. "Yeah, I don't think I believe you either, Ashland."

He threw his hands in the air. "I just got a little out of my head with the blood. Of course sharing is fine, love. Felix and I will take care of you. I know you want us both."

"Come here then," she purred, pulling off her shirt and bra and tossing them on the floor.

We moved like we were puppets on a string. She was the puppet master. Ash had his clothes off in record time, and we both tucked our wings away to make more room for all of us on the bed. We lay on our sides, Palmer between us. Unable to resist any longer, I gripped her chin and turned her face toward me. I had to taste those lips.

A husky moan left her mouth as I pressed our lips together. She tasted like cherries and beautiful nightmares. After a moment, I pulled back and turned her face to Ash, loving the way she stared up at him like she was high from just the amount of sexual chemistry in the room.

"Kiss him, baby," I whispered, sliding down and leaving a trail of scorching kisses along her body. Despite being toned, Palmer had full, sexy as fuck thighs and an ass that I wanted to take a bite out of. After ridding her of her damp panties, I tossed her legs over my shoulders and shoved my face against her cunt. "Fuuuck, I could get high from your scent." Cherries and a sharp bite of something metallic, like iron or steel. Our own little danger berry.

"I can smell how good it is from up here, Lixy. Make her scream for it," Ash said with a growl, making our girl squeal as he pinched her nipple roughly.

My tongue slipped out, and I laved a path from bottom to top, loving the slickness of her, the fucking sweetness. I hadn't gotten a chance to taste her last night, and my eyes rolled back when she bucked up, grinding her cunt against my mouth.

"Let me touch you, Ash," she gasped, reaching for his dick. He got up on his knees to give her better access, and she pumped his cock with her small hand, earning herself some deep groans of appreciation from the big, blond demon for her trouble.

I fluttered my tongue, which I knew felt like a vibrator on a sensitive clit. "Oh gods," she moaned, writhing her hips faster, chasing that release. I knew firsthand how good that damn tongue felt, since Ashland loved to tease me with his. Another burst of her sweetness hit my mouth, and I savored my reward.

"That's it, love. Come all over Felix's pretty face and then we'll fuck you... but not until you fucking come."

Jesus, there was something so hot about him when he went all psycho dom. I squeezed her hips, sucking her whole clit between my lips and letting out a deep groan.

"Yes, yes, like that, please, *please!*"

Her back bowed and she lifted her ass off the bed as her orgasm wrecked her, but I kept hold of her little body, not wanting her to come for a second without my mouth on her. Pride sizzled down my spine as I gazed up at her pretty body laid out before me, knowing that the sated expression on her face was thanks to me. I could see how Talon had the urge to knot her; she was too tempting.

"Felix, oh my gods," she panted as the grinding of her hips slowed. "That was... wow."

I grinned up at her and licked my lips. "Can I do it again?"

She laughed, wiggling away from me. "Too sensitive. Dick time."

"You heard the girl." Ash scanned her body, then lifted his gaze to me. "How do you wanna do this?" I leaned over and dug around in the nightstand drawer for a second before finding what I was looking for. Lube. I held up the bottle for Palmer and Ashland to see. "Where are you in this setup?" he asked, lifting a brow.

I didn't need to think about it. "Middle."

Ash smirked. "Deal."

"Whoa," Palmer interjected. "What is happening?"

"Don't worry, little rabbit. I told you we'd take care of you, didn't I? And you came so prettily just now. Felix and I have a plan, but first, I want to feel your wet pussy wrapped around this dick. It's all I've been able to think about since last night."

"Fuck yes." Palmer rolled over, pushing Ashland down on his back. I laughed at the way his eyes widened. "What? I'm taking what I want, demon boy. Lay still and let me use you."

"Fucking hell," I cursed, stroking myself as I watched. "Who are you?"

She tossed a look at me over her shoulder as she sank down, taking Ashland deep within her body. "A woman you'll never forget."

That was the truth. Ashland groaned as Palmer swiveled her hips to her own rhythm, bouncing and rocking, using every inch of his cock for her pleasure. I loved the noises of determination that spilled from her perfect, red mouth and the way Ash's fingertips sank into the meaty flesh of her hips, hers digging into his pecs as she used his body for leverage. They were sinfully hot together, and my dick wept at the sight.

"Fuck, fuck, slow down or this is going to end sooner than I'd like." Ash gripped her hips, holding her still. He glanced up at me, fire blazing in his eyes. "Toss me that lube." I threw it over, my anticipation rising over what was to come next. "Here, love. Get my dick nice and slippery, yeah?"

Palmer dismounted Ash, eyeing the lube. "It's uh... It's been a while." She popped the lid and squirted some of the liquid into her hand.

I couldn't help but laugh at the apprehension in her voice. "Don't worry, baby. It's not for you."

Her eyes widened as she looked from Ash to me. "What?"

"Oh, don't be sad. I'll have this ass. Soon, just not tonight. I want to properly train you to take me—to take us—especially if it's been a while." He reached for her hand and wrapped it around his length, moving it up and down, coating himself. I greedily eyed the way his cock seemed to look bigger than ever with her small hand wrapped around it. Knowing she was helping him get slick so that he could fuck me had me biting my lip and swallowing a growl. "You are going to get on your hands and knees so Felix can fuck you. And while he's fucking you, I'm going to slide deep inside his ass and fuck you both."

"Holy fucking shit," Palmer breathed.

I laughed at her reaction, but her desire was evident in the way her lips parted. Those blue eyes were now lost in the black depths of her blown pupils.

"Yeah, you into it, baby?" I trailed my fingertips along the smooth skin of her inner thigh, loving the way her body seemed to get even hotter.

"Mmmhmm," she hummed, twisting her palm around Ashland's dick. As sexy as it was to watch, I couldn't wait another fuckin' second. I needed them both. *Now.*

"Come here, turn over." I tapped on her hip, and she rolled onto her front, putting that juicy ass on display for us. "Damn," I praised, roughly grabbing a cheek and squeezing. "I can't wait to watch this bounce on my dick."

She tossed a look over her shoulder that was pure seduction. "Then hurry up and fuck me, Felix."

Ash barked a laugh as we all repositioned ourselves. "Get those hips up, love. Show us that pretty pussy."

Palmer moaned and promptly got on her knees, keeping her head low. It was one of the best views I'd ever seen, that was fucking sure. I closed in behind her, and with one thrust I sank my cock completely within her hot body, both of us shuddering at how gods damned good it felt.

My thighs and hips flexed as I pumped my hips slowly, hitting her with firm, deep strokes that forced her breath out each time. This was so much better than her mouth, and the thoughts my brother had leaked while he pounded her last night suddenly made so much sense. So tight and warm—my cock wanted to live here forever.

A tap on my thigh reminded me that we weren't alone, and I spread my legs apart a little further. I never let it go too long in between bottoming; even when I wanted to get myself off, I still used a plug or something. It just felt too fucking good not to. I loved the stretch and how full I felt taking something within my body.

Ash and I had fucked more times than I could count. Sometimes we'd pick up another guy and fuck around with him all night, or sometimes it would be a woman. It depended on our moods as much as anything. Sometimes Mishy and Talon would play, too.

Sharp nails raked down my back, and I growled. "Don't fuck with me, Ashland."

"Wouldn't dream of it, Lix," he whispered against my ear as he pressed his hard cock against my ass.

"Fuck, you two are hot," Palmer breathed, looking over her shoulder, her eyes bouncing from my face to Ash's.

"We know," Ash replied before licking a line of fire up the side of my neck. His big hand applied pressure between my shoulder blades, pushing me down against Palmer. When he was satisfied, he sighed in delight. "Hold still."

"Telling a man to be still when his dick is inside a woman seems like cruel and unusual punishment," Palmer mused, not hiding her disappointment at my suddenly frozen state.

I gritted my teeth. "Oh, it fuckin' is, trust me." A wet finger tapped against my ass, and it was hard to remain still. Palmer swiveled her hips, creating some delicious friction that didn't require me to move at all. "You're a witch," I told her, loving the way she felt wrapped around me.

"Obviously." I couldn't see her face but I heard the grin. "Nobody said I couldn't move."

Ashland's finger pushed in, and I groaned at his filthy words. "That's it, take me in. Fuck, you're tight."

"Quit fucking edging me and get your cock in there, man," I gritted out between clenched teeth. Between Palmer writhing her hot pussy around my dick and Ashland playing around with my ass, I was done.

"Aww," he cooed, ramming another finger deep, making my body jerk forward, deeper into our girl. "Did this slutty hole miss me?"

"Oh my fuck, I'm going to come," Palmer moaned, and her cunt rippled around me.

"Tell me, Lixy. Tell me how much you want my hot load dripping out of your body. Tell me you're a dirty boy who plays with his ass and thinks about this cock right here." His heavy length slapped my ass cheek.

I squeezed my eyes shut, dropping my forehead onto Palmer's shoulder. "Ash..."

"Tell him, Felix." Palmer's hand reached up to grip the back of my neck as she whispered in my ear, "Tell him how he has two sluts here who need fucking." She was going to kill me with those dirty words... She turned her head, then tugged me down and pressed her mouth against mine, licking and nipping. I sighed in bliss against her lips, relaxing myself in preparation for what was coming.

With a growl, I broke our kiss, reaching back and gripping Ash's thigh. "Fuck me—*now*." The fucker smiled against my back and nudged me with the head of his cock. As he pushed in, I shivered, loving the feeling.

"Tell me what you're doing, Ashland," Palmer rasped, wiggling around beneath me.

"Mmm, I'm about halfway in. Our boy is tight as fuck, and the way he grips my dick is criminal."

I couldn't take it anymore. I pushed back and impaled myself completely, making all three of us gasp. "Yesss," I hissed, rocking my hips. I wasn't going to last long, not with Palmer's sexy as fuck body pinned beneath me and Ash behind me.

"Yeah, fuck my dick, you little whore. You should see the way your body swallows me, Lixy," Ash grunted, gripping my hips hard.

"Oh my gods," Palmer cried out. Our words in combination with my movements were a lethal combination. Fuck it. I picked up speed, slamming into her harder, which in turn had Ash railing me even deeper. His hips snapped forward as mine pulled back, and my body was building. Higher and higher.

"Are you sluts going to come for me? Gonna give me my prizes?" Ash swiveled his hips, and he hit my prostate, making my eyes roll and my balls tingle.

"I'm coming... Oh fuck, I'm coming," Palmer whimpered frantically, her head thrashing back and forth on the pillow.

I snarled. "Yes. Milk my cock, baby. Gonna fill you up so full." And she did. She clenched around me so violently, it verged on painful. "Ah, shit yeah. Like that."

I understood now why she'd triggered Talon into wanting to knot her. That fucking grip. I couldn't even bring myself to imagine how good it would feel, locking her to me. Pressure was building at the base of my dick in a way I hadn't felt before, and I wondered if it was simply my imagination. *Who is this girl?* The sensations died down as Ash railed into me harder, and I submitted to the intense feeling of fucking and being fucked.

"Fucking gorgeous when you come, love. Now watch me make Lixy blow.' He picked up his pace, holding me still. Palmer's body was still trembling and fluttering; all I could do was take the pounding and enjoy the swell of euphoria in my veins as my orgasm built.

"Come for him, Felix." Palmer's hand somehow found my throat and she squeezed, cutting off my air. Ash's other hand came around and covered hers, squeezing both of us. "Fuck him harder, Ash. He's a slut who needs to be fucked hard."

Yeah, that did it. My eyes rolled back, and my cock spasmed, sending rope after rope of my cum deep within her wet pussy. I could feel my ass clenching Ashland, needing his release just as badly. With a roar, he pulled my head back by my hair and sank his teeth into my neck, releasing his grip around my throat so I could breathe. Warmth filled me as he flooded me with his load. His tongue lapped at his teeth marks, and we all convulsed together as a group.

"Holyyyy shit," Palmer sighed, her body going completely limp.

"Hmm, yeah," I agreed, unable to formulate a more articulate response while I got my breath back.

"Damn, that was sexy as hell." Ash pulled out of me, flopping over to the side. He sprawled out across the mattress, looking like a sculpture. "You two are fire together," he murmured, wiping the sweat from his brow.

I rolled to the opposite side and wrapped a palm around Palmer's waist. "I think we were all fire just now."

Ash chuckled. "Can't argue that."

"Can you two shut the fuck up? I'm in post-orgasmic bliss right now and your jabbering is ruining it for me," Palmer snapped, and I leaned back to look from her to Ashland.

"Damn, you're cold, baby."

"You have no idea, man. She says the meanest shit, and I'll be damned if it doesn't get my cock up every fucking time!"

"Shut. Up. Asshole." She buried her face in the pillow, but I caught a glimpse of a smirk. Aha. She might act like she hated us, but she didn't. Not really. I was surprised by how much I liked that. I was always a bit of a loner. I mean, I had the guys, but I never had any desire to do anything more with other people aside from hook up. One and done. Everything else just seemed like too much work, especially when I knew that my boys were my real family. Maybe that was why Palmer was so alluring? All of us were intrigued by her—which was a first for us—and the ideas of what could be were already swimming in my head.

Ash stretched and sat up. "Right, well, I better grab a quick shower. I have a bit of work to do, so if you need a nap..."

I definitely did need a nap. I'd been up all night and most of the day working on that damn piece. My eyes tracked him as he moved around the room, grabbing his clothes. "Yeah, I could use some sleep."

He paused at the door. "Forgot to tell you. Fight night tomorrow."

That brought a smile to my face. "Perfect."

"Thought you'd like that plan. Booze and blood to get some jaws to slacken..."

"What's it going to take to get yours to tighten?" Palmer grumbled into the pillow, and my mouth fell open in shock. Ashland and I met each other's eyes. His expression wasn't as carefully guarded since she couldn't see him, and he looked every bit as shocked as I felt. Then the two of us started laughing like a couple of idiots.

"Oh, little rabbit. You're a poisonous little thing, aren't you? It's okay, my dick still wants you."

A small middle finger shot up into the air, and Ash winked at me before spinning out of the room. I settled back into the pillows and tugged the blanket up, covering my lower half. After a few moments, Palmer picked up her head and glanced around before turning to grin at me.

"Thank fuck, he's gone. Are we going to sleep now?"

"Yeah, I need it," I admitted, rolling onto my side to talk to her easier. Her eyes were the prettiest shade of navy blue that popped with her dark hair. A few soft freckles were sprinkled over the bridge of her nose, giving her an almost cartoonish look combined with those big eyes. Like a princess in a fairy tale. I wasn't going to tell her that though—I valued my balls.

"What the heck is that all about?"

"What? The painting?"

She huffed. "No, not the painting. The staying out for hours on end, painting the side of a fucking lighthouse, not returning phone calls or texts to let anyone know you're alright..."

"Okay, okay. Fuck," I breathed, running a hand down my face. "Sometimes I get in my head. It's how I unfuck my brain."

"Unfuck your brain. I like that description. So what's it like?"

It didn't seem like she was teasing me, or hell, judging me. She seemed interested in what I had to say. "Um, well... I don't particularly like blood. As you saw earlier. It's not just blood though. I just don't like feeling... dirty."

"So we won't be mud wrestling any time soon?"

My eyes flew to hers just in time for her to wink at me, and my heart rate settled. I barked a laugh. "Fuck no."

She shrugged and her eyes fell shut. "Okay. So you got blood on you or something last night?"

"Eh, not exactly. It's a long story. But it sent my brain for a walk down memory lane, and I just didn't want to deal with it, ya know? So I grabbed my shit and came here. The others know that when I disappear like that it's because I'm creating."

A small scoff left her tired body, like she didn't believe what I was saying. "They seemed kind of worried about you." Her eyes remained closed but she scooted a little closer.

"Nah, baby. Nobody's worried about me. That's how I like it. I can do my own thing that way, and no feelings get hurt. Art is an escape for me. From reality, the past, whatever. It's the only thing in my life I've had that I could completely immerse myself in, and have it be all mine. When I'm creating, I go into this... shit, how do I describe it? It's like subspace, I guess. All I can see is the project, the brushes or lines of my art, and I can't stand stopping before it's complete."

"That sounds nice. Like your own hidey-hole safe space in your brain. It's gorgeous art, ya know? So much of it too, so you probably take a lot of time-outs, hmm?"

I thought about that for a second. She was right. Some people had a physical location that made them feel like I did when I was doing art. I had my brain and my ability to hyperfocus.

As I formulated my thoughts, the sound of her breathing changed, and I realized she'd fallen asleep. Why the fuck had I told her all of that? I wasn't the kind of guy who shared a lot of information, especially not personal sort of shit. Definitely not with a woman I'd just had a threesome with.

And yet, she hadn't looked at me like I was a freak. In fact, it was almost as though she understood on some level. Part of me wanted to wake her up and find out what she thought about my phobias. Then again, I was working on accepting the fact that it didn't matter what anyone thought about it. *This is who I am; it's who I've always been.*

Self-acceptance was a freakin' bitch.

Sleep was calling me, the sounds of Palmer's breathing luring me to oblivion. It took a few minutes, but I pushed everything from my mind and let myself slip under.

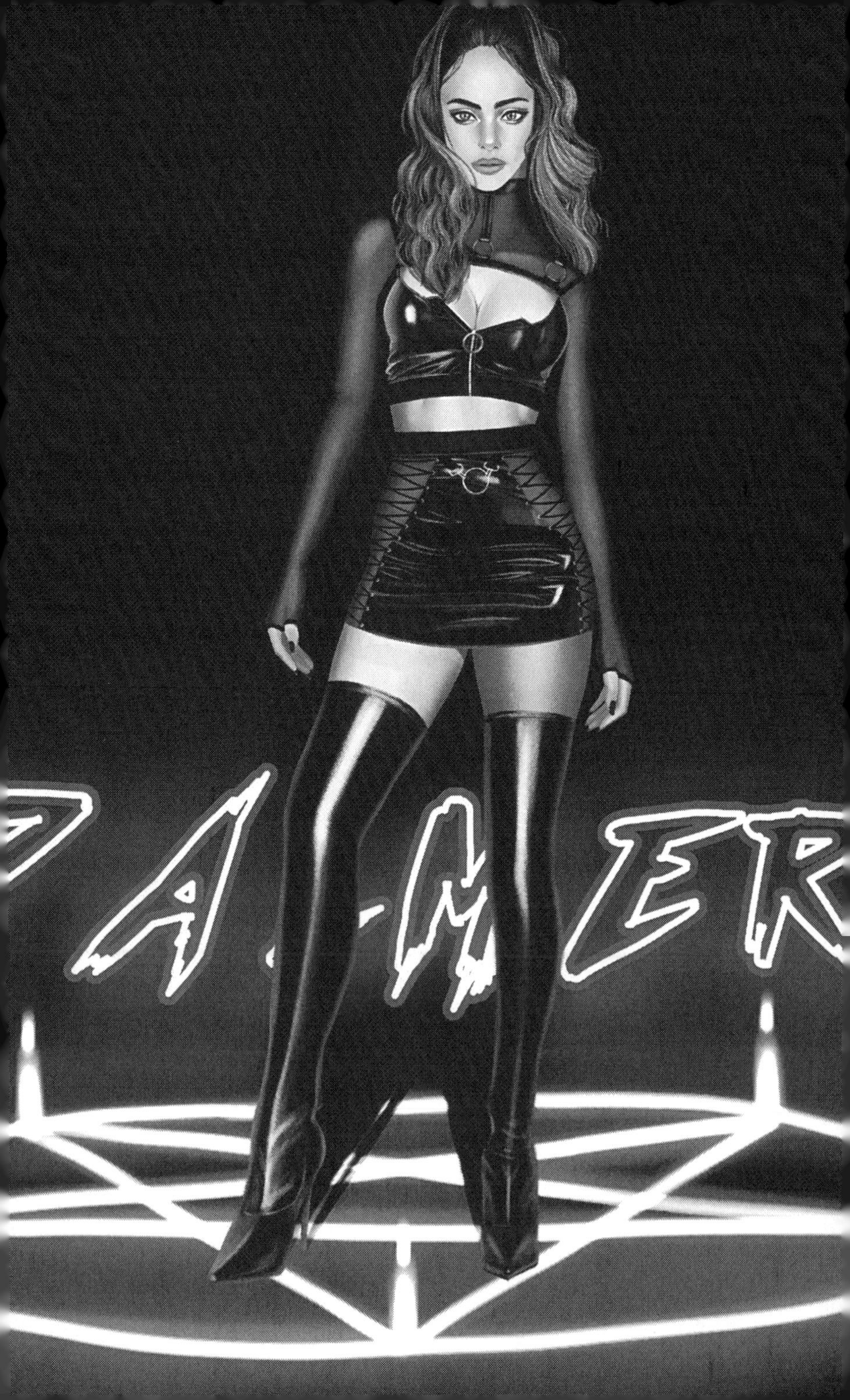

PALMER

Chapter Fourteen

Vibration woke me, and my eyes flew open. Blinking quickly, I saw the room slowly come into focus.

"Right," I said softly. I was in the lighthouse.

"I usually am, yes."

I gasped and sat up, finding a very naked Felix lying on his back and his also very naked twin... *Wait. What?*

"Talon? What the fuck are you doing?!"

He sighed dramatically. "Well, funny story. I went to my meeting and whatever, but then I got bored waiting around. I thought you might be out here so... here I am. Though I am a little sad I missed the sexuals."

My eyes widened. "Are you fucking insane?!"

"I mean..." He shrugged. "It has been brought up before. I like the term 'pleasantly delusional' if I have to go with a label."

I glanced over at Felix, who was still sound asleep. I guess after a lifetime with a madman as a twin, you'd evolve or something to be able to sleep through anything.

"He'll be out for another few hours, easy. Man, you looked so cute cuddled up with your head on his chest. Such a vision, the demon and the bunny," Talon mused, giving me a very wide, completely inappropriate smile for the situation.

I couldn't deal with his mind games right now. "Where's my phone? I think someone was calling or messaging?" I started feeling around in the blankets. "And I do not cuddle."

"Oh, the vibrating? Yeah, about that—"

I tossed the blanket back and froze when I came face to face with a neon blue... tentacle? "*What the hell is that?*"

Talon sat up and snatched the thing, tossing it across the room so it vanished behind a chair. "Remember when I said you looked really fucking good all naked and—"

"Talon, so help me..." The vibrating started again from the other side of the room. "Is that what I think it is?"

"Oh gods, okay. Misha has the remote. It's a little game we like to play. He tries to make me ink against my will. Get it?"

"No!" I held out my hand, cutting him off when I saw his mouth open. "No, I do *not* get it! Whatever sex games you want to play with Misha, be my guest, but I want to know why you were doing this in bed, right next to me, while I was *sleeping?*"

"Bun-bun, I didn't do anything. Yet. I simply had the tool on my person—or next to my person is more accurate—in case an opportunity came knocking. Don't be mad, I wouldn't have done it without you. Definitely would have woken you up, which is more than I can say for *you* not extending an invitation to *me* before you did whatever kind of shish-kabobbing happened with my brother and Ashland!"

"Shish-kabobbing?" I was going to murder this demon. Yes. I was going to take that butt tentacle and stuff it down his throat. "It's none of your damn business what I was doing!" The tentacle vibrated its way off whatever padded surface it had landed on and was now extra loud against the wooden floor. "And *why* is that thing on?"

Talon hopped out of bed and sped over to the toy, snatching it off the floor. He turned and pointed at me with the tentacle like it was a wand and he was the bigger, crazier, sexier Ronald Weasley. "Were you or were you not shish-kabobbed?"

Ashland chose that moment to materialize out of thin air—that was going to take some getting used to—and froze in place, looking from Talon to the tentacle, then over to me. His brows lifted as he pulled his bottom lip between his teeth. "Oh, are we playing squid games? Last time I played, the tentacle wasn't used like that, Tal. You need to stick it—"

"You are all fucking psycho!" I hissed, jumping out of bed and grabbing my clothes from the floor, nearly falling over as I tried to pull them on as quickly as possible. "I'm going to take a shower. Alone. Someone better get me some gods damned food too for when I'm done, because you don't want to see me hangry."

I stormed over to the stairs and heard the two of them mumbling.

"And I will put a hex on all of you if you even think about serving me calamari!" I raced down the steps, heading for the bathroom I'd used before. It wasn't until I was halfway down the last flight of stairs that I saw Misha lying on the couch with a goofy ass smile, fiddling with his phone.

Oh my gods, the remote to the tentacle!

"Seriously?" I yelled before my foot even hit the final step, causing Misha to snap into action and bolt upright. "Yeah, bet you're surprised to see me. Thought I was busy playing hide the tentacle up Talon's ass?!"

Misha stood up and stuck his phone in his pocket. "Clearly, his plan didn't work."

"Clearly." I turned and walked away. "I'm going to shower." Maybe I hadn't slept long enough, because man, I was feeling especially bitchy at the moment. *A hotel might be a good idea for a night or two... Get my shit together and get some space from these crazy fucking idiots.*

"Hungry?"

My walk on the angry side halted so quickly, I was surprised the sound of brakes squealing didn't emanate from my body in some way. I looked back over my shoulder, narrowing my eyes at the smug fucker who was holding up bags of takeout food. Everyone knows it's best to eat that stuff when it's still hot.

"Whatcha got there?"

Misha set the bags down on the dining table. "Eat first. Then shower." He started removing boxes and setting them out. He was wearing a skintight, black T-shirt with camo pants and black boots. Typically, if I saw a man wearing camo outside of the military or the wild fucking wilderness, I steered clear, but it just looked perfect on Misha. As far as I was concerned, he belonged in the wild wilderness with how damn big he was.

"Fine. I'll eat... but then I'm showering and after that, I need some alone time." I sat down, and he handed me a box and a bottle of water. I opened the water, eagerly downing half of it in one go. His intense stare was on me as I lowered the bottle. "What? You wanna say grace or something?"

He slowly sank into his seat and continued staring, one eyebrow raised. It was almost like he wanted— *Oh. Ugh. Manners.*

"Thank you," I said, trying to ignore how gross it felt to be thanking one of the demons I was here to expose. I mean, I was pretty positive they'd killed two men last night—that I knew of. Misha didn't respond, just opened one of the boxes and started devouring the contents. Flipping open my own, I didn't even try to stop the groan of satisfaction that came out when I saw the buffalo wings and french fries. Pretty sure I didn't even take a breath or blink, because when I finally did suck in a huge breath, six wings had been picked clean and half the fries were gone.

Glancing up, also for the first time since I started, I saw a literal pile of bones in front of Misha as he tore into another wing. Holy shit. *Well, when you're seven feet tall and three hundred pounds, I suppose your intake would have to be fairly large.*

"Want another?" he asked gruffly, grabbing a wing and holding it out to me.

"Oh no, no. I'm good. Was just taking a breather," I explained, and he nodded, starting right away on polishing that one off. I figured it was as good a time as any to ask some questions since it was only us at the moment. "This place is pretty cool. Has Felix had it long?"

Misha swallowed his bite and shrugged. "A while."

Oh, okay. Good. Excellent information.

"Renovations must've been a bitch..."

He grunted. In Misha-speak, he could be agreeing, disagreeing, or just acknowledging that I'd spoken. I opened my mouth to ask another question, but he pushed my food toward me. "Eat."

"I'm full."

"One more."

I really didn't want to eat more, though it wouldn't kill me if I did. It might also put me in his good graces, so I grabbed the smallest wing and started munching on it. Tearing off the final bite of meat, I tossed the bones down and wiped my hands.

"Good work, *kukola*," Misha said, seeming pleased. I had to assume it was because I'd listened to him and ate more. The guy obviously had an obsession with the amount of food I ingested.

Kukola? I was going to have to google that one later.

"Do you think you could drop me off downtown after my shower? I have a few things to do..."

"Nope."

"I'm sorry, what? What do you mean nope?" I stood and placed my hands on my hips.

"No. No way. Nope. Never happening."

My eyebrows nearly touched my hairline. "Are you being a smart-ass right now?" He didn't even act as if I'd spoken; he simply began cleaning up our food. I hated being ignored. "Misha! Why won't you take me downtown?"

With all of our trash in a bag, he walked around the table and into the kitchen. I followed him. And by followed, I mean I was practically attached to his ass, so when he stopped suddenly, I ran right into him.

"Oof." It was like walking into a brick wall. "You can't just keep me locked up like a prisoner or—"

Misha moved fast. I barely had time to brace myself before he'd spun around and grabbed me, lifting me up by my thighs so I had to wrap my legs around him. In seconds, I had my breath taken away for the second time when he slammed me against a wall.

"Misha, what—"

"Quiet. I don't repeat myself. Ever. So you better listen." My eyes widened, and I ignored the heat that ignited in my belly at his roughness. I never liked being bossed around, and was usually quick to let it be known. So why then, when Misha did it, did it make me question a lot of things about myself?

As I stared into his eyes, I saw the change. He wasn't the Misha who had been gentle with me, the one who'd fed me while I sat on his lap. Was this the man everyone called The Carver? I had to admit, I hadn't seen anything yet that indicated he deserved such a brutal nickname. However, I always trusted my instincts, and right now, they were telling me that this guy wasn't fucking around. Licking my lips, I nodded once, slowly.

"You. Aren't. Leaving. Do you understand? You know what we are, and not only that, you still fuck us after knowing. You aren't running away. Even if you tried, I would hunt you down and drag you back!" Our noses were practically touching as he raged, his anger palpable. "I don't know what kind of witch you are, but I am fucking bewitched, woman. So no, you don't get to do what you've done, and then skip off to wherever the fuck!"

My eyes widened as he stared me down. *Bewitched? I've bewitched him?* My chest felt tight at his declaration, like my heart was split into two and at war with itself. One side wanted to pulse with feelings of warmth and the other side was already throwing up impenetrable ice walls, since eventually, this would have to stop. I would need to kill them if necessary. Why did that idea suddenly make me feel sick?

I shook those thoughts away and focused on the guy pinning me to the wall. His body was trembling, his eyes locked on mine. "You're so mad..." I whispered.

"Because you're being selfish," he said, his voice returning to its normal, growly tone.

"So what?" I tossed my arms up, frustrated. "I live with you guys now? What about my stuff? My apartment? My pet?" I didn't have an apartment, but they didn't need to know that. But I did have a duffel bag with a few clothing items and emergency essentials that I had stashed in a little tiny storage locker at a storage facility on the outskirts of the city.

His grip tightened on my hips. "Have I not made it clear yet that whatever you want, I will get for you? Tell me your address and I'll have your stuff collected."

I closed my eyes and rested my head back against the wall. "You still can't do this, Misha. It isn't right."

Apparently, he didn't care if I thought it was right or not because his response was a deadpan expression, before he finally narrowed his eyes, giving me a calculated look. "Why haven't you tried to escape? Why do you still let us near you after knowing what we are?" He brought both hands to my face and forced me to look at him. "Tell me!"

"You guys are the leaders of one of the most notorious gangs in the country. I already knew you were monsters—was I really supposed to be that fucking surprised that you look like them too?"

"Monsters? You think we're monsters?" He chuckled quietly, and the hairs on my arms lifted. "We're worse, *kukola*."

"Yeah? Well, I'm not scared of you." I lifted my chin defiantly.

He raised a thick brow. "You think you can handle me?" He leaned in, and I felt his breath against my neck a second before he whispered, "I would wreck you."

I hated backing down, and if I was really honest with myself, I didn't want to. I wanted to push Misha to see what he was capable of. He'd been pretty thoughtful of my needs the entire time, and I was very curious about his nickname.

"You can fucking try, you big asshole."

There are moments in life when you make a decision and you know right away if it's the right or wrong one. When Misha closed his eyes and pressed his hips forward, driving his massive cock against my clit—clothes be damned for all the good they did—I still felt pretty good about my rebuttal. When his eyes flew open at the little moan that escaped my lips, they were glowing orange, and I started feeling a little wary. When the black shirt he was wearing ripped to make way for his leathery, black wings, and his horns started to grow, I wondered if I was the fucking idiot here.

There was nowhere for me to go, pinned between the wall and a demon.

He lifted a hand to reveal long, black claws that were probably just as sharp as his knives, and when he sliced my shirt down the middle, causing my tits to fall out, I had the sudden urge to scream. Were these his real weapons of choice when he was busy carving people up?

"You think you're safe with us?" My nipple tightened as he dragged the tip of his claw over the tip. "Nobody is safe with us, *kukola*. For some reason, they like your fire. Lucky for you because normally, they'd have slaughtered you by now."

I tried not to react to his words, to the deep bass of his husky voice... but I was positive he could smell, if not feel, the dampness that had grown between my legs. "Well, Mishy bear, that works out great for me, because you know something? That fire is who I am at my basest level. That fire is how I am right here, right now. Without my fire, I'd have been nothing but a swirl of smoke in the wind by now, and I'd rather fucking die than let that flame dim for a second. Especially just to make some fuckboy demons feel more alpha male about themselves." I grinned at his growl, letting him know I was deliberately poking the bear, so to speak.

I wound my arms around his neck and sank my hands into his hair before tentatively drifting them toward the top of his head, seeking his horns. Would they be hard as bone? Cold or warm?

"If you touch my horns right now, you're not leaving this wall before I fuck you against it," Misha growled, his orange eyes staring at my face intensely.

A dare, perhaps? He was telling me straight up what would happen if my hands continued the path they were on. I could stop and walk away, but if I continued... I'd basically be giving him the green light to fuck me.

"I mean it, *kukola*. I'll split your little cunt in two right here." He leaned forward and nudged my cheek with his nose. "As a male who wants to give you what you need, I'm struggling to hold myself back."

"Misha." I sighed in bliss as he rolled his hips, driving himself against me.

"I know what you need. Grab my horns and hold on tight, little doll. You want a monster? You've got one right here."

I didn't get a second to deny his words. It would've been lies anyway. He was fucking right. My fingers wrapped around his thick, black horns, and the noise that erupted from his chest was pure beast. It was deep and rumbling, and I felt the vibrations through his horns. They were warm, almost too hot to touch, but holy shit, the way he responded to the slightest pressure by my hands was worth it.

Reaching between us, he undid his pants and let them fall to the ground. Those damn claws came in handy again when he sliced the crotch of my pants right down the middle, completely exposing my wet pussy.

"Fucking dripping for my monster cock, aren't you?" His hand gripped my hair as he tilted my head back. "Gonna stuff you with it, *kukola*. I want your eyes right here. Watch how I stretch you."

I glanced down just in time to see his dick press against my opening. But when I looked closer... that wasn't a dick. Squinting, I saw his cock, hard and thick between us, and then I saw the appendage dipping around us. It seemed to start out thin and then it widened quite a bit. It was a dark green color that reminded me of a forest. "Mish... what?"

"My tail," he answered immediately, unsurprised by my reaction. "You don't just start the game without warming up, little doll." He winked, and I cried out as his tail slid deep within me.

"Oh my gods," I panted, tightening my grip on his horns. The sensation was so different to a regular cock. The ridges and bumps along his tail seemed to ignite every one of my nerve endings with each movement.

"Mmmhmm, the best part about getting fucked by a tail is the range of motion."

The what now?

"Ah!" I bucked my hips forward as Misha's tail began cycloning within my cunt, bringing my pleasure to dangerously high levels. The wicked smirk on his face told me he knew exactly what he was doing to me. I'd never come in my life without clitoral stimulation, but I knew that was about to change.

"That's a good little doll. I can feel your pussy quivering already. Give me my cum, pretty bunny."

"Fuuuuck," I moaned as the orgasm gripped my entire body. I literally felt my cum running down the crack of my ass, and I was pretty certain that was also a first. Misha withdrew his tail, leaving me clenching around air, and my mouth went completely dry when his tail moved up to face height, his molten gaze holding me frozen in place as his tongue flicked out, lapping up my essence.

"Best thing I've ever tasted," he rasped, wrapping his lips around the tip of his tail as if it were a cock. It was one of the most erotic things I'd ever seen. The way the veins in his forearm bulged as he sucked my taste from himself... Fuck. I wanted him to grip me as hard as he was holding his tail.

When a deep rumble spilled from his throat, I couldn't take it anymore. A soft whimper from me had his orange eyes snapping to my face, and his tail slipped from his mouth, leaving his lips shiny and swollen. "Hold on to me tight. Squeeze my horns *hard*."

I did as he asked, really tugging on them as I lifted myself up a bit on his body. Suddenly, both of his hands were on mine and squeezing, hard—showing me how hard he wanted me gripping him. Just as I was about to ask if it hurt, Misha's body shuddered. The amount of pressure we were applying seemed extreme, but I swallowed my words and watched as one of his hands left mine and wrapped around his hard cock, practically strangling it. "Fuck me. Feels so fucking good."

In that moment, I decided that watching this absolutely beautiful and huge demon come apart between my legs was one of the most empowering things I'd ever experienced. My hand snaked between us, and I grabbed his wrist, pulling his face toward me with the horn I was still gripping. "I need you now, Misha."

The corner of his mouth lifted, and I leaned in. Since we were so close, it was easy for me to lick his lips. Misha chuckled deeply, and then the hand that wasn't holding his big dick wrapped around my throat. I was well and truly pinned when he pressed his lips against mine, igniting sparks of heat and zings of electricity throughout my body. The way he kissed me, it was sinful and yet familiar, like we'd done it a hundred times before. I moaned as he sank his teeth softly into my bottom lip before he turned my face to the side and whispered in my ear. "Put my cock inside your cunt, *kukola.*"

Stars above, this fucking man... male. Demon. Sweet and filthy. Quiet and bossy. Thoughtful and wicked. I was so fucked.

He released the hold he had on himself so I could take over. I gripped his length, and a little trepidation worked its way through my body when I realized I couldn't quite touch my fingertips together around his girth. As though he heard my thoughts, he gripped my chin and leaned in, capturing my mouth in another blistering kiss that felt like so much more than just fucking. It felt like he was staking a claim on my mind, my gods damned soul. I'd never forget this moment, and I'd never forget him, regardless of how things eventually would end between us.

"Can't wait to bounce you on this fat cock, I want to watch it disappear within your little body, doll."

"Fuck, Misha... I don't know—"

With a snarl, he batted my hand out of the way. "I do know." He lined himself up and surged forward, breaching me slightly. I whimpered at the small burning sensation. "Relax, doll. Picture me pumping in and out, each thrust has me getting slicker from your cum, and your body is taking more and more because you. Need. Me. Don't you?" His hips rolled, and he was right—with each movement, he went deeper.

"Fuck, fuck," I cursed when it seemed as though his dick got wider.

"Breathe. You're doing such a good job taking this demon cock. Fucking made for me to fill..."

I squeezed his horns so hard, my knuckles turned white, and then it was as if my body accepted what was happening and allowed him to go all the way. We both froze and breathed heavily against each other, adjusting to the feel of one another. I gasped as his tail moved across my hard nipples, adding to the sensory overload in the best possible way.

"Mishy," I breathed, looking into his glowing eyes. "Fucking move, now."

He laughed but didn't move at all. How was he able to fight the urge? I couldn't. Fuck this—if he wasn't going to move, I would. My hips rolled, and his chuckling died immediately.

Large hands gripped my hips as he encouraged me to find my own rhythm. "That's right, ride my cock. Fuck, you take me so beautifully."

We must've looked ridiculous. This massive demon and small woman attached to him like a leech. At that moment, I didn't care.

"Fuck! Hold on," Misha barked, spinning us off the wall and walking us over to the table. He laid me back, letting me stretch out. All the while, his cock remained inside of me. "Scream when you need to, *kukola*."

Then he fucked me, in a way that I'd never experienced before. His black wings fanned out, and it seemed as though his hips moved so fast that they blurred. All I could do was lie there, gripping the edge of the table and taking it. And, as he predicted, scream. The stretching pain that I'd experienced at first was long gone, and all I felt now was overwhelming ecstasy. It was almost unbearable.

When I finally felt capable of opening my eyes, his were right there, watching my face and taking in every single reaction. His own face had changed; his demon form was in complete control right now. The angles of his face had become sharper, more menacing. A literal demon was fucking me harder than I'd ever been fucked before, and all I could think about was how amazing it was.

"Misha!" I felt sudden pressure that was building, like I needed to pee. Right now. "Oh fuck, I'm gonna…" His thumb landed on my clit, and suddenly, there was fluid. Everywhere. My body convulsed and shook, while Misha continued thrusting.

"Fuck, that was the hottest shit I've ever seen," Ashland announced, making me jerk in Misha's hold. I looked over to see him, Felix, and Talon standing there, watching.

Misha growled and fisted my hair. "Don't look at them. You look at me while I claim you."

"Please," I begged, not sure what exactly I was begging for. I could barely hear Felix and the others talking about how I'd just squirted all over the place, but I didn't dare look over at them. It was honestly something that I'd never done before, but I didn't have time to feel embarrassed—or any other emotion—with the way Misha was fucking owning me.

"Squeeze me, *kukola*. I'm not gonna last..." Misha shivered as I reached for him, roughly pulling him down to me by his fucking horns. I swore I heard some groans from the others, and I made a mental note to do more horn grabbing in the future.

Misha slammed into me a few more times, and I raked my nails down his shoulders, loving the way his large body felt atop mine. "Come for me, big guy."

His cock jerked and seemed to vibrate, sending pulsing jets of hot cum deep within me. It triggered another orgasm for me, and we shook, panted, trembled, and cursed as we held onto each other, riding the waves of euphoria.

After a moment, Misha lifted his head. I pressed a kiss to his lips and whispered, just for him, "Well, you act like a monster, look like one, and yeah... you definitely fuck like one."

He grunted and smirked. My brow furrowed when instead of his cock softening, it seemed to... swell? Misha pulled out of my body so fast, my vagina almost got whiplash.

Okay then...

I watched as he walked away from me and went straight to the sink to get a glass of water. My head rolled to the side, and I saw the other guys standing there with strange expressions. *What? Were they jealous?* Well, they could fuck off. I'd fucked all four of them in less than twenty-four hours.

"Well, I'm going to have that shower now..." I slid off the table, literally. Grimacing, I turned to see the damage. "Fucking hell."

"Like my brother said," Talon piped up. "You are one messy Bun-Bun. Don't worry, I'll clean up your love liquids."

I held up a hand. "Talon. Never say 'love liquids' ever again."

He laughed, grabbing some paper towels and a bottle of cleaning spray. I had a feeling I hadn't heard the last of that term. I held my head high and attempted to walk with dignity to the bathroom, but heard snickering behind me. I tossed up both middle fingers, because yeah, I was definitely walking like I'd just straddled a strapping oak tree.

After an incredibly long and hot shower, I felt awake and ready to figure out a game plan. Whatever was going on with that guy, Frank, from last night, plus the whole corpse cruise thing... It seemed important. I needed to figure out what kind of shipments they were getting. It was proving difficult to do anything without one of them tailing me though.

A soft tapping drew my focus up to the small, circular window above the toilet. "What the hell?" I waited, and sure enough, it happened again. Someone or something was tapping on the window.

I lowered the lid of the toilet and climbed up. The glass was lightly frosted, but I could just make out the dark shape and had to stifle my squeak of excitement. Undoing the hook latch, I opened the window. Snake, my crazy, undead, squirrel familiar, scurried inside and jumped right onto my chest, rubbing his little face against my neck.

"Oh, Snake. I was worried about you! I mean, I knew you'd be fine, but I didn't know when I'd get to come find you with all of this shit going on." He chittered away, like the good little buddy he was. "I might need to introduce you to them. I just don't see any other way at the moment. If I don't, you and I won't be able to work together much, or even see each other... Plus, you'd be awesome to have with me. We're a team, right?"

Snake's tail fluffed, and he made a little titter of agreement. Snake couldn't talk but I could pick up on his feelings about things. He could understand me, which was invaluable in times like these. Right now, he was just happy to see me.

"Awesome. Well, heads up, they don't know what my powers are yet. I'm still not sure I want to tell them the full extent, so would you be offended if I told them I found you this way? Not that I brought you back?" He didn't have a problem with that, thankfully, but I still felt the need to explain. "I've decided to use my abilities and magic to speak to their victims. Earlier today, I talked with a ghost who had some valuable intel. If they know what I can do, they'll just get paranoid."

Snake's whole body shivered in agreement with that. He was familiar with how weird people could get when they found out about my affinity. Anything that dealt with the dead or making a connection was a priceless gift to so many people. Asrael and my other mentor, Laurie, had shown me stories of other spirit witches who'd been kidnapped and trafficked.

We made great spies for obvious reasons, but there were plenty of people out there who just couldn't let go of someone who'd died. Knowing there was a chance you could talk to them again? It drove a lot of people to madness. It was really in my own best interest to keep it secret.

"Okay, I need to get some clothes." I wrapped the towel around myself, and Snake took his usual spot on my shoulder. I threw open the door and stepped out, finding everyone in the kitchen. The others were eating their food, but paused when I walked in.

"What in Saturn's balls is that?" Talon demanded, pointing at Snake.

"This is Snake. My pet squirrel. Well, it's more than that. He's my familiar."

Ashland shifted, staring at Snake and then glancing at me. "Little rabbit," he said carefully, wiping his hands on a napkin. "I hate to have to tell you this but... that squirrel is missing about forty-five percent of his skin."

"Looks kind of dead, actually." Felix took several steps back, clearly wanting to get as far away from us as possible. Ah, the germs thing. Snake chose that moment to hiss at Felix, clearly not appreciating the assumption that he was dead.

"Look, he's not dead. He was sent to me like this. We don't know what he's been through, so let's try to be respectful?"

"It's a squirrel," Talon pointed out, his brows pinched in confusion. "Do they even have feelings?"

"Well, this one does! So be nice."

"Let me get this straight." Felix held up a hand. "Your familiar is a skeleton squirrel who has feelings?"

I blinked. "Looks like your ears work. Any other questions?"

"I mean, is it dead? It's gotta be dead," Ashland stated firmly, crossing his arms. "And where the fuck did it come from? How did it get in here?"

"Ah, well, he was tapping on the window in the bathroom, and I let him in. It's not a big deal, right? He's a good boy, aren't you, Snakester?" I lifted a hand and tickled the side of his neck that still had fur.

"I do not trust creatures who display their under-armor. It's unsavory," Talon announced, hopping up to sit on the counter.

I scoffed. "Your dick bag was practically hanging out in that little skirt you were strutting around in last night!"

Talon slowly turned his body to face me. "So you're telling me you noticed? Fuck, I was starting to get concerned I was losing my touch, my edge, my mojo! That's a relief. Fuuuck!" He flopped backwards, sprawling out across the workspace like a starfish.

"I don't even know why I talk to you, honestly," I griped, rolling my eyes.

Misha shrugged. "It's his superpower."

"To stun every person he encounters so thoroughly that they question their own sanity?"

Ashland threw his head back and laughed. "Ya know, that about covers it, little rabbit."

Talon lifted two middle fingers. "Suck my ass. What are you? A couple of wiseguys?" His smirk told me he wasn't actually offended. I didn't want to see what Talon could be like if he was actually pissed.

"Right, well, now that you've all met Snake, it won't be surprising when you see him around. Just don't eat any pickles or Skittles when he's around. He has literally poked children in their eyes with those little hands to steal food, and that stuff, in particular, makes him go rabid. Trust me on this. He will fuck you up." I glanced over at Snake, who was now sitting on the counter, looking around at the guys. His ears flicked, and I stepped back.

"See? He knows what I'm saying. He heard the words, so now he's on high alert."

They all looked at me like I was insane. That was fine though, because I'd be the one laughing and saying "I told you so" when they were walking around with face scratches and bite marks.

"So, what's the plan today?" Felix asked before taking a bite of his fries.

Talon sat up again. "It's fight night! Rhodes is back at Haunt, preparing."

"Wait, I thought fight night was tomorrow night?" I was positive it was. *Why did they change the date?*

Ashland and Felix laughed, and Misha stared at me like I was missing a few marbles. "Love, it already is tomorrow. You slept like the dead. A whole day."

"What? There's no way. That isn't possible," I sputtered, looking at the windows and seeing the sunlight. "I never sleep that long."

Ash shrugged. "Guess you needed it then."

That made no sense. From my best guess, I would've fallen asleep just after two. I thought it had only been a few hours. "What time is it?"

"Eleven now. You woke up around eight-thirty," Talon supplied.

I had no idea how I'd slept so long, then woken up without even realizing it was a new day. That had never happened before... but there wasn't much I could do about it now. Had they drugged me somehow? Knocked me out so they could go do whatever nefarious shit they didn't want an audience for?

"You okay?" Misha was leaning against the fridge, staring at me.

"Huh?" I shook my head, trying to clear the fog I felt. "Yeah. Yeah, I'm good. So what happens on fight night?" I reached out to Snake, who was adjusting to his surroundings and currently sniffing the counters hard enough to make himself light-headed.

"Only the best entertainment these parts have to offer!" Ash boasted, spreading his arms wide.

Felix stood and dropped his food container into the trash. "Fight night is whatever you want it to be. Gangs from the surrounding cities come, and beef is settled in the ring. You don't need to worry though—you'll be safe as long as you stay close and don't wander off."

I crossed my arms. "Damn. You guys are seriously misogynistic. Stay by my side, little woman. Don't try to fight, girl. You couldn't possibly defend yourself, silly female."

"Uhh, I don't think anyone said that." Talon threw a confused look at the others.

"Oh please. It's not something you have to say directly. It's all about how you act. And when you guys act like I'm some delicate flower, it makes me want to kick you in the balls."

Felix grimaced. "Hey, I was just trying to put your mind at ease. Fight night is a lot, and we don't recommend that *anyone* walk around alone. Man or woman. Demon, witch, human. Doesn't matter. It would be stupid as fuck not to listen. Got it?"

Oh, Felix wants to be authoritative now?

"Let it go, *kukola*," Misha whispered, and something about the seriousness of his gaze made me back down. There was something more to this for Felix. I was going to find out what it was.

"Okay then. I won't wander off. One problem though... I don't have any clothes to wear to this thing. I don't have any clothes at all right now, actually. Can we do something about that?" I pointed to the towel still covering my body.

Talon shot Misha a look. "The fuck, man? You didn't give her the stuff?"

Misha's cheeks reddened a little. "Got distracted."

"Yeah, we heard. And saw." Felix grabbed a towel and a bottle of cleaning spray and began cleaning all the surfaces, eyeing Snake apprehensively.

"What stuff?" I looked at Misha expectantly. He sighed and walked over to the front door. It was only then I noticed the shopping bags. A lot of fucking shopping bags. I followed Misha, feeling the others' eyes on me as I approached the big guy.

Mishy turned and held out the bags. "For you."

"All of this is for me? What is it?" I crouched down and opened a bag, gasping when I saw a lot of clothes. Another bag held socks, bras, underwear, and in another, sleepwear. It was a whole gods damned wardrobe. "Misha," I whispered, suddenly overcome with emotion. It was dumb and made no sense, but nobody had ever bought me more than a cupcake or a secondhand band T-shirt from the thrift shop.

Not that I hadn't appreciated the band T-shirt from Hunter when we were thirteen. He'd scraped together five bucks and surprised me with the shirt and a birthday cupcake. We hadn't gotten much money from Montague for personal items when we were kids. A yearly amount was deposited into our accounts, but it really wasn't much. They provided pretty much everything we needed. So this... This was unexpected and completely new to me.

And here was this demon. An actual, honest-to-stars *demon*, and he'd bought me an entirely new wardrobe. Plus the beautiful bunny knives he'd *made for me*. Unbelievable. I'd been sent here to find out what these monsters, these criminals, were up to. The way my research made it sound—the way Asrael had made it sound—was that they were nothing more than brainless beasts who killed, tortured, and destroyed. I was quickly learning there was a lot more to this entire situation, which was confusing. So fucking confusing... but I couldn't tear my eyes from the bags.

Misha mistook my silence, and he rose, not giving me a chance to speak. "You hate everything? I knew it!" He ran a big hand down his face and turned to the guys. "Talon, burn it all."

My mouth fell open when Talon pulled a lighter out of somewhere and flicked it on. I snapped out of my frozen state when he took a step toward me and my treasures. I jumped up and blew out the flame, giggling like a madwoman as I launched myself at Misha, wrapping my arms tightly around his waist.

"I love everything. Thank you," I breathed, closing my eyes and breathing in his tobacco flower and steel scent. I waited for what felt like hours, standing there, breathing him in. His body started to relax, turning him from an oak tree into a squishy Mishy. I decided I'd save that nickname for a later time.

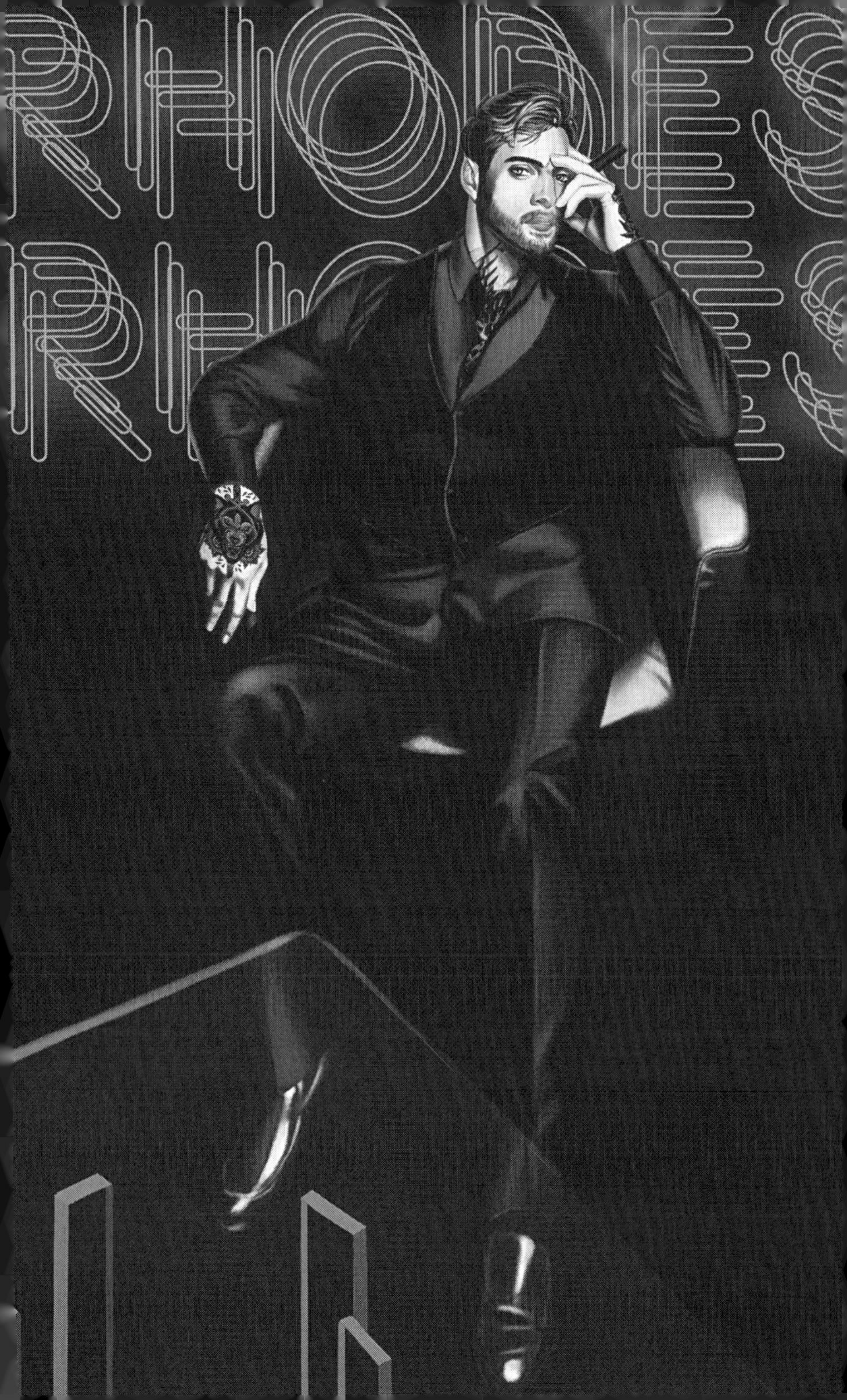
RHODES

RHODES

Chapter Fifteen

Those pussywhipped assholes had gone to chase after that witch. At least, that's what I was assuming, since I couldn't find Talon or Misha after they'd failed to show up for our morning workout. Ash had texted last night to let us know that they were at the lighthouse and that Felix was fine. Another manic art episode.

I was glad he was feeling better. I'd known immediately when I saw him in the showers after dealing with Frank that he was spiraling. Felix was just the kind of guy who kept his struggles close to his chest and didn't talk about his emotions—ever.

I took a sip of my coffee and couldn't stop the smile that took over as I thought about how strange genetics were. Talon was basically the polar opposite to Felix. Extroverted, loud, obnoxious, Tal lived like the wind. Never in one place long, his presence could be as gentle as a breeze or as intense as a huge gale of icy air that took your will to live.

A pair of hazel eyes flashed in my mind, and my smile faltered. Not a day went by that I didn't see them, full of fear... and also acceptance.

Sighing, I pushed the image of those eyes out of my head and headed to my office. It wasn't raining, which was fucking lucky. It seemed to always be raining. I didn't have any clients today, but my mind operated best when I was in my office.

I preferred to walk, especially since it was such a short distance. Didn't make sense to me to go through the hassle of dragging out a car or bike for such a quick walk. The others loved their automobiles though. We didn't have them in Besmet; they weren't necessary. All demons could fly, and if you were injured or elderly or needed to travel a great distance, you could always jump to whatever destination you needed. Much easier than the way these idiots lived.

I adjusted my tie as I rounded the corner, seeing my pride and joy come into view, The Edge. I admired the red brick exterior and the large picture windows that gave passersby a look inside. Of course, the windows were bulletproof. I liked natural sunlight when it came around, but I wasn't a fucking fool. Too many enemies out there who could decide at any time that today was the day to try and kill The Exiled.

My barbershop was my baby. Call me vain, I didn't give a fuck—there was nothing that compared to a fresh cut and shave, and every man who came in here left feeling like a million bucks. Not only that, the atmosphere was relaxed and I'd gained a steady crowd of regulars who liked to pop in and hang out. Several of them belonged to the gang, but there were also the old men who hung out just as frequently.

The bell at the top of the door signaled my arrival to my two employees, who were currently hunched over the table in the center of the shop.

"Morning, boss. This box of donuts was on the step when I got here about twenty minutes ago. Your name's on the card. Here ya go," Hawthorne told me, handing over a small, blue envelope. I peeked around him, my brow pinching together as I wondered who the fuck would send me donuts.

"Oh, a secret admirer?" Briar teased.

I rolled my eyes. "Don't start, Bri." She held her hands up, feigning innocence. I wasn't fooled. The girl was a gods damned troublemaker, but it was part of why I liked her so much. She had the same the-world-can-get-fucked attitude that I had, though hers had a freshness to it that only youth could provide. I was just a cranky, old bastard.

"I'll be in the office. Got some work to do. Here." I reached into my vest pocket. "Fight night tonight. Here's some tickets."

"Aw, hell yeah. I've been waiting for another fight night. The last one was—"

I held up a hand. "Yeah, yeah, we all remember the last one."

Hawthorne chuckled, shaking his head. "Not so sure about that, boss. That poor fucker... I don't think he even remembers his own name."

"Yeah? Well, the ring isn't for fucking posers," I barked. There had been a bit of an incident at the last event, and one of the fighters learned a hard lesson. Don't act tough and talk shit if you can't back it up, and always, *always* keep your chin tucked.

"I don't know why you insist on snapping at us like that, boss. We're like, your *only* friends." Briar flipped open the donut box lid, and both she and Hawthorne instantly gasped, scrambling backward. "W–what the fuck?!"

"That's *sick*," Hawthorne forced out, trying not to gag.

Immediately, I was on high alert. I focused my hearing and got closer. "Fuck's sake," I muttered, seeing what they were so disgusted by. There were donuts, but they were covered in mold and swarming with maggots and ants. "Burn it out back. I need to make some calls. Let me know right away if you see anything suspicious outside."

"You got it." Hawthorne slammed the lid shut with a grimace and disappeared with the box out back.

"You good, Bri?"

She looked up at me and rolled her eyes. "If you think that's the most fucked-up thing I've seen this week, then you don't know the city we live in, bossman."

"Touché." I left her at her station and made a beeline for my office. I'd never admit it to Hawthorne or Briar, but I was glad I had them. They were both part of the gang, but they didn't do anything illegal—they just did hair and ran the shop for me.

Hawthorne had been with me pretty much from the start. I'd liked him straightaway; his sense of fashion was very mid-century and I appreciated a man who took his appearance seriously. He'd arrived with no barber training, so I'd taught him everything I knew. He took to it like he'd done it in a past life.

Briar, on the other hand, had been a fucking disaster when she first came into my life. No dad to speak of, just a crackhead mother who'd lost custody of her when she was thirteen. Being the force that she was, Briar became a runaway after her first foster home experience ended with her stabbing the foster dad in the cock with a stick. As in, an actual fallen stick from the trees surrounding them in the woods where he'd planned to do very bad things to her.

Little fighter had taken off, hopped on a ferry, and ended up here in Port Black. I found her one very cold morning lying on the front step of the shop, looking like a skeleton. I wasn't intending on letting her in, but when I'd stepped over her to open the door and she'd called me a heartless comb-over-having motherfucker, it made me pause. Even I had to admit that was one hell of an insult, especially for a child.

Long story short, she'd ended up apprenticing beneath Hawthorne and me. The kid was a natural. Now, three years later, I was more than a little protective over the little fireball. Hawthorne too. Loyal, hard-working, dependable employees were something I tried to hold onto.

My body relaxed slightly upon entering my domain. The mahogany bookshelves and large desk gave off a natural wood aroma, and the large, chesterfield sofa added that hint of leather. The industrial vibe carried from the shop to my office with the exposed pipes and colors, but there was just something about being able to come in here and relax.

The main difference here was the smell, which wasn't as strong as usual today, so I quickly lit one of my custom-made candles I ordered from the shop down the street. Blood orange and cedar. I suddenly felt like I could breathe easier as the scent permeated my office, reminding me of things that I should've let go a long time ago. Unfortunately for me, I'd learned that I was a masochist.

Sighing, I sat at my desk and stared at the envelope. The handwriting didn't look familiar. I reached for my letter opener, which had a crystal demon on the handle, a gift from someone years ago.

The card inside was plain white. Nothing on the front or back to give any clues. I took a breath and opened it. The writing looked like chicken scratch, almost making my skin crawl. Had a child sent this shit? No grown being would write that poorly.

Then I scanned the one sentence, and my skin really did crawl.

"I know things nobody else knows..."

My eyes scanned that sentence back and forth, back and forth, probably a hundred times. *Fuck. There's no way anyone knows. It's impossible. We've been so careful. Why now?*

What the fuck did this mean, and what was with the fucking donuts?

Leaning back in my chair, I fired up my computer, quickly accessing the security cameras we had set up, hoping to catch a glimpse of this sneaky asshole. I rewound the footage and sped it up, freezing it at five-thirty-six this morning. Someone dressed in all black—it was impossible to tell anything concrete about their build—had left the box, but they were wearing a ski mask, hiding their face and hair. Of course.

My eyes bounced around the frame, looking to see if anyone else was waiting in the background, when suddenly the person got spooked by something and scrambled back, like they'd seen something truly terrifying.

What the fuck did you see?

I backed up the footage and played it again in real time. The space to the right of the door seemed to shimmer, like looking through leaking gas. *What the hell is that?*

My phone rang, breaking my focus. Ashland's picture popped up, which was a selfie he'd taken of himself blowing a kiss. Fucker was always changing his contact photo, but I was thankful that this time it wasn't his ass or nipple or his damn dick.

Rolling my eyes, I connected the call and leaned back in my chair. "What?"

"Is that any way to greet your best friend?"

"Sometimes you really fucking annoy me, Ace."

Shit. The ensuing silence told me he'd heard my slip-up.

"Sorry, brother. Old habits and all."

He sighed. "Yeah. Just make sure it doesn't happen where anyone else could hear."

"You really think he doesn't know? Ash... Come on, man."

"Listen, we'll be heading home soon. Did you get a chance to look through anything yet?"

I didn't like the way he'd sidestepped my question, but it wasn't like he was suddenly going to enjoy talking about his family. I had to respect that.

I pulled up a new screen on my monitor and gave it a quick scan. "Nothing that stands out, but I'll look closer, don't worry. Does she suspect anything?"

"Nah, but it really doesn't seem like she uses her phone much. That's weird, isn't it? The girls at the club can't put the fucking things down."

"If there's something to find, I will. We can't risk exposure right now. We're so close to the endgame, Ash. Think with your head and not your cock."

He snorted. "Nothing wrong with some hanky-panky. Look, I have to go. Just... take it easy today—we have a big night tonight. I want everyone at full alert."

We hung up, and I found myself going back and forth between the stupid fucking card and Palmer's phone information. I'd taken the liberty of cloning her entire device, so I now had access to everything that was on it. Anything incoming, any activity, I'd see it all as it was happening.

Sighing, I took a small key from my pocket and opened the large desk drawer, lifting out a metal briefcase. After inputting a code and using both a fingerprint scanner and retina scanner, I watched as the case popped open.

My fingertips trailed over the little vials of green gas that was going to completely change the fucking game. Over my dead body was some smart-mouthed whore going to come in here at the finish line and turn everything to shit.

She was here to stay for now, since she knew what we were... but I wanted to know who the fuck she was. Including *what* she was. Where she came from, and if she was a threat. Keeping my crew, my brothers, safe—that was most important to me. I'd been caught off guard one time. One fucking time and...

I clenched my jaw when those haunted hazel eyes made another appearance in my mind.

Let's just say, I'd made a vow that I'd never be taken by surprise again. That's how I operated. I didn't believe in second chances or comebacks. With me, you got one chance. Betray me, fuck me over? You might as well be a gods damned ghost, because you were that dead to me. And there was no coming back from it.

I saved the video clip, deciding against sending it to the others. There was no need in getting everyone all worked up over something that might just be a dumb fucking prank. The unease in my gut told me it wasn't, but if that was the case and someone actually had found out...

I tried to tell myself it wouldn't be a big deal. That was what I'd told myself for years, even though I knew it would be. Fuck. Groaning, I ran a hand down my face. No time to worry about that right now anyway; I had to get ready for tonight. With one last look at the vials, I shut the lid on the briefcase and returned it to its safe spot.

"Boss?" Hawthorne poked his head through the door tentatively. "I knocked a few times. Everything okay?"

He had? Damn, I hadn't even heard it. "Yeah, kid. All good. Did you get rid of that shit?"

"Yeah, all taken care of. Want me to have some of the crew hang around for a couple nights? See if anything else happens?"

I nodded and stood, pocketing my phone. "Good idea. Just a couple low-level lookouts is fine. We'll need muscle tonight at the fight."

"I'll see ya tonight, boss." He turned and headed to the break room, probably to get more coffee. I made my way back out front and found Briar working on braids for a kid I knew she went to school with.

"Yo, goodbye to you too, bossman!" she called out, and I had to hold in the laugh that wanted to burst out at the shocked look on the other kid's face. I could swear sometimes Briar just acted like that for shock value.

I kept walking at my brisk pace, waiting until I was halfway out of the door before lifting a hand in a half-assed wave.

Fucking hell, I really hated small talk. What the shit was I thinking starting up a business as a barber? That was all people did in there, try to make small talk. Briar tried to tell me all the time that it was just my "tough guy act." That I was a big softie on the inside. It took a lot—and I mean a fucking lot—for me not to gag when she said it.

Eh, it wasn't anything to worry about right now. I had time to burn, and it was still early enough that I could grab a nap and get some extra rest. I was going to need it.

Ash, Felix, and myself were bumping to some music as we flew down the highway on our way to The Valley. There was an old barn on some abandoned property that the gangs in the area had kind of claimed as a ceasefire location. Violence was allowed only in the ring, and if you broke the rules, your own gang leader or leaders were held accountable for your public punishment.

The only accepted fighting outside of the ring were lovers' quarrels, but even then it was frowned upon. It was ridiculous how many fights broke out between males over pussy, and having the women fighting over dick was even worse. If we punished everyone for that, no one would come to fight night. That was why I stayed way the fuck away from all of that nonsense. I just wanted to fight.

I turned in my seat to look at Felix, who was lounging in the backseat. "How ya feeling?"

"I'm good, brother. More than good, actually. Did a shit ton of painting, had some hot sex... I'm set. How about you? You ready?"

I cracked my neck and twisted back around in my seat, ignoring the sex comment. "I'm always ready."

"Oh, ho, ho. A cocky boy. Better watch yourself. Last thing you want is to underestimate anyone," Ash told me, switching gears and getting off the freeway. Our location was rural, and we still had about fifteen minutes to go.

"So what's the plan?" Felix leaned forward, glancing between Ash and myself.

Chuckling, Ash shook his head. "You always do this, Lix. We've gone over the plan so many times. Do you think something changed from the last time we went over it, which was"—he glanced at the time on the console—"four gods damned minutes ago?!"

"I get a little anxious, you fuckball. Now quit being a couple of turd sprinkles and tell me the plan!" Felix fired back, an almost-snarl edging his tone.

This got Ash's attention, and the crazy fucker actually lunged. Legit lunged toward the backseat, completely taking his hands off the wheel and removing his eyes from the road as he grabbed for Felix.

"Ashland! You gods damned fool!" I grabbed the wheel and straightened the SUV a moment before it would've gone off-road.

"Wanna try that again, Lixy?" he taunted, giving zero shits about the fact that we now had no driver.

Felix grunted, then rasped out a "Fuck you."

Oh sweet fucking Jupiter. Ashland was crawling into the backseat now, spewing all kinds of filth about how he was going to fuck some manners into Felix. The car started rolling down a hill, picking up some serious momentum.

"Shit," I cursed, climbing over the console and slipping into the driver's seat just in time to hear Ashland's moan.

"Yeah, little bitch. You wanna talk shit? Can't do that too well with my fat cock in your mouth, can you?"

"You crazy cunts! It's not like we're in a moving fucking vehicle or anything! Couldn't you have like, I don't know, pulled the car over and then fed him a dick sandwich, you prick?!"

Ash roared with laughter, making me want to strangle him. "This is not my fault, Rhodes. You heard the way he was talking to me." He sucked in a sharp breath. "Fuck, use your teeth again and you'll regret it."

"You pull a stunt like that again and *you'll* regret it!" I bellowed, glaring into the rearview mirror and meeting his gaze.

"I heard Ash the first fuckin' time. Gods damn!" Felix grumbled, his words muffled due to obvious reasons.

I gripped the steering wheel hard enough to crack my knuckles. "I wasn't talking to you, Felix!"

Ashland piped up, meeting my eyes in the mirror with a serious expression. "Maybe you should get your dick sucked, man. Might do you some good." His eyes rolled back, and I looked at the road with a huff, slowing down as the old dirt road came into view. "Get on your knees, Lixy. Rhodes will see what he's missing when my cock hits the back of your throat."

I rounded the turn probably a little too fast, if their curses were anything to judge by, and I cackled as I made sure to hit every fucking pothole and rock I came across.

"I'd hold off on putting any appendages in anyone else's body, lest you desire some unexpected pain! Don't fuck with me!"

Felix's head popped up. "Please, please get laid tonight, you grouchy fuck."

I flipped them both off, pulling up to the front of the barn. The leaders all got prime parking, and sure as shit, we had our usual two spots waiting. The grounds were already crawling with people and cars.

Killing the engine, I scanned the crowd I could see lined up, waiting to get inside. There were a few of our people mixed in, but they wouldn't have been able to see us, thanks to the blacked-out windows.

"Alright, let's do this." I opened the door and stepped out, waiting for the back doors to open. They didn't. I leaned down. "Hey, what— Oh, for fuck's sake."

How did they even move that quickly?

"I'm gonna do this right here first." Ash smirked, bringing his hand down hard on Felix's ass cheek. With his other hand, he lined himself up and surged forward at the exact moment I slammed the door shut.

Maybe I did need to get laid. I quickly adjusted my junk and walked around to the back of the SUV, opening the trunk and grabbing my bag.

"All those people over there know I'm in here, dicking you down like the dirty cum slut you are."

Bloody hell. I closed the trunk and headed for the side door, wanting to avoid the crowd for now. The guys were like brothers to me, and while I enjoyed watching them fuck other people, it just didn't hit the same watching them together. Plus, I was already a little on edge.

Throwing open the side door, I stepped inside. I was surrounded immediately by people. The scent of sweat, booze, and anticipation hung in the air like a fog. Ignoring them all, I walked over to my locker and dropped my bag. I'd learned a long time ago that this area back here was the best place to overhear conversations and find out information that never should've seen the light of day.

Almost everyone back here right now were fighters. Some spent their time training, and then an hour before the fights got started, the fighters' girls or guys were allowed back here. That was typically where the intel came from. Alcohol, weed, Molly... You name it, someone was on it. I didn't like drugs, but the ease with which people ran their damn mouths while on them? That I did like.

"There he is! I was wondering when you were gonna show up, handsome." I'd barely turned around when my face was smashed against the largest pair of tits I'd ever come across.

"Priscilla," I mumbled, trying to breathe.

Releasing me, she held me back at arm's length. "That's no way to address a queen, sugar. I know I taught you better than that."

I smiled. "Apologies, Queen Prissy. Forgive me?"

Her dark skin was practically fucking sparkling with all of the glitter and—I looked closer—tiny rhinestones around her bottom eyelashes. One thick, perfectly sculpted eyebrow raised, and her chin tilted up. I didn't know if she was about to bitch slap me or kiss me. She studied me, holding her stern expression a couple of seconds longer before it melted away and her eccentric, happy self returned. "Of course, of course. When I saw you over here, I wanted to come tell you about the lineup tonight."

Queen Prissy was the HBIC during fight nights. The only reason I knew that meant Head Bitch In Charge was because she had a sash made with that on it. Talon had been trying for months to steal it, unsuccessfully. She was neutral as far as gangs went, but I knew she liked us the best.

"Well? Who's getting fucked up tonight?" I cracked my knuckles and followed her over to the table where she kept her books.

"Looks like some guy named... Skippy." She glanced up at me through her incredibly thick, rainbow eyelashes.

"Skippy?" I deadpanned. "What? Am I fighting a man or his Jack Russell terrier?"

Prissy coughed to hide her deep laugh. "Belongs to Buzzard's crew. Never heard of him before. Good luck. You're fight six." Buzzard was the head of a crew from a city forty-five minutes south of Port Black. He'd earned his name because rumor had it that whenever he showed up, bodies would inevitably start hitting the ground. I preferred my own origin story, which was that he looked like a gods damned big bird with a weird floppy neck and a beak-like nose. Add in the slight hunch of his shoulders, and yeah, I'd think a buzzard had fucked a hooker and birthed that son of a bitch.

"Thanks, Queen. See ya out there," I said, shooting Prissy a wink and heading back to my locker.

Crouching down, I unzipped my bag, looking for my tape and water bottle. I froze when my eyes landed on the small blue envelope sitting at the very top of all of my things. I stood and looked around, trying to see if anyone was watching me. This definitely hadn't been here when I walked inside. Someone had placed it here while I was talking to Prissy.

My heart was pounding, but when I didn't see anyone blatantly staring at me, I crouched back down and snatched up the offensive correspondence. Opening it quickly, I found the same blank white card as earlier, but the note scrawled inside was different.

Secrets are cancer, so here's a truth. I know yours. They were never meant for you!

What the fuck? My hand shook, and I dropped the card back into my bag, wiping the sweat from my brow. *How? How do they know?* This was bad. I needed to figure out who the fuck was sending these and fast. They needed to be eliminated.

I pushed away my internal freak-out and straightened to my full height. Whoever did this was here, right now. If they thought they could get in my head and fuck with me, distract me? They were fucking *wrong*. I was going to win my fight, I was going to find out the information we needed in regards to Scorpio and his bullshit attempt to take us down, and I would find out more about this little witch and what was so gods damned special about her.

It was then that a dark thought settled in the back of my head. Was she connected to this? *She just shows up and suddenly I start getting these notes?* Yeah, I didn't believe in coincidences like that.

My demon purred at the promise of getting to do what we did best—stalking the shadows to find out the secrets nobody wanted brought to light.

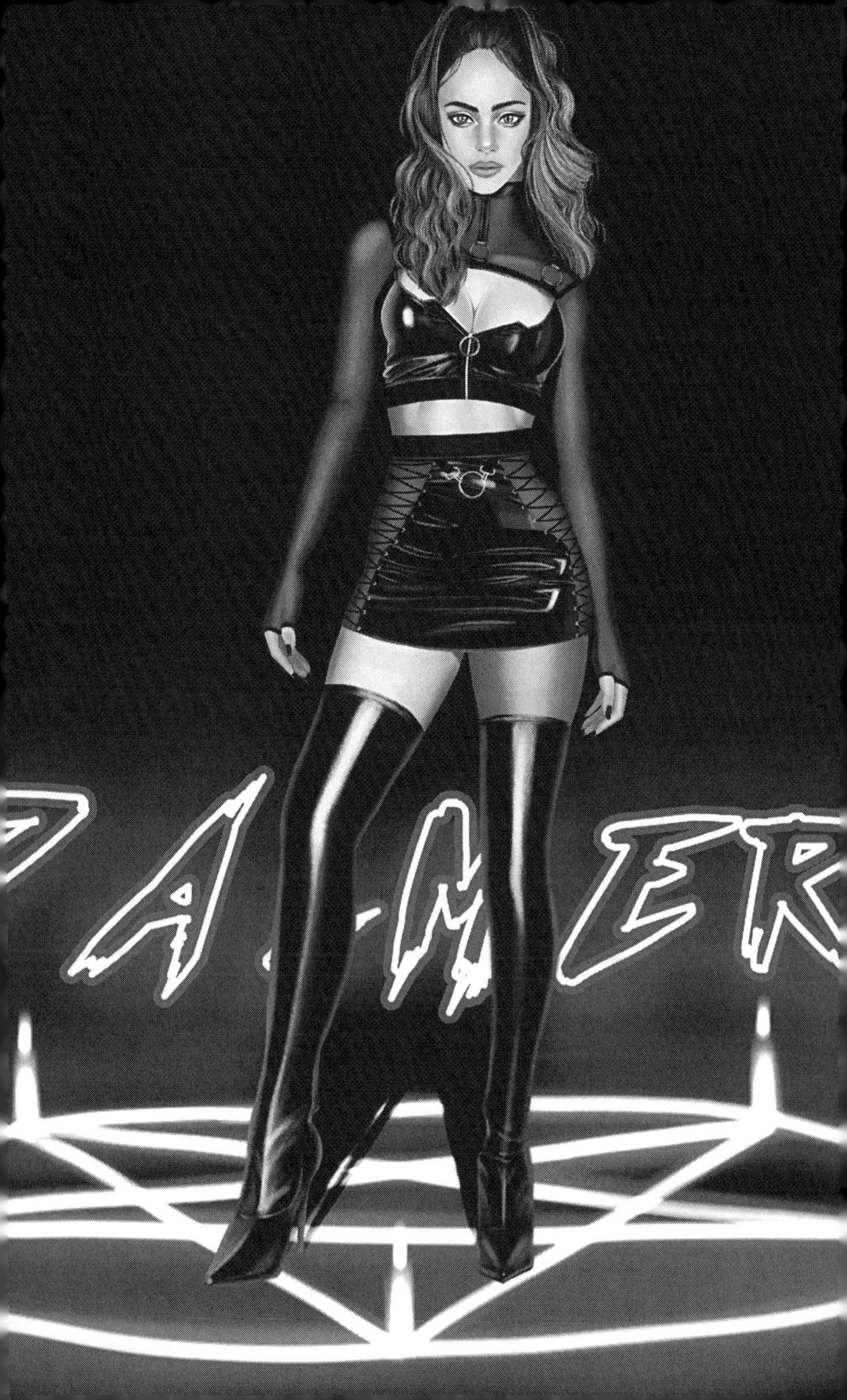

PALMER

Chapter Sixteen

"I just don't understand why I can't drive this one," I pouted, pointing at the shiny crotch rocket.

Talon groaned. "Listen. This is tradition. You'll ride right here on the back while I drive." He was dressed in a pair of purple, latex pants that hugged his nuts tighter than a squirrel clinging to an acorn at the height of winter solstice.

I huffed, crossing my arms. "Please. Your balls will be getting windburn the second we hit a bump and those ridiculous pants split open."

Talon's mouth fell open in disbelief. "Ridiculous? I think you meant sexy as fuck! And haven't you ever heard of Spandex? Gods, what planet are you from?"

"Where did you even get that shirt?" I pointed to the black tank he was sporting, which had a neon orange silhouette of a woman's body bending over. She had a bunny tail and ears, and the word beneath her read *#fuckbunnies*.

"I made it. Don't worry, I have one for you too. In fact, I made one for each of us," he giggled.

Over my dead body would I be wearing that shirt.

"Where's Misha? And why are we riding this... thing?" I'd only ever seen such a thing in cartoons.

The elevator dinged behind us, and Talon grinned. "There's the big guy now."

Misha stalked across the concrete floor, a black backpack strapped to his back, tactical black pants with a million pockets and hidey-holes, and oh my fuck. The shirt.

"No. Nope. We're not leaving here with you wearing that!"

Talon jumped up and clicked his heels together like he was a freaking leprechaun. The big demon didn't even react to Talon's show of excitement. "The shirt looks perfect. I think the 3XL was the way to go, but if you keep hitting those weights..." Tal trailed off and shook his head sadly, swinging his leg over the bike. "It's going to make things a lot more complicated to dress you properly."

Rolling his eyes, Misha walked over to me. "You sit here." That was all he said before lifting me by the waist and depositing me behind Talon. "Helmet." A second later, he buckled the chin strap of a helmet, wiggling it around on my head to make sure it was secure.

I glanced around, confused when Misha rounded the bike, instead of walking over to the shiny, pretty one I wanted to take. "No fucking way," I whispered. Oh yeah, Tal and I were on a fucking sidecar motorcycle. And if my eyes weren't deceiving me... Misha was going to ride in the sidecar.

"What is it, Bun-Bun?" Tal glanced over his shoulder, checking to make sure I was okay.

"Uh," I started, staring wide-eyed at Misha as he somehow folded himself like a lawn chair into the sidecar. The entire thing shook with every movement he made. Suddenly, the only thing I could picture was Kronk from that one Disney movie being squeezed into that little rollercoaster cart with batshit crazy Yzma, and I died. "Oh my gods," I wheezed, sucking in a breath while they stared at me like I was the weirdo. "Is that your *groove?*"

"*Kukola,*" Misha warned, narrowing his eyes.

"I'm sorry, I just—" I wiped the tears away and held my midsection, which was now aching from the laughing fit. "Why are you riding in there?"

Talon fired up the bike before responding to my question. "Mishy can't see the best at night, Bun-Bun. Also, what's wrong with him riding in the seat that allows him to do what he does best?"

I looked back at Misha, who was now spinning a few blades between his fingers. "What's he going to do with those?"

The bike roared, and we shot forward out of the underground garage. "We're doing a drive-by on the way out of town! Stinky Pete needs a reminder about who runs this shit!"

My arms wrapped around Tal's waist as we cruised through the city. I hadn't heard of a Stinky Pete before in my research, but there was a Peter Baleman. A fifty-something-year-old water mage who had never taken up with The Exiled. He had an old, car repair shop on the edge of town and basically had to pay a tax to the gang in order to stay and do business there. Word on the street was he was a real asshole and liked to walk a fine line, pushing boundaries when only men who had a death wish would do such a thing.

I tried not to look over at Misha, because I had to choke down my giggles every time. Unfortunately, when we arrived at our destination, I had to look to my right to see where we were pulling into. A car shop. So Stinky Pete was Peter Baleman. As I looked, I caught a glimpse of Misha and realized he was wearing huge goggles. Fucking massive, bug-eyed...

Gunshots pulled my attention away before I lost my shit laughing again, and I saw that two men had just come out of the garage, firing semi-automatic weapons at us.

"Talon! Fucking go!" I screeched, panicking because he was doing the exact opposite of going anywhere. In fact, he slammed on the brakes.

Misha sent a handful of daggers flying through the air, the momentum from the braking giving the deadly accurate weapons even more power. I didn't think that should be allowed. Like, for the sake of humanity. It just wasn't safe. That dude was lethal with blades; he didn't need any power ups.

One of the men firing at us was struck in the neck, blood spraying instantly from his throat as he dropped the gun to grab his neck.

The other one, well, he died immediately when one of Misha's daggers stabbed him right through the eye.

"Don't be a little bitch, Pete! Get your ass out here! We just want to have a little chat!" Talon shouted, remaining in his seat. Neither he nor Misha bothered getting up. Either they were incredibly confident in the outcome of whatever this was... or they were cocky fuckboys who were about to get me killed.

One of the garage doors opened fast—someone had raised it manually, and that someone walked out a moment later with his hands in the air. "Apologies. Didn't know it was you guys. Been having some trouble with thieves."

Pete had gray hair and a big belly. His greasy jeans were held up by a pair of equally greasy suspenders. He had the kind of face that could have been seen as approachable at some point in his life, but not now. The wrinkles that had formed in the shape of a scowl told that story easily enough.

Talon tsked. "See, I just don't know if I believe ya, Pete. If you've been having so much trouble, why didn't you let us know so we could help you out? That's exactly why you pay tax. You get to operate a business, remain an unattached entity in our city, and you get our protection. Doesn't add up, does it, Misha?"

Misha didn't answer, he just unsheathed another dagger and began spinning it slowly, eyeing Pete like a cat watching a mouse. Pete's face paled as he suddenly realized he was in trouble.

"See, Pete, word on the street is that you've been skimping on reporting your income." Pete opened his mouth to argue, and Talon held up a hand. "Your *full* income. It's not that hard, Pete. You know we get our cut, no matter what."

"I–I d–don't know who you've been getting your intel from—"

A woman walked out of the garage, much younger than Pete but clearly a mechanic. Her blonde hair was braided in two long rows and she wore a backwards snapback hat that had seen better days.

Pete glanced over at the woman, who crossed her fully tatted arms and leaned casually against the side of the building. Understanding dawned on me about ten seconds before it did for poor Stinky Pete. His employee had sold him out. Tal and

Mish were still as statues as they waited for the man to piece it all together.

"You! You fuckin' b—" *Thwack.* His voice was cut off, along with the spray of water from his palms that never got beyond a sprinkle.

Pete stumbled back from the force of the hit. A dagger protruded out of his chest as he fell to his knees, mouth opening and closing like a fish out of water.

"Yeah, me. You're such a pathetic piece of shit, Pete." The woman approached the dying man, circling him with a sneer. "How long have I worked here and put up with your sexist fucking bullshit?" She moved like a rattlesnake, punching him right in the nose. "You shoulda known, you thieving cocksore. Port Black belongs to The Exiled. So do I."

Pete's eyes nearly bugged out at that little nugget of information. The woman waved her hand, and a wrench that was on the hood of a car zipped through the air, landing right in her open palm. My mouth dropped as she whacked him over the head with it hard enough to make my own head hurt.

"Fuck yeah, Lucille! Fuck him up!" Talon cheered, and Lucille definitely did. By the time she was done smashing Pete to smithereens, she was sweating and panting like she'd run a marathon.

"What's her affinity?" I whispered to Misha.

He smirked. "Selective magnetism."

Interesting. Lucille was busy wiping the sweat and blood from her brow as she walked over to us, laughing. It didn't strike me really as an appropriate time for laughter, but it seemed like everyone in this city just did whatever they wanted, social expectations be damned.

"Can't tell you boys how long I've wanted to do that. Fuck me, it felt good. I'll drop off the money owed tomorrow?"

"Sure thing, Luce. Feel free to change whatever you want around here. Exiled property now. Good work." Talon shifted on his seat, giving Lucille a clear view of me for the first time.

"You boys didn't tell me we had a guest," she said with a flirtatious smirk. "What's your name?"

Two low-pitched growls were her answer, and I smacked Talon on the arm. "Don't be rude!" I leaned around him and waved. "Hi, I'm Palmer."

"Charmed," Lucille replied, eyeing Talon and I with what looked like surprise. "Well, I guess I'll be seeing you guys at fight night? I'm gonna clean up and head down there. I'll call the cleaner about that." She tipped her chin to indicate Pete and his two men.

"We're heading there now." Talon started the engine and backed up. "Oh," he called out. "Lucille? You ever flirt with my girl again, you'll regret it. Understood?"

Lucille nodded, and I had to give her credit, she didn't cower. "Apologies. I didn't realize. I meant no disrespect, boss. Won't happen again."

"Wonderful." Talon grinned at her so wide, I wondered if it hurt his mouth. Then we were off, speeding through the streets once again.

About ten minutes and one very long, dusty road later, we arrived at a huge barn, otherwise known as 'The Valley.' Mostly because the barn itself was in the middle of one. Talon parked and helped me off the bike, his eyes constantly scanning our immediate surroundings.

"So Pete was stealing money?" I asked, wanting to see if he'd talk more about what had just happened.

"Yeah. Lucille was our inside man over the past few years. We suspected something was going on but could never prove it. She's a hell of a mechanic though, and her affinity for magnetism enables her to create the perfect tool for any job. Stinky was a fuckin' sexist and I'm sure she put up with a lot from him in her time there. Giving her that garage was the least we could do. Loyalty is rewarded. Always."

Misha came around to stand at my back, and I looked up at him. "But I thought you gave people a chance to like... fix things? The guy at the club that night..." The big guy snarled at the mention of the man he and Ashland had stabbed in the neck at the club.

"What? He could've gotten his debt erased, so why not Pete? I still think it's pretty fucked up to just kill someone like that."

Talon sprang forward, making me stumble back into Misha. "Listen here, Bunny. You're talking about shit you have no idea about. We don't do anything without a reason."

"Okay, fucking hell, Talon. Back the fuck up. I was just making conversation!" I pushed him squarely in the chest, forcing him back a whole inch. Small victories. He smiled and leaned down, crowding into my space. A large hand settled against my stomach, and Misha tugged me closer.

I could count the freckles on Tal's face as he grinned in that unsettling way he often did. "Does it seem silly to kill sick fucks who like to do bad things to little kids?"

"W–what?" I stumbled over the word, because that was basically the last thing I'd expected him to say.

Talon nodded. "That's right, Bun-Bun. That fucker in the club? A boy's mama came to us a couple of weeks back with some evidence that Jack was up to some really sick shit. Naturally, we wanted to make an example of the scum and publicly execute him, but this boy's mama, she begged us not to reveal his crimes. Know why?"

My stomach clenched in disgust. I had a feeling I wasn't going to like what he was about to tell me.

"Jack was her husband, and the victim? Her son. His own *stepson*, Palmer. If we'd outed him as a child molester, everyone would've been able to guess who he'd victimized."

"So you did it the way you did to... protect them?" My mind was kind of exploding at the moment, like a huge firework.

Talon tilted his head and studied me. "Well, wouldn't you have done the same thing? Jack did owe us money—that was true. We did offer him a chance to clear his debt, but Ash fuckin' knew he'd never follow through with it. Too much pride. So in the end, a pedophile was wiped from existence, and our loving citizens got another example of why you don't fuck with us."

I knew my mouth was open in shock, but I couldn't seem to close it. Damn. All the things I'd thought about them, all the things I'd read... But then there was Pete. Curious, I asked, "And Pete? Was he a sick fuck, too?"

Misha snorted behind me. "No, *kukola*, Pete was a thief and he smelled like horse shit."

Aaaand they're back to being psychos. But they kill child predators, too. They're not complete psychos. I was giving myself mental whiplash with all of the waffling back and forth I was doing lately. What was six months of this going to do to me?

Without another word, we started moving as a group toward the entrance. I moved on autopilot, allowing my feet to carry me as if I was floating, because my head was spinning. Just when I thought they had maybe a shred of humanity in there—doing what they did for that kid—they go and kill a man because he smelled like horse shit.

"Please tell me they have alcohol here," I mumbled as we skipped the line and entered the mayhem. I needed a few shots of liquor. Who the fuck really were these demons and why the fuck had Asrael sent me here? I really wasn't convinced they were as bad as I'd been led to believe.

"We don't do anything without alcohol. Let's grab you a drink and then find Rhodes." Talon slipped his hand in mine and guided us through the throngs of rowdy people.

A fight was already going, and the energy was high and heady. It had been too long since I'd gotten to use my fighting skills, and I'd have been lying if I said I wasn't feeling the itch. Especially in this setting. It reminded me of the training center at Montague.

"You good, Bun-Bun?" Tal asked, putting his face right in front of mine. We'd stopped walking and were standing at a wooden bar, complete with dancing men and women and a few bartenders.

"Yeah, yeah. I'm good. I'll take whatever liquor is available." Tal looked at me for a couple seconds before nodding and slamming his hand down on the bar. All three bartenders scrambled to get to him the quickest and take his order. The one who won out was a woman with huge tits and jet-black hair. Her lips were painted red, and she batted her eyes at Talon so hard, I thought her fake lashes might double as a pair of wings and carry her skanky ass away from—

Wait. No. I'm not jealous. I have no reason to be jealous. And yet...

She leaned in to whisper something in his ear that had him laughing. I slowly looked up at Misha who wasn't looking at Tal, but down at me. He lifted a brow, as if to ask me the question I was already asking myself. *Are you going to allow this?*

The others at the bar were already whispering and pointing at this bitch's display. She stepped back and smiled, telling him she'd be right back.

Talon turned to find me glaring at him. "What? Steph is getting the drinks, it'll just be a second."

I nodded. Idiot was clueless. It was fine. *He isn't yours. That's ridiculous.* So why was I watching Steph's every move as she poured the drinks? Why did I want to climb over the bar and smash a bottle over her head every time she looked in his direction?

Talon and Misha were talking about something, but I was zoned out. All I saw was red. Blood red. Until I saw *him.* Just sitting there casually, down the end of the bar top—the ghost from the bathroom. He lifted a hand and waved at me before his eyes shifted to where Talon had been. He frowned, and my gaze snapped over just in time to see Steph put a shot glass between her fucking tits and make a come hither motion with her finger.

Oh hell fucking no.

I pushed my way next to Talon at the bar. Steph glared at me like she wanted to chop off my head, but Talon glanced over at me and smiled. "Oh hey, Bun-Bun," he said, opening his arms like I was going to just snuggle on in there like a bug in a rug.

"Oh hey, Talon. Mind getting out of my fuckin' way?" His brow furrowed as he dropped his arms and made a spot for me between him and Misha.

Before anyone could react, I hopped up on the bar and literally launched myself like a fucking panther at the skanky bitch. She squealed and tried to escape me, but that wasn't going to happen.

"By the moon, Bunny!" Talon shouted at the same time onlookers started cheering, screams of *cat fight* piercing the air. I didn't care. This cunt was going to learn right here, right now... along with everyone else.

She hit the ground hard, the liquor nestled in her cleavage spilling all over her as she sucked in gasping breaths, trying to regain the air I'd knocked the fuck out of her.

Reaching down, I took the shot glass out of her titties and snagged a bottle of tequila from a low shelf. I poured myself a shot and downed it just in time for Steph to try to buck me off. Sighing, I tossed the glass over my shoulder, hearing the shatter behind me, which felt strangely like the shattering of my sanity. I lifted the bottle and downed a hefty amount, relishing the burn.

"Get off of me, you crazy bitch!" Steph screamed, flailing her arms at me.

I raised my hand and then swung, connecting with her cheek and sending her face flying to the side. The crowd actually went quiet after that. It tended to happen when people realized there was someone unstable in the ring. Also, slapping a bitch hard enough to knock a layer of makeup off her face did tend to get some fucking respect.

Enraged, she tried to strike back at me, but I grabbed her wrist and twisted just hard enough to let her know that with a little more pressure, I could break it. "Don't let me catch you trying your whore shit on what belongs to me again, or next time I'll slice your nipples off and wear them as earrings."

Oh my fucking gods, did I just say that? I threw my head back and cackled at the mental image.

"Crazy bitch," Steph muttered, holding her cheek.

"You have no idea. And trust me, you don't want to." I hopped up, smoothing down my clothes.

Talon and Misha were standing there, but they were no longer alone. Ash and Felix had now joined them. Tal and Ash had feral grins on their faces while Felix smirked. Mishy looked stone-cold, arms crossed, and I knew at least one of his hands was gripping a dagger.

"Which one is off-limits?!" some chick at the bar yelled, and I narrowed my eyes at her, ready to go another round. She yelped and covered her nipples before ducking down and disappearing from sight. I supposed it was a valid question though, and I looked at these demons who had made me crazy. These monsters who had flipped everything I thought I knew upside down and had me questioning everything. *Everything*.

"All of them are off-limits!"

The reaction was a mixture of gasps and booing. Some jeers were made about me being a crazy bitch groupie who just wanted to choke on Exiled cock. I memorized that chick's face for later. On some level, I couldn't believe I had just attacked that woman like that, but on the other hand, it was honestly as if something inside me had taken over. If I hadn't intervened when I did, and she put her lips on him? It was scary to admit to myself, but I was pretty sure I might've killed her.

I'd just publicly claimed the five leaders of one of the scariest gangs in the country. As far as I knew, no other 'outsider' could say they'd ever done the same. It explained the bitter Bettys who were eyeballing me, probably planning my demise.

"Tal?" I looked down to see Steph pouting, holding her cheek as she spoke. "Do you want me to have security remove her?"

I tipped my head back and howled with laughter. "I'd like to see you fuckin' try."

Next thing I knew, Talon was hopping the bar and picking me up, wrapping my legs around his waist. My hands sank into his red hair, and his blue eyes twinkled with desire and mischief.

"I'm harder than an over-toasted slice of bread right now, Bunny," he purred into my ear and rolled his hips, demonstrating his point.

"I can feel that. If you don't want murder here tonight though, you better tell all these motherfuckers that you're mine."

Tal leaned back, bringing a hand up to fist my hair. "Is that what I am? Yours?" He leaned in and licked my lips, causing them to open on a gasp.

"Aren't you?" I challenged, darting in and nipping his bottom lip.

Grinning maniacally, Talon spun around so he was facing the crowd. "Exiled dick is off-limits!"

The crowd clearly didn't like that, and Ashland yelled out over the boos, "Just the five of us. Anyone else's dick status is their own fucking problem!"

The crowd cheered again, and the noise grew to deafening levels as Talon plopped my ass down on the bar, claiming my mouth in a brutal kiss that I felt down to my toes.

"Alright, quit sucking face. We have work to do." Rhodes's voice broke through the sexual tension, and I felt like barking at him. Dickhead.

Talon broke the kiss, smiling against my mouth. "You're so gods damned sexy. Later, I want to eat your pussy for like eighty-six minutes. Pencil me in. I'll see ya around, Bun-Bun." With that, he hopped over the bar and disappeared, swallowed up almost immediately by the crush of bodies.

"You just told the entire fucking world that my dick belongs to you," Rhodes sneered, getting in my face.

I rolled my eyes. "It was easier to include you than to try and explain that I'd never want to claim the stuffy fuck who probably wears tighty-whities."

If steam could blow out of someone's ears like the cartoons, Rhodes would've been puffing like a geyser. The best part was that I knew he wore tight, little, red boxer briefs, thanks to our night in the maze, so I took immense satisfaction in fucking with him.

"Look, if you happen to find a nice dick you want to sit on, I'd be happy to let the gent know that you're not included in my little harem, but I just don't see anyone here lining up, Monocle. Hey, don't you have a fight soon?"

Just then, a deep, raspy voice cut in before he could answer. "Rhodes, darling, bad news. It seems as though Skippy decided to indulge a bit too much tonight and is currently nodding off in the tall weeds behind the barn."

Rhodes pinched his nose in annoyance. "Well, what now?"

"What now? Aren't you going to introduce me to your girl? I heard that you're all together, like one big happy, sexy crime family."

I smiled at the statuesque, glittering queen, immediately deciding I liked her based on her sense of fashion and the fact that she seemed to take no shit. "Yeah, Daddy. Introduce me."

The drink that Rhodes had just taken promptly sprayed out of his mouth, and I reached behind me, snagging a napkin from the bartender's stash. "Here ya go." I fluttered the napkin at him and turned back to his friend. "Hi, I'm Palmer."

"Queen Priscilla, at your service. It's so nice to see the boys actually trying—" Rhodes slammed his glass down, making Queenie P pause. "Boy, I know you are going to lose that piss-poor attitude and quit this rude behavior in the next ten seconds or I will flatten you. You boys all think you're so bad, so tough. Well, let me tell you, I can—and will—bend you over this knee and light that ass up."

Imagine my shock when Rhodes actually looked ashamed and apologized. "I'm sorry, Queen Prissy. I just needed this fight tonight, okay?"

"He does, ya know?" a voice whispered in my ear, and I knew without looking that it was him. That fucking ghost. The hot one.

I didn't respond, because obviously I couldn't without looking like a real psycho. Rhodes and Queenie were talking about who he could fight, but I was zoned out, thanks to Ghost Dude who was now sitting right beside me.

"I'm just saying, he needs to blow some steam off. He is wound up. Look at the veins in his arms popping out."

They were totally bulging. I didn't know what that had to do with me though.

"I know," the ghost continued with a sigh, crossing his ankles and swinging his legs. "You're probably wondering why you should care. It's just, in my experience, a man who is that primed to explode should let that steam out in a safe environment before he goes boom. Come to think of it, you also look a little tense."

I snorted softly, covering it up with a cough when Rhodes glanced at me. When he looked away, I took a gamble and whispered as fast as I could, "I've got a lot going on right now. Can you fuck off?"

The ghost laughed. There was something so familiar about the sound, but I couldn't place it. "Fight him."

"What?!" I blurted out, not able to catch myself from saying it out loud.

"I was telling Queen Prissy here that you and I are not together, and that I'm not even sure that this is an appropriate place for you to—"

Oh, this macho man wannabe was about to learn.

I hopped down from the bar and crossed my arms. "Put me down. I want to fight." Queenie P let out a surprised chuckle of delight and scanned her clipboard.

"Absolutely not!" Rhodes barked. We both ignored him.

"I'm afraid I don't have any open fights. All of the women—"

I cut her off. "I want to fight *him*." I pointed to Rhodes.

"Have you lost your shit? First, you attack that woman, and now you want to fight me? *Me?* No fucking way."

I bumped up against his chest. "What? Scared to get your ass whooped by a girl?"

"Miss Palmer, I really don't think it's a good idea. Rhodes is one of the best fighters that we've had come through here, so it would be dangerous and irresponsible to allow—"

"Do you allow coed fights?" I asked, not taking my eyes away from his, even though I wasn't addressing him.

"Well, yes, but—"

"Then write my name down. If you'll excuse me, I have a fight to prepare for." I saluted Queenie and flipped off Rhodes, then walked away.

It wasn't until I was well and truly into the fray of the rowdy crowd that I realized I'd done exactly what Talon and Misha had told me not to do.

Wander off alone.

There was no going back now. I'd made my mind up, and that was that. Plus, Rhodes really needed to be put in his place. I was sick of his better-than-thou attitude. The hell had I done to him? I ignored the little voice in the back of my head that was saying something about the fact that I'd infiltrated his family with the intent to do some fucked-up things... but he had no proof of that. So I didn't get it.

I started to make my way over to the rings so I wouldn't miss the fight when it was time. As I scanned the setup, I spotted a small frame with little spiky, blonde pigtails. *No way.* She was watching a particularly brutal fight between an extremely tall woman and an incredibly short man. One of the woman's legs were as thick as both the dude's legs put together, but I knew better than anyone that size didn't necessarily mean you were going to come out on top.

Stepping up next to the girl, I glanced down and made sure it was her. It definitely was Cherry, my friend I'd made the night of the party at Haunt.

"Interesting matchup," I said, loud enough for her to hear me over the noise.

She looked at me, and her eyes widened. "Oh my gods! Girl, you're alive!"

I chuckled. "Last I checked, yeah. Why wouldn't I be?"

Cherry grabbed my forearm and pulled me a few rings down where it was marginally quieter. "Okay, we all saw them take you wherever they took you and that typically doesn't bode well for people!" She was looking around nervously, as though one of the guys was going to pop out and bust her ass for talking to me.

"Oh, right." I supposed that would've been ominous to anyone watching. It also felt like it had been weeks since that night, not the few days it was in reality. "Well, I'm just fine, as you can see."

Cherry looked unconvinced. "So what happened? They took you for a tea party?"

"Something like that," I replied, winking. "Do you live around here?"

"Pfft, unfortunately. I have a small studio on the east end of town. Nothing fabulous, but it's clean and it's mine."

"That's all that matters, right?" I smiled at her, surprised by how much I enjoyed talking to her. Maybe it was all of the big dick energy I'd been immersed in over the past few days, but socializing with another woman was doing it for me right now.

Cherry blew a bubble with her gum and nodded. "Got that right. Happiness is in the eye of the bear herder."

I choked on a laugh. "What?" She waved me off, giggling. Cherry was clearly a tiny bit intoxicated. So was I though, so we made a good team.

"Hey," she said, sobering a bit. "Do you want to like, exchange numbers? There's karaoke tomorrow night at this little sports bar by my apartment, if you're looking for something to do?"

I needed this connection. At first, I thought it would just be to pump her for information about the city, the people who lived in it, and the demons who ran it... but I was starting to realize that if I was going to be here for a little while, a friend might not be so bad. I'd never had many friends. I wasn't the best at it. Too abrasive, too untrusting, but I always, always had Hunter.

My heart squeezed as I thought of my best friend. He hadn't been happy about me being put on this mission solo, and even had a discussion with Asrael about his decision. Pissed me the fuck off that he got involved in something that wasn't his business, but aside from Asrael, he was the only family I felt like I had.

Then the one time at the academy when I'd taken a chance and decided to live a little bit, it had completely exploded in my face. Memories of the entire chain of events liked to assault me at unsuspecting times. Like now, hearing the cheers of the crowd, the sounds of flesh on flesh, bodies hitting the mats...

Hunt sank down beside me on the mat, both of us sweaty and panting like dogs in a desert. "Holy fuck, P. What a workout."

I quickly wrapped my hair up on top of my head and secured it before spreading my legs so I could stretch my muscles out. "I need the ice bath later."

"Same. My right quad feels like it's burning," Hunter complained, rubbing his leg and wincing through the pain.

We sat there, the two of us stuck together like glue. Everyone else was so cliquey, and I had no desire to play social mind games. I was here with one thing on my mind. Revenge.

"Hey, I heard we're getting a new instructor today," Hunter said, continuing his stretches.

I hadn't heard that. Strange. "Who is it?"

He shrugged. "Some guy. I think his name starts with a B, but I could've heard that wrong. You know how the rumor mill works around here."

Just then, the doors to the gym pushed open and Asrael strutted in, his arm slung over the shoulders of a guy I had never seen before. He was gorgeous. Not that I cared about shit like that, because like I said, revenge. But my traitorous eyes drifted back to the new guy just to find him staring at me. He couldn't have been that much older than us.

His hair was short, and he was definitely as tall as Hunter. The other girls were going to be all over this dude in a matter of...

"Hi!" A series of greetings were called out by several different female recruits.

I shook my head and stood up, ignoring the flock of girls who had swarmed Asrael and the new guy. So predictable. Why not just suck his dick right now?

Hunter barked a laugh, and some of the girls gave me a dirty look. "What?"

"Didn't mean to say that out loud, P?" Hunter teased, getting to his feet as well.

"Eh, fuck them. You know there will be dick sucking." We walked side by side toward the doors and just made it out when a deep voice had us stopping.

"Hey!" I spun around to see new guy jogging over to us, leaving the gaggle of girls open-mouthed and staring daggers my way. "Sorry, I uh, didn't get your names back there."

I glanced at Hunter, who was looking smug as fuck. "Sup, bro. I'm Hunter James. Welcome to Montague."

The guy lifted his chin in that bro way that bros do. "Slade. Slade Porcino."

I put my hands on my hips and eyed Slade suspiciously. He unsettled me a little, and I wasn't completely sure why. Was it because he was hot as hell? Maybe. Regardless, I didn't like it.

"Well, Slade, welcome to Montague," Hunter said again with a grin. He was always so welcoming and approachable. I wasn't sure why he even bothered hanging around with me. "This is Palmer. Don't mind her, she's kind of a rude asshole at times."

My head snapped in his direction. "Fuck you, Hunt." I wasn't sure what I was more annoyed about, the fact that he gave this dude my name or the fact that he called me a rude asshole. Probably the name thing. I was a bit of a rude asshole, to be honest.

"Well, it's nice to meet you both. What do you do for fun around here?" Slade asked, and his eyes glittered with anticipation. It had me taking a second look at the guy standing before me. First impressions had led me to believe he was a kiss ass. A golden boy type, with his thick black hair and greenish-brown eyes.

"I guess that depends on what your definition of fun is, Porcino." I didn't want to use his first name. We weren't on that level yet. "And anyway, aren't you faculty? Hanging around with students doesn't really seem appropriate."

He grinned roguishly, and I tried to ignore the way my heartbeat sped up. "I'm not faculty yet. I'm here on an intern basis for six to twelve months. Plus, if you didn't notice, the other staff aren't exactly young."

He wasn't wrong. He would be the youngest by far. Whatever. If he wanted to hang out with us, it didn't bother me in the slightest.

"Let's walk and talk, man. We were headed for the cafeteria. You hungry?" Hunter asked, starting to walk away.

Slade pinned me with his intense gaze. "Actually, yeah. I'm starving." He walked past me, close enough that I could feel the heat of his body. Not only that, I could sense his power. He was incredibly strong, and with those looks, dangerous as fuck.

Thing was, I was all of those things too.

The crowd grew louder, drawing me out of my head. I realized the focus was on the ring to our left, where one of the fighters was knocked out cold while the other strutted around beating on his chest like Tarzan. Male posturing at its finest.

"I don't think he's gonna be waking up any time soon." Cherry shook her head, then turned back to me. "So? How about karaoke?"

"I'm down." I reached into my bra and dug out my cell phone. I rattled off my number to her, and a second later, a text came through with just a cherry emoji. Clever. I saved her info and tucked my phone away again.

"We'll have a good time," she promised, scanning the room. "Oh, for fuck's sake. Listen, I gotta go. I'll message you tomorrow. Sorry!" Cherry ran off, her tiny body making it entirely too easy for her to disappear completely. I assumed she saw something she wanted a piece of.

"New here?" A deep voice came from behind me, and I whipped around, feeling for my bunny blades I had strapped to my thigh. The man behind me was pretty damn tall and he felt moderately strong, magic-wise. Though I suspected in a place like this, a lot of people were shielding their true capabilities.

Stars, where are all of these big boys coming from lately? And what's with the fucking masks? About half of the people in this place were wearing some form of mask.

"You could say that," I responded, looking back out at the fights.

Only the guy's eyes were visible beneath his black, leather mask, which had an assortment of silver studs and spikes decorating nearly the entire thing. In the dim lighting, it was hard to tell much about him, other than that he had dark eyes. Even his hair was covered with a hoodie.

"New in town and you've already laid claim to The Exiled? That's impressive. Not an easy feat, considering the amount of pussy and cock they get thrown at them on the daily."

"Oh? What? Is your cock one of them? That why you're over here talking to me?" I bit out, feeling possessive for some reason, and really not appreciating this guy's tone.

He laughed, and it was full of gravel. His voice didn't sound like a natural one, more like the kind of voice you'd have after smoking heavily for thirty years. "They fuckin' wish but no, they're not my type."

I snorted and rolled my eyes. "Sure. I'm pretty sure they're everyone's type."

"I saw you walk in, and I've thought of nothing else since," he confessed, stepping forward and crowding me.

I stepped back. "Wow, I'm honored. I managed to keep your focus for a whole what? Hour and a half? Sorry, bud, but as you already know, I'm not on the market."

His eyes flashed with something dark, like his real self was being held back within the confines of his public persona, just waiting to bust out.

"And in ring six, we have a new fighter, taking on none other than the champ himself, Rhodes!"

I grinned at the guy as he glowered at me. "That's my cue. Gotta run. You have a nice night now." I turned on my heel and raced toward ring six. I felt those dark eyes on me the entire time. Whoever that dude was gave me the creeps, and not the creeps that got my panties a little wet—the kind of creeps that weren't so nice.

I ran right up to the ring, only to be caught around the waist by a fuming Misha. "Where the hell did you go?"

"Put me down, Misha," I growled, wiggling in a lame attempt to get away.

"And you're fighting him?" He sounded exasperated, like he was finally seeing me for the first time. A complete wild card that no man or beast would ever control.

"Sure am. Here's my phone." I pulled it out of my bra and shoved it in his face, forcing him to put me back on my feet. "Hold that for me while I whoop some ass, okay?"

I groaned when I heard my name being shouted by someone else. "Bun-Bun, do you have a death wish?" Talon reached me first, with his brother and Ashland on his heels. They all looked varying shades of pissed off.

"And you!" Ash roared, pointing a finger at Rhodes who was warming up in the ring. "Of all the possible opponents!"

"She is responsible for this, not me. So fuck all the way out of here if you think otherwise. I'd rather fight any other opponent, trust me on that," Rhodes spat with a sneer in my direction.

"Listen, baby, if you are hell-bent on fighting, we can find you a more evenly matched—"

I shoved my finger in Felix's face, cutting him off. "Just stop. All of you! Sit your asses down and shut up."

Ashland's eyes glittered with the promise of consequence for speaking to him like that, especially in front of all of these onlookers, but I was done. I never much liked being weak—being weak was what led to me not being able to save my family. That familiar feeling of shame and remorse started to spark in my chest. As hard as it was, I tried to not think of my parents often for this exact reason.

People had always told me that it would get easier with time. Time heals all wounds and all that shit. The only thing time had ever done for me was make it harder and harder for me to remember the sound of their voices telling me how much they loved me. How fucked was it that while those little whispered words of love faded, the sounds of their screams from that night got louder?

No. I'd never be weak again. Being weak had also led to me underestimating someone who I thought was— *Fuck. No. Not going there right now.* Point was, I wasn't weak, and even pretending to be made me feel sick to my stomach. People treated you differently when they thought you weren't capable.

I was capable. Of everything. I'd worked my gods damned ass off to be able to do absolutely anything I wanted. Maybe it made me egotistical that I wanted them to acknowledge my worth. They were badasses in their own right, but so was I. Maybe I'd even have a better shot at fully infiltrating them if they thought I was on their level.

Everyone sat down, except for Misha, who leaned down and put his mouth to my ear. "I told you not to wander off, *kukola*." I shivered at his words. "I'm already looking forward to making sure you don't do it again."

My eyes widened as he leaned back and stared down at me. He was probably going to use that big dick to teach me a lesson.

"Are we fighting or what? I'm bored." Rhodes's snarky voice pierced through my thoughts.

I rolled my neck, enjoying the crack that followed. I was going to enjoy every second of this.

"Let's do it, Monocle!" I called out, turning my back on the other four demons, who were staring at me like I'd just said my last words.

"Stop bloody calling me that. I don't even own one of those vile accessories."

I hopped up into the ring. "Mmhmm, sure. Can you even see properly when you're not wearing it?" I knew taunting him could be dangerous. If he fought better when he was enraged, it was definitely a shit decision, but sometimes I could rile my opposition enough to throw them off their game.

All I could do was hope that I hadn't made a huge mistake in challenging him.

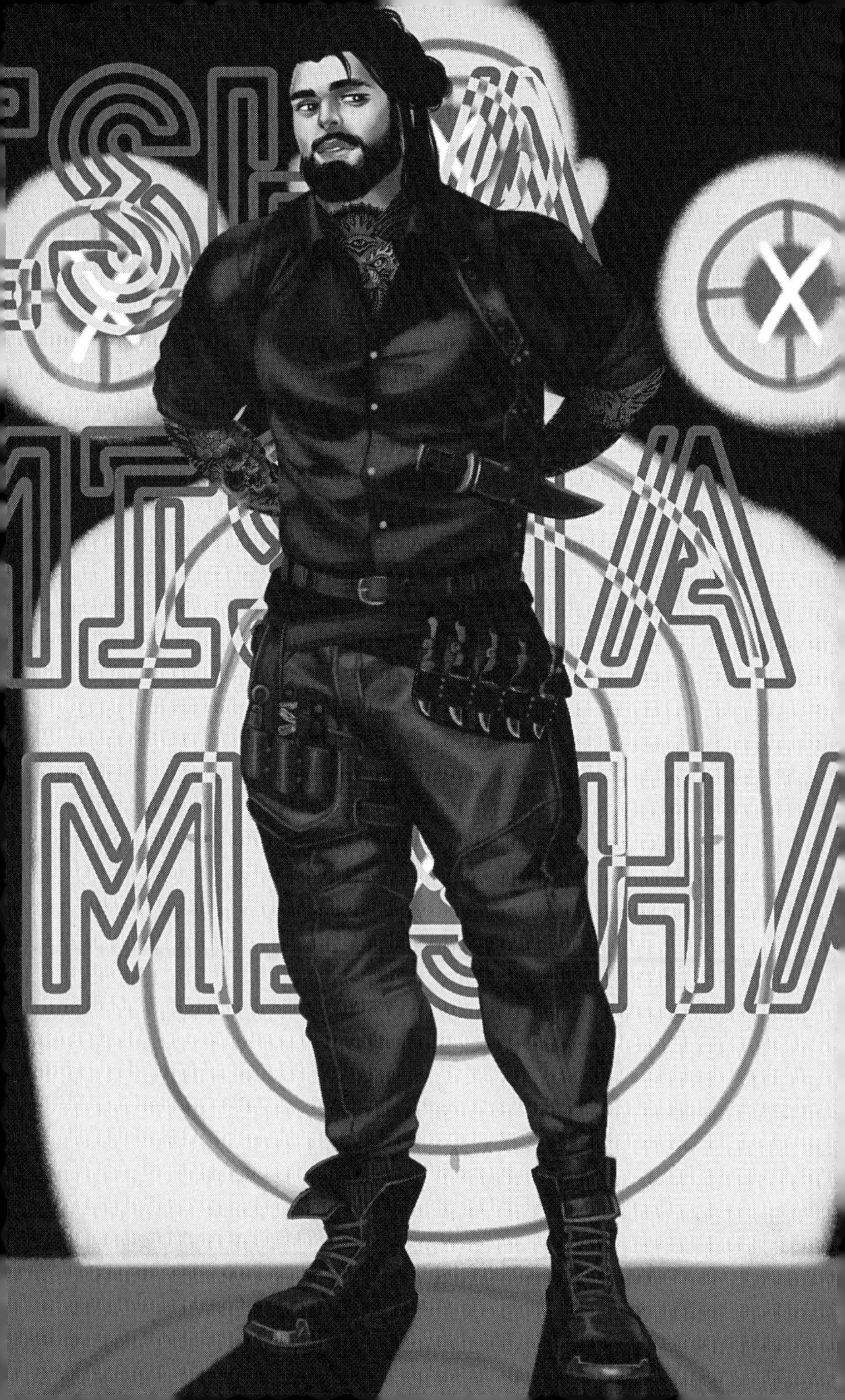

MISHA

Chapter Seventeen

I fisted my hands, trying to chill the fuck out. I was beyond pissed. After Palmer had kicked that chick's ass, I saw her talking to Rhodes, so I figured I would use that opportunity to do a little recon. It wasn't easy for me to go unnoticed, but the fact that I didn't speak a lot made people feel safer to talk with me in listening distance.

I wasn't deaf. Hell, I wasn't even mute. I just didn't see the point in talking to the majority of fucking idiots that plagued the realms.

It seemed I got lucky when a group of people from Scorpio's crew started talking about the group of members who went out the other night and didn't return. Standing against the wall, I pressed myself into the corner, letting the lighting hide me. Dark shadows fell over my body, making this the last place anyone would be looking. Especially with all the skin on display around the place... I made a mental note to get Palmer out of here before the night devolved into a massive orgy. It'd happened before. Scratch that—it happened every fucking time.

What did it matter though? Maybe she'd want to stay and fuck around. As soon as the thought crossed my mind, I pictured all of these fuckers eyeing her body as I bounced her on my cock, and a snarl built in my throat. Gods, she'd looked so sexy this morning, stuffed full of me. The way she'd fucking gripped me was one for the record books.

"I don't know, they're definitely up to something. Shipments aren't the usual shit."

That snapped me out of my flashback. My gaze locked on a young dude, probably sixteen at most. Fuckin' new bloods, always running their mouths. I stepped out from my dark corner, and the kid spotted me right away, his eyes getting comically large. I didn't say a word; I didn't have to. With my arms at my sides, I was able to just run my fingertips over the blades strapped to my thighs.

"Fuck," the kid cursed, all color draining from his face. His friends looked like they were seconds away from shitting themselves. Wouldn't surprise me in the least. Stranger things had happened.

I memorized his face, deciding I'd hunt him down later tonight when things were a little more chaotic. He'd think he was safe by then, and he'd probably be tipsy as fuck. Perfect.

Flashing a smile at him that was a thousand percent more demonic than human, I walked straight through their group toward him, as though I was going to flatten the little bitch. He actually let out a squeak, and at the last second, I side-stepped him, narrowly missing him.

I could hear their gasps of relief and shock over what had just happened, and I rolled my shoulders and cracked my neck. Sometimes it was too easy.

Making my way through the fray, I headed back to the bar, only to see that Palmer was no longer sitting where she'd been when I left. Rhodes, however, was pounding whiskey. That shit didn't even get us drunk. I stormed over to him, scanning the crowd in search of my little doll.

"Where is she?" I barked, jabbing him in the ribs.

"Ow, what the fuck?" He turned to me with an unreadable expression. "The crazy witch ran off somewhere. I'm not her fuckin' keeper."

My blood heated to boiling in the blink of an eye. "What did you just say?" I couldn't have stopped the growl in my voice if I tried.

As it was, I was having a time trying to keep my damn demon under control.

"She's crazy, Misha. I don't know how else to say it. I didn't trust her before, but she is honestly certifiable. She's fighting tonight—did you know that was her plan?" My brow furrowed, and Rhodes let out a sardonic laugh. "Oh yeah, and guess who she's going up against?" He lifted his whiskey and downed the entire thing.

"Over my dead body!" I boomed, scaring the people in our direct vicinity.

"Good luck convincing her otherwise. She wouldn't take no for an answer."

I got in his face. "You are not fighting her. You are not touching her."

"You know the rules, man. You get in the ring? You fight. I'll go easy on her, how about that?"

The urge to punch him in his handsome face was strong. So strong. But if I did and knocked him out—which I would—then a new opponent would be selected for Palmer. It could be anyone. And after she'd publicly claimed us, all the gangs knew she was ours. They'd love a chance to throw their best fighter in there to fuck with her. If that happened, this would be the last fight night because I would literally tear this place apart with my bare hands.

Looking out again, hoping to spot her, I saw something else interesting. Her friend from the other night was trying to break up some kind of altercation between a group of people before it got into illegal fight territory. Still no sign of Palmer. I was two seconds away from climbing up on the bar when the PA system came on, announcing Rhodes's fight.

He gave me a serious look and slapped a hundred down on the bar before saluting me and heading for the ring. I followed. "I'm fucking serious, Rhodes. Don't fuck with me."

He spun around, getting up in my space now with a sneer. "You're all so deep in this bitch's pussy you might as well live there. And *you* nearly knotted her!" he hissed at Talon, earning a snarl in response. "You all look like fucking fools, Misha. We're The Exiled.

We're not the kind of men who can be kept." His eyes trailed down my body and back up. "You know this. Why are you doing this to yourself? She isn't gonna stay."

His words were venomous, and I felt the poison hit me like a punch to the gut. "You don't know that," I replied lamely.

Rhodes laughed, shaking his head. "Don't I? She knows what we are," he whispered. "She won't stay. It'll end up being too much. We'll end up being too much."

I pinched the bridge of my nose. "You're wrong. She accepts me like this."

"Keep telling yourself that, big guy. At the end of the day, we have each other and that's it. Now, if you'll excuse me, I have a fight." The asshole walked away, looking like a god with the way people were carrying on about him. He might act like he didn't like the attention, but I knew his egotistical ass loved it.

A flash of dark hair caught my attention, and I spotted Palmer darting through the crowd, heading for the ring. *Oh, little doll, you've been such a bad, bad girl.*

She broke through the crowd and was one step away from launching herself up into the ring when I snatched her around the waist. My blood pounded in my ears, and I desperately tried to get control of myself. "Where the hell did you go?"

Palmer squirmed against me. "Put me down, Misha!" She was pissed, but so was I.

I glanced up to see Rhodes warming up, and I just cracked. "And you're fighting him?" This had to be an alternate universe or some kind of punishment for all the bitches I'd knifed over the years.

"Sure am. Here's my phone." She shoved it in my face, and I was forced to set her down. "Hold that for me while I whoop some ass, okay?" Where the hell had she been storing this thing?

That was when I heard Talon. Also pissed. Everyone was pissed. Ashland and Felix arrived with him, promptly turning their anger to Rhodes.

I blocked out their bickering. I had one concern and that was making sure that she didn't get squashed. Rhodes was an absolute beast in the ring, which was why every set of eyes was on us right this second.

Palmer barked at the others to sit down. Maybe I was included in that order, but like fuck that was happening. I crossed my arms and studied the dark-haired wildcat as she worked through whatever emotions were running through her. It was maybe the most expressive I'd ever seen her.

She paced back and forth, and when she reached me again, I took the opportunity to let her know she could act tough all she wanted, but there were going to be consequences for disobeying a rule and putting her safety in jeopardy. Leaning down, my lips barely brushed the shell of her ear. "I told you not to wander off, *kukola*. I'm already looking forward to making sure you don't do it again."

And I was seriously looking forward to it. For some reason, my little doll felt the need to prove herself right here, right now. Whether it was to herself or to us, I wasn't sure. She stared up at me, processing my double-edged threat. I loved how those deep blue orbs always managed to look surprised when something dirty was said to her.

She and Rhodes traded barbs as she hopped up into the ring, and I was impressed at her skill level when it came to shit talking. Palmer never should've shown up wearing bunny ears—something more aggressive was much better suited. Like a tiger or a bear.

"Can you believe this?" Ashland grunted, joining me by the ring.

I made some kind of noise in response.

"I want to fucking whoop both of their asses for this stunt. I'm barely containing myself, Mish. What the hell is happening to me? I've never had control issues!"

Queenie P started belting out the rules to the crowd, who was surging like a pulsing wave of energy. "There's only two rules! No magic and no fuckin' weapons!"

Palmer held up a finger to Rhodes, signaling she needed a second before bouncing over to where Ashland and I stood. "Almost forgot I had these on me. Keep 'em safe?" She produced the bunny daggers I'd made for her and handed them over with a grin full of mischief. Before either of us could respond, she was gone, back to circling Rhodes like she was the viper and he was the mouse.

Moments later, the bell dinged. It felt like every soul in the building took a deep breath.

Ash reached up and gripped the rope, flexing his forearms. "She makes me crazy."

I felt for him, because I was starting to feel the exact same way. I watched with whatever I had left of a heart in my throat as the two circled each other.

"Look, little one, how about I just stand here and you can take a few free swings? Then I'll put you in a chokehold until you blackout, and we'll call it a day?" Rhodes offered, keeping his eyes locked on the little fireball who was clearly ready to detonate.

The crowd was a ball of anxiety. Word had no doubt spread that this was the woman who had claimed The Exiled for her own, and with the way the rumor mill worked, no doubt the story was that she'd killed Steph behind that bar.

"Anyone ever tell you you're a prick?" Palmer fired back, riling the masses even further.

Rhodes laughed and bounced on his toes. "Just that I have a big one, little girl. Quit fuckin' around and fight me. You were so eager before."

Ashland and I both watched as a transformation settled over Palmer. Her face lost all traces of what made her her. She became expressionless, except for the fire in her eyes as she stared down Rhodes.

"Oh shit," Tal murmured, as he and Felix joined us. "She's got that crazy look."

Rhodes lost his patience first and darted forward, throwing a punch. Palmer spun, easily dodging him, but he hadn't been really trying. More of a warmup. He came for her again, and this time she held her ground, waiting until he struck out. She ducked, landing a punch to his stomach.

"Oh damn," Felix murmured, leaning in closer. "I didn't expect her to land a single hit."

Judging from the look on Rhodes's face, neither had he. Recovering quickly, he plastered a grin on his face. "You know how to fight, little one? That's a decent right hook, but you'll have to do better than that."

She only smirked before making her move. Her fists flew, and it was all Rhodes could do to block her relentless blows. She faked him out, spinning to the right and kicking out with her left leg, landing another hit. A solid kick to the back, knocking him forward, right above us.

"What the fuck?" he growled at us, accusation flaring in his eyes, like we'd known she could fight like a ninja. Palmer was walking around, waving her hands, pumping up the crowd. Rhodes was still glaring at us when she launched into a roundoff, back handspring, crossing the mat in record time. As soon as her feet hit the mat, she twisted and pounced on his back, scaling him like he was the oak tree in a childhood backyard.

He snarled, grabbing her calves and forcefully throwing her backward. I held my breath, but she somehow pulled it together, doing a back tuck and landing on her feet. Rhodes dropped low and spun his leg out, sweeping her right off her feet. She was prepared for that too, catching herself easily before she faceplanted.

She rolled onto her back just as Rhodes bent down, reaching for her. Her fist flew up, popping him right in the mouth. I side-eyed Ashland, whose jaw had dropped so low, he could've deep-throated an orc cock.

Rhodes brought his hand to his mouth, and when he brought it forward, there it was. First blood. The little doll had drawn first fucking blood. The two of them were on their feet now, staring absolute fire at one another.

"How's the lip feel?" she taunted.

He was done going easy. Using a burst of his enhanced speed—which was technically against the rules—he quickly landed a hit.

"You motherfucker," Palmer cursed, spitting a wad of blood out of the ring onto the floor. She grinned though, showing off her bloody smile, and I groaned.

"Fuck me, that's hot," Ash gritted out, eyeing our girl hungrily.

"How's the lip?" Rhodes mocked, winking at her.

Then, all hell broke loose. For two minutes straight, they threw everything they had at each other. Both of them were covered in blood and bruises. It made no sense; the type of fighting skills she had weren't learned in some backyard brawl. This was professional-level fighting, and I realized she should have fought us much harder than she had that night in the maze.

They were stumbling around now, both exhausted beyond what was productive. They swung at the same time, neither one bothering to block the incoming hit. Probably because they were too fucking tired. Their punches landed at the same time, knocking both of them stupid.

"Fucking idiots," Ash rumbled, white-knuckling the rope now.

At least they were both finally on the fucking floor, and the ref could count it down.

"Both of you better stay the fuck down or so help me," Ash barked at the two panting fools in the ring. Palmer whimpered and rolled onto her side, which drew a strangled sound from Ash's throat. "I can't be in here. I'm two seconds away from shifting. I need some air. Get them into a car and get home."

Felix was practically vibrating as he stared at the blood everywhere. Usually, it only really bothered him if it was on his body, but it always hit differently when it was people you cared about who were bloodied.

"Tal, why don't you and Felix ride back on the bike?" I asked, working through a plan of action in my mind.

He nodded. "Yeah, you can carry them out and ride in the SUV with Ash. Good plan." Talon tapped Felix on the shoulder, snapping him out of his daze. "Let's go, bro. We can get some first aid shit set up for when they get home."

Felix's face was so pale, I was concerned he was going to pass out.

"Hey, Lixy!" Talon slapped him, getting him out of his head. I literally saw the moment his brain came back online.

"The fuck, man?"

"Let's go. We need to set up at home so we can play doctor tonight." Talon clapped his brother on the shoulder and then walked away, heading outside. Felix tossed one more look back at Rhodes and Palmer, wincing at the state of them.

"See ya in a bit, Mishy," he said, giving a half-assed wave as he followed Talon.

"And it's a tie tonight between these two! Who would've thought the woman who captured his heart could also knock him on his ass?" Queen Prissy chuckled into the microphone, earning plenty of laughs from the crowd.

I stepped up onto the platform and swung my leg over the ropes. Staring down at them, I shook my head. Palmer though, crazy ass that she was, cracked a smile that was stained red. She really looked like she'd gone ten rounds with the devil and ended up winning the right to sit on the throne.

"How'd you like that, Mishy Bear?" she slurred, barely able to talk. Whether that was from swelling in her mouth or a head injury, who could say? Probably both.

"You're a liar," Rhodes breathed, holding his ribs as he sat up.

She laughed and then groaned. "And you're a little, baby, monocle bitch who just got his ass beat by a woman."

"Enough." My tone was dark and final. I was annoyed with both of them, putting on this bullshit fight—it showed discord between our crew. I didn't like it at all. I bent down and scooped Palmer off the mat like roadkill. "I'm taking her out to the car. I'll be back for you."

"Fuck that. I can walk myself," Rhodes replied, pushing himself to his feet and swaying. I wasn't going to argue with the stubborn bastard.

"If he can walk, I can walk too," Palmer challenged, wiggling in my arms.

My demon woke up, zeroing in on Palmer. I needed her to shut the fuck up. Breathing hard, I left the ring, ignoring the shouts from the crowd. "I swear to all that's cosmic, *kukola*... If you don't stop moving and shut your mouth, I will turn that ass redder than the seventh circle of hell and then stretch it out with my hand."

I didn't look down. I couldn't see her face right now. All I knew is she'd stopped moving and didn't say another word. *Good.*

We busted out of the barn into the cool night air, and I sucked in a deep breath, not slowing as I stomped over to the SUV.

"Put her in the backseat," Ash ordered, opening the door for me. "Where's Rhodes?"

"Coming." I slid her as gently as I could into the vehicle, but she still cried out. I didn't like the sharp feeling it gave me in my chest. Maybe I was having a heart attack. No, impossible. Demons never had heart attacks. Though other demons didn't have a fucking Palmer to deal with.

I was steaming now, I was so pissed off. Honestly, I wasn't even sure what it was that had me so mad. The fact that we'd looked like idiots? Nah, I didn't really give a fuck what anyone thought about us.

"Here, ride up front," Ash told Rhodes, who had just limped his way over to us. He helped him get in the car and then shut the doors, turning to me. "You want to drive or sit in the back?"

I clenched my jaw. "Can't get in there. Meet you at home in a bit."

"Misha," Ash warned, and I snarled.

"You don't want me in there. I said I will meet you at home," I repeated, hoping that he'd let it drop. I was at my max right now and needed to blow off some steam before I could think straight.

"Alright, alright," he acquiesced. "Just be careful."

I grunted and slipped through the dark field of cars like a phantom. The woods were calling my name, and that's precisely where I was going.

Seeing Rhodes and Palmer both bloodied and beaten had done something to me. It had been a fucking long time since I'd seen Rhodes looking anything less than perfect, and it was that little witch who had stomped him. Incredible. And concerning.

As I passed by car after car—several of which that were shaking, thanks to the people fucking inside of them—the urge to destroy shit rose up within me until it was all I could think about. My muscles were coiled, ready to strike, and I needed to completely exhaust myself before even thinking about returning to Haunt.

Finally, the tree line came into view. Twigs crunched beneath my boots as I approached the woods. I could already hear the scampering of animals through the brush as they scattered, sensing the incoming predator. Night had fallen long ago, and it was increasingly darker within the cover of the trees.

My horns were done waiting, and they sprouted, making me growl. It always felt like such a relief to let my natural form come out. About a quarter of a mile into the forest, I spotted a fallen tree that would be perfect for what I needed. Luckily, it had snapped in half so there was a section that was about three feet long. Grunting, I hoisted the tree trunk over my head, loving the strain against my muscles. With a burst of power, I launched it through the forest, narrowly missing other trees.

Learning to control my anger was something I'd struggled with for most of my life. I suppressed a roar that wanted to escape when I thought about the two men who were responsible for my anger issues. Ironically, one of them had taught me control. For the longest time, I'd thought I had someone in my corner. Someone who actually gave a fuck, but in the end I was wrong.

It had been several years since King Thane's soldiers came to retrieve me from my father's house. They came back for me four years after that first visit. Four years since that day my father locked me in the cellar as punishment. Four years I had to endure his increasing abuse for ruining his life.

He was beyond livid when the soldiers finally returned and were only interested in taking me back to the capital of Besmet, Naryian.

I laughed to myself every time I thought about how enraged he'd been, the way he'd lashed out at the soldiers and looked like a complete fool. If I was a better blacksmith than him at age ten, then I was like a fucking master at age eighteen. Not to mention, when my powers had shown themselves a few years back, I'd made it my personal mission to use my father as a test subject as often as possible.

Sleep walkers were rare, which just added to my value for the monarchy. Not only could I create the most lethal and lightweight blades in the realm, I could also slip into dreamscapes and fuck with people's realities. Since then, I not only created weapons, I became one.

I was in my workshop on the castle grounds, enjoying the peace and quiet of a cool summer morning, when he showed up. Stumbling in through the wooden Dutch door, he tripped over a bucket I kept by the door for trash. All I saw was a flash of red hair, and I hopped up off my stool, catching the person before they hit the ground. Or worse, my tools.

"Fucking hell, I'm sorry. Didn't see that bucket there and—"

I wasn't listening. I was too busy staring down at the man I'd caught. He'd thrown his hand over his eyes, clearly embarrassed. I could see his pale skin and the freckles that dotted his face. Slowly, he separated his fingers and peeked out at me with one strikingly blue eye.

"Well, they certainly know how to feed the boys around here, don't they?" he muttered, dropping his hand and righting himself so he could stand on his own. I was still staring at him like a dumbstruck idiot; I couldn't seem to stop myself.

He was just so... pretty. I'd never seen a man look anything less than rugged and rough. This one was almost feminine with his soft facial features, the high cheekbones, and slightly slanted eyes. His long, red hair fell in waves well past his shoulders.

"I didn't uh, hurt you, did I?" he asked shyly, biting his bottom lip. My eyes zeroed in on that point of contact. What would it feel like to bite his lip like that? "Well, um, I really am sorry. You look kind of pissed off, so I'll just fuck off."

He turned and walked a few steps before I snapped out of my little episode. I caught up with him easily, reaching for his arm. He gasped when I gripped his bicep and turned to face me again.

"Look, I might be smaller than you, but I bet I'm faster than you. If you try to beat me up, I will poke you right in the eyes, mark my words."

Not sure what I was expecting him to say, but it wasn't that. For the first time in years, I laughed out loud. It sounded atrocious. Like I had glass in my throat or I was a dying cat. Not to mention it startled me so fucking bad, I clapped a hand over my mouth in shock, silencing the horrid noise.

As much as I thought I was over my past, the fear that had been instilled in me for years sprang to life. My laugh served as a spark to start the wildfire of my PTSD.

My ass hit the floor first, and the next thing I knew, I was covering my head with my arms and trying to make myself as small as possible—which, given my size, was a fucking joke.

"Hey, hey," the guy whispered. "What's wrong? I'm not going to hurt you."

In my panicked state, I saw his feet come closer, and it helped me process where I was—because he was barefoot. My father never wore anything other than boots and he hated being barefoot. It wasn't him. I wasn't there anymore.

"Sometimes my brother has panic attacks. It can be scary, I know. Just focus on breathing in through your nose and out of your mouth. Here, do it with me." He crouched down and locked those blue eyes on mine, and I found myself trying to match his breaths. "Good job, man. Now I'm going to be really pissed off if you come out of this shit and try to beat my ass. I mean, I can be really petty, just warning you. I also hold a serious grudge. We just got here yesterday, so I'm still getting used to the layout which is how I ended up barging in here."

Good grief, he talked a lot. Like, a lot a lot. At some point during his ramblings, the panic receded and I felt like myself again.

"Wow, you look so much better. Scary shit, right? I always feel bad for my brother when he gets one, but I try to be supportive and not make it worse. He's got an issue with germs and shit. Not like actual shit, I mean, ya know—not feces. Well, come to think of it, he probably does have a problem with legit shit." He stared off into the distance, deep in thought.

How does a man look so pretty? *My brain had been scrambled in a matter of minutes, thanks to this guy.*

He snapped his head back to me. "You don't talk much, do you?" He tilted his head to the side and waited. I shook my head. "Do you talk at all?" I shook my head. "Damn, okay, this is making more sense now. That laugh from before—did it hurt or scare you or something?"

I shrugged and pushed myself to my feet. I was done talking or thinking about that little slip-up. I had work to do, and some red-headed chatterbox wasn't going to throw me off.

Turning my back on him, I got back to my tasks. I was just about to bring my hammer down on the iron I was working with when he hopped up on my fucking countertop. I froze, the hammer in midair, and slowly turned to look at him. His legs were swinging back and forth, like he didn't have a care in the world.

"Blacksmith, huh? So you mainly make weapons? Doesn't that ever get"—he paused and wiggled his eyebrows—"dull?" I blinked. He threw his head back and laughed like hell. "Get it?"

Was he crazy? He might be. Just what I needed in my life, more crazy people.

"Is that how your muscles got so big? You swing that hammer around all hours of the day and night?"

Glancing over, I found his eyes scanning my body. Heat raced up my neck. I was a big guy, I always had been. Catching the attention of girls was never a problem, it was dealing with the punk ass boys who liked to tease me for not talking that usually caused any potential relationships to fizzle out.

Was he making fun of me? It was kind of pathetic that I couldn't tell.

"You must be swinging something around to be built like that." He whistled, then winked at me. That heat that was spreading up my neck had reached my face now, and I knew he could see it. "Oh my stars, I never introduced myself. I'm Talon. I'd ask what your name is, but I know you won't answer. Oh, I know! Maybe you can spell it on my hand. Like, with your finger?" He thrust his hand out and batted his eyelids.

Fuck. Okay. I put down the hammer and held onto his wrist. He wasn't pulling away in disgust so maybe he really did want to know my name. Swallowing roughly, I took my index finger and wrote an M.

"M?" he guessed, and I nodded, moving on to the next letter. He got them all right, and after I finished writing out the name, he grinned. "Misha," he whooped triumphantly, and I ignored the way my heart picked up speed as I watched his excitement. "I love your name. It's very you. Badass and unique—fits you perfectly."

That might have been the nicest thing anyone had ever said to me that wasn't directly pertaining to my work as a blacksmith.

"Talon?!" a deep voice called from somewhere outside of my shop.

He slid off the counter and brushed off his ass. "I have to go. Thanks for the fun."

Go? Where was he going? Was he... leaving? Absolutely not.

"I'll come see you tomorrow? Same time? We're here for the foreseeable future, so it looks like you're stuck with me for a bit." Talon smiled and skipped to the door. He turned back at the last moment, hesitating a second. My brow furrowed, because he didn't strike me as the kind of person to censor his words. "Your laugh... It's pretty great. Anyway, see you tomorrow."

Then he slipped out of the door, leaving me in a state of total fucking chaos.

Talon became my first friend in that moment, and he didn't even know how much he boosted my confidence with one conversation. That was Tal, though. He had big feelings and he loved hard.

A few hours after that, Asrael came out to the shop to check on my progress with some new blades. He took the opportunity to talk about the new brothers who'd arrived and how he wasn't convinced they were worth shit. They seemed weak and soft. They needed to prove themselves.

Asrael was one of those people who felt comfortable spewing whatever was in his brain at that moment, knowing I wouldn't repeat it. He looked over my work and gave me a smile. "These look fantastic, Misha."

His compliments always made me feel really good about myself. After so many years of being told I was a fuckup, any sort of positive feedback was almost like a drug to me.

"How's the anger been since we last trained? Are you feeling less on edge with regular sessions? It's important that you don't let your emotions rule you."

I sighed. It wasn't that the training wasn't helping. It really was, but there were times that my anger got the best of me and no amount of tiring myself out or fighting was going to stop it. When that happened, it was best to just get the fuck out of my way and let me rage.

"Well, I noticed that there haven't been any more trees ripped out by the roots, so I'd say we're making progress."

I grunted, not convinced, but Asrael had been the only constant source of positivity in my life. I found that I really didn't want to let him down.

"You're doing great, Misha. You have so much going for you and it's all right in here." He poked my chest. "I believe in you—you know that, right?"

I nodded, because I'd never believed anything with such conviction in my life. He was the only one who had ever believed in me.

"Good, that's good. Come, let's practice, I want to try some new techniques..."

The castle grounds faded from my sight, and the dark woods came back into view. I shouldn't have been surprised to see three trees lying on the forest floor, their trunks shattered. I was breathing heavily, and when I looked down, a small slice of moonlight cut through the clouds, showing me that my knuckles were wrecked and bloodied.

A twig snapped, and I spun around, snarling. My tail flicked in warning as my muscles coiled, ready to fucking strike. Silence greeted me, and I was just about to chalk the whole thing up to an animal when I heard an 'oomph.'

In a flash, I pulled my wings, tail, and horns in, darting through the forest in the direction of the sound I'd heard. I could hear their heartbeat now, practically taste their fear.

There, just ahead, was a person sprinting back toward the barn, but they weren't going to make it. I was on them before they knew it, slamming into them and taking us both down to the ground.

"Please don't kill me, oh my fuck. Oh please!"

I slammed my hand over the idiot's mouth and got a look at their face. A slow grin took over as I realized it was that teen from earlier. The one who'd been talking shit—this little prick had the balls to try and spy on me?

"Be. Quiet," I whispered. "Or I'll gut you right here."

The kid's eyes widened, but he nodded. I removed my hand, staring down at him. What the fuck was I going to do with him? Kill him? Ugh, he was just a kid... but I couldn't really let him go back. Not when I knew he'd seen me.

"Look man, I didn't see shit."

I raised a brow. He'd just admitted that he did, in fact, see shit.

"I'll just... go. Yeah? I think that would be good for both of us." He got to his feet and actually started inching away.

Nah, this wasn't going to work. But I knew he was one of Scorpio's recruits, and he clearly knew something about us from what I'd overheard. Sighing, I wiped my palms down my shirt. Clearly, the kid was coming with me.

"Please don't punch me. I'm not built like those trees and they never even did shit to you!" I advanced on him, and he stumbled back over a branch. "Oh gods, my body would just explode like a water balloon if you hit me that hard. You know that, right? Fuck, of course you do, you're The fucking Carver!"

Rolling my eyes, I grabbed him by the back of his shirt, gripping his upper arm with my other hand. I pictured Haunt in my head—the basement, to be precise—and let the sensation of jumping take over my body. We didn't get to use this power nearly as often as I'd like since we were banished to this realm, and it always gave me a rush using it after a while.

It was as if our bodies were pulled into a black void, swirling colors speeding past as we fell at what felt like supersonic speed. The kid was screaming, and I was worried he'd piss himself. I didn't know if anyone had ever done that in the void before... What would happen to the liquid?

A second later, we landed in my office in the basement of Haunt, and I grabbed the trash can beneath my desk, shoving it under the kid's face. Just in time too, because he lost his dinner immediately.

"What the fuck are you? Where are we?" His eyes were wide as he looked around, wiping his mouth with the sleeve of his shirt. Gross. Fucking teenagers.

I headed for the door, pulling the kid along behind me. We had holding cells for these kinds of situations—that's where he was going to have to wait for now. The lights were motion-sensored, so they kicked on as we walked deeper into the basement. It was mostly long hallways and concrete floors on this side, with the maze being on the opposite side.

I came to a stop in front of a metal door, and the kid broke out in tears. "Please, I'm too young to die."

The door creaked as I pulled it open, revealing a pretty gods damned nice little cell, if I was being perfectly honest. All the times I'd ever been held in a cell, they were never anywhere close to this nice. It was something I'd insisted on when we built this place.

The people we put in these cells were kind of in Exiled limbo. Not totally bad, not totally good. Therefore, it didn't sit right with me to not treat them somewhat humanely. However, if someone ever fucked me over to the point that I'd want to throw away the key, I'd rather just torture them for a few hours, get my rocks off, and then kill their ass. I saw no point in letting traitors or scumbags breathe the same air as me or my boys.

"Get in," I barked, shoving the kid's shoulder. "I'll be back later." I shut the door, blocking out his pounding as I made my way over to the elevator. His screams were muted, thanks to soundproofing. Thank fuck. Little punk was probably screaming his ass off in there.

There were more important matters to deal with right now. Mainly, the woman who was upstairs at this very moment, bleeding all over our apartment. For the first time in a very long time, I was a little concerned about my temper.

Studying my hands that were cut to shit, I waited for the elevator. A ding alerted me that my ride had finally arrived, and I stomped inside, scanning my palm and hitting the button for our floor.

Leaning my head back against the wall, I closed my eyes and sent up a wish to the fucking stars, the gods, the freaking wizards that be, whoever was listening, that nobody pushed me. That I'd be able to regain my control I'd worked so hard for, because nobody—and I did mean nobody, in this fucking realm or any other—could handle me when I went berserk.

TALON

TALON

Chapter Eighteen

"Lixy! We'll need more bandaids and I don't know, those stretchy fabric things!" I yelled up the steps, hoping he could hear me. I'd sent him to raid the medicine cabinets the second we got back. We were easily the first ones here, and adrenaline was riding my ass hard.

Sweat was beading on my forehead, but the last thing I needed was to drip-drop into my poor Bun-Bun's wounds. I had the perfect fix though. I sprinted through the house, heading for the kitchen. Every house I'd ever been in had a junk drawer in the kitchen, and this place was no exception. There was no shortage of treasures hidden in this little hidey-hole.

"Ope. Shit." I cursed when I pulled the drawer a little too hard, and some batteries and rogue paperclips went flying onto the floor. "Where are you, you absorbent circular contrap— AHA!" I pulled the sweatband out and held it triumphantly in the air. Neon blue was going to look bitchin' with my eyes and complexion.

I slipped that baby on and was about to reach for my phone to get an ETA from the others when I felt eyes on me.

"What the fuck?" I spun around and came face to face with none other than Viper. The reptile squirrel. His little beady eye slowly looked up and eyed my sweatband. "Look, Scales, this one is mine.

There might be a wristband or something in that drawer but that's up to you, bro."

He chittered at me and flexed his little creepy fingers.

"I usually draw the line at harming animals, but this was my brilliant idea and I will straight fuck a bitch up if you think you're getting it."

The poser snake blinked his one eye. Or at least, I think he would have, if he had an eyelid to go with his eye. But alas, he didn't, so suddenly I was locked in a staring contest with a woodland creature who probably didn't even get dry eyes!

"Why do we have to do this right now, Python? I'm a terrible loser. In fact, I refuse to lose." My eyes were already starting to feel like someone had thrown sand in them, but I stuck it out. "Oh my gods, can you just look away? I feel like this is a challenge or something and I don't like it." I threw my hands down on the counter, but the fucker didn't even flinch. Lowering my voice, I leaned in. "Listen, I don't want to kill you, but you're the one making the decisions here. It's up to you, man. You have three seconds to look away or it's game over."

His tail pulsed. What did that mean? Hysteria was rising in my body now, and I didn't know if Bun-Bun would ever forgive me for killing this insanely alpha squirrel.

"I have a tail too, motherfucker. It's bigger than yours, just so you know. How about you give up and I'll show you?"

Nothing. I waited another two seconds for good measure, then launched myself at that arrogant little nut-muncher.

"Talon?"

I was sprawled out on the countertop looking like the snack I was, so I rolled onto my side and propped my head up on my hand. "Oh, hey. Didn't see you there, big guy. Been here long?" I fluttered my eyelashes and immediately winced. My eyes were now so dry, they felt like pearls that had been lying in the sandy ocean for years.

The sound of little tiny nails, belonging to quite possibly the most entitled creature in all the realms, scurried softly along the tops of the cabinets. *I can hear you, motherfucker. This isn't over.*

"Are they here?" Misha demanded, ignoring my sexual posing completely.

Pouting, I sat up and shook my head. "Not yet. Should be anytime. I've been waiting for the call. He'll need help getting them up here, right?"

Misha opened the fridge and pulled out a bottle of water. As he tipped it back, quickly draining it, I noticed his hands.

"Misha!" I gasped, hopping down and rushing over to him. He tried to pull his hands away from me, but that wasn't happening. "What the hell?" Anger blanketed me completely in the time it took me to see that his knuckles were destroyed. Blood was drying all the way down to his elbows. "Who the fuck am I killing tonight? Give me a name, big guy."

Misha's shoulders seemed to drop, which confused me. Clearly, he could handle himself, but I would always have his back.

"Hey, what's wrong, Mish?"

Usually, fighting got him riled up. Carving someone up was like a bloody Viagra for my big boy. Something was off.

"It was me, Birdie." He pulled away and turned on the water in the sink. My heart swelled at the nickname; it had been a while since I'd heard it. He always fell back on it when he was feeling vulnerable.

Sliding up behind him, I wrapped my arms around his waist. "What was, Mishy?"

"I did this to myself."

Oh. Oh fuck.

"Are you okay?"

"I haven't lost control in years, but tonight, I fucking blacked out in a rage. Maybe I need to be—"

I cut him off, ending that line of thinking right the fuck now. "Absolutely not, and don't bring that up again. I know it's hard for you sometimes, because you think you need to be perfect all the damn time. That's how you grew up and it's been so hard to break free of those unattainable expectations. Nobody here—and I mean fucking *nobody*—expects you to be perfect. Or for you to be in control all the gods damned time, Mishy. It's not possible."

He sucked in a deep breath, and I could feel the pounding of his heart. Seeing Mishy sad always hit me like a bullet straight to the heart.

"It'll be okay. You're okay now, right?" I asked, rubbing my hands up and down his stomach, trying to distract him.

"Yeah," he grunted, shutting the water off.

My phone started ringing a second later, ending our conversation. For now.

"You here? Yeah, okay. See you in a few." I hung up just as Felix came into the kitchen. "Ash is here with the others. There were some guys downstairs, so they're going to help Rhodes get up here. Ash has Palmer."

Felix dumped everything in his arms onto the kitchen island, and we got to work organizing our supplies. Then the elevator dinged, and we all took a collective breath. What a shit show.

"I'll go see if they need anything," Felix suggested, rushing off.

Misha was about to follow but I grabbed his wrist. "Come here, you brute." I pushed him down onto a stool and began cleaning his hand. I'd wrap it after I got it clean. "Remember when I used to do this in your shop?" I asked, recalling how we'd be in this exact position.

He snorted in response, not flinching as I began dabbing at his knuckles with a washcloth. "How could I forget your bossy attitude?"

"You needed to be bossed around! At the rate you were going, you were going to end up fatally wounding yourself." I finished up the cleaning and spread some ointment over the cuts. Some were fairly deep, but thankfully we healed quicker than humans.

"Why now, Birdie?" Misha asked, his voice so low I almost didn't hear him.

I carefully wrapped bandages around his hands and then looked at my best friend. "I don't know. I think we're all on edge because we're making progress, ya know? We're so close to finishing it. Plus, it's been what? Ten years since we were in Besmet? We knew this was coming at some point."

Demons could exist outside of Besmet, though most chose to stay in our own realm. It was more comfortable for us to be in our natural forms, which we didn't have to hide there. Demons weren't exposed to humans in Besmet, only mages and witches, and we liked it that way. For a lot of demons, it was easy enough to travel back and forth between the realms, if one decided to stay here longer.

We didn't have that luxury. We physically couldn't return to Besmet.

It was also common knowledge that the longer a demon stayed away from Besmet, the greater the risk of complications arising. That's when companies like Radical Incorporation and Montague Industries stepped in. When a demon was tagged as being rogue or feral, they were taken into custody or eliminated.

"I'm surprised we made it this long, Mishy. It just means we need to work harder and finalize this gas. There's only a few more tweaks—we're so close."

He didn't look convinced, and I didn't have time to work harder at it because right then, Ash came storming in and laid a completely limp Palmer down on the kitchen island.

"What the fuck?" Misha snarled, standing so fast his stool fell backward. "She was talking when I left. Now she's unconscious?"

Ash started stripping off her clothes, revealing dark bruises and some terrible-looking patches of raw skin. Felix and Rhodes came around the corner next, Rhodes looking almost as shitty as my Bun-Bun.

"Why isn't she waking up?" Ash's eyes were panicked as they landed on Misha. "Can you reach her?" With a firm nod and a grumble, Mish snatched his toppled stool and straightened it, taking a seat and letting his own eyes close.

"What the hell were you thinking?" Felix snapped at Rhodes, pushing him down on the stool furthest away from Misha. Probably wise.

"She wanted that fight. As you can see, your little princess isn't as much of a helpless girl as you all like to make her out to be," Rhodes barked, grabbing a few towels and wiping his face. His lip was split and swollen twice its normal size, so he sounded even douchier than normal. "Wouldn't take no for an answer."

Ash growled, running his hands gently down her torso. "You didn't have to fuck her up this badly."

"Do you not see how I fucking look?!" Rhodes roared, blessing all of us with his horns and wings.

"Don't hurt yourself, old man. Sit the fuck down," I chided, flipping him off when he snapped his teeth at me.

Palmer whimpered, and I planted myself at her head, letting my fingers slip through her hair. She had a nasty cut along her hairline, which looked like it could use some stitches.

"I'll be fine, thanks for asking. While I'm showering though, maybe think about why this woman can fight at that level and chose to hide it from us." Rhodes limped out of the kitchen like a pissed-off cat, and Felix looked torn. I could tell he was upset by the way his shoulders were bunched up, as well as the pinched expression on his face.

"Lixy, can you gather up some clean clothes for her?" Ash stared down at the girl who had taken over our fucking heads. "I'll carry her upstairs in a few minutes."

"Yeah. Of course. Is she going to be okay?" Felix asked softly, like he was scared of the answer. I didn't blame him.

"She fucking better be," Ash growled like the devil himself.

My brother left to complete his task, and I sighed, wrapping my arms around Ashland. Poor guy tended to get bent out of shape when it came to injuries involving one of us. It wasn't pleasant, but I wasn't going to be a little whiny grump about it either.

"She's probably just exhausted," I assured him. "She fought like she was a demon herself—did you not see that shit? It was epic." And it was. I'd never seen another female fighter as talented.

"And what about Rhodes's theories? Why did she hide it?" Ash asked quietly.

I let him go and shrugged. "Aren't we all hiding things? Have we known her long enough to be demanding all of her truths? What if she wanted the same from us?"

He was quiet, staring down at our girl. "Let's just hope this was the biggest secret she has. She already knows our biggest one."

"What? That we're demons? Nah, that's just our biggest secret from society. It's different from our own personal secrets."

Suddenly, Misha's eyes flew open and he reached out for Palmer, grabbing her just as her eyes flew open and a scream tore out of her body that was so awful, it hurt my bones.

"Shh, *kukola*, shhh. You're safe. You're safe." Ashland and I stared at each other with matching serious expressions while Misha stroked Palmer's hair.

Swift footfalls alerted us that Felix was incoming, likely having heard that horrible noise she'd made. "What the fuck is happening?!" he bellowed, sliding into the kitchen in only basketball shorts, aside from his leathery black wings.

"I'm not exactly sure," Ash said slowly, eyeing Misha and Palmer.

That seemed to snap her out of whatever mental episode she was having, because she pushed away from Misha and sat up with a groan. "I'm fine. Bad dream." She chuckled, then winced in pain. Misha looked like he was clenching his jaw so hard, he was in danger of breaking his teeth. "Wow, I feel like I got hit by a truck."

"Are you serious right now, love? That's all you have to say?" Ash crossed his arms and leaned against the counter, staring her down.

Felix came closer and stood before her. "You're hurt, babe. Let them look at your injuries. You were fucking unconscious."

She waved her hand. "No, I was just sleeping. I think you're all blowing this out of proportion."

Hmm. Now I was getting a teensy bit pissed. Misha audibly scoffed. Our Bun-Bun had no idea how thin the ice was, and she was stomping around without giving a thought to the danger.

"Sleeping, she says," Ashland mocked. "Pull up your shirt and look at your bruising. You have a gash along your hairline that needs stitching, for fuck's sake. Blowing it out of proportion, my fucking ass."

She lifted her shirt and patted her flat tummy. "Looks fine to me." We all looked. There was very minimal bruising, and it appeared to be lightening up with each passing second. "Thanks for getting me back here safely. As you can see, I'm good. I just need a shower and bed."

The little bitch actually slid off the island and then stretched, reaching her arms up as high as they could go. I watched as her eyes caught a glimpse of something in Misha's front pocket, and she reached out to snatch her bunny blades, sighing contentedly.

We all eyed each other for a second, then everyone moved. Palmer screeched as Ashland grabbed her, locking her arms against her torso. Kicking, she tried to headbutt him. She might have been able to fight like a demon, but she wasn't strong like one.

"What the hell are you *doing?*" she demanded, turning her fiery stare on me as Misha wrestled the blades from her pinned hand.

"What are *we* doing? Listen, Bun-Bun, I'm not sure if you cracked your head too hard in that ring tonight, but you're acting like a complete asshole with a dash of delusional on top of that hot mess sundae."

Felix bent down and grabbed her ankles, suspending her between him and Ash as they walked through the apartment. Misha and I followed closely behind.

"I have no idea what you're talking about, Talon! Where are you taking me?"

"It's the fact that you are still lying to our faces that really astounds me, Bun-Bun. You had some wicked injuries that are now magically healed. You have fighting skills that rival ours, and you didn't say shit about that, ever. In fact, you didn't even *try* to escape us in the maze, did you?" I pushed, my tone taking on an angry edge.

I wanted answers right the fuck now.

They carried her up the stairs, and Ash directed us to his room. He had the right kind of... tools for this. I'd talked him down from this earlier, but that'd been before she'd gone all Nurse Nightingale on her own body.

"Since you're fine and everything, you won't object to a little game?" Ash asked darkly.

"You're all dicks. All of you. What's wrong? Feeling intimidated now that I beat Monocle? You want to put me in my place, is that it?"

Felix laughed. "Damn, you really come up with some hurtful shit sometimes. Who hurt you, baby?"

Misha snarled and pushed everyone out of his way so he could open the doors to Ash's space. Something had him ready to go feral for the second time in one night. *What the actual fuck is going on? Are we becoming werewolves? Is it a full moon?* I only liked to pretend to be a dog sometimes—usually when I was getting railed at the same time—but I didn't really want to be one.

"We're not turning into gods damned werewolves!" Felix snapped at me, picking up my thoughts. I leaned in and bit his shoulder. "Ow! The fuck?"

"Well, first of all, I didn't like your tone. Secondly, if I'm a werewolf, now you are too. That's how it works. Read a fucking book, Lixy."

"I hate you all so much!" Palmer shouted, still trying to escape.

"Hush, *kukola*. Or you will hate us more before long," Misha warned, and his voice was so deep and demonic that it sent a wave of excitement down my spine. He was such a big, bad boy when he wanted to be. Usually, he didn't like to let the bad part out, because ya know, people tended to die or get maimed. But ooh, I loved a good adrenaline rush.

Misha switched places with Ashland, who stood before the massive seven-foot-tall mirror and did some kind of hand motion. A green light illuminated the border of the mirror, and it swung open, revealing Ashland's secret room of depravity.

"Oh, I think *the fuck* not!" Palmer screamed as we entered, allowing her to see the extent of the space.

Ash glanced around, ignoring her. "Hmm, what do you think boys? I'm leaning toward the St. Andrews cross."

"I will fuck you up, Ashland. The second they release me—"

Felix chimed in, speaking over Palmer. "I think I'd like to see her strung up on the cross."

"You're all going to pay for this, I swear. You can't even congratulate me? Like 'Oh, Palmer! You're such a bad bitch fighter—you looked hot as fuck whooping Rhodes's ass tonight!' And I'd be like, I know, right? Thank you! Now give me my winner's orgasms."

I tilted my head at her. "Do you think we can gag her? Just like, for now?"

"Yes," Misha piped up, eyeing Palmer with dark promises in his gaze. He and Felix fought to get her arms straightened, securing her wrists to the cross. She was spitting mad, breathing hard, and sweating by the time she was fully restrained.

"Stop fighting, Bun-Bun. We just have some questions, okay?" I pushed some of her hair out of her face, and the little beast tried to bite my hand. I snatched it out of her reach just in time. My eyes widened as a thought sprouted in my head. "Oh fuck, of course. Makes sense," I mumbled to myself.

"What makes sense?" Ashland demanded, looking between me and Palmer.

"Earlier, I was wondering what was going on with everyone acting crazy, and then I thought 'oh shit, what if we're turning into werewolves?!'"

"Not this again," Felix groaned, and I flipped him off.

Palmer was staring at me just as intensely as everyone else at this point. "Well? What's your theory here?"

"*She* is a werewolf. Did you not see her just now?"

Ash sighed. "Talon. Get the fuck out." He pointed at the door.

My mouth popped open. "Excuse me?"

"This is a serious fucking situation and you're being a serious fucking idiot!" He ran his hands through his hair and tugged, making it stick out in all directions. I wanted to tell him he looked like he'd been hit by lightning, but thought better of it when I saw his eyes taking on a red hue. Dude was losing it.

"If you think I'm letting any of you touch me, you're crazier than I thought!"

Felix laughed darkly. "Who said anything about touching you?"

"Trust me, love. You don't want my touch right now. I want to turn your ass red, I want to make you scream under the kiss of my flogger. I want you to stop FUCKING LYING!" Ash roared, his shirt ripping from his body as his wings burst out, his horns growing rapidly right along with his height.

For the first time since we'd met her, Palmer actually looked a little scared.

"I think we all need to calm down before anything else happens," Felix suggested, eyeing Ash warily. Even Misha was vibrating with emotion, though whether that was rage or something else, I had no idea.

I cleared my throat. "I vote we leave her here. She can think about her behavior while we chill out and clear our heads. Then we'll get some answers."

Palmer's attention snapped to me. "Leave me *here*?"

"Good plan. I'm out," Ash growled, his eyes never leaving our little bunny as he stormed past and disappeared through the door.

"Wait!" she cried, flexing against the restraints.

Felix stepped up and cupped her cheek. "We all need a breather, baby. You'll feel better after, you'll see." He dropped his hand, and her mouth opened in disbelief.

"You can't just leave me here!"

"You better have some answers for us when we come back, Bun-Bun. We're not big on touching women who don't want it, but those who aren't friends are enemies, so the rules don't really apply. And by touching, I mean using some… creative options to get the truth." I let my gaze fall to the Wall of Depravity, as I liked to call it. Whips, floggers, chains, ropes, some questionable dildos…

Her eyes darted to Misha. Her last hope at getting out of this, though I already knew it'd be pointless. "Mishy, please." Her voice cracked, and I lifted a brow. Nothing had really seemed to bother her before now—in fact, I'd expected anger, not whatever this was. "Please don't leave me like this."

He stopped right in front of her. "You are making me insane. I haven't felt this out of control in decades. It can't continue, *kukola*. I'll be back in a while."

"No, no, let's just talk now. Ask me anything! I'll answer! I promise!"

Misha pressed his lips together, shaking his head as he removed the bunny blades from his pocket and laid them down on a bench, looking pained. Together, we walked over to the door and then she really started to flip out.

"Fuck you guys! How dare you? I don't even know why you're so pissed! You could actually fucking talk to me instead of acting like a bunch of pricks!"

Misha walked out, and I gave her one last look before stepping through the door and letting it shut, cutting off her insults and hateful declarations.

The others were waiting, hanging out in Ashland's bedroom now. Ash was starfished out on his bed, staring at the ceiling. Felix was pacing, his anxious energy rolling off of him in waves.

"Was it just me or did she seem genuinely distressed?" I asked, rubbing my jaw with my thumb as I thought over her reaction.

"Nah, she did... but was it an act? My mind is so fucked right now." Felix sighed and walked over to the window. The city lights were all glowing brightly, lighting up the dark night.

Ash rolled over onto his stomach. "How long do we give her?"

"As long as it takes. We need to check on Rhodes," Misha grumbled, his shoulders sagging as he left the room. My big boy was a sad boy, and I didn't like it one bit.

We filed out after him in search of Rhodes. I didn't like that we'd found out two major secrets from Palmer in one night. She could fight—like, ninja-level fight—and she could heal herself. We'd all been obsessed with her immediately, but I had to wonder if maybe we needed to tone it down going forward.

Yeah, I was obsessed. Addicted. Wanted to lick her pussy from dusk til dawn and then roll around in her scent like a dirty dog... but I also didn't tolerate disrespect. Lying was the quickest way to piss me off.

I just had to hope that this little punishment would set her straight. If not? Well, she was still stuck here, and that was a long time to try to keep secrets from me. We hadn't gotten to where we were by letting things slide. She was no different. She couldn't be. We couldn't afford any fuckups.

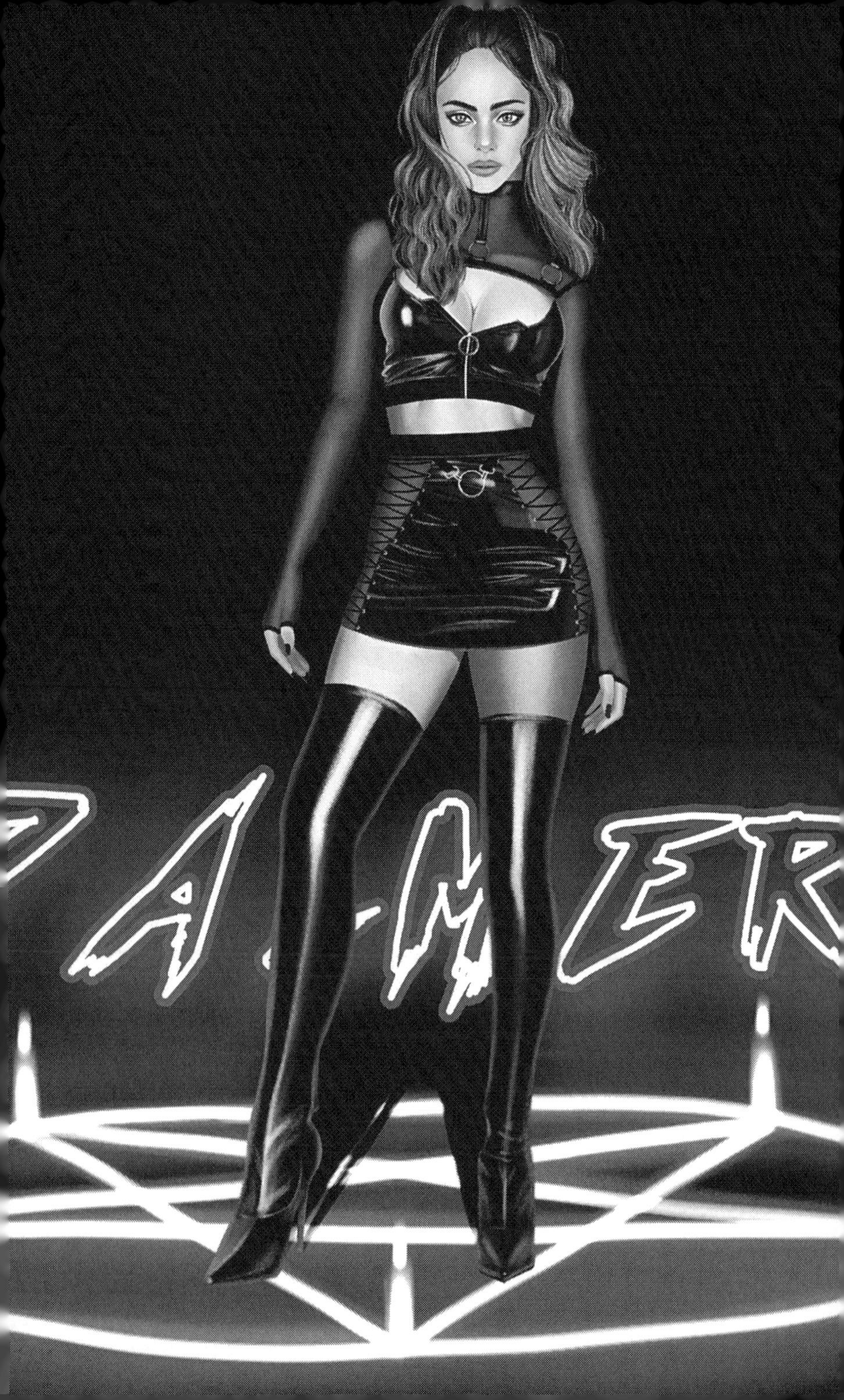

PALMER

Chapter Nineteen

They left me. Motherfuckers tied me up like a sacrificial lamb and left me in this... this... I glanced around, trying to control my breathing, but it was a battle I was losing. *You're stronger than this, Palmer. You've faced much worse. It's okay, just breathe.*

That was the fucked up thing about PTSD. Sometimes, no matter how rational you were with your thoughts, you could still get sucked into the vortex of trauma and there wasn't a damn thing you could do about it. The dream I'd just had while I was unconscious hadn't helped. It was never a fluid dream, always just snippets and flashes of memories—yet another way I wasn't in control.

"Come on, push harder, Vale! You're slacking, and one day it'll end up costing you out in the field!"

I gritted my teeth and pushed through the pain, spinning and landing a roundhouse kick on Slade's shoulder.

"Yes! Atta girl! Again."

Sometimes, I really fucking hated Slade, but since he'd taken over our fight training, my body had never been in better shape. I'd made so much progress, and I knew Asrael had noticed. I'd even managed to take Hunter down to the mat last week for the first time.

"Is that all you've got?" Slade taunted, bouncing out of reach.

I snarled and lunged forward, intent on slapping that smug smile off of his face. He stepped to the side and had me pinned down beneath him on the mat in a matter of seconds.

"Ugh!" *I slammed my hands down beside me in frustration.*

He hopped up and held out his hand. "You did great. Every session, you're showing progress. You're learning how to channel that anger you hold onto, so once you can hone that, you'll be a fucking force."

Sighing, I slipped my hand into his and let him pull me to my feet. It was after hours. Asrael had mentioned that he noticed how hard I'd been working lately. I'd wanted to keep that up, so had asked Slade if he'd be willing to give me some private lessons a few nights a week.

Panting, I headed for a bench and sat down with a groan. My legs felt like jelly.

"Here. Drink your water." *Slade handed me my water bottle, and I guzzled all of it. He chuckled.* "I wonder what it's like to drink with you—if you drink alcohol like you drank that water just now, that could be either a disaster or a lot of fun."

Wiping my mouth with the back of my hand, I leaned back against the wall. My skin was glistening with sweat, and a cold shower sounded like heaven. "Too young to drink, remember?"

He crossed his arms and looked down at me, his expression unreadable. "It's easy to forget sometimes," *he said quietly, dropping my gaze. My face suddenly felt much warmer, and not from the physical activity.*

My phone vibrated and I leaned over, fishing it out of my backpack. "It's Hunt. I'm meeting him to study." *I glanced at the clock on the wall.* "Fuck, I'm late." *I answered the call and quickly told Hunter I was just leaving the gym. After hanging up, I stood and started gathering my things, well aware of Slade standing right next to me.*

"Here," *he said, bending down and snagging my backpack before I could. He held the arm straps out, waiting for me to turn around. What was going on here? I sighed and turned, letting him slip the straps over my shoulders.*

"Thanks. For the fight and the uh, hag help. Oh my gods, the bag help."

Slade threw his head back and laughed, something he didn't do often. "Wow, that was brutal, Vale. I'll think of that moment at random times for the rest of my life and cringe for you."

"Hey, fuck you!" I laughed and shoved his chest. He grabbed my wrists, tugging me with him as he stepped back. I found myself locked in his dark eyes, and suddenly the air felt very heavy, like it was hard to get a full breath of air into my lungs.

He released my wrists with a smile. "Good work today, Vale. See you on Thursday." Then he just turned and walked away, leaving me confused as hell.

*****

Two days went by, and I pushed the encounter with Slade from my mind, chalking it up to dehydration. At seventeen, nearly everyone I knew was fucking or dating, or obsessed with one of the two ideas. I wasn't interested in either of those things. Hunter had recently started dating this new girl, and I was pretty sure she was jealous of our friendship. She was constantly giving me dirty looks and texting him whenever we were hanging out or studying.

For years, the other recruits had teased us, assuming that we were in a relationship simply because we were always together, but that was ridiculous. Hunter was like a brother to me. We'd had this conversation before, laughing at the idea of us dating. Couldn't a girl have a best friend who was a boy without having romantic feelings toward him?

Not only that, Hunter had a type, and I loved teasing him about it. The thicker the thighs and ass, the more interested he was. Swear to the stars, a big ass was like a magnet for my bestie. He always laughed me off and said something about how he'd need a woman with meat on her bones to be able to handle him. I'd usually gag and pretend to throw up in the trash can.

I pushed through the doors to the gym and immediately saw Slade there, wrapping up his knuckles. He was shirtless, and it bothered me that I looked a little bit longer than I ever had before.

"Hey, hope you're ready to eat the mat!" I shouted, announcing myself and trying to replace the tension I was feeling with shit talking.

He turned and lifted a dark brow. "Are you giving yourself a pep talk, Vale? Because you should know by now I don't eat mat. Ever."

"First time for everything, Porcino," I sang back to him, slipping on my gloves.

We never used our powers or any magic during these training sessions. With advancements being made daily from humans who were scared of the magical community, we needed to be able to fight without them, on the off chance that we were ever disabled magically during a fight. Before graduating and being allowed into the field, we'd all have to pass mock missions where the instructors would literally use whatever newfangled shit the humans had come up with to disarm us.

There were separate classes that were nothing but magical fighting tactics, but Slade didn't teach those and I was already advanced with those lessons. My affinity really didn't help me much when it came to fighting anyway, but learning basic spells and blocking techniques were still important.

We hopped into the ring, and an hour later, I was well and truly exhausted. Slade looked like he was barely sweating.

"How do you do that?" I panted, scowling at his ability to look so put together after the fighting we just did.

He took a big drink of water. "Do what?" My water bottle was sitting next to him, so he picked it up and brought it over, holding it out to me.

"Look like"—I waved my hand at his body—"that."

He laughed, and I tried to ignore the way my lower belly fluttered at the sound. "I'm not sure if that's a compliment or an insult?"

I rolled my eyes and downed some water. "It's just, I feel and look like a drowned rat, yet you look like you're ready to go out to dinner or something."

"Well, I don't usually go to dinner shirtless," he teased, leaning against the wall.

"Me either." *My eyes bugged out as I processed my words. "I mean, of course I don't. Do that. Shirtless. Most things I do while wearing a shirt is what I meant."*

His eyes twinkled. "I know what you meant. Do these sports bras count as shirts, though?" Slade reached out and plucked the strap of my blue bra, which was the only thing I was wearing as far as a top was concerned.

"Yes," I squeaked and cleared my throat. "They do count."

Slade hummed. "Are you hungry?"

"What?"

"Well, you mentioned dinner and it is getting late. I'm hungry. Are you?"

I was going to say no, that I needed to get back to my dorm and study for finals, but that wasn't what came out of my mouth.

"I'm starving."

***

Slade started taking me out to dinner after every training session. Hunter was off with his girlfriend, so he was never suspicious of anything going on. It was nice. Slade listened to me when I talked about my fears and plans for the future. How I wanted revenge for the deaths of my family. How my affinity was problematic since the spirits weren't always friendly.

He was always interested in hearing more about that, because his power was similar in a way. He had a mind control ability. It was rare as hell and pretty scary, to be honest. He'd done a little demonstration for me one time after I pushed hard, wanting to see what he could do.

Slade was incredibly powerful. All he had to do was touch your skin and he could control your mind. It was more effective if the person didn't see it coming, so it would be harder for them to get their mental shields up to fight against his invasion. Though I'd be lying if I said it wasn't difficult to keep him out even when I knew it was coming. It didn't surprise me; Asrael only recruited the best to work for Montague.

We were seated together in a booth at an Italian restaurant in the next town over. "My body is killing me," I whined after the server walked away.

"You've been working really hard. I saw you last night..."

"What? You spying on me now?" I joked, taking a sip of my Diet Dr. Pepper.

Slade leaned back in his seat, keeping his eyes on me. "For your information, I was walking back home after a date and saw you through the windows of the gym."

"A date? You went on a date?" I asked skeptically, not sure I believed him. In all the months he'd been at Montague, he'd never shown interest in anyone... and there had been plenty shown to him.

"Yes. I do have a social life outside of our sparring." He didn't sound offended, but there was something to his tone that was off.

The server brought our salads, and we sat in silence as we started chowing down. After a few minutes, I took a break. "Well, who was it?"

He paused with his fork halfway to his mouth. "Who was what?"

"Your date."

"Nobody of importance. I won't be going out with her again."

I laughed and stabbed a tomato with my fork. "Yikes. That doesn't sound good."

"Eat your salad, Vale."

Our conversation turned to other things after that. The techniques I'd been working on, the ones I'd mastered, things Slade thought I could improve on. Before I knew it, the restaurant was closing. We'd sat and talked for hours.

That was my favorite thing about Slade—how easy it was for me to open up to him. It was different from how I felt around Hunter. Something new. There was a freedom to the way Slade made me feel. He never judged me, just encouraged me.

As we walked to his SUV, his phone started vibrating, and I saw him glance at the screen and then silence it. Frowning, I wondered if it was his date from last night.

So what, Palmer? He's a grown ass man, he can date if he wants.

Slade opened my door and I slid into my seat, swinging my legs in so he could close it behind me. As he walked past the front of the vehicle, I saw him look at his phone again and then he brought it to his ear.

I watched him pace back and forth for a moment, before running his hand down his face. Then he pocketed the phone and got into the car.

"Everything okay?" I asked, feeling kind of awkward.

"Yeah. Uh, is it okay if I drop you off at your building tonight?"

My brow furrowed. Usually, he'd park at his building and then insist on walking me back to mine.

"Sure thing," I bit out in a clipped tone, reaching for my seat belt. Was he going to see her again, whoever she was? Were they going to fuck? Suddenly, the food I'd eaten wasn't sitting so well in my belly.

Slade reached down and rested his hand on the gear shift, the veins in his forearms shifting beneath his skin as he drummed his fingers against the leather. His thumb began stroking back and forth, back and forth over the smooth surface, and I stared, transfixed. Is that how he would touch her? Did he fuck her last night?

Oh fuck. Am I jealous?

My gaze snapped to Slade, and the air seemed to crackle when I found his intense hazel eyes boring into mine.

"You good, Vale?" he asked, his voice deep and gritty. I squirmed in my seat and broke the stare in favor of staring out of the window. I remained silent. I didn't trust myself right then, who knew what would come out of my mouth if I opened it.

Suddenly, the car jerked to the left, bumping as he drove the car down a little dirt path. "What the hell are you doing?" I reached out and braced myself against the glove box.

He slammed the brakes and threw the SUV into park. "Palmer. I can't take it anymore. You're driving me insane. It's impossible to read you." Slade looked a hundred times more serious than I'd ever seen him before.

"What are you talking about?" I glanced around, still alarmed at the off-roading he'd just put me through in the middle of the night with no warning. "I thought you were taking me home?"

A growl of frustration left him, and I didn't know what to say. "That was the girl from last night. On the phone," he said quietly.

My stomach sank. "I figured that."

"She wants me to come over. Do you know why?"

I swallowed. "I can guess."

"And you don't care? That doesn't bother you?"

"Should it?" I whispered. My heart was pounding. "Why are you asking me, Slade? Why does it matter if I care or not?"

"Because I don't fucking want her, Palmer! I can't stop thinking about you. All day. All the time. Tell me I'm way off base here. Tell me you don't feel it too."

My mouth popped open. Of all the things he could've said, I wasn't expecting that. The car suddenly felt too small, too confining. I scrambled for the door handle and tugged on it as I hit the release on my seat belt, throwing myself out of the damn SUV and into the night air. We were in some secluded, little, pine forest just off the country road.

Slade's door slammed seconds after mine, and I spun around and pushed him away just as he reached for me.

"How dare you!" I pointed my finger at him. "You're my trainer. My friend...."

"I'm still those things. I just want to be more than that. We'd be so good together, Vale. You know it."

"Asrael will kill you," I fired back.

Slade shook his head. "He doesn't need to know."

I laughed. "He knows everything, Slade! He probably knows we're here right this second, having this stupid as fuck conversation! You're ruining our friendship right now."

"You're scared, I can see that. I think we're just two sides of the same fucked-up coin, but we're whole together. Telling you how I feel doesn't ruin anything. I know you feel it too. I can see it when you look at me."

My chest was heaving, but I let him reach for me. I let him pull me in and wrap his arms around me.

"You were going to drop me off and what? Go fuck that girl?" I had to know. I stepped back and stared up at the guy who was terrifying me right now. He was scaring me, because I'd never felt these things before.

"I thought about it. It would've made me sick to do it. That's why I had to know about this, do you understand? If you didn't feel it, then I was going to force myself to move on."

That created a mental picture of Slade with a girlfriend, one that he spent all of his free time with. She'd be the one he took out to dinner after training, not me. We wouldn't have this anymore. Panic gripped me; I couldn't lose Slade. Hunter wasn't around much these days, and I'd be alone...

"Slade," I choked out, emotion taking over. I hated crying. I hated needing anyone.

"Hey, hey. It's okay." He tipped my chin up, and his thumb traced my jaw softly. Each pass felt like another rock landing heavily in my belly.

I shook my head. "Don't leave me, okay?"

He studied my face as he stepped closer to me. "I will never leave you. I couldn't even if I wanted to. You're in my head now, and I don't think I'll ever get you out."

I barely had time to suck in a breath before he bent down and pressed his lips against mine. I'd never been kissed before. He was soft, yet hard at the same time. The little whimper that escaped my mouth sounded nothing like any sound I'd made before, and Slade used that opportunity to slip his tongue past my lips. His groan made me feel things in my body that I was positive were witchcraft.

His lips left mine in favor of my neck, and the ache between my legs was at an all-time high when his tongue skimmed my throat.

"Slade," I breathed.

"You taste better than I dreamed," he murmured.

"Promise me I won't lose you. Promise me," I demanded, grabbing his face with my hands so I could look into his eyes. The

fear of something going wrong, of this blowing up in my face, of not having Slade in my life anymore... I couldn't cope with that.

"I swear it, Palmer. You're stuck with me." I nodded, and he tucked some of my hair behind my ears. "Come on, let me get you back. You have an early class tomorrow." My brain was foggy and my body needy as he led me back to the car.

That night set me on a path that I should've seen coming. All of the feelings of doom, loss, dread, and just general badness... I ignored them.

For months after that, Slade and I had this secret relationship. We'd train together and then go out—that wasn't different. Over time though, I'd sleep over at his place. We'd watch movies and make out. He knew I was a virgin and he never pushed me.

My routines were changing. I went from being attached to Hunter all the time to barely seeing him, and that was hard for someone who valued structure. So any chance I had to see my best friend, I greedily took.

At first, it didn't seem to bother Slade, but after the fourth or fifth time of me not being able to spend the night because I had plans with Hunter, he started acting pissy. I wasn't sure exactly when it happened, but I began to dread telling him that I was going to hang out with Hunter. He'd get quiet and it made me uncomfortable, though he never actually wanted to talk to me about what the problem was.

A few weeks later came the night of my eighteenth birthday. Hunter was away on another assignment, and I was spending the evening with Slade. Tonight was an important night. I was ready to have sex with him. I'd gone into town last week and bought some lacy lingerie, hoping that he'd like it. Slade was so important to me, and I wanted him to know.

I was waiting out front of my building, wearing a sexy black dress I'd bought that paired great with the lace I had on underneath. My phone started ringing, and I smiled when Hunter's face popped up, immediately connecting the video call.

"Happy birthday, beautiful! Daaamn, look at you. Are you going out tonight?"

I felt myself blush. "Maybe I am," I teased.

"Wish I was there. Eighteen is a big one. I'll be home next week though, and I'll take you out for a birthday dinner then. Sound good?"

"Sounds perfect." I glanced past my screen and found Slade glaring at me. Shit. "Hey, Hunt, I gotta go. Thanks for the call."

I hit end and stuffed my phone in my bag, happy to see Slade. He was dressed in a black suit with a black shirt underneath and a matching black tie. He looked delicious.

"Hey, handsome," I greeted my boyfriend, stepping closer so I could wrap my arms around him. His body was rigid, but I hugged him anyway and murmured, "Hunter called to say happy birthday."

The muscles in his back rippled. "Yeah. I heard. And he wants to take you out on a date next week and he thinks you're beautiful. Am I missing anything, Palmer?"

I jerked back and stared up at him in confusion. "What? No. That's not—"

"Do you love him?" he demanded, crowding me against the wall. My heartbeat was racing like a hunted rabbit as he completely invaded my space.

"Of course I love him. He's my family, Slade. You're being ridiculous and acting jealous for no reason!" I couldn't believe he was behaving the way he was.

His eyes trailed down my body, taking in my outfit. The sharp glint in his eye told me he wasn't done yet, and I braced myself for whatever his next accusation was going to be. "Is that why you wore this dress? Because you knew he'd video call you?"

I shoved his chest, a flare of anger finally flickering to life as the hurt, confusion, and fear settled. "Back up!" I needed him to take a step away from me. I was two seconds away from going into fight or flight mode, and knowing me, it was going to be a fight. I felt cornered, like he was deliberately trying to intimidate me. "Why are you acting like this?"

"I don't share, Palmer. I can't help but feel like I'm having to share you with another man. I don't fucking like it and I won't tolerate it," he snapped, slamming his hand against the wall.

"I've told you a hundred times, he's like my brother. I'm allowed to have other people in my life, Slade!"

My mind was spinning, and nothing was making sense. He hadn't been like this when we first met, or when we'd first started training together, or going out... Why was he doing this?

"He wants you!" His nostrils flared and his jaw jumped. He looked utterly deranged, and my throat tightened as I accepted that I was looking at a stranger. Clearly unable to stop himself, he kept going. "I know he wants you! He wants to fuck you—"

I didn't think. I just reacted. My palm landed hard against his cheek, shutting him up. We were both so stunned that we just stared at each other. I watched Slade's eyes go from shocked to dark and scary in the blink of an eye. A flash of red drew my focus, and I watched as a line of blood ran from the corner of his lip down his chin. I'd made him bleed.

"I think you should go, Slade." I swallowed the urge to apologize, to ask if he was okay. Because I wasn't. He'd hurt me more than he knew.

"That's not happening." He stepped out of my path, giving me a view of his car that he'd parked along the street. "Get in the car."

I shook my head, trying to stifle the tears that were wanting to fall. "No."

"Gods dammit, Palmer. Get in the car. It's your birthday and I'm taking you out."

In that moment, it was like the stars themselves twinkled brighter just to shine a light on how blind I'd been all these months. Slade didn't look sexy to me right now. He looked pissed off, scary, unstable. And why? Because Hunter was my friend?

I didn't move, my feet and eyes remained frozen to the sidewalk. I couldn't even look at him right now.

His feet shuffled, and he took a step closer to me. I immediately moved back, putting myself against the wall again. "I'm sorry, sweetheart. I didn't mean those things. Can we please just go?" He sounded so sincere. So sorry for his behavior...

My heart was breaking, because I knew deep down that this was the real Slade. Everything was starting to become clear. "This isn't working for me." My voice was so soft, I wondered if I'd said the words out loud.

"What did you just say?"

The first tear fell. "I said that we're over, Slade. I can't do this with you."

He reared back, almost as though I'd physically slapped him a second time.

"I'll, uh, see you around." I started walking away, rounding the corner to my building when I was whipped around and pressed against the rough bricks. My exposed shoulders and back scraped against the rough surface, and I yelped, opening my mouth to scream but a large hand was suddenly pressing against my lips, silencing me. My frantic gaze bounced around before landing on Slade's enraged face.

"You don't get to just walk away from me. I said I was sorry. You just— You make me so crazy. I see the way guys look at you, and all I want to do is gut them because you're mine. You'll always be mine!"

I shook my head, trying to get air into my nose, but I was in such a state of panic that my body wanted more oxygen than it was getting. My vision was blurring.

"I fucking love you, Palmer. I know you love me too. Don't be scared of me, I'd never hurt you. Never."

He removed his hand and replaced it with his mouth before I could get even a strangled cry for help out. I fought against his hold, not wanting his mouth on me. The taste of copper exploded on my tongue, and I remembered that he'd been bleeding.

"No," I tried to say, but it came out more as a garbled groan.

"See? You do love me, Palmer."

I did? Yes. I found myself nodding. "I love you, Slade."

He cupped my cheek. "I've waited so long for you to say that." I felt his cock press against my stomach. "I know you want me. I *want you so bad it hurts me, Palmer. Tell me you want me, that you want to feel me. That you want me to be the only man to know what your body feels like."*

My brain felt fuzzy, almost like I was drunk. Then I realized he was using his magic... against me. To control me. I was desperate to get away, but this was so much stronger than the other time he'd shown me his affinity. I wanted to tell Slade that I wasn't feeling well, but the second I opened my mouth, I was telling him how much I wanted him to be my first. That I'd bought lingerie especially for him, for tonight. His eyes lit up like the fireflies I used to catch in the backyard with my parents... before...

"You're perfect. So perfect for me," he praised, kissing me again. "Let's skip dinner. I want to feel this sexy body against me and then, after I really mark you and make you mine, I'll order some food. Come on, let's go." He slipped his hand in mine and led me to the car.

I didn't fight. I didn't want to fight. All I wanted was whatever he wanted. He was happy and so was I.

Tears were running down my cheeks as I came back to reality. My body shivered. I was just so fucking exhausted. That was the first time Slade had used his affinity on me. He took great pleasure in me doing whatever he wanted, saying whatever he wanted to hear.

There were times though, where he'd imagine some slight against him, and he'd think I needed to be punished. Slade's favorite punishment was tying me up and leaving me in dark rooms for hours on end, not knowing when or if he would return.

There were two things that triggered me like a hit of adrenaline straight to the vein. Having my mental state altered against my will, and being restrained and abandoned. The panic was ingrained.

That had been the worst part about being Slade's zombie. There was always an undercurrent of awareness, this little voice beneath all of the bullshit reminding me that the things I was doing and saying weren't me. That I was being used. Abused. Raped.

So it was no wonder I had a traumatic flashback after being tied to this damn cross and left completely alone.

Or so I thought.

"Bad past, huh?" my new sidekick ghost asked, his form coming into full view as he got closer.

I sniffled. "How could you tell?"

He chuckled, and for the first time, I noticed his hair was deep mahogany. I bet when he was alive, it would've been the prettiest deep red in the sunlight.

"Been there, done that. You're okay now. Wherever you were in your mind, that's not reality." He was so matter-of-fact about it that I felt myself taking a deep breath, giving my body the precious oxygen it needed to chill the fuck out.

I sighed. "No, my reality is worse than my ghosts. I'm in too deep with a group of psychos who are probably going to come in here and rape me. Or kill me. Or both. Who knows."

His eyes narrowed. "Yeah, that's not happening. Neither of those things. I won't allow that." Once again, that matter-of-fact tone took over, and I wondered if he'd been considered arrogant when he was alive. Or had he managed to pull off confidence without the negative connotation arrogance often carried?

I rolled my eyes and tugged on my restraints. "And how are you going to stop them, ghost man?"

"Ghost man, huh? Is that my name now?" he teased, his lighthearted attitude working to slowly override my anxiety.

"Well, I don't know your name."

He smiled. "Jasper. My name is Jasper. Wow, it's been a very long time since I've introduced myself to anyone."

"I'm Palmer, though I suppose you already know that."

He shrugged. "Might've heard it a time or two."

"You seem to know a lot about these guys," I muttered. I needed to figure a way out of here.

"They're pretty interesting to watch. It can get boring being stuck like this, ya know? Need to find entertainment where I can."

"They're all mad at me."

Jasper paced back and forth in front of me. "I don't know about all that. I'm not sure mad is the right term."

"Oh." I laughed sardonically. "No? So this is what they do to women they aren't mad at?"

"Hurt is a better word. I think they're hurt that you lied to them."

Hurt? I'd hurt *them*?

"They're demons! They do horrible, despicable things all the time with no remorse!"

He crossed his arms and pinned me with a serious stare. "And? What? That means they don't have feelings? That they can't feel hurt or betrayal? And the things they do, you have proof of that, or is that just the rumor mill working?"

My mouth opened and closed as I thought of what to say. "I saw them kill a man!"

"Why did they kill him?"

"That— That's irrelevant. You can't just go around killing people."

"And your employer? You think they aren't out there killing everyday?"

My eyes nearly popped out. "What do you mean, *my employer?-*"

Jasper huffed a breath, staring me down. "I'm not blind, Palmer Vale."

My blood turned icy. *He knows my last name?* "I'm wondering if you're even a ghost now. What the fuck?!"

Ghosts were not usually this coherent. Or lucid. Especially not a lengthy amount of time after their death.

I narrowed my eyes. "What are you?"

Jasper laughed. "A friend."

"I don't need any of those. I tend to get fucked over by them."

"Considering you're the only one who can see me or speak to me, I think you're pretty safe here."

"And I'm supposed to just take your word for it? If you know I'm here for my employer, then I've been made and that puts me in an extremely dangerous position."

Jasper tilted his head and looked pointedly at the ties that were binding me to the cross. "I'd say you were already in a precarious position before I showed up."

An idea came to me, and it was hard not to get my hopes up. But if Jasper wasn't like other ghosts, then maybe...

"Hey, do you think you could untie me?"

He pushed off the wall and sauntered over to me. "I'm a ghost. I haven't been able to touch or feel anything since I died."

I shook my head in frustration. "I know that. I know more about ghosts than I care to. My point here is that you're different. Did you know that? At first I thought you were just like any other spirit, but you're not really decomposing and your mind seems intact. I've never seen that before. So, it's worth a shot, don't you think?"

"I think you're going to be disappointed." And yet, he reached for my wrist. Both of us seemed to be holding our breath in anticipation. "This is stupid," he muttered.

"Just try, okay? If it doesn't happen, then we're no different than we are right this second. But if it does?"

An icy sensation tickled the soft skin of my wrist, and I sucked in a breath, my wide eyes snapping to his. Soft, barely there pressure against my skin... but I felt it. I felt him.

"By the moon," he whispered, staring at the point of contact with wonder. "How is this possible? Your skin, it's like silk..." He dragged two fingers down the underside of my arm, spreading more of that chilly sensation, though it seemed to be lessening the longer he touched me.

"Jasper," I gasped, noticing the color returning to his skin. "What's happening right now?"

"A miracle..." He made his way to my face, and I saw the way his hand trembled as he brushed his fingertips against my cheek, his expression one of awe as he searched my face. "Incredible."

Color was coming back to his form, showing me his pale skin, the way his cheeks turned a deep shade of red, and his pretty eyes that were a deep, pine green interspersed with flecks of light brown. They reminded me of a forest of Christmas trees.

"Jasper, can you undo the ties?" I knew he was having a big moment, but I really wanted out of here before those fuckheads came back.

"Oh, right." He blinked a few times, snapping out of whatever trance he'd been in. I held my breath when he grabbed the ties, and could've cried with joy when he actually began undoing them. "This is insane. It shouldn't be possible. I wonder..." He dropped the knot he was working on, leaving me still tied up, and walked over to the side table. I watched him try to pick up a dildo with no luck at all. His hand moved right through it. Even his color looked as if it was fading again.

"Why isn't it working now?" He looked to me like I had answers, which I didn't. I was just as confused as he was. I had never in all my life turned a ghost corporeal. "So, it's connected to you. You have the ability to make me whole."

I shook my head. "I have no idea why this is happening, but no, I don't have that ability. Dead is dead. I can communicate and I can help you cross. That's it."

He pointed at me. "But that isn't completely true, is it? What about your little furry friend? 'Dead is dead' didn't apply to him, did it?"

"He's an animal. It's not difficult for me to reanimate animals. You're a spirit without a body. There's nothing there for me to reanimate! Now can you please untie me and we can continue this discussion afterward?"

"Sure, but I want to make a deal. If you're the only thing I can physically touch, or I can only feel things if you're also touching them, I want thirty minutes a day."

"Thirty minutes of what?!" I pulled against my binds, hoping he'd loosened one of them enough that I could slip my wrist out.

"Uninterrupted touch time."

"Are you nuts? I don't have a spare thirty minutes to let you feel me up. That's ridiculous and you know it."

He crossed his arms. "Fine. Looks like you're stuck here. I'll see ya around."

I could've hissed, I was so pissed off. "Wait, wait. Don't go. I'll give you ten minutes a day. No touching my tits, ass, or pussy. Got it?"

"Fifteen minutes."

"Ugh, fine. Get me out of here."

Jasper was all big smiles as he practically skipped back over to me and began untying me. Once the final knot was released, I was ready to move, but first things first. I dashed over to the bench that held my weapons. After securing those babies to my thigh, I glanced around and then lifted a brow at Jasper. "There has to be another way out of here that doesn't involve going through that door."

"There is. It'll cost you though." Excitement laced his tone, and I groaned. I hated being indebted to anyone.

"If you weren't already dead, I'd be very tempted to kill you right now."

"I'll get you out of here, unseen, for five minutes added to my daily total. Twenty touch minutes, total."

I growled. "Fine. Get me out of here."

Jasper took my hand and led me over to a wardrobe. He went ahead and opened it himself, since apparently as long as he was touching me, he was able to touch other objects too. I glanced inside, curious about what he could possibly want to bring with us from a closet in a sex room.

"Alright, in you go," he said, holding his arm out for me to walk past.

I shot him a skeptical look. "What now?"

"This wardrobe has a false back—that's the way out of here." He looked really proud of himself for having such inside information.

"You fucking with me? If this is like some Narnia bullshit and you're pranking me, you should just—"

He pressed his index finger to my lips. "Shh." I froze, hearing the creaking of floorboards. Too close. "Get in the damn wardrobe!"

I hopped inside, immediately starting to believe him when he pulled the doors shut behind us using handles attached to the insides of the doors. "There's a little switch right around... here!" With a soft click, the back of the wardrobe swung open, revealing a staircase.

"Holy shit," I said in awe as we stepped through. "That was by far the closest to Narnia I ever got."

Jasper laughed and started walking down the steps. It looked like any other stairwell in an industrial building, except there were no windows. Instead, there were the backs of paintings, as well as sections of see-through glass—which I assumed were one-way mirrors—and wooden boards, which were likely the back of a piece of furniture.

There were access points to this escape route from every floor. Multiple escapes, even. Since they could fly and jump like spider monkeys, the escape points were all over the walls. Some fifteen feet above the stairs. Luckily, the one we'd used was only two feet above the landing.

"How often does this get used?" I whispered to Jasper, stealing glances upward and preparing for one of the guys to appear perched like a gargoyle.

"Often enough that you should probably speed up."

"Great," I muttered, picking up the pace. "How many floors until we reach the bottom?"

Jasper was quiet for a moment, and since he was in front of me, I couldn't see his face. "Depends on where you're wanting to go. Do you want to leave? If that's the case, there's a door coming up that we can sneak through which will bring us out on the first floor."

"What's the first floor? Is that Haunt?"

"It is, but it's closed for the night since it's fight night. Should be a ghost town right now." He turned back and lifted his eyebrows, laughing at his own joke. I couldn't help the little huff of amusement that I let slip.

I had to think. Did I really want to leave? If I did, how easy would it be for me to get back in? What if me leaving pissed them off to the point that they decided I wasn't worth the hassle? On the other hand, they'd tied me up against my will in a fucking sex closet and left me there. After I'd begged them not to. All arrows were pointing to *fuck them*.

"First floor would be great. I need to get out of here and think. I can't do that here with them taking over my brain. Is that a demon power? Mind control or like, I don't know, the ability to make people unable to resist their sexual prowess? I like sex. I love sex...

but I've had more sex in the last week than I've had in the last six months, no contest. And let's be real," I panted, starting to get winded as we continued down the stairs. "I was fucking these guys at really inappropriate times, and oh my gods, Jasper. The things we were doing to each other..." He stopped so abruptly that I slammed into his back. "Ow, what the hell?"

"You want to talk about sex with the man who has been dead for an unknown amount of time and just regained his ability to touch?" Turning to face me, his hazel eyes bored into mine, and I shook my head.

"Sorry. I wasn't thinking. I just haven't had anyone to talk to about all of these feelings! I can't even call my best friend right now. Who knows when I'll be able to talk to or see him..." I wandered behind Jasper as we started descending again, feeling kind of shitty about my situation. Pity party for one.

We came to a stop in front of a glass panel. "Here we are. This is the voyeur room in the club."

I eyed the one-way glass and rolled my eyes. "Classy. I bet Monocle likes to stand out here and beat his thing." Jasper let go of my hand with a gasp.

"Excuse me?" a deep voice demanded, and I slowly spun around until my eyes landed on a very scowly Rhodes who appeared to have been stepping out of an opening about halfway down the next flight of stairs when he either heard or saw me. Just perfect timing. "What the hell are you doing in here?"

"Oh, well, I was doing some exploring. I found this little hole in the wall, so I let my curiosity get the best of me and here I am."

Rhodes looked like hell. The bruising on his face was fading, but he clearly hadn't showered yet because there was dried blood on his face and neck. I tried to school my features into a mask of innocence, but that got harder and harder to do as the big guy stalked up the stairs toward me.

"You just don't know how to tell the truth, do you, Palmer? Every time you open that pretty, little mouth, it's to spew more lies and bullshit, isn't it?" He cocked his head to the side and stared down at me. Jasper was standing halfway up the stairs, a pinched expression on his face.

"I don't know what you're talking about, Rhodes. You've had it out for me from the very first moment we saw each other. Honestly, I think you're jealous." There was something about this demon that made it impossible for me to hold my tongue. That might've made me a shitty spy, but I was beyond the point of caring or being able to fix it.

"I have questions and you're gonna fuckin' answer them right here, right now. And if you lie to me, little girl? I will make sure it's the last lie you ever speak, do you understand me?"

I stepped closer to him, bumping him with my chest. "How about this for a truth? Fuck. You."

Seriously, fuck him. I wasn't going to just stand here and let him talk to me like that. I stepped to the side and made it one step closer to the door when I was yanked backward by my hair.

"Ow, what the fuck?!" I shrieked, twisting around with my fist ready to smash into his nose.

"I'm done with these bullshit games. I want answers and I want them right fucking now, or so help me." His body seemed to be expanding before my eyes. His demon was very close to the surface right now, so I had to swallow the urge to tell him to piss off again. I wasn't telling him shit, but he didn't need to know that.

"Fine. What do you want to know?"

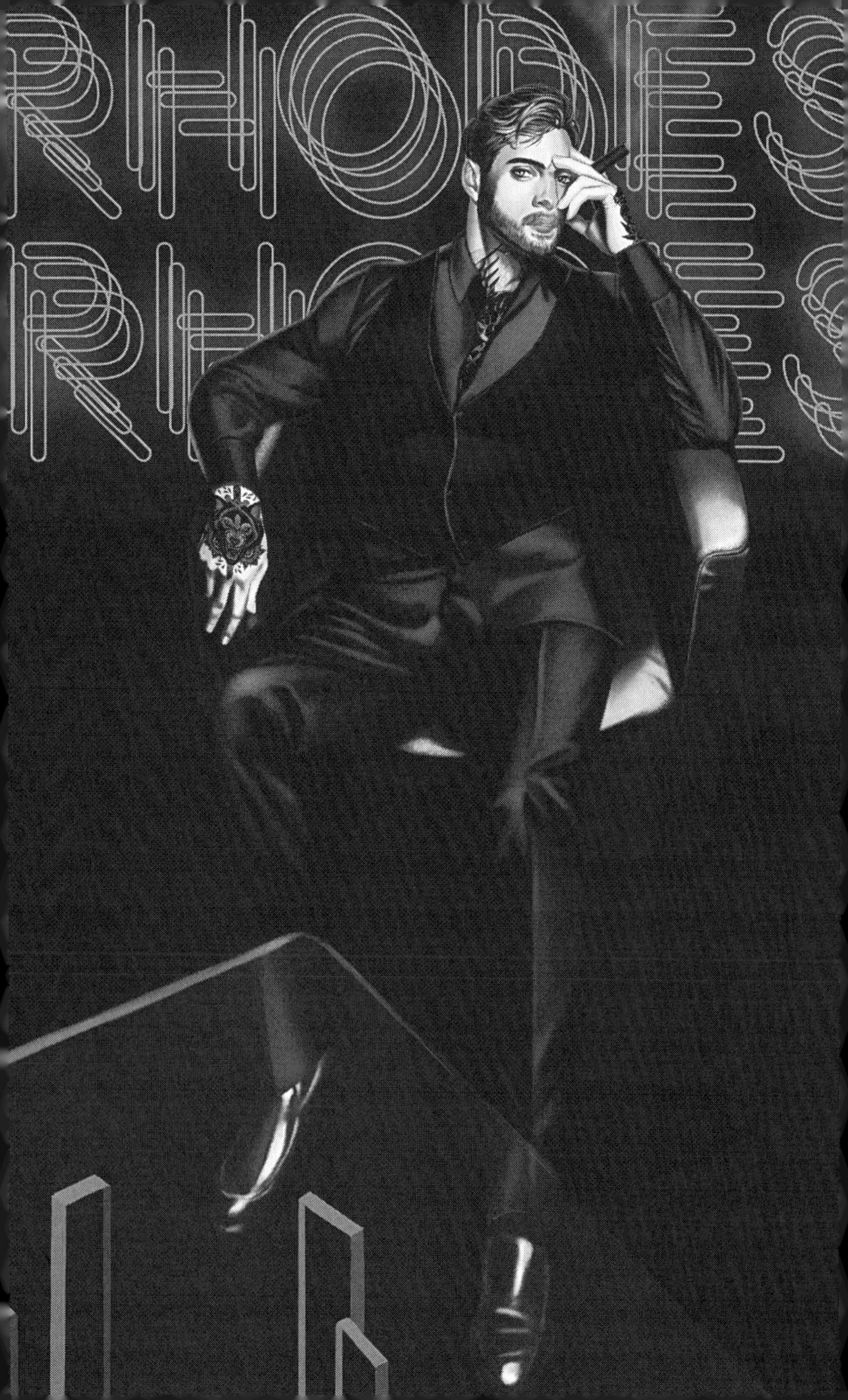
RHODES

RHODES

Chapter Twenty

"What do I want to know?" I laughed darkly. "Everything."

She shifted her weight, popping out a hip and crossing her arms. If defiance had a face, it would be this woman's right here. My palm practically itched with the urge to spank her.

"Well, ask away. I don't have all day for your temper tantrum."

I narrowed my eyes, wondering what exactly she'd been through in her life that gave her bigger balls than ninety percent of the people I'd ever encountered. We'd shifted in front of her, fought in front of her—hell, I'd fucking fought *with* her—and yet she had no fear. A person without fear was a loose cannon. Reckless and unpredictable. I didn't have time for any of that shit.

"How'd you learn to fight like that?" I guessed starting out easy was wise because I knew if she felt cornered, she'd lock herself down in a heartbeat.

She shrugged. "Started learning martial arts as a kid. Earned my black belt in karate when I turned sixteen, and I study several other different fight styles."

"A black belt at sixteen is impressive. Why did you hide that?"

"I didn't hide it. It's just not exactly something I lead with when I meet new people." Her gaze shifted from my face to behind me, and I looked over my shoulder, not seeing anything there.

"I see. Well, you had a perfect opportunity to use your skills in the maze, yet you didn't give away a thing that indicated you had any training."

That was the part that really confused me. After she saw what we were, she didn't fight very hard to get away... and as far as I knew, she didn't even attempt to escape once Misha took her upstairs after the hunt. No, something wasn't adding up.

"What can I say?" She held her hands out at her sides. "I wanted a night with The Exiled, same as everyone else in that damn club. Why is that so hard for you to believe? Even now, I can see the doubt in your eyes."

"Oh, I don't doubt that part, little girl. Your cunt was weeping for my boys before they even suggested the maze." I shook my head when her mouth opened, ready as ever to argue with me. "Don't try to deny it." I leaned in, an inch from her face. "I smelled how wet you were."

A slow smile spread across her face. "Get the fuck out of my face, Rhodes. I'm two seconds away from throat punching you and pushing you down this flight of stairs."

I laughed and straightened my back so I was once again towering over her tiny frame. There'd been a moment there in the ring when I'd actually felt a surge of something resembling respect. I probably would've given her credit where credit was due—if I didn't feel like she was full of fucking shit and lying about everything. It was hard for me to find a worthy opponent that wasn't one of the guys.

Since she was still being evasive about the fight skills, I asked the next question I was really interested in. "What's your affinity?"

"That's rude as fuck, you know?"

I cracked my neck. "Yeah, I don't fucking care. Answer the gods damned question."

"I see dead people," she said in a sugary sweet tone that grated on my last fucking nerve.

I pinched my nose and shut my eyes, trying to calm myself down. I'd had enough of her sass. "Palmer, listen. I'm beyond playing these games with you. What. Is. Your. Affinity?"

"You deaf? I told you, I see ghosts. Spirits. Whatever you wanna call them."

Was she serious? She certainly looked like she was serious, though I knew deep in my bones that this woman was a liar and loved to fuck with me. Rile me up. Well, it wasn't going to work this fucking time.

"I know you think I'm an idiot, just like you think the others are. They fell to their knees for you so damn easy, didn't they? You don't want to tell me what your affinity is? I'm not surprised." I ran my thumb back and forth over the dark stubble on my jaw as I considered what to do next.

Palmer was shaking her head at me with disgust on her face, but her tricks weren't going to work on me.

"They had you tied up in Ash's room. How'd you get out of there?" I snapped my fingers. "Aha! One of your ghost buddies help you break out?"

"Yes, actually. He was very helpful in my escape. At least, he was until I got fucking caught by a cigar-toking troll beast."

"What the fuck did you say?" I clenched my jaw. "Actually, no, never mind. I don't care. Just tell me how you got out of that room without help. Do you have some kind of fire magic that burned through the binds?"

Palmer looked two seconds away from clawing my eyes out, but we both knew that for every hit she got, I'd get one right back. "Fine. You want a play-by-play? Those fucking monsters carried me into Ashland's sex room—and by the way, if there's ever been other women in that room, he will never fuck me in there. Honestly, that's just sick; I can't imagine letting him stick who knows what inside of me in a room his whores have been in."

I bit the inside of my cheek to keep from smiling. "You do know his actual dick has been inside other women before?"

Her eyes flared with rage. "I will smash your balls if you ever say something that disgusting in my presence again."

"I'll add delusional to your toxic personality traits. Continue with my play-by-play, please."

"Right, so they were all pissy over me knowing how to fight, and then I woke up on the kitchen island with all of these injuries, so I healed myself. That really threw them over the edge, so they tied me to a St. Andrew's cross. You would've thought I killed their family pet or some shit. I deserved congrats and butt pats for the way I demolished your ass in the ring, but no—"

"Wait a second. You healed yourself?"

She pulled up her shirt, revealing her smooth torso with no sign of bruising or cuts. "Yeah. It's part of my affinity. I think the ghosts—"

"For fuck's sake, enough about ghosts. Continue with this bullshit tale. I want to see how many more lies you can spew in the span of two minutes."

"That's when they left me up there. Said I needed to learn a lesson or some shit. I begged them not to leave, and I *do not* fucking beg. Do I look like someone who begs, Rhodes?" She paused, smoothing down her shirt. "There's this ghost—" I growled under my breath at her persistence. "Fine, this man, if that makes you feel better? He popped up and we started chatting, then he let me out and said he'd help me get out of that room. Now I'm here."

"Right." I pursed my lips together. "And where is this man now?"

"Behind you, near the door." Palmer pointed to where she was staring earlier. All that greeted me was an empty staircase.

"There's nobody there."

She sighed dramatically. "I know that. I'm the one who sees ghosts, not you. I didn't expect you to be able to see him, idiot."

Alright, so Palmer was a little unstable. Considering who I lived with, instability didn't tend to bother me, but paired with her addiction to lying... it wasn't something I could ignore.

"Stop doing that!" she shouted, and then giggled, covering her mouth with her hand. "What? I already told him I can see you, why should I hide it anymore?"

"Are you serious right now?" How was this my current life situation? She wasn't even paying attention to me anymore. Instead, she turned and started walking toward the door to the voyeur room, carrying on a one-sided conversation with herself. "Excuse me?" I grabbed her arm. "We're not done talking."

"Your rudeness literally knows no bounds. As you can see, I'm now having a different conversation. Just because Jasper is a ghost that doesn't mean you get to disrespect him—"

It was as if someone had dumped water in my ears. Her mouth was still moving, but her words were lost to me. I must have misunderstood, misheard the name. I knew she was speaking, but I wasn't hearing. It was like I'd been sucked into a riptide, my body being tossed back and forth beneath the waves. My heart was racing, and blackness danced at the edges of my vision.

I knew I should ask her to repeat what she said. I needed to know if my mind had just played a horrible trick on me, or if this witch was about to meet the real Rhodes. The one who lived deep inside, the one I locked beneath two-inch, thick, steel chains behind a ring of hellfire.

"Are you okay? You don't look so good, Monocle. Maybe you should sit down?"

The whooshing sound gave way to a high-pitched ringing. "What did you say his name was?"

"Jasper."

A roar exploded from my chest, and I squeezed my eyes shut, seeing those hazel fucking eyes. The ones that haunted me. My shirt shredded as the chains holding back the beast shattered and the demon within me took over, stretching his muscles. My body grew five inches taller and my wings snapped out, a twenty-foot span that ensured no prey could escape. My fingers shifted, growing into long, deadly claws that could slice through skin, sinew, and tendons like butter.

My vision went completely black, and I blinked. The blackness faded after a moment, leaving a red haze, and I realized I had the lying witch by the throat, pinned up against the wall. She was kicking and clawing at my arms, but I felt nothing.

Slowly, I slid her body up the wall, until her feet were barely touching the ground. The coppery scent of blood hit my nose, and my mouth watered. My claws must've done a little damage.

"Where the fuck did you hear that name?" I snarled, showing her my sharp teeth. Her eyes were bulging, and her face was getting darker, but I was only seeing in red. "Who sent you here? Fucking *tell me!*"

I released her, and she crumpled to the stairs, sliding down to the landing. I prowled after her, eyeing her as she lay on the floor, coughing and sputtering. "He told me his name," she choked out, sounding like a dying frog.

"How fucking dare you come here, into our gods damned house, into their beds? Do you think this is a fucking game?!" I was thankful we were surrounded by concrete, because the furniture would've been shaking with how loud I was being. There was no longer any logical thought. Just rage. Red-hot fucking rage.

I bellowed at the top of my lungs, all of the anger, pain, and hurt flying out of me after years of repressing those emotions. Breathing heavily, I looked down at the witch at my feet. Over my dead body would she use this to wreck my boys.

She was scooting backward now, trying to put distance between us. Finally, she was afraid.

"You think you can come in here and what? Just save that name for the perfect moment? Drop that bomb on us when we're vulnerable? Who the fuck sent you?" I tossed my head back and laughed darkly. "Oh my fucking hell, it was him, wasn't it?"

"Rhodes, please, calm down..."

"Calm down?" I took a step closer to her. "Calm down?" I repeated as I squatted down. "Felix and Talon have finally, *finally* made progress. Ashland isn't as hateful, Misha is talking a little more... and you think I'm going to let you blow that up?"

"I don't know what you're talking about..."

"*SHUT UP!* Just shut the fuck up! Enough of this!" I grabbed her and lifted her by the back of her shirt. "You can go tell your boss that I've been getting his little notes, and he can suck my fat fucking cock. You're going to walk out of the front door and get the *fuck* out of my city. And when the boys see that you're gone? I'm going to tell them that I didn't see a thing. That you must've been a lying bitch all along and you've run away. I mean, that part will actually be true. But you aren't going to succeed—they'll never know that you were walking around here dropping the name of their dead fucking triplet, and I'll have saved Felix and Talon the pain of having to kill a woman they seem to actually care about."

Tears were welling in her big blue eyes, and her bottom lip trembled. "Rhodes, I honestly didn't know. I swear, I'm a spirit witch and I—"

"I swear to fuck, Palmer. I am two seconds away from gutting you, and I'd much rather have you run like the little rat you are back to your master and deliver my message. Now get the fuck out of my sight. If I *ever* see your face in this city again, I will drag you through the streets and set an example that will be whispered about forever."

The tears finally lost their battle and started falling down her cheeks. She stumbled over to the nearby door and tugged it open. I felt like I was on fire; there was so much anger and adrenaline in my body.

"I'm going... but I want you to know something, Rhodes. I know what it feels like to lose your family, so I would never use my affinity to cause pain to those who have to go on living without their person... or people. And I do care about the others, so go fuck yourself."

She wiped her cheeks with a small laugh as she stood straighter, and I watched her calm, confident mask slip back on. With her chin held high, she slipped through the door, shutting it behind her. I watched through the one-way glass as she walked through the room. She never looked back.

Once she was out of sight, I pulled out my cell phone, opening the security app to make sure she actually left the damn building.

What the fuck just happened?

Palmer walked right out of the club doors like I told her to, and I immediately switched to the camera that gave me a view of the street out front. Slowly, my demon calmed down, letting me begin to shift back into my human form. I didn't like letting the demon take over, because clearly I had some anger issues, and I knew that going full-on demon escalated my emotions, making me overbearing and unmanageable. And yet, I didn't feel remorse for what I'd just done. Not one bit.

I figured she must be working with someone, because the timing of the blue envelopes told me she wasn't the one delivering them. It could be one person or several, though.

Honestly, I should've recognized her fighting style. She was a carbon fucking copy of the man who had ruined our lives. But throwing Jasper in our faces and using a woman to infiltrate us? I couldn't wait to fucking end Asrael.

I climbed the stairs and slipped through the secret door into my room before falling back on my bed with a deep sigh. My body was tired from the fight, from shifting, from the emotional fucking hit I'd been blindsided with.

She was gone, and I was pretty positive I'd scared her bad enough that she wouldn't dare come back. The only thing I wished was that I could spare my friends the hurt they'd inevitably feel when they realized she was gone. I was thankful I could soften the blow though; they didn't need to know about the bullshit she'd tried to pull, using Jasper's name like that.

It was too difficult to talk about Jasper, so we just... never did. What used to be six was now five, and it didn't matter how much time passed, the sting of his loss was never going to lessen.

There were regrets. Of course. Jasper had warned me about the risks—if Asrael found out what we were doing... Foolishly, I'd ignored his warnings. We'd both ignored common fucking sense, and it had cost Jas his life.

Asrael never knew it was me that Jasper had been sneaking around with, and thank fuck he never found out, because the rest of us wouldn't have made it out of Besmet alive. As it was, we'd had a hard enough time escaping the castle after Jasper died and we realized what Asrael had done. Tal and Ash had been ready to shred him right then and there, but he was too strong for us to attack without a plan.

We'd slipped through the realm, mainly at night, using our unique abilities to go undetected and to get out of dicey situations. The nights were dark, and our minds were even darker. Eventually, we made it to a resistance camp and got to work helping them figure out ways to overthrow Asrael and the monarchy. King Thane was still on the throne, but that didn't mean shit when you had a sociopath for a brother. I was amazed that Thane's son, Bram, hadn't met an untimely end in some sort of "accident," since he was the sole heir to the throne.

My phone vibrated, snapping me out of my thoughts. I dug it out of my pocket and saw a text notification from Hawthorne. It was early morning, but he often got started at the shop before the sun came up. I opened the message and scanned the words, sitting up as I did.

This was taped on the front door this morning.

I clicked the picture to enlarge it and growled at the sight of a blue envelope with my name on it. Fucking bastards. But if Asrael was behind these little notes, then that would mean that he did know about Jasper and me. This seemed like an underwhelming reaction from him. I'd fully expected him to materialize before me and kill me outright if he ever found out, not leave fuckin' notes to taunt me.

I pressed my palms to my forehead and groaned. My gods damned head was pounding from trying to figure out what the hell was going on, and I knew my headache was about to become exponentially worse since I could already hear pounding footsteps and shouting from the boys. They knew she was gone, and they would be heading in here next.

They couldn't know that I'd seen her before she left. I threw the covers back and dove under them just seconds before my bedroom door was practically blasted off the hinges.

"*WHERE IS SHE?!*" Ashland roared, charging into my room like a rabid wolf, his eyes darting around like I was hiding her in plain sight. My door made a creaking sound, and the top hinge came loose, leaving it hanging at a very awkward angle.

"What the fuck, man?" I pointed at the fucked-up door. "Where is who?"

"Palmer," he snarled, sniffing the air. I braced myself for the hit I knew was coming because I suddenly realized he was going to scent her all over me. His wings expanded, and he launched himself at me, knocking me out of bed. He lowered his face, scenting my chest and neck. "You smell like her. Where is she?"

"Ash, you need to get the fuck off of me. Now." I spoke as calmly as I could, not wanting to escalate his already fragile state of mind. Whenever we got too pissed—or too much of any emotion, really—it could trigger a feral reaction, much like what I had just been through.

Howls drifted to us through my ruined doorway, and Ash threw his head back and practically wailed. *For fuck's sake.*

"Listen, Rhodes, I'm telling you right now... If you know something, you need to tell me. I need to know where she is." His hands were shaking, and if I didn't know better, I would've questioned whether he was on something... or withdrawing from something. Why was he so weak over this lying bitch?

"I smell like her because she was all over me earlier during that fight. You know this," I explained, pushing him off of me. "Where was she last?"

The others barged in as I stood up, and started filling me in on what I already knew. That she'd healed herself, that they tied her up in Ash's room and when they went back in to get her, she was gone. And now nobody knew where she was.

Misha was stone-faced as he stood against the wall, while Talon and Felix seemed especially distraught, given the way they were pacing and bouncing on the balls of their feet. Ash was tapping away at his phone, likely sending out alerts to our crew to keep an eye out for her, asking if anyone had seen her in the building.

I knew the exact moment he opened the security app and saw her walk out of the front doors. His jaw ticked and his eye twitched. He didn't want to believe it, even though the proof was right there in front of his face.

"She left," he said with no emotion.

"What?" Talon demanded, walking over and grabbing his phone. Felix and Misha watched over his shoulder as he played back the video.

Felix ran a hand through his hair. "Maybe she wanted to go to the store or something?"

Ashland snorted. "She's gone."

"But how can you be sure? She could've just gone for a walk to clear her mind or—"

"No," Misha said quietly. "She begged, and we didn't listen."

Everyone was quiet after that, and my phone vibrated again. I pulled it out, ready to tell Hawthorne to chill about the fucking envelope, but the notification was for an email, from a sender who wasn't in my contacts. My brow pinched, and unease began to build as I opened it.

Just thought you should know... your girl is a snake.

Below that sentence was a picture of Palmer from that first night at Haunt, standing in line outside of the club, wearing that damn bunny mask. Frank—the rat who'd been working with Scorpio—had his arm around her waist as she laughed. It looked like he was bending her back slightly... to kiss her?

What the fuck? My head felt like it was going to explode. I thought back to when Frank had shown up at the VIP area. He'd gotten handsy with her. Was that all a fucking act? A ploy to do what, get her an in with us? Was that part of their fucking plan?

"Yo, Rhodes, you alright, man?" Felix asked, waving his hand in front of my face.

"She was a rat," I gritted out, pissed off all over again. Now I had confirmation of what I already knew, but actually seeing it was a slap in the face.

"Don't say that," Talon barked. "I know you don't like her, but calling someone a rat—"

"Look for yourselves," I snapped, shoving my phone into Felix's hands. His face fell when he saw the picture.

Tal grabbed the phone next, his horns growing slowly as he stared at the screen. Misha looked for only a second before turning on his heel and heading for the door. His fist slammed into the wall, leaving a huge, ugly hole to match my fucked-up door.

"Mish, we need to talk about this!" Felix yelled at his retreating back, but the big guy didn't stop.

Ashland was sitting on my bed with his elbows on his knees. Talon offered him the phone, but he shook his head. "I can't look at that right now." His leg was bouncing up and down, and I knew his mind was going a mile a minute. "She lied."

"She did," I replied gravely.

"She broke our deal and ran."

I nodded. "Yes."

Ash looked up, his eyes now completely black. "I want her found and brought back here. I have questions, and then we can decide what to do with her."

"Ashland," Felix murmured, taking a step closer.

"No, Felix. Don't fuckin' start with me. I will never tolerate liars!"

Talon was walking in circles, his red hair sticking out in every which way. "There has to be a reason for it... She wouldn't do this. I just know she wouldn't."

"You don't know that, Tal," I said, trying to be gentle about it but fuck, the proof was right here. And paired with what I knew on top of that? The bitch was guilty.

"Let's go find her." Ashland hopped up and stormed out of my room. I followed him, trying to think of some way to stop him—at least for now—but the stars intervened, and his phone rang.

"What?" he snapped at whoever was on the other end. "It's done? Are you sure?"

Talon and I shared a wide-eyed look. "It's done" could only mean one thing.

"We'll be there in twenty minutes. Yep. Sounds good. Bye."

Ashland slowly turned around, a maniacal grin on his face. "Well boys, the hunt will have to wait for now. That was Balor. The gas is ready, and we're needed at the lab, stat. Asrael's latest stunt seems to have sped the timeline up substantially."

"*Fuck yes!*" Talon fist-pumped the air, and I cracked a smile for the first time in what felt like days. National media had released a ton of press coverage on Montague Industries and the great strides that the CEO, Asrael Montague, was making in regards to cellular manipulation.

"Right, listen to me and listen good. All thoughts of Palmer are getting pushed to the very back of our minds right now. We've waited too long, worked too fucking hard to let our plans get derailed over a traitorous cunt." Ashland glanced at Felix. "Go find Misha and tell him what's up. We're leaving in five minutes."

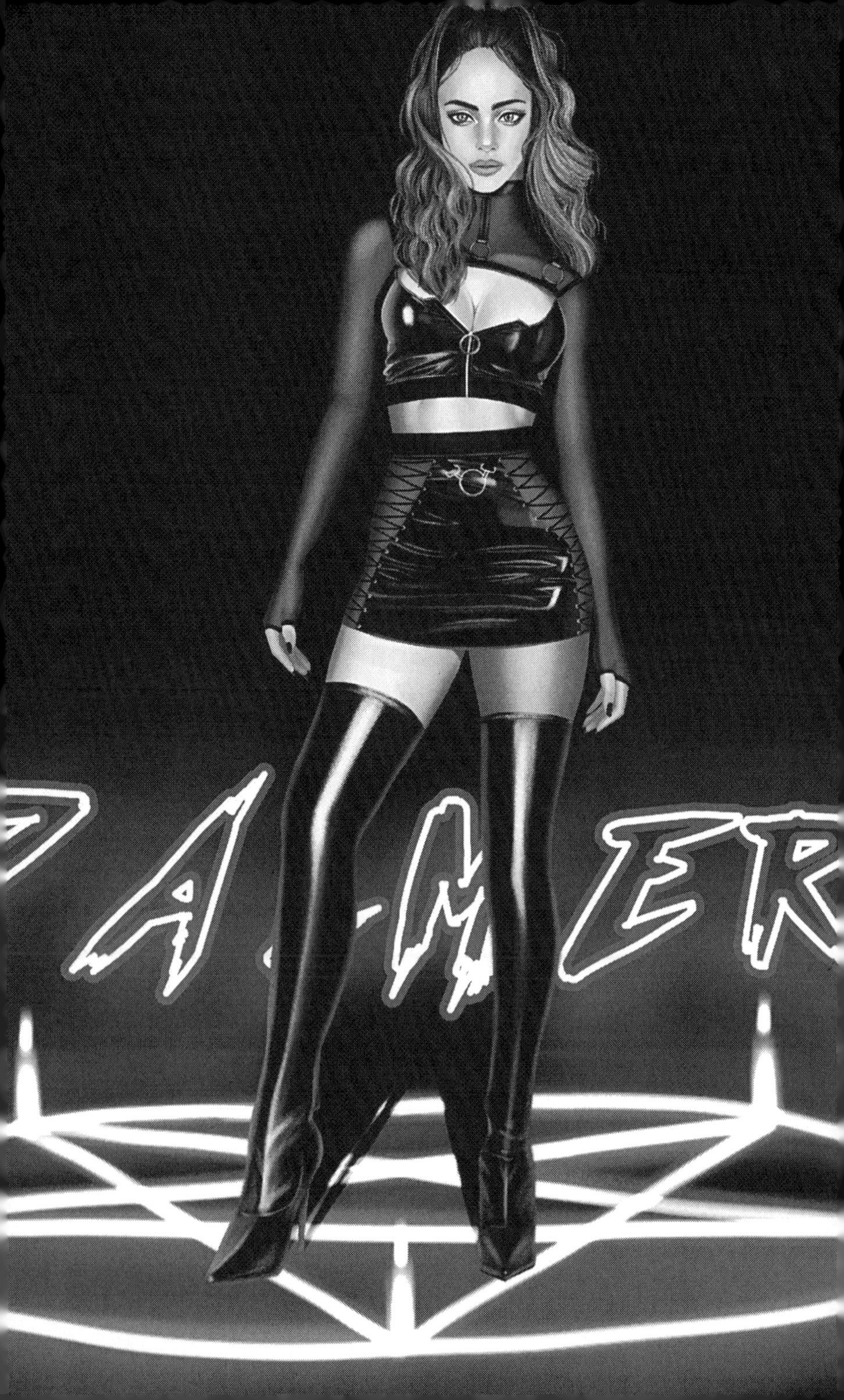

PALMER

Chapter Twenty-One

Tears stung my eyes as I wandered down the street, and that pissed me off more than Rhodes being a Grade A dick. I was furious that he'd affected me enough that I fucking cried—in front of him, no less. I'd had no idea that Talon and Felix had a brother, nor that he was dead. Where was all of that information when Asrael had set me up for this fucking assignment?

Having all of the facts was critical to completing a mission successfully, and I was furious that I'd been caught so off guard. I needed to figure out a new plan, and I needed to fucking think. And sleep. Gods, I was so damn exhausted.

A small squeak was all the warning I got before Snake landed on my shoulder. "Hey, buddy," I murmured, reaching up to give him some scratches under the chin. That was the nice thing about Snake—I never had to worry about him. He somehow always managed to get out of sticky situations, and it really helped that he was so agile.

Raindrops began to fall from the gray clouds, making me groan. Perfect. Just what I needed. I needed to find a place to crash for today, maybe a little longer if possible.

What had happened to Jasper? Speaking of the ghost, his ass conveniently wasn't here with me for me to rage against. Smart on his part. Why hadn't he told me who he was?

I picked up my pace, not thrilled with the heavier rain that was starting to come down. An awning over one of the businesses a block away was calling my name. Snake abandoned my shoulder in favor of a tree he could huddle in and ride out the storm clouds. Little traitor.

"Son of a bitch," I swore, once I was safely underneath and protected from the downpour.

"Awful weather, isn't it? I'd never be able to live in such a shithole city, but if it's raining in Brussels..." a deep voice said, and I reached for my bunny blades that were luckily still on my body.

A man seemed to appear out of thin fucking air at the opposite end of the storefront. He wore a well-fitted, dark blue suit with a matching hat, the brim angled down over his eyes, not giving away much of anything. His side profile wasn't familiar, and my fingers wrapped around the handles of the daggers.

The man tsked. "Ah, don't forget who taught you how to use blades in the first place, young lady."

My heart skipped a beat as my brain finally caught up. Smiling, I replied, "If it's raining in Brussels, then it must be snowing in Barcelona." Brussels was Asrael's city code name. Mine was Barcelona.

Staring out at the deluge pouring from the sky, I sighed a breath of relief. When dealing with shapeshifters, it was important to have a system in place to verify identity, otherwise you could literally be talking to your arch-enemy and be none the wiser. At Montague, we'd established code names for ourselves to be able to verify our identity to other agents in the field. Shapeshifters were rare, but Asrael had made sure we knew that they were out there and that they were sneaky.

Asrael was all about pushing your abilities to the limits to see what you were capable of. By pushing his own, he'd mastered the ability to shapeshift. He was incredible.

I exhaled a shaky breath. Asrael was here. *Here.* I felt so much relief knowing that someone who knew me, who cared about me, was here at this moment when I was feeling so fucked-up. I slowly moved closer, noticing when he looked up that his normally dark eyes and hair were now golden and a gray-blue respectively. It always boggled my mind, knowing this was Asrael but having him look so wildly different...

"I didn't want to risk it, even in the rain. There are cameras everywhere," he explained, gesturing at his new face that was now complete with a beard. Asrael was always impeccably groomed—he never normally had long hair or a beard.

"Everything okay?" I asked, biting my lip. If he was here, it likely didn't mean everything was great. Hopefully, he'd just wanted to see how things were going.

He leaned back against the bricks and crossed his ankles. "Mostly. With you here, it's not like I could call or email. Curiosity has gotten the best of me though. What have you found out?"

I sighed. "Well, true to their background files, they have a lot of criminal dealings. I've witnessed murder, as well as illegal shipping and receiving, and yeah, they're all crazy as hell."

"That's all?" he asked, lifting a brow.

"For now, yes. To be honest, I'm having a hard time knowing what to look for when I don't know exactly what I'm supposed to be focusing on." My stomach was twisting uncomfortably as I thought about betraying them. The way Rhodes had gone off and threatened me... I'd found out really fast that I didn't like the way it made me feel. I felt lower than low.

"You look conflicted, Palmer. Are you having issues?"

I blinked, shaking away their faces from my mind. "It's just, with all due respect, sir... They're honestly not as bad as I thought. They're insane, sure. Dangerous, irrational, but for the most part, they think things through before acting."

Asrael tossed his head back and laughed. "Not as bad as you thought? Did you not just tell me you witnessed murders?"

"Well, yes, but he was a pedophile and they—"

"Palmer, listen to yourself. You're justifying murder right now, which goes against everything you learned in training. Now, what about these shipments?"

I cringed hard on the inside because he was right. Wasn't he? In training, we'd always been taught right and wrong. Good and evil.

Black and white... But what happened when the black and white bled together and created a beautifully confusing hue of gray that housed five demons who were making me question everything? I had to shut down those thoughts. Especially in front of Asrael. The last thing I wanted was to be pulled from the assignment.

Clearing my throat, I answered his question. "Ashland blew up a boat full of bodies of a rival gang, who'd been stealing crates and spying on whatever shit they're moving. Scorpio's gang from West Harbor? There's a war brewing there and it's going to get bloody. I can sense it."

I knew I needed to ask him about Jasper, if he'd known. The thing was, he had to have known, but there was a big part of me that wanted to keep pretending that Asrael was clueless about him. Otherwise, he'd deliberately kept crucial information from me and sent me half-cocked into a fucking complicated assignment.

"What are they shipping and receiving that's different from the norm?"

"Wish I knew, but I haven't exactly had a chance to investigate. This is my first time alone since the party at Haunt."

Asrael crossed his arms. "Are they suspicious?"

"No, more like obsessed," I confessed, thinking of all the ways they'd shown their level of obsession over the past week.

He chuckled. "I knew they would be. Look at you—you're beautiful. I don't think there's a man out there who could resist you."

"What's the endgame here, sir?" I needed to know. I'd come into this thinking I was going to kill them at the end, but truthfully, I didn't know if that fit anymore.

"Same as before. I need you to figure out what's so goddamn special about these shipments and then we can meet again to discuss. This is a time-sensitive situation, Palmer. Everything's been moved up. I need answers and I need them *now*. Do you understand?"

I chewed on my bottom lip. Same as before. So he wanted me to kill them, end of story. Could I do that?

"You know," he continued slowly, waiting for me to give him my attention. "There was a reason I wanted you on this job. It's not because you were the best recruit from your class. It's not because of your unique affinity, and it's not just because you're my favorite."

My eyes stung a little at that last little bit. *His favorite.* I knew he cared about me and oftentimes had shown me favor over other recruits, but to hear it...

"Oh, sweet girl. Didn't you know that? I admit, I'm not the greatest at expressing my emotions, but I do care about you. So much so that I made sure that you were prepared to go into this and come out successful in your mission for revenge."

I turned and faced him, pushing my wet hair to one side and wringing it out. "My mission for revenge? What does that have to do with anything?"

"I'm going to ask you to keep an open mind as I explain this. Just know that I made what I felt was the best decision as your guardian and mentor. Sometimes we have to wait to learn the truth of things until we're prepared to bear the weight of it."

My throat was already tightening up, and I had a horrible feeling settling in the pit of my stomach. Whatever he was about to tell me, I knew it was going to be horrible.

"When I first told you about The Exiled and started preparing you for this assignment, there was a reason. You trained so hard, Palmer. Worked yourself to the point of exhaustion to make sure you were fit for this."

"I already know all of this," I murmured.

"You do, but I felt the need to remind you because the truth is, I know who murdered your parents, Palmer."

If words had the ability to physically assault you, I would've just received a jab to the throat, a kick to the gut, and a right hook to the cheek. It felt as though the ground was going to open up and swallow me whole.

"You have to understand, I didn't tell you back then because it would have driven you mad. You would have wanted to seek out vengeance immediately, without being ready, and that would've ended in disaster. So I kept the truth from you, buying you time. I hope you can appreciate that."

If he didn't tell me and instead had me begin training for this? That means...

Oh gods, no.

"They're charming, aren't they?" he murmured sadly, shaking his head. "The most vile creatures usually are, unfortunately."

My body broke out in a cold sweat. *There's no way.*

"The reason I'm telling you this now is because I can see they've... affected you. Don't let them into your head, Palmer. They're killers, with no remorse or moral code. Everything they do is calculated to ensure it benefits them and nobody else. They're not on your side. I am, and I always will be."

My world spun on a new axis and my heartbeat roared in my ears, but I still heard him, somehow, even though his voice sounded small and far away.

"I have to get back to headquarters now, but I'll want you to be ready with a report as soon as possible. I'll be back when I can." He walked over to me without hesitation, hugging me tightly.

I was pretty sure shock was setting in, because I didn't feel it. Not really. I watched the water fall from the roof like a curtain, blocking the outside world from me. I couldn't be sure how much time passed—could've been seconds or minutes—but when I finally opened my mouth to ask Asrael how he knew, I was alone. Completely fucking alone in a rainy city that reeked of lies and deceit.

They were the ones who'd broken into my childhood home and ransacked the place? The ones who'd killed my parents while I hid in a kitchen cupboard? A cupboard which I stayed inside of for days before I was found.

Water built in my eyes, wanting to fall heavy and hard just like the rain. But no. Absolutely fucking not. My stomach cramped as the words Asrael had spoken replayed in my head, like a sick soundtrack of my traumatic past.

And then, oh gods. I clapped a hand to my mouth, fighting the urge to retch as flashes of the things I'd done with them came crashing through my fragile mind. The way I'd moaned and thrashed around on their cocks, the way I'd secretly loved their attention and gifts, their possessiveness and craziness. Stumbling over to a trash can, I heaved and heaved, as though I could vomit up the memories of their touches on my skin. If I threw up my tarnished fucking soul in this gods damned trash can right now, I knew it still wouldn't be enough.

And then the betrayal slammed into me. Asrael had sent me here, knowing that I'd probably end up fucking them? My parent's killers?

My head was swimming, but I had to figure something out. I wiped my mouth with the back of my hand and took a few shuddering breaths. A hotel. That's what I needed. I'd get myself a room, get cleaned up and refreshed. Make a new game plan. Get back in there and make them pay. Yes.

That was what needed to happen, and if Rhodes wanted to get all King of Hell on me again, I'd take pleasure in shooting him in the dick or stabbing him in the neck.

Resolved with my new plan, I darted out into the rain, trying to look for a taxi. Headlights were heading my way, so I got as close to the road as possible without standing in the street. Visibility was shit but I needed them to see me. I needed a fucking ride out of here.

The lights got closer, and I brushed the water off my face, only for it to be replaced a second later. I sighed at the sight of the lit up taxi sign on top of the vehicle and waved my hands frantically. The car slowed, and I hopped in.

"Oh thank the fucking stars," I groaned, trying to get my soaked hair out of my face. "Sorry that I'm soaked. I kind of got stuck in the storm."

"No problem," the driver said.

"Can you take me to the nearest hotel just outside of the city, please?" I reached for my pocket to see how much cash I had on me when the locks on the doors engaged. Confused, my eyes flicked to the front of the car, connecting with a familiar pair of greenish-brown eyes.

The man turned in his seat to face me, and I was frozen. Completely fucking frozen. A black mask with silver spikes covered his nose and mouth. Just like it had at fight night.

"You know, I was a little hurt that you didn't recognize me before," he said, and I shook my head in denial. "But you know who I am now, don't you, babe?"

My eyes widened as he lifted the mask and flashed me a smile that I'd seen a hundred times before. A smile that had fooled me. A smile that was actually sharper than any knife I'd ever handled.

"Oh, come on, don't be afraid. You made me promise when we first got together that I would never let you lose me. I'm keeping my promise. I've missed you so much, and now I can show you. Didn't you miss me? Tell me that you missed me and thought about me all the fucking time, babe."

I couldn't speak. It honestly felt like I was choking on my own tongue.

"*TELL ME!*" he roared, and I jumped.

"I missed you," I whispered, trying to stop my body from shaking like a leaf.

He smiled again, making my blood run cold. "Say it again with my name this time."

Tears were already trailing down my cheeks, but he didn't care. He never did. "I missed you, Slade."

He moaned and shifted in the driver's seat. "I always loved hearing my name come out of your mouth, but I liked it so much better when you were naked and underneath me. Let's fix that, hmm?" He turned back around, putting the car in drive. "Oh, and I have some exciting news. You can call me Slade or you can use my new name—I think you'll like it. Has a certain sense of danger to it. Do you know what it is?"

Slade was taunting me. He'd always loved playing games with me, asking me questions I didn't know the answers to and forcing me to answer, only to make me feel stupid when I got them wrong. But this time, I had a sickening feeling that I did know the answer. Pieces were shifting into place before my eyes, and little bells were going off like fireworks in my head.

"Oh, come on, Palmer. You know it... Fucking say it."

My fingernails dug into my palms as I clenched my fists together. "Scorpio."

Slade laughed maniacally and hit the steering wheel with both hands in quick succession. "Yes! Fuck, you're so smart. Always were. Do you know how long I've waited for you? Mmm, my cock has been hard for you for years. I want you to know right now that while we were apart, I only fucked women who reminded me of you."

Bile was rising up, burning my throat. First, I had to find out that I'd been fucking the men who'd killed my family, and now I was back in the clutches of my stalker and abuser.

Slade ran his mouth for fifteen minutes straight. That was how long it took to reach wherever he was taking us. He told me how he'd watched me leave Haunt earlier and followed me. That once he found out I was officially in Port Black, he'd started keeping eyes on me immediately. That he knew I'd sense him being close and would sneak away to be with him.

He was crazier than ever, and I was beyond fucked. The worst part was that my body seemed to be frozen with shock. No matter how much I repeated in my head that I was a badass bitch, a trained killer, nothing worked. One second of being back in his presence had cracked my head like a fucking egg.

"We're home." He turned and grinned at me. "Now listen, until I can be sure I can trust you, I'm going to keep you secluded. Can't have you trying to topple our kingdom before I get you back into the right state of mind, and unfortunately, I have a few things to tend to before I can heal you."

Heal me. That's what he used to call it. When he'd force his blood into my mouth and mind-fuck me, making me believe I was in love with him. Making me have sex with him, doing whatever he wanted to my body. He said I'd let others get in my head and turn me against him, so I needed to be healed of those false thoughts.

Whenever he'd take control of me, it was like some part of me, deep down, knew that something wasn't right. That I didn't want the things he was doing to me or making me do, but I was helpless to stop. All he had to do was tell me to do something and I was lost. My free will was gone. He would tie me up and leave me for hours in the dark. It was like being drugged and unable to control yourself—your mind, your actions, every part of yourself ended up crushed under the weight of that addiction.

"Out of the car, babe," Slade ordered, and I saw he'd gotten out and walked around to my side to get me out, all without me realizing. I got out slowly, my body feeling like it was made up of jello and paper tape.

Oh gods, he wants to heal me.

Years ago, I'd found out very quickly that Slade's blood really was like a drug. I'd turned into a shell of a person, desperate only for him. For what he could give me.

I had to get out of here. If he used his blood on me, I was a goner. I almost hadn't made it out last time; I'd just gotten lucky. I had Hunter back then. Right now, I had...

Them. The fucking murderers.

But what I'd told Asrael was true. They were obsessed with me. Not Rhodes, but the other four—Ash, Talon, Felix, and Misha. They wouldn't just let me disappear. They'd look for me. I knew they would, and they'd find me. They'd get me out of here.

"Welcome to your kingdom. I've been busy building this empire. I'm going to make you my Scorpion Queen, babe." We were at some sort of industrial park, with warehouses and factories scattered around. Most were in a state of disrepair, but this building looked like the central hub. "Here we are." Slade unlocked a door, and then grabbed my wrist, pulling me inside. "This is where you'll be staying. For now. How quick you get to move into our room depends on your behavior."

Our room. Our room.

"Don't cry, babe. I know you missed me but don't worry, I'll be back as soon as possible. Perhaps a shower while you wait? I can't wait to get reacquainted with your body, so get freshened up for me, hmm?"

I couldn't stop my mouth. "No."

The creepy smile fell from Slade's face. "Excuse me?"

All of the trauma, the fear—it bubbled over. "You're not fucking touching me, you psychopath!" I screamed the words so loud that they echoed around us, hanging in the air like shards of glass.

Slade didn't move. He didn't flinch or even so much as blink... and then suddenly, he did. His arm stretched out and he grabbed my throat, slamming me down on the bed. "I'm not touching you?" he asked, incredulously. "I'll fucking touch you whenever I want, you little bitch. Look at all of this that I built for us. You think you can tell me what I can or can't do?"

My vision was going blurry as I clawed at his arms, desperate to get away from the hardness pressing against my core as he pinned me down.

"You ungrateful cunt. You know something? I was prepared to force my blood into your body, to heal you now so you won't have to suffer, but I think this time I might wait until you earn it. I'll make sure you're begging for me to give you the tiniest little taste, just to make you accept that this is your gods damned life now, Palmer. You were always mine. MINE!"

His hold loosened, and I sucked in air desperately.

"And then I had to see you being the slut you are, publicly claiming five men in front of hundreds of people. I mean, it was a risk I had to be willing to take... that you might develop feelings for them."

"What?" I rasped.

He chuckled. "Oh, right. I better explain. You see, when Asrael kicked me out of the academy, I needed another plan. So I came here, because I knew you'd be coming eventually. The Exiled were always going to be your target, so I had to be patient. But fuck, I am not patient anymore. I knew Asrael would be interested in any information about The Exiled and what they were up to, so I started spreading rumors. That they were shipping and receiving different shit. I even found a perfect rat, poor Franky boy."

I felt nauseous. Slade was way more involved in this than I could've imagined, and every sentence out of his mouth made me feel more and more fucked.

"And that invitation to the party! Genius, right?"

My mouth parted as I remembered the bouncers looking at me like I was nuts when I tried to give them my invitation. Nobody else had them. *Fucking stupid. Stupid.*

"The bunny ears really were a nice little touch."

"They're going to kill you," I choked out, my voice hoarse.

Slade got off of me finally. He stood beside the bed, staring down at me. "Who? The Exiled?" he scoffed. "For what? They don't know I have you."

"They'll figure it out..."

At this point, they were probably my only hope of getting out of here. Asrael wouldn't know what happened to me or would even connect Scorpio to me. Why would he? I'd have to tolerate The Exiled a little longer, just long enough to get the fuck away from Slade.

"And what? You think they're going to be upset that I took you away from them?"

"They're obsessed with me, Slade. You didn't account for anyone else becoming as obsessed with me as you are."

He cocked his head to the side and reached into his pocket, producing a phone. "That's where you're wrong. I've had years to think about everything, Palmer. Take a look at this." He turned the phone around and showed me the screen.

It was me, the night of the party at Haunt. I remembered the guy who'd bumped into me as he walked by, nearly knocking me over. Someone had taken a picture of us at the perfect moment. To anyone looking at this photo out of context, it would appear that I was involved with this man. I was bent back slightly and his hands were on my hips, keeping me upright.

"What the fuck is that?"

"Not what, babe—who. Don't you recognize him? That's Frank! The rat! And you're in his arms, staring up at him moments before he kissed you!"

"He never kissed me!"

Slade shrugged. "The Exiled don't know that. I think I'll just"—he tapped his thumbs over the screen—"send this off to

Rhodes and let them decide for themselves if you're trustworthy or not."

"*NO!*" I screamed, scrambling off the bed and launching myself at him. I needed to get that phone before he sent that fucking picture. He batted me out of the way like I was a gnat, and I hit the ground with a cry of pain.

"Too late, babe. It's done. So if you had any grand ideas of them coming to your rescue, you can fucking forget about it. Now, as I said, you can have some of my blood whenever you're ready to ask me nicely. But either way, I will be back for you in a little bit. So take a fucking shower and get yourself together." He turned and walked away.

I couldn't stop the sob that tore from my throat. *Oh my gods...* I couldn't go through this again. I couldn't be his victim again.

"You'll love me again, you'll see."

The door slammed shut, and I broke apart into a million pieces. Maybe if I let myself break, it wouldn't hurt so badly when he did it again.

Continue Palmer and The Exiled's story by clicking here!

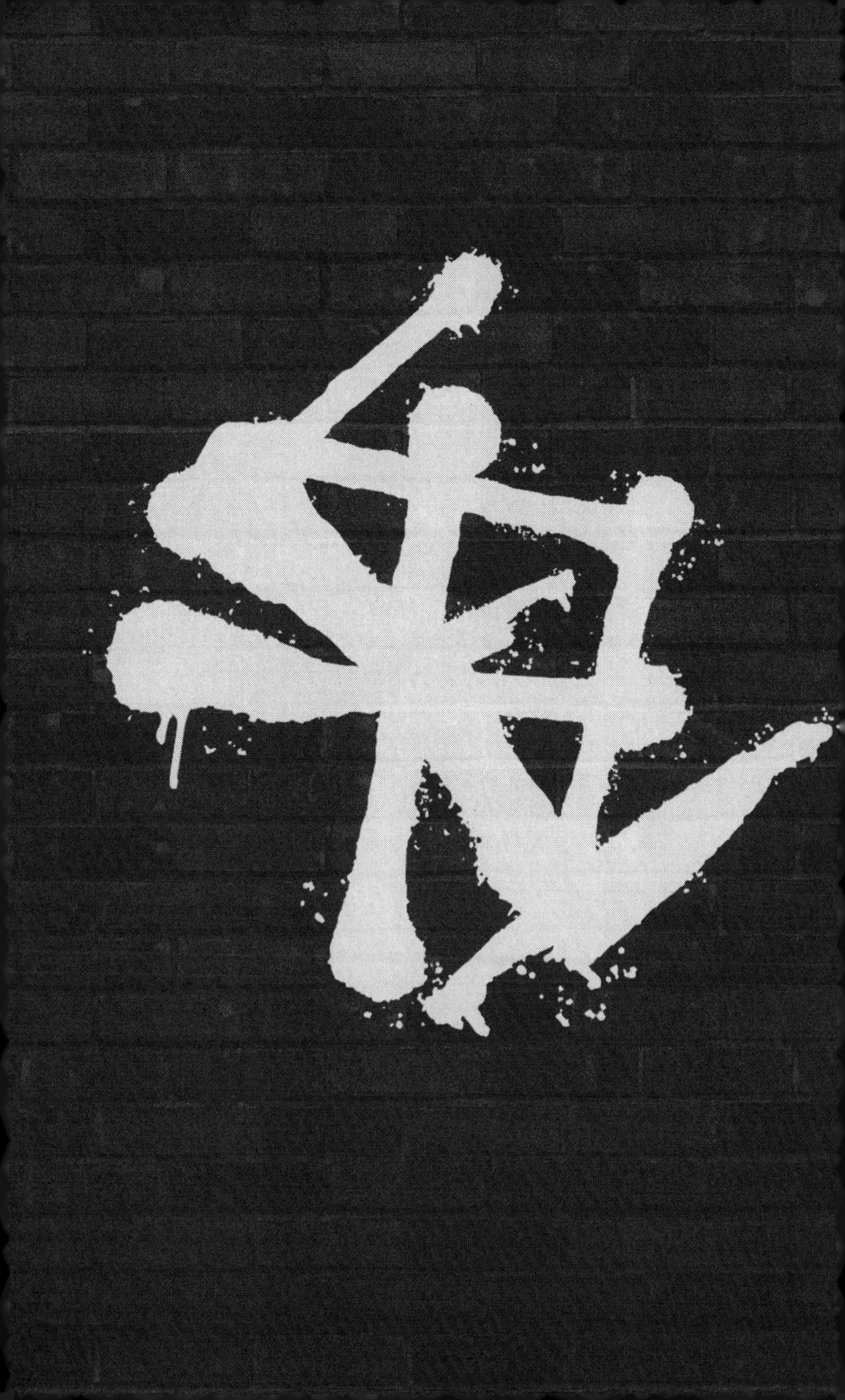

AUTHOR NOTE

Well hello there, little rabbits.

I see you've made it to the end of the first part of our journey together.

Are you mad about that epic ending? Aww, come on, you know you love the way that adrenaline was pumping through your veins. What a rush. Did you feel it? That energy that builds and builds as you near the end of the book, knowing something big is coming? Damn, I love that part.

So where will this story go next? Will our guys find Palmer before it's too late? Will Scorpio force his blood on her once again? And what about that shocking news from Asrael? What a mess our characters are in!

Make sure you pre-order book two, Demons In My Head! Pay no attention to the date, I'm giving myself a wide time frame for my own sanity.

Join us in the Demons In My Bed Spoiler/Discussion Group on Facebook!

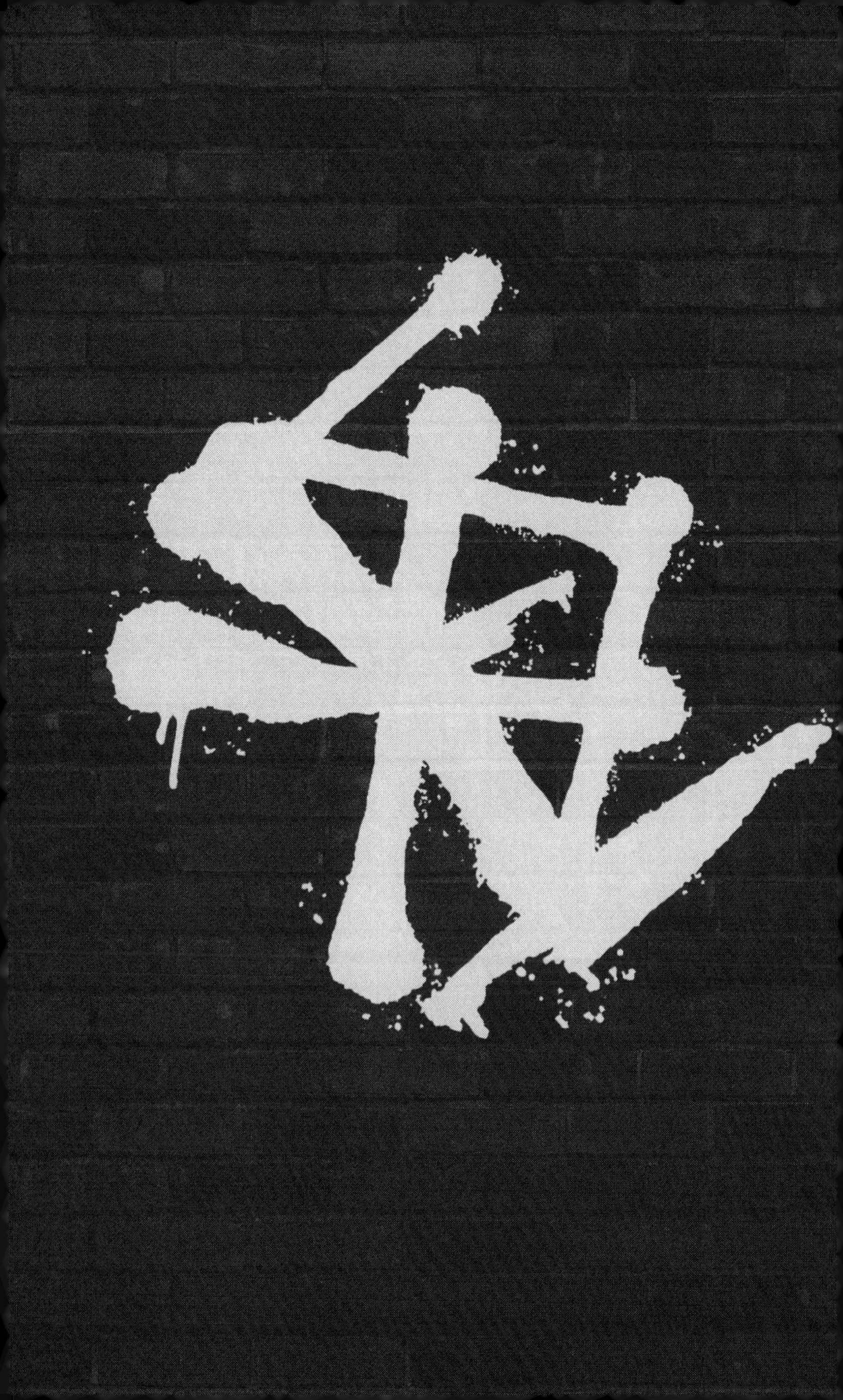

THANK YOU

This story has been a journey, to say the least.

I first bought covers for this before The Magic of Discovery was even published! So, a year and a half ago. That's how long I've been kicking this story around in my head, slowly building the ideas and characters until they felt right. It was starting to feel like release day would never arrive, but now it has, and I am so fucking thankful to each one of YOU for giving me the time I needed to write their story. I literally went into a phase of mourning after finishing Emerald Lakes and it took time to come out of that funk. Not once did I feel harassed about needing to write faster or quicker. I love this book community that we have created together that's full of love and acceptance.

To my husband and my kids, thank you for being patient. Thank you for being understanding that sometimes Mommy can't go do all the things because she's busy writing. But more than that, thank you for being my biggest cheerleaders, the ones who always tell me how proud you are. I love you.

My editing team! You guys... I don't know what I'd do without you. Cassie, Raewyn, Polly... the three of you take my 90k plus word hot mess manuscript and shine that baby up! Seriously, you the real MVP's.

My PA's, Robin, Jess, Polly... thanks for putting up with all of my last minute shenanigans and for keeping me on track.

Sometimes. I am a rebel, after all! You'd all do well to remember it! HA!

To the lawn gargoyles who helped get my house ready to go on the market while I was writing this beast of a book, don't worry, boys. Your story is coming. Thank you! Mike Bomboris, my dear friend and realtor, I never would've finished this book if it weren't for your help during a super stressful time. I love you so much.

I'm sure I'm forgetting people but rest assured, you are appreciated greatly and I love you ALL.

東

ABOUT BRITT

Britt Andrews is a paranormal romance author who focuses on the reverse harem genre. After being laid off of her job in April 2020 due to the COVID-19 pandemic, she decided to take a leap of faith and attempt her lifelong dream of becoming a published author. She hasn't looked back since. Her debut novel, **The Magic of Discovery**, has hit #1 Best Seller in four different categories on Amazon and has received hundreds of five star ratings. She's often mingling with her readers in her Facebook reader group, Britt Andrews' Magical Misfits.

When she's not writing, she is wrangling her three young children and living her best mom life with her supportive husband (yes, he's read her books). They also have two chihuahuas and each day is a wild, chaotic adventure that keeps things interesting. Britt can be bribed with tequila and Mexican food. *wink, wink*

Britt Andrews hopes to bring stories to life that readers can relate to. She strives for inclusivity in her writing and female empowerment. Hopefully, while reading her work you feel more confident in yourself, learn to accept yourself for who you are, take responsibility for your own life and grab it by the balls until you get everything you want.

We're all Queens worthy of a kingdom and a sexy King... or two... or three... or four...

東

STALK BRITT

Follow me on:
Amazon
Facebook
Instagram
TikTok
Bookbub
Goodreads
YouTube

Britt Andrew's Magical Misfits Facebook Group

Website

Subscibe to Newsletter

Become a Patron on Patreon

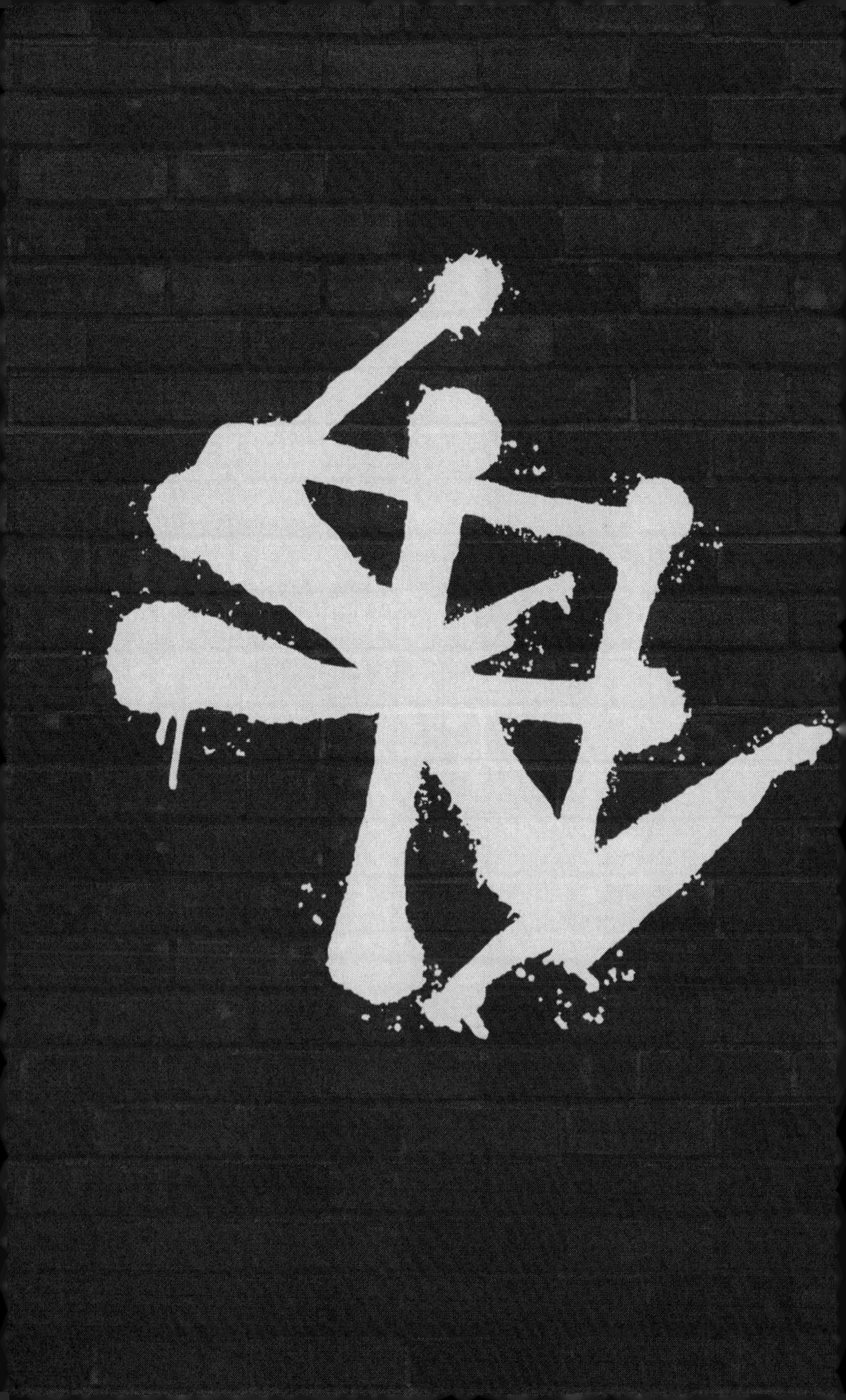

ALSO BY BRITT ANDREWS

Paranormal Reverse Harem
The Emerald Lakes Series:
The Magic of Discovery
The Magic of Betrayal
The Magic of Revenge
The Magic of Destiny
The Magic of Eternity
Sapphic Monster Romance Novella
Little Green Vines
Contemporary MM Romance
Diamond Dreams With Maya Nicole:
Catching Kalen

BOOK 1
THE MAGIC OF DISCOVERY
EMERALD LAKES
BRITT ANDREWS

I'd had hope, something that I never would have given a second thought if she hadn't fucking pushed me. Then she humiliated me. *Broke me.* Now, I was going to find her and break her. The final conversation we had face to face constantly played over and over in my head, and I couldn't just banish it and move on with my life, my never-ending existence.

"Khol." Laura looked up at me when I entered our bedroom. She'd moved in with me only six months ago, but now a suitcase was open on the bed, almost full of her clothing and toiletries.

"Where are you going, darling?" Walking around the king-sized bed, I reached out for her, wrapping my arm around her waist and pulling her into me. She melted against me like butter, and my heart warmed. I loved this woman. I dropped a chaste kiss on the top of her strawberry blonde head.

"I have a business trip I have to take. My boss called, and while it's been fine working remotely for the last several months, I'm needed in person for this job," she explained, running her fingernails down my back. "I wish I didn't have to go. I'll miss you. And I'll miss this." She cupped my erection with her palm and squeezed, summoning a moan from deep within my chest.

"How long will you be? Don't forget we have our engagement party in two weeks. It would be a bitch to have to reschedule at this point," I reminded her, my hands kneading her voluptuous ass. Gods, the woman was sculpted.

"I could never forget, Khol. It should take four to five days, tops," she reassured me as she closed the lid on her suitcase and zipped it up. I lifted it off the bed and put it on the floor for her.

"I've gotta get down to the airfield. My jet is waiting. I'll let you know when I land." She wrapped her lean arms around my neck, rose onto her toes, and planted her lips on mine.

That was the last time I saw her in person. The other five times had been through shitty camera snapshots using facial recognition software. I'd never come close to catching her slippery ass, but now I knew she was keeping secrets. Someone had put protection spells down to keep me out of that town. The guys had had no problem crossing that imaginary boundary, which just backed up my suspicions that this particular spell was keyed to me.

Or others like me. Now that's an interesting thought.

Sloane had texted me earlier to let me know they'd arrived, gotten settled, and were coming up with a game plan to tackle this mission. The kid was hardworking, one of the best I'd ever employed, but so was every single spy in my company. He was just easier to manipulate into doing this for me. He

constantly sought approval, fame, and glory. He didn't do anything just to conquer it; he wanted to be the fucking legend. I'd read his file.

I knew everything there was to know about all of my elites.

Sloane Sullivan, thirty years old. Pyro mage. Top ten percent of his training class. Anger issues, loyal, broken family, only child. Master of wards.

Fischer Bahri, thirty years old. Cognitive mage. Interrogator, ability to not only read emotions but also push them, alter memories, hypnotize. Valedictorian of his training class. Loving family, one sister and two nieces.

Cameron Jacobs, thirty-one years old. Storm mage. Protector, fierce fighter, relentless. Can manipulate weather within a seventy-five mile radius with the ability to create more localized storms. Generates lightning from hands. Severe childhood trauma. Fear of loss.

Kaito Mori, twenty-nine years old. Shifter mage. Black panther: Bagheera. Heightened sense of smell, vision, and hearing. Oldest of five children. Struggled with depression in the past.

Pacing around my apartment, I swirled my glass of whiskey. Finding out about this town had me completely obsessed. I'd yet to have a lead

this promising, and it was all I could think about. Once I found her, I could be free of this fucking weight.

Come out, come out wherever you are.

Chapter One

Saige

The Devil. I was staring down at the Devil. *Well, that's just a fantastic start to my Saturday.*

At least he's in tarot form and not an actual manifestation of the dark lord?

Gran had insisted she do a three card tarot reading for me this morning before I left for the shop, so I indulged her request as I finished drinking my coffee. Ah, sweet coffee, the root of every witch's power supply.

"I knew something was brewing! I felt it throughout my body from the moment these starry eyes opened this morning," Gran proclaimed. She slammed her tiny hand down on the table for emphasis, causing me and our filled to the brim coffee cups to jump.

I gave Gran a killer side-eye, but she was much too far down her own rabbit hole to pay any attention to my facial expressions. She started clapping her hands together, squealing like she did every time a man stepped foot on our property. *Any* man. Even her ex-husband who she momentarily forgets that she can't fucking stand. Gran has got mad love for the 'D.'

"Your emotional body is the Fool. Are you ready to take new chances? Experience change? Find a new man?" Gran's eyebrows rose up so high at

the end of her question I thought they were going to blend right in with her wild and curly copper hair. Even her fine wrinkles seemed to be trembling with

excitement. That's just how she was though, eccentric and unapologetically free. I wouldn't change her for the world.

"Gran! You know there isn't anyone in this town that I'm interested in. Even if there were, that piece of shit Bryce would do nothing

but cause all kinds of drama just to make sure that I never got laid again solong as I live in Emerald Lakes," I retorted, stirring sugar into my liquid gold. My ex, Bryce, had been a two-year complete waste of time that I had only freed myself from six months ago. He was a total shithead. I'd taken my dear friends, Frank and Arlo, with me when I'd ended things, just in case.

"I'm so glad you're out of his clutches, but you don't need to kill the coffee mug, dear," Gran replied as she reached out and grabbed my hand to stop my violent cycloning motions. "And fuck Bryce, he's nothing but a limp dick noodle wand."

I laughed suddenly, startling my pet arctic fox, Maven. He released a low angry growl and lifted his head from his bed in the corner of the kitchen. I could always tell when he was pissed because his tail fluffed up to three times its size.

"Aww, don't be mad, Mave. Come over here, boy," I called out to him as I patted my thigh in encouragement. He hopped up and lazily meandered over to where Gran and I were sitting at the breakfast table. My long red hair spilled over my shoulders as I bent over to scoop him up. He nuzzled into my

chest as I ran my fingers through his thick, silky, white and gray-streaked fur. Lifting my mug to my lips, I sipped the warm liquid and settled into the

wave of contentment that burrowed deep in my heart. Gran, Mave, coffee... the three loves of my life.

"The Sun is lining up with your spiritual body. Positive outcomes, child. Success and optimism! Today is going to be a star-blessed day," Gran continued, moving down the line of cards, not fazed by Maven's antics at all. They didn't always see eye to eye anyway, so if they wanted to ignore one another, that was totally fine by me.

"And as for your... physical body..." She waggled her eyebrows and pinned me with her cornflower blue eyes. "We have the Devil. Sexual. Lust." Gran enunciated the last two words as she jammed her one hundred percent non-threatening index finger down onto the face of the card.

"Yeah, or materialism or envy or obsession and addiction. I highly doubt I'll be getting lusty over anybody, Gran." I stood up and took my empty mug to the sink to rinse it out.

"Dick addiction is a real affliction, Saige," Gran said in a serious voice.

By the stars, what is she? A rapper?

"You'd know since you're the Queen of Dick Addiction. If there was a figurehead for Dick Addiction, your face would be on it. The Twelve Steps of Dick Addiction with Bette Wildes," I bantered back at her, chuckling as I continued cleaning up breakfast.

"More like," Gran paused, already laughing her ass off at her coming joke, "The Twelve *Inches* of Dick Addiction, heyoooo!"

We both were dying now, and I felt fortunate that I had such a witty and fun grandma in my life. Wiping my eyes, I scolded her, "Gran. You're going to make me late to the shop. No more dick jokes."

"Awwww, man. You're no fun. But fine, I'll put a lid on it," she gave in with an eye roll, standing up from her chair. "But only until I see you for dinner."

She had raised me and was truly more of a mother to me than my actual birth mother, who had last blessed us with her presence about two months ago. It was the first visit in two years, but that wasn't unusual at all since she worked for a big magical firm on the other side of the country. Regardless of the physical distance, we'd just never had the typical mother-daughter relationship. My birth mother had only been nineteen years old when she'd gotten pregnant with me. My biological father was your stereotypical deadbeat, a one night stand. Laurie (yes, I call her Laurie) always told me that she didn't know who he was. They'd hooked up at a party, and she'd had no way of contacting him after that night. Lucky for me, my gran was an out of this world person, and I never found myself lacking when it came to feeling loved or taken care of.

I turned to put my mug back in the cupboard and caught my reflection in the glass of the large window that ran the length of my countertop. High cheekbones, full lips, and a slight upward turn on the end of my nose... those were all *my* features. Not Laurie's and not some sperm donor I'd never met. I'd always been relieved that I wasn't a carbon copy of Laurie, looks or otherwise. I mean, sure, we shared some things like our red hair, the arch of our eyebrows, and the shape of our faces, but that was where the similarities ended.

Movement outside broke me from my thoughts, and I watched a handful of baby bunnies hopping and playing in the yard. Scanning our wide property, I took in all of the different gardens that covered most of the acreage, ending with the large flowerbed closer to the house. That was when I noticed a row of my tulips had wilted, the blooms sagging so low they were brushing the dirt. *What the hell?* Those were in absolutely perfect condition last evening! I'd been planning to give them a couple more days to grow before I cut them to sell at my magic shop, The Mystical Piglet or The Pig, as the locals had so lovingly shortened it. *I'll have to remember to check on them when I get home from work later.*

Hearing Gran shuffling away since she knew I would be taking off soon for work, I continued to maneuver around my eat-in kitchen, grabbing some snacks to bring with me. Fishing my phone out, I checked the weather forecast for the day. *Perfect. Seventy degrees and sunny.*

"Oh, damn it." The sound of Gran's exasperated voice drew my attention as I walked around the kitchen table and took a right, intending to meet her on the back porch where she always entered and exited my cottage. She had her own sweet set-up along the back tree line. "I completely forgot that I got a phone call yesterday after dinner from a man who wants to rent the apartment above the shop. He already paid the first three months' rent and the security deposit. He's due to arrive at The Pig at ten. Here, take these herbs with you." Gran picked up an overflowing bag that was sitting on the countertop and shoved it at me. Fresh greenery peeked over the top of the bag, the scents of basil, sage, and oregano mixing together.

"A heads up would've been nice, Gran. I'm going to have to rush now," I huffed with fake annoyance, heading back to gather the rest of my things.

Following me, she chuckled. "Just keeping you on your toes, child." Her phone started ringing, and she silenced it with a curse. "I've got to get home. Had a bit of a rager last night, so there are streamers all over the living room and that lightweight Randy Roger passed out in my bathtub. This is the third time! No more tequila for him. I'm the umpire of drinking and questionable decisions, and I call them like I see them. Three strikes, you're out!"

The dude's name was *not* Randy Roger. It was Roger, and I'll let you guess why she threw the other name in there. In any case, Gran had bequeathed that name unto the man, and thus, he was now Randy Roger to everyone in town.

Throwing everything I needed into my backpack, I slipped it onto my shoulders. Glancing at the black cat clock that was ticking happily along on my kitchen wall, I groaned when I realized I really was going to have to rush.

"It's already 9:45! I'll be back later, and I'll call if there are any questions," I called out as I slipped my feet into my favorite pair of shoes. "Come on, Maven! We gotta hurry," I yelled to my little furry friend as I ran out the old screen door.

* * *

I could hear Gran cackling as the screen door slammed shut behind us. *Sick woman laughing at how much I'm going to be sweating by the time I get down there.* Shaking my head, I hopped on my pastel blue bicycle while Maven leapt into the large wicker basket attached to the handlebars. He never missed an opportunity to freeload, and my gods, he looked cute doing it.

"Maven, don't crush those herbs! Watch your tail, son!" He gave a chirp in response and then squirmed down into the basket, that damn tail now pulsating like a pissed off squirrel. *Sometimes he can be such a moody little bastard.* I pushed off of the brick pathway that led to the main road in front of my cottage. It was a beautiful day for gardening and witching, which happened to be two of my top five favorite things. Frank and Arlo, my two handymen who hauled our items down to our shop, had already been by and picked up today's fresh supplies. We typically left a clipboard on the side of the shed and marked things that needed to be loaded up and taken into town each day. It was mid-May, so most of our produce wouldn't be ready for several weeks yet. Good thing we had more than just your usual vegetable fanfare at The Pig.

A grocery store, we were not. I carried everything from smudge sticks, to moonstones, crystals, bulk spell supplies, tonics, elixirs, and I did tarot readings here and there. Selling in-season produce was just a little extra income for me, and it always sold extremely well. Fresh-cut flowers were also a hot commodity, and in a couple of months, I would be up to my tits in blooms.

The bicycle tires bumped along our rocky stone driveway, a path I had walked down a million times. Riding into town was just easier, and it usually only took about ten minutes. I just might make it in time, which would be a good first impression. Whoever this guy was, we were going to be seeing each other a lot, and starting out on the right foot would set the stage going forward.

Thankfully, most of the ride was a straight shot, so I didn't need to worry about going uphill. *Thisbody is not about that type of life.* I was curvier than your average woman, but that was just my build. I was in shape since gardening outside and doing most of my own home improvement projects kept me fit enough. Squats were something I had a love-hate relationship with, but with squatting being a near-constant gardening maneuver, my ass and thighs were thicccc. *Yes, with four c's.*

I assumed the renter was coming in from Portage Falls, one of the closest areas with more business opportunities than my small town of Emerald Lakes. It was about ten hours south, and I'd only ever heard of the place. I had never actually set foot more than twenty miles outside of Emerald Lakes. In fact, I'd never felt the need or the urge to. When I'd taken my mastery classes, I attended a university that was only ten miles from the cottage. I'd also commuted to save money and so I'd be able to help Gran with the upkeep around our sizable property.

The wind picked up then, blowing my hair off of my neck and breathing life into my body. I loved everything about being outside; I was a green witch, after all. Deriving my power from the earth and the sunlight, I was able to create vegetation and other natural growing items, like crystals and moonstones. The sun's rays hit my skin, sinking down to my bones, and I groaned. The feeling of my muscles being energized by the glorious golden orb was intoxicating. Nothing like that first blast of vitamin D in the morning to set you up for a fantastic day. My mind thought back to Gran's tarot reading. It seemed the stars felt I might be getting some of the more fun vitamin 'D' soon. *I fucking wish.*

Entering the downtown area, the road gave way to a designated bike path. Moving my bicycle onto the smoother asphalt, the ding of a bike bell drew my attention to the opposite side of the road.

"Hi, Saige! Hi, Maven!" a cute, tiny voice squealed, and Mr. Grumpy Fluff let out a low growl, not bothering to raise his head in acknowledgment. Ignoring him, I slowed to a stop and greeted the seven-year-old blonde across the street.

"Hi, Annie!" I called back, waving to her and her mother before adding, "Come by the shop later. We have a fresh batch of basil and the moonstones that you asked about last week, Miranda."

"Sure thing, girl. There's a reason you're everyone's favorite magic shop owner in Emerald Lakes!" Miranda gave me a wink and a smile as she began walking again with Annie pedaling in front of her.

Ha. I'm the only *magic shop owner in Emerald Lakes. But yeah, I'm pretty awesome. All the asspats for me.*

Miranda was my only friend who still lived in town; everyone else had left for one reason or another: schooling, careers, marriage, or just craving a change of scenery. She and I had grown up together, and it never mattered how many days went in between us texting or seeing one another. It always felt like we could pick right up where we had left off. I didn't know what it was like to have a sibling, but I'd imagine it would be like my bond with Miranda.

A loud rumble came from behind me, and I swiveled on my seat to see who would be driving so loudly through downtown. Oh hell, a moving truck with the words 'Get Your Move On' sprawled across the side barreled past me. A colorful tattooed arm was hanging out of the window, and I glanced up, my gaze connecting with a pair of emerald eyes. It was like time slowed to a crawl, and I couldn't bring myself to look away. *Who the hell is that guy?* The truck passed me, and I sped up, curiosity taking over. *Is that my tenant?*

My shop was sandwiched in between two other businesses. To the left was Mr. Vladescu's crystal shop, and to the right was a bookstore that was owned by Madame Winston. I lifted my hand in greeting toward Mr. Vladescu who was just opening up for the day. Being such a small town, we were able to keep pretty cushy hours, most businesses opening between 9:30am and 10:00am.

Slowing to a stop, I hopped off my bike in a practiced move and walked it the rest of the way to the bike rack, no need for a chain since crime was basically nonexistent here. It was hard to get away with anything illegal when the town's residents had likely watched you grow up and knew where you lived. Maven leapt fluidly out of the basket and into my waiting arms. Frank and Arlo were already at work, stocking the produce stands in front of the large picture window that looked into The Pig. Green ivy climbed to the roof and blended beautifully with the deep red bricks that housed my livelihood. A continuous beeping alerted me that the moving truck was backing into the alley beside our row of shops, and I quickly ran inside to grab the keys for the upstairs apartment.

The dark hardwood floors creaked as my favorite flats quickly flew across the boards, my left hand trailing along the smooth twenty-foot-long wooden bar that I used as my sales counter. Floor to ceiling shelves lined the entire wall behind the bar. Having such a perfect setting for it, I'd enlisted Frank and Arlo's help to set up a mixing station so that I could whip up different elixirs, tonics, and potions for customers as needed. Once a month, I hosted 'Witching Hour,' an event that nearly the whole town attended. I ran specials on different items and mixed up magic shots, always a big hit.

With a quiet yip and eager squirm, Maven jumped from my arms, running straight to the back of the shop where I kept his food and water bowls. Figuring the keys were likely in the spelled safe we kept under the counter, I ducked down and unlocked it with a flick of magic, the safe recognizing me and popping open. The bell that was attached to the front door began to chime, announcing a customer, or in this case, a tenant. Sensing their magic immediately, the hair on my arms stood straight up. It felt like fingers reaching out to me, seeking, caressing, and I hadn't even seen these people yet. *They must be really fucking powerful.*

"Just one minute! Grabbing the keys..." My hands wrapped around the keyring, and I'd just spelled the lock when a thump sounded from the

bar top, jerking my head up. When a face appeared right above me, I startled, releasing a shriek and falling backward onto my ass. A smiling man stared down at me, his almond-shaped eyes sparkling like onyx. Jet black hair fell playfully over his eyes, and his mischievous grin only served to spotlight his

defined high cheekbones. *Beautiful.*

"Kaito, don't scare the poor girl," a deep voice chastised.

The man above me, who I assumed was Kaito, gave me a sheepish look. He still had a playful glint in his eye as he said, "Sorry, didn't mean to spook you. This is a really cool shop." Disappearing momentarily and just as quickly reappearing beside me, he held out his hand to pull me up. I grasped it and was instantly propelled upward, the momentum had me putting my palms out and catching myself on his chest.

"Hi, I'm Kaito, but you can call me Kai." He looked down at me and canted his head to the left, a move that instantly struck me as animalistic in nature, reminding me so much of Maven when he was studying something. His hands were wrapped around my wrists, barely an inch of space between our bodies. I knew I should back up, but my brain felt like sludge and my feet wouldn't listen. My heart was pounding so hard I wondered if he could hear it. Kai exhaled.

"Actually, you can call me whatever you want..." My eyes rounded when his grip tightened on my arms as he leaned in slightly, effectively destroying the inch of space that had been between us, his nostrils flaring as he inhaled deeply.

"Kai." That baritone voice from before broke the spell like a splash of cold water in my face. I pulled my hands from his grasp and took a step back, smoothing the front of my shirt down just to make sure I wasn't showing any skin.

We both looked to the front of the store, but the morning sun was shining brightly through the window, and all I could make out was a large, dark silhouette that was illuminated with golden rays. Turning back to Kai, I stuck my hand out to him. "Welcome to Emerald Lakes, I'm Saige. I'm not usually this clumsy, but I've only had one cup of coffee this morning, and my gran only let me know about your arrival approximately twenty minutes ago. She owns the apartment, but she's old and really fucking nuts, and I'm rambling, so can you just shake my hand now?" My mouth was going a mile a minute, but he just grinned at me with a blindingly perfect smile.

Now that I was no longer pressed against him, his eyes rapidly dropped from mine to my feet and then back. I wore a black shirt that said *I hope thistle cheer you up* and a pair of skinny jeans. A laugh broke free from his throat as he took my hand and pulled me close to him once again. I swear to gods, I stopped breathing.

"I love your shirt," he said as he leaned down to put his mouth next to my ear. "The answer is yes, by the way," he added softly, which caused my brows to furrow in confusion. With another flash of that blinding grin, he explained, "It did cheer me up."

It appeared that we had a Grade A flirt here.

Back away, Saige. Red alert. No, vagina, do not do that zingy thing. Looks like another night of digging around in my nightstand to see which electric weapon, I mean TOY, will be pleasuring me.

Problem was that everyone in this town knew everyone, and it was no secret how my old relationship had fared. Most had been extremely supportive, but you always had *those people*, the ones who made excuses for men who got off on preying on women. At this point, there honestly wasn't anyone in town I was interested in, so my toys and I were quite well acquainted.

A deep throat clearing made me jump, breaking the intense eye contact between myself and Kaito. He held onto my hand, gently tugging me around the corner of the bar and up to the front of the shop.

"Saige, this is my best friend, Cam. Cam, this is Saige," Kai sing-songed.

I pulled my hand out of Kaito's and giggled. *What the fuck was that?* Taking Cam's offered hand, I tilted my head up to look at him. *By the moon, this one is a giant of a man.* Light brown hair with glittering strands of gold was twisted up into a topknot on his head. The arm that was extended toward me was covered in colorful rune tattoos. *This is moving van man.* My stomach bottomed out when our hands connected; it felt like an electric current was moving through my bloodstream, tethering me to him. His piercing emerald green eyes were staring at me so intensely I could feel my blush darken at least seven shades. I probably looked like a fucking strawberry. *Be cool, Saige.* I pulled my hand back, flipped my hair over my right shoulder, and put my hand on my hip. *No, do the other hip. This feels off, switch back. Yes. That's the pose of power. Now hit him with the scrutinizing stare from hell.*

"Hello, Saige," he rumbled. A delicious shiver worked its way through my body. "Do you have the lease agreement and keys so we can start moving in as soon as possible? I'm feeling a storm coming in later this afternoon, and this hair cannot handle that type of abuse." He winked at me when he said this, and I nodded at him like a bobblehead doll.

Laughter came from beside me, and my brain caught up with what I was doing. *Gods dammit! There goes my authoritative stance.*

"Oh! Yes, forgive me. So, my gran was um... not forthcoming at all regarding who was going to be renting, so which one of you is our new tenant?" I drew out the question while pointing between the two men.

My inner witch was jumping up and down, rolling around on the floor, laughing maniacally, and doing hip thrusts. *Please just let it be one of them, please just let it be one of them.*

"Actually, it's me, Cam, Sloane, and Fischer." Kai smirked, the cocky twist of his lips saying he knew exactly what I'd been repeating in my head.

Well, poop sticks. I'm fucked.
*****

Click here to keep reading the complete five book series!

Printed in Great Britain
by Amazon